# DRUMMER BOY

# Scott Nicholson

Copyright ©2010 Scott Nicholson
Haunted Computer Books
ISBN: 978-1451588491

**Haunted Computer Books**
**P.O. Box 135**
**Todd, NC 28684 USA**

CHAPTER ONE

The Jangling Hole glared back at Bobby Eldreth like the cold eye of the mountain, sleepy and wary and stone silent in the October smoke.

"Th'ow it."

Bobby ignored Dex's taunt as he squeezed the rock and peered into the darkness, imagining the throbbing heartbeat that had drummed its slow rumble across the ages. The air that oozed from the Blue Ridge Mountain cave smelled like mushrooms and salamanders. He could have sworn he heard something back there in the slimy, hidden belly of the world, maybe a whisper or a tinkle or the scraping of claws on granite.

"Th'ow it, doof."

Bobby glanced back at his heckler, who sat on a sodden stump among the dark green ferns. Dex McCallister had a speech impediment that occasionally cut the "r" out of his words. Dex was so intent on pestering Bobby that he failed to note the defect. Good thing. When Dex made a mistake, everybody paid.

"I hear something," Bobby said.

"Probably one of them dead Rebels zipping down his pants to take a leak," Dex shouted. "Do it."

Vernon Ray Davis, who stood in the hardwood trees behind Dex, said, "They didn't have zippers back then. Nothing but bone buttons."

Dex sneered at the skinny kid in the X-Men T-shirt and too-tight, thrift-store jeans that revealed his pale ankles. "What book did you get that out of, V-Ray? You're starting to sound like Cornwad," Dex said, using the class nickname for Mr. Corningwald, their eighth-grade history teacher at Titusville Middle School.

Bobby hefted the rock in his hand. Though it was the size of a lopsided baseball, it weighed as much as the planet Krypton.

Probably even Superman couldn't lift it, but Superman wouldn't be dumb enough to stand in front of a haunted hole in the ground, not while he could be boning Lois Lane or beating up Lex Luthor.

Dex and Vernon Ray were thirty yards down the slope from Bobby, in a clearing safely away from the mouth of the cave. Not that any distance was safe, if what they said was true. The late-afternoon sun coated the canopy of red oak and maple with soft, golden light, yet Bobby shivered, due as much to the chill emanating from the cave as from his fear.

"I've been to the camps," Vernon Ray said. "My daddy's got all that stuff."

"That's just a bunch of guys playing dress-up," Dex said.

"It's authentic. 26th North Carolina Troops. Wool pants, breech loaders, wooden canteens—"

"Okay, Cornwad," Dex said. "So they didn't have no goddamn zippers."

"Daddy said—"

"Your daddy goes to those re-enactments to get away from you and your mom," Dex said. "My old man drags me along, but you always get left behind with the girls. What ya think of that, Cornwad?"

During Dex's bully act, Bobby took the opportunity to ease a couple of steps away from the mouth of the cave. The noise inside it was steady and persistent, like a prisoner's desolate scratching of a spoon against a concrete wall. The Hole seemed to be daring him to come closer. Bobby considered dropping the stone and pretending he had thrown it while Dex wasn't looking. But Dex had a way of knowing things.

"Bobby's chicken crap," Vernon Ray said, changing the subject away from his dad and deflecting Dex's attention. "He won't throw it."

*Good one, V-Ray. I thought we were on the same side here.*

Dex tapped a cigarette from a fresh pack, then pushed it between his lips and let it dangle. "Ah, hell with it," he said. "You can believe the stories if you want. I got better things to worry about."

Relieved, Bobby took a step downhill but froze when he heard the whisper.

"*Uhr-lee.*"

It was the wind. Had to be. The same wind that tumbled a gray pillar of smoke from the end of Dex's cigarette, that quivered the bony trees, that pushed dead autumn leaves against his sneakers.

Still, his throat felt as if he'd swallowed the rock in his hand. Because the whisper came again, low, personal, and husked with menace.

"*Uhrrrr-leeee.*"

A resonant echo freighted the name. If Bobby had to imagine the mouth from which the word had issued—and at the moment Bobby was plenty busy *not* imagining—it would belong to a dirty-faced, gaunt old geezer two hundred years dead. But like Dex said, you could believe the stories if you wanted, which implied a choice. *When in doubt, go with the safe bet. Put your money on ignorance.*

"To hell with it," Bobby said, throwing extra air behind the words to hide any potential cracks. "I want me one of those smokes."

He flung the rock—*away* from the cave, lest he wake any more of those skeletal men inside—and hurried down the slope, nearly slipping as he hustled while feigning nonchalance. One more whisper might have wended from the inky depths, but Bobby's feet scuffed leaves and Dex laughed and Vernon Ray hacked from a too-deep draw and the music of the forest swarmed in: whistling birds, creaking branches, tinkling creek water, and the brittle cawing of a lonely crow.

Bobby joined his friends and sat on a flat slab of granite beside the stump. From there, the Hole looked less menacing, a gouge in the dirt. Gray boulders, pocked with lichen and worn smooth by the centuries, framed the opening, and stunted, deformed jack pines clung to the dark soil above the cave.

A couple of dented beer cans lay half-buried in a patch of purple monkshood, and a rubber dangled like a stubby rattlesnake skin from a nearby laurel branch. Mulatto Mountain rose another hundred feet in altitude above the cave, where it topped off with sycamore and buckeye trees that had been sheared trim by the winter winds.

He took a cancer stick from Dex and fired it up, inhaling hard enough to send an inch of glowing orange along its tip. The smoke bit his lungs but he choked it down and then wheezed it out in small tufts.

The first buzz of nicotine numbed his fingers and floated him from his body. Relishing the punishment, he went back to mouth-smoking the way he usually did, rolling the smoke with his tongue instead of huffing it down. His head reeled but he grinned toward the sky in case Dex or Vernon Ray was looking.

"We ought to camp here sometime," Dex said, smoking with the ease of the addicted. He played dress-up as much as the Civil War re-enactors did, though his uniform of choice was upscale hoodlum—white T-shirt and a windbreaker that had "McCallister Alley" stitched over the left breast pocket. Three leaning bowling pins, punctured by a yellow starburst indicating a clean strike, were sewn beneath the label. Dex's old man owned the only alley within 80 miles of Titusville, and about once a month Mac McCallister was lubed enough from Scotch to let the boys roll a few free games.

"It'll be too cold to camp soon," Vernon Ray said, constantly flicking ash from his cigarette like a sissy. Bobby was almost embarrassed for him, but at the moment he had other concerns besides his best friend maybe being queer.

Concerns like the Jangling Hole, and whoever—or whatever—had spoken to him. *The wind, nothing but the wind.*

"Best time of year for camping," Dex said. "I can get my old man's tent, swipe a couple six-packs, bring some fishing poles. Maybe tote my .410 and bag us a couple squirrels for dinner."

"There's a level place down by the creek," Bobby said.

"Right here's fine," Dex said, sweeping one arm out in the expansive gesture of someone giving away something that wasn't his. "Put the tent between the roots of that oak yonder. Already got a fireplace." He booted one of the rocks that ringed a hump of charred wood.

"I don't know if my folks will let me," Vernon Ray said.

"Your dad's doing Stoneman's, ain't he?" Dex dangled his cigarette from his lower lip. "Since he's the big captain and all."

Stoneman's Raid was an annual Civil War re-enactment that

commemorated the Yankee incursion suffered by Titusville in 1864. The modern weekend warriors marked it by sleeping on the ground, drinking whiskey from dented canteens, and logging time in the saddle on rumps grown soft from too many hours in the armchair.

If they were like Bobby's dad, they spent their free time thumbing the remote between "Dancing With The Stars" and "The History Channel," unless it was football season when the Carolina Panthers jerseys came out of the bottom drawer.

"Sure," Vernon Ray said, voice hoarse from the cigarette. He flicked his smoke twice, but no ash fell. "Mom will probably go to Myrtle Beach like usual."

"The beach," Dex said. "Wouldn't mind eyeing some bikini babes myself."

There was a test in Dex's tone, maybe a taunt. Perhaps Dex, like Bobby, had been wondering about Vernon Ray. "What ya think, Bobby? A little sand in the honey sounds a lot better than watching a bunch of old farts in uniform, don't it?"

Bobby's gaze had wandered to the Hole again and he scanned the crisp line where the dappled sunlight met the black wall of hidden space that burrowed deep into Mulatto Mountain. As Dex called his name, Bobby blinked and took a deep, stinging puff. He spoke around the exhaled smoke, borrowing a line from his dad's secret stash of magazines in the tool shed. "Yeah, wouldn't mind some sweet tang myself."

Dex reached out and gave Vernon Ray a chummy slap on the back that was loud enough to echo off the rocks. "Beats pounding the old pud, huh?"

Vernon Ray nodded and took a quick hit. He even held his cigarette like a sissy, his pinky lifted in the air as if communicating in some sort of delicate sign language. Vernon Ray, unlike most of the kids at Titusville Middle School, already had a hair style, a soft, wavy curl flopping over his forehead.

Bobby wished he could protect his best friend, change him, rip that precious blonde curl out by the roots and turn him into a regular guy before Dex launched into asshole mode. When Dex got rolling, things went mean quick, and Vernon Ray's eyes already welled with water, either from the smoke or the teasing.

"I heard something at the Hole," Bobby said, not realizing he was speaking until the sentence escaped.

"Do what?" Dex leaned forward, flicking his butt into the cold, dead embers of the campfire.

"Somebody's in there."

Dex twisted off a laugh that sounded like the wheeze of an emphysema sufferer. "Something jangly, maybe? Bobby, you're so full of shit it's leaking out your ears."

Vernon Ray looked at him with gratitude. *Bambi eyes*, Bobby thought. *Pathetic.*

Bobby put a little drama in the sales pitch to grab Dex's full attention. "It went 'Urrrrr.'"

Dex snorted again. "Maybe somebody's barfing."

"Could have been a bum," Bobby said. "Ever since they shut down the homeless shelter, I've seen them sleeping under the bridge and behind the Dumpster at KFC. They've got to go somewhere. They don't just disappear."

"Maybe they do," Dex said. "I reckon those wino bastards better stay out of sight or they'll run 'em plumb out of the county."

The shelter had been shut down through the insidious self-righteousness of civic pride. Merchants had complained about panhandling outside their stores and the Titusville Town Council had drafted an ordinance against loitering. However, the town attorney, a misplaced Massachusetts native who had married into the fifth-generation law firm that had ruled the town behind the scenes since Reconstruction, dug up some court rulings suggesting that such an ordinance would interfere with the panhandlers' First Amendment rights.

Since the town leaders couldn't use the law as a whip and chair, they instead cut off local-government funding and drove the shelter into bankruptcy. Vernon Ray had explained all this to Bobby, but Bobby didn't think it was that complicated. People who didn't take the safe bet lost the game, simple as that.

"Even a bum's not stupid enough to sleep in the Hole," Vernon Ray said. "Cold as a witch's diddy in there."

Dex grinned with approval. "That why you didn't th'ow the rock, Bobby Boy? Afraid a creepy old crackhead might th'ow it back?"

"Probably just the wind," Bobby said. "Probably there's a bunch of other caves and the air went through just right."

"Sure it wasn't the Boys in Blue and Gray?" Dex said, thumbing another smoke from the pack. "Kirk's See-Through Raiders?"

"Like you said, you can believe the stories if you want." Contradicting his bravado, Bobby's gaze kept traveling to the dank orifice in the black Appalachian soil.

They should have stuck to the creek trail and not followed the animal path into the woods. The trail was the shortest distance from the trailer park where he lived and the Kangeroo Hop'n'Shop, a convenience store run by a family that Dex called "The Dot Heads." Bobby wasn't sure whether the family was Indian, Pakistani, or Arabian, though one of the daughters was in his English class and had a lot of vowels in her name. Dot Heads or not, it was the closest place to buy candy bars and football cards, not to mention sneak a peek at the oily, swollen breasts flashing from the magazine covers.

Half an hour before, the boys had made their ritual Saturday visit, flush with pocket change collected over the course of the week. While tobacco had become a controlled substance on the order of liquor and Sudafed, even in the tobacco-raising state of North Carolina, not all packs were kept on shelves behind the cash register.

A promotional two-pack of Camels, shrink-wrapped with a lighter, was perched on the edge of the counter by the ice cream freezer, and as Bobby had paid for a Dr. Pepper, Dex swept the package into the pocket of his windbreaker. Bobby caught the crime out of the corner of his eye, but the middle-aged woman at the register, who had a slight mustache riding her dark, pursed lips, was focused on counting pennies.

"Let's smoke 'em at the Hole," Dex had said, once they were out of sight of the store. Neither Bobby nor Vernon Ray had the guts to protest.

The Jangling Hole was half a mile's hike up rocky and wooded Blue Ridge terrain. Bobby had been there before with his two pals—after all, who could resist the most notorious haunted spot in the county, especially during Halloween season?—but they usually just eased around it and went to the headwaters of the creek where you could hook rainbow trout all year round, because no wildlife officers ever hoofed it that far back into the hills. That was back before Budget Bill Willard, the famous local photographer, had bought the property and posted "No Trespassing" signs all over it.

Dex had knocked down the first such sign he'd seen, unzipped his trousers, and urinated on it. Then he'd cajoled his reluctant merry band of pranksters to the Hole. After Dex had dared him to "th'ow" the rock, Bobby had no choice but to march up to the crevice, which was as wide as a pick-up truck. Nobody in his right mind would go near the cave that harbored the spirits of—

"Bobby?"

At first he thought the voice had come from the cave, in that same reverberating whisper that reached into his ears and tickled the bottom of his nasal cavity. But it was Dex, arms folded, chin out, squatting on the deadfall like a gargoyle clinging to the edge of some old French cathedral.

"You going to pretend it was them Civil War ghosts?" Dex said, letting one eyelid go lazy as if suggesting they could play a good one on Vernon Ray.

"I'm bored." Bobby's mouth was an ashtray, tongue dry as a spider web, nicotine ramping up his pulse. He'd wished he'd saved some of the Dr. Pepper, but Dex had knocked it from his hands as they'd crossed the creek.

"What you guys doing tonight?" Vernon Ray said.

"Your momma," Dex snapped back.

"I claim sloppy seconds," Bobby said, though his heart wasn't in it.

"For real," Vernon Ray said. "Think you can get out for a movie?"

"What's playing?" Dex said, faking a yawn and showing his missing molar.

"Tarentino's got a new one."

"We can't sneak into that, dumbass," Dex said. "It's rated 'R' for racks and red blood."

Bobby was about to suggest a round of X-Box, anything to get away from the cave, when Vernon Ray held up his hand.

"Shhh," the curly-haired boy said. "I hear something."

Bobby couldn't help sneaking a glance at the Hole, wondering if Vernon Ray had heard the whisper. Dex groaned. "Jesus, not you, too, V-Boy."

"Serious."

"That's the roaring of your own fat skull." Dex stood and looked down the slope into the woods, where the animal path widened. He blinked and flung his cigarette away as he turned and bolted.

"Over here!" came a shout. The rhododendrons shook along the edge of the clearing and a man in a brown uniform burst out, breaking into a run. Bobby caught the gleam of metal on the man's belt.

*Cop. Crap.*

His heart jumped against his ribs and fluttered like a bird in a cat's mouth. His dad would bust his ass good if he got in trouble with the law again. Dex headed for the back side of the mountain, where the steep slope bristled with brambles and scraggly locust trees, cover fit for a rabbit but little else.

The overweight cop was after him, wheezing, shouting at him to stop. Vernon Ray, who had fled down the path toward the creek trail, froze in his tracks at the command. While Bobby was still deciding which way to run, a second cop emerged, the brown-skinned store owner beside him.

"Is them," the store owner said. The cop, a young guy whose cheeks were blued with stubble, put his hand on his holster, no doubt weighing the wisdom of drawing on a couple of kids.

As the second cop hesitated, Vernon Ray cut to the right, through a shaded thicket of hardwoods and jack pine. He was soon out of sight, though his route was discernable by snapping branches and rattling leaves. The cop took three steps in pursuit, and then apparently realized Bobby would be easier prey.

Bobby took a backwards step. As a Little League All-Star, he could dash ninety feet between bases with no problem, and the safety of the woods was only half that distance. Dex would get away clean, he was as slick as a snake in a car wash, but the swarthy cop would probably net Vernon Ray if Bobby fled. And Vernon Ray was Honor Roll, the pride of the trailer park and Bobby's best friend.

"Hold it right there, son," the cop said, though he was barely a decade older than Bobby. The stem of his sunglasses was tucked in one pocket, the lenses like a second pair of accusing eyes. Sweat splotched the cop's underarms, and the badge caught a stray bit of sunlight as if God had signaled a secret moral message.

Bobby wanted to tell the cop he was innocent, to sell Dex down the river and take a plea, to beg the hairy-eared store owner's forgiveness. But no words came, his feet had grown roots like the trees around him, and his senses were as heightened as they'd been during the first rush of nicotine. *Had there been so many birds before?*

The cop smiled in condescension and triumph, and Bobby blushed with anger. Titusville was full of meth addicts, lock bumpers, and check kiters, and Bobby was pretty sure Louise Templeton was running a trailer-park whorehouse three doors down from his home, yet the local peace officers had nothing better to do than hassle kids.

Of course, his jacket already had three lines in it, and though as a juvenile he'd had it all written off because the courts called him an "at-risk youth," bad habits had a way of coming back to bite you on the ass.

"Don't worry," the cop said, reading the anxiety in Bobby's eyes. "We just want to talk."

"I make charges," the store owner said in his high-pitched, thickly accented voice. "I run fair trade."

The cop waved him back. "I'll handle this. It's only a misdemeanor, not a hanging offense."

It was the same smug crap the probation officer, the school counselor, and the principal all dished out. They'd poke around for some reason to explain the delinquent behavior, and though Bobby had only a passing knowledge of Freud, he'd picked up enough to feed the crap right back. Unhappy home, poverty, what they liked to call "an adjustment disorder," and the likelihood of substance abuse became not reasons to whip his ass into shape, but excuses for screwing up. Not only was his troubled streak explainable, it was practically expected. And who was *he* to disappoint so many others who had such a deep interest in his future?

The cop was close enough that Bobby could smell his aftershave, Old Spice or some other five-dollar-a-pint pisswater they sold at

Walmart. The store owner's pudgy fists were clenched, his dark face flushed with the anger of small-change violation. Hell, Dex could have paid for the smokes, that was no prob, Dex not only had a generous allowance but he was the biggest weed dealer at Titusville Middle School. He always had some spare jack in his pocket. But what the Dot Heads and the cops and the do-gooders didn't understand was that stealing was just more *fun*.

And Bobby had nothing better to do on a Saturday afternoon than sit through a booking and a lecture and then Dad's trip to bail his ass out of trouble again. Beat the hell out of X-box any day. And, he had to admit, an arrest would get him away from The Jangling Hole and the cold whispers and—

"*Aieeeeeee.*"

A scream ripped from the other side of the ridge, where the cop had chased Dex. It was followed almost immediately by a gunshot, the sharp report silencing the birds and riding up above the wind.

The young cop's face erupted in what might have been shock, but Bobby saw just a little pleasure in it. The cop was as bored as Bobby, and "Shots fired" was almost as good as "Officer down" when it came to law-enforcement hard-ons.

The cop grappled with his holster and had his mean-looking piece in his hand by the time he brushed past Bobby and headed around the Hole. Bobby and the store owner were left looking at each other, neither knowing what to do.

Bobby shrugged. "It was just some smokes, man."

The store owner stamped his foot and started jabbering a mile a minute in some exotic language, but he shut up quick when the second shot rang out.

CHAPTER TWO

Vernon Ray was nearly to the creek, wondering if it was safe to pop out onto the trail, when he heard the shot. *Surely they wouldn't shoot anybody for shoplifting, would they?*

Unless Dex had been packing. Dex McCallister had a bad rep to maintain, but his record was pretty clean. That had more to do with the bully's instinct for self-preservation, as well as his dad's lawyer, than it did criminal cunning. Vernon Ray was Dex's pet target, but Bobby's defense was worth all the "Batman and Supergirl" comments Dex dished out. Vernon Ray had to admit, nobody else at school picked on him these days, and though Dex still got in a little jab now and then, it was a better deal than have a hundred other goons riding his case. All because he was different.

*Just because . . . .*

*Just because nothing.*

Now push had come to shove, and Vernon Ray could either be a piss ant little coward the way Bobby and Dex expected, or he could circle back out of the safety of the woods and see what had happened. He wasn't up for bravery, the kind of action-movie horse dookie where the wimp suddenly overcame his inner nature out of loyalty, love, or just plain recklessness because it fit the plot. But maybe he'd have a cool story to tell his classmates, and if Dex did eat an appetizer of hot lead followed by a dirt sandwich, Vernon Ray could put a great spin on it.

Even better, maybe Dex had shot one of the cops. Vernon Ray could get a lot more mileage out of that, put it out there as a Bonnie-and-Clyde story. Of course, inevitably he'd be cast as Bonnie, but better to live forever as a marred legend than to sit in the corner with his thumb in his mouth until the end of high school. A shooting was a much bigger attention-grabber than a bunch of ghosts that probably didn't exist, and even his dad would want to know the gory details. Even if it was just for a week, there would be something in Titusville bigger than Stoneman's Raid and Capt. Jefferson

Davis's brass balls.

He was still weighing his options when the second shot rang out.

*Bobby?*

Vernon Ray wiped the sweat from his palms and began retracing his steps. The forest was in full flush, hung in that verdant phase of late autumn when the leaves screamed of death, and he had to push the pine and undergrowth away from his face. A scratch on his cheek stung with the promise of infection, and his chest heaved from exertion. But this wasn't about him and his suffering. This was about buddies, the Three Musketeers, the Unholy Trinity, the Good, the Bad, and the Ugly, every little comic-book fantasy he'd ever concocted.

Hell, it was about belonging. Bobby and Dex were the closest things he had to friends. Sure, his parents were still together, unlike practically every other kid in the eighth grade, but they might as well have mailed in their parental love like cereal box tops to Battle Creek, Michigan, for all the good it did him. So if Dex and Bobby needed him, he'd be there.

And, truth be told, he was pretty damned ashamed about bolting and abandoning his best bud. An arrest on his record would earn him some props at school and a lecture from his dad, the Captain. Then again, inner nature was nature after all, and maybe you couldn't really change the boy you were or the man you were bound to be. He was a chicken-tailed, limp-wristed little sissy like they all said.

Dapples of sunlight made a crazy disco ball in the treetops overhead as he ran. A couple of sirens wailed up from the valley below, probably half of Titusville's on-duty contingent cutting its way to Mulatto Mountain. Vernon Ray strained his ears for the crackle of cop walkie-talkies. No follow-up shots had been fired, suggesting that Dex probably hadn't staged a dramatic "They'll never take me alive" showdown. Dex would make a perfect subject for a Frank Miller graphic novel, the cautionary tale of a good boy gone wrong, assuming he hung around long enough to grow a personality and then was able to come back from the grave and seek vengeance.

By the time Vernon Ray backtracked the quarter-mile uphill to The Jangling Hole, the old campsite had been abandoned. Maybe Bobby was already headed to the sheriff's office, sitting in the back of a cruiser and cussing under his breath. They could charge him with being an accomplice or receiving stolen goods–if sucking down stinky, chemical-soaked tobacco counted as "receiving." But even the clod-headed ex-jocks who populated the field of law enforcement were smart enough to know chasing juveniles was a thankless and fruitless chore that rarely led to conviction.

A shout came from beyond the trees, maybe three hundred feet away. Dex must have stirred up the cops, provoked them, craving all the attention like a suicidal drama queen at a drag show. Sometimes it just didn't pay to hang out with a goon. But Vernon Ray would lose either way: a black mark on his record would help stifle the "sissy" label, but for sure Dad would bust his ass and Mom would go into one of her patented sulks.

But the deal breaker was his buddies' reactions. He was a little ashamed for running off like that, but instinct had taken over. It was probably too late for redemption, and Dex had a long memory for such things, but Bobby was a little more flexible. Bobby had been his best pal since daycare, when they'd snickered through Mrs. Underwood's version of "Three Billy Goats Gruff," or what Dex had called "Th'ee Billy Goats Gwuff," at least until Lori Stansberry laughed at him and he bloodied her nose, after which Dex never mentioned that stupid old story again. Nor did any of his classmates.

So Dex could sink or swim on his own, nobody had a problem with that, especially Dex, but Bobby—

"Psst."

Vernon Ray looked around, peering under the heavy thatch of laurel, galax, and briars and across the jumbled shelves of gray granite. But he knew the sound hadn't come from the forest. And the cops would have bellowed, not whispered. Vernon Ray whispered in return. "Bobby?"

"In here."

*Confederate Christ on a battle flag, was he really dumb enough to hide in the Hole?*

Vernon Ray squinted against the afternoon sun, which had reached a low-enough angle that it slanted through the canopy, throwing a mystical, ethereal light against the leaves. By contrast, the dark slit of the crevice was as foreboding as a woman's womb. "Where's the cops?"

"I dunno. The other one took off after the second shot."

"Come on out of there," Vernon Ray said.

"I can't."

"Why the hell not?" Vernon Ray strained his ears, but all he heard was the caw of a solitary crow and the wind crawling low in the pines. He expected the cops to jump out from cover at any moment, or maybe the foreign store owner with his incessant, rapid-fire vexation. He couldn't believe Bobby would corner himself like that. Maybe his pal was waiting it out, hoping to ride the darkness until sundown, then sneak down the mountain and head for home. A high price for a lousy cigarette.

"You gotta see this," Bobby said, and it sounded like he had moved deeper into the mouth of the tunnel, because the echo died with a stifled sigh and Vernon Ray had trouble hearing him.

"I'm not going in there," Vernon Ray said. "That's the *Hole*, for crying out loud."

Bobby didn't answer and Vernon Ray took a reluctant step closer. He was now maybe fifteen feet from the opening, closer than Bobby had been earlier when Dex had urged him to throw the stone. Even from that distance, he could smell the Stygian stench of the cave as its clammy, insidious air oozed around him and embraced him, pulling him closer.

Depending on which version of the myth you believed, The Jangling Hole was either an inviting refuge or a sinister maw that would swallow all who entered. According to his dad, the Hole had been a Civil War hideout for deserters of both camps, a gang of raiders brought together by a schizophrenic Yankee colonel. In that cramped darkness, there was no room for conflict, as neither the Confederacy nor the Union stirred much loyalty among the isolated mountaineers, who had little use for government of any kind. Apparently no artifacts had ever been found there, so the legend was mostly written off as the wistful folly of those who found the past more alluring than the bloody, televised tempest of their own times. People like Capt. Davis.

But lack of evidence had never killed a good legend. The cave had earned its name from reports of clinking tools and the jangling of knives against mess kits and canteens. Vernon Ray, who had read plenty of Weird War and Tales From The Crypt comics, figured the cave was as likely to be haunted as any other piece of ground, and Civil War battle sites were notorious for their paranormal activity.

He'd been plenty curious, but never brave enough to enter. Until now.

The thick air seeped from the cave's mouth and blended with the healthy, green atmosphere of the forest. He wondered how Bobby could even breathe in there, much less move around without a flashlight.

He raised his voice, figuring the risk of cops was lower than the risk of getting closer to the cave. "Hey, Bobby!"

No answer. His pal had disappeared like Alice down the zombie rabbit hole.

*Okay, Straight-A Brain, give me something useful here besides algebra functions and the roster of Gettysburg commanders.*

He had a few choices. He could go find the cops, wherever they were, and report Bobby missing, which would leave Bobby hating his guts; he could high-tail it home and call Bobby's dad, which would probably put Vernon Ray's own ass in a sling; or he could go inside the cave—just a few feet—and summon his friend again.

He was still undecided, though he'd edged another step closer to the narrow entrance, when he heard the soft patter of rain on leaves. That made no sense, for though the weather in the Blue Ridge mountains could change dramatically, sometimes delivering the worst of three different seasons in the same day, the sky was mostly clear at the moment. Yet another faint rumble rolled across the black dirt of the mountain, suggesting a thunderstorm on its way.

*Great. A few bolts of lightning at this altitude and I'm pretty much guaranteed to be trapped in the Hole with Bobby. Or zapped to Asgard and Odin's throne.*

The pattering grew louder, and Vernon Ray looked up,

expecting water droplets to splash in his eyes. But the air was dry and free of static, though cooling with the approach of sundown. The rumble swelled, taking on a resounding quality, but it was topped by a steady staccato. Now Vernon Ray placed the sound, though it had no place in this primal environment.

The rattle of a snare drum.

Often in the Civil War re-enactments, one of the counterfeit soldiers' kids was decked out in a little uniform, round-topped kepi tilted low over the forehead, leather boots dusty and scuffed. The kid would either be the drummer boy or, less often, the flag bearer, since flags were heavier and slightly more dangerous in simulated battle. A flagstaff could dip and knock a foot soldier on the head or joust a cavalryman out of the saddle. But a drum—well, a drum was just plain cute.

Not that the Captain had ever invited his son into the camp, or let him wear one of the miniature uniforms in the memorabilia collection. Years ago, they used to travel to the events together, though Vernon Ray and Mom were strictly spectators. From Manassas to Spotsylvania to Harpers Ferry to Marietta, they had kneeled in the shade eating picnic lunches while mock battles raged and a layer of black-powder smoke settled over the field. Though most re-enactments featured a civilian attachment in period clothing, the women in cumbersome hoop skirts and the children in knickers and ragged cotton blouses, Vernon Ray was soon consigned to being a spectator only, and eventually his dad stopped taking him along altogether.

Vernon Ray had been jealous of those boys who actually got to participate, especially the drummers. Sometimes, an entire corps of boys, some of them with wrists barely as thick as their drumsticks, would stand in the morning sun and roll out marching cadences. When the action began, a few of them even got to die, flopping on the ground while carefully tossing their snares to the side or dragging themselves toward enemy lines as if sporting deep, imminently fatal wounds. Vernon Ray, who probably knew more Civil War history than all of them put together, had yet to put a boot on such hallowed territory.

But he had taught himself how to roll out a snare cadence, his right wrist turned upward, his left wrist flexing gently. His sticks on the nylon skin made the same percussive rhythm as the one now welling from the cave. He knew the drill, and this was its beat.

Somebody in the Hole was tapping out a marching tempo, and as far as Vernon Ray knew, Bobby had never touched a drum in his life.

CHAPTER THREE

Two shots. Them peckerwoods were at it again, poaching on the low backbone of land that ran up Mulatto Mountain. Hardy Eggers started for the shotgun in the closet, but then remembered two unfortunate details that he'd done a decent job of burying over the last couple of months.

One, the sheriff had pretty much warned him against hauling out the shotgun every time trouble showed up, ever since he'd run off that last batch of suits from Elkridge Landcorp, LLC. Hardy figured the initials stood for "lily-livered cowards," but the legal documents probably spelled out some long-winded horse manure drummed up in a Yankee law school.

Hardy hadn't been aware that it was a crime to step out on the porch armed for protection when a bunch of squirrel-eyed strangers pulled up in a long, shiny Cadillac. The sheriff explained that such shenanigans constituted "communicating a threat," which apparently trumped the trespassing charge Hardy could have sworn against the suits. To Hardy, it had simply been a case of marking territory and cutting the need for chatter. They wanted him to sell and he wouldn't sell for a barn's worth of gold bullion and a lifetime's supply of Louise Templeton, not that he had much demand for her particular ware in his old age.

Two, the upper side of the mountain was no longer in the Eggers family. Brother Tommy and sister Sue Ellen had sold off their portions of the family birthright to Budget Bill Willard, who built his fortune as a photographer with pictures on calendars, postcards, and the pages of "Southern Living" magazine. Budget Bill, who was second-generation local, parlayed his makeshift camera shop into a cottage industry and then had gone into land development. The stumpy, bald-headed peckerwood was known for his scenic shots of old-timey mountain farmsteads, but now he was using the money to bulldoze those very sites and turn them into second-home subdivisions for flatlanders who drove too slow and talked too fast.

Hardy figured he was probably the only coot in Pickett County to see the irony in Budget Bill's career trajectory; only a hypocrite would pretend to celebrate the thing he was actively destroying. But that was Budget Bill for you, and his type of crime was not only tolerated but written up big in the papers and showered with plaques from the Chamber of Commerce, like he was some sort of hero. Just went to show you could get away with murder as long as you did it with a camera or a bank note or a bulldozer instead of a gun.

*Two shots, though.*

October was too early for squirrel hunting, and the elk that gave the developers their fancy-pants subdivision name had been extinct for two centuries. Daniel Boone and his pack of musket-toting tourists had accomplished in ten years what the Cherokee hadn't managed to do in a thousand. And Hardy figured by the time Budget Bill's group of bankers and lawyers were done, not even a skunk would be left on Mulatto Mountain.

There was one other possibility, but he liked that one even less. The Hole had been quiet for years—ever since they'd taken a piece of his son—but who could say what would happen when bulldozers scraped and gouged ill-rested ground? And whether the family's skeletons might rattle and dance free of the closet?

Hardy parted the curtains and peeked out, just to play it safe. He still clung to a herd of short-horns, even though the Republicans had stomped out farm subsidies and pretty much guaranteed farmers would have to sell off their property eventually. The cattle were grazing in the blue-green grass under the soft autumn sky, all accounted for, so nobody had been taking pot shots at the livestock. And nothing hungry had come out of the dark cracks in the mountain to haul off some fresh, writhing meat on the hoof.

A thump came from the stairs, the irregular clatter of shoe leather on wood. His wife Pearl was limping down, arthritis and all. Hardy had tried to talk her into moving their bedroom to the first floor of the farmhouse, but she was having none of it. Their four-poster bed, hand carved from cherry, had withstood forty-three years of loving and fussing, and she saw no reason to go rushing into change. Besides, Donnie was on the second floor and moving him would be a mite harder.

The thumping stopped and her face peered over the banister, eyes as bright as marbles despite the lines around them. "What's going on?"

"Somebody shooting on the mountain."

"No need to go whipping out your pecker. It's none of your affair."

"It is if they're hunting out of season."

"You can't have it both ways, hon. You expect people to mind their own business when it comes to your land, but when it's the neighbor's, you got to go sticking that big snout right in it."

Hardy touched his nose. It wasn't *that* big. Besides, the feature ran in the family, and the Eggerses had been prominent back when property and healthy livestock, not money, were the measure of a man. "Well, it ain't been their land long."

"Tommy and Sue Ellen did what was best for their futures. They got kids in college. Not everybody's as hardheaded and stuck in the past as you are."

"Shit fire," Hardy said, letting the curtain drop and not bothering to mention Donnie's chances of attending college were about the same as a pig playing banjo. "I guess I need something to get riled over in my old age."

"You're better off tending to your blood pressure," Pearl said, finishing her descent of the stairs. He went to her and gave her a kiss on the cheek, despite the fact that he'd kissed her no more than an hour ago, when they'd been fooling around up in the marriage bed. Hardy hadn't been able to work up enough to give either of them satisfaction, but he figured he ought to try once a week or so whether he felt like it or not. Pearl, loyal partner that she was, never once complained or ridiculed him, just said a long snuggle was plenty enough intimacy for her. Hardy had hinted she might try out some of those battery-operated contraptions they sold right out on the drugstore shelves, but she only giggled and said an old dog like her was way past any new tricks.

He was about to ask if she wanted a cup of tea—she liked her Lipton's warm with a teaspoon of sugar and a dash of half-and-half, which he thought was Massachusetts foolishness she'd got out of some magazine or other, but it was her only vice and not much of one at that—when she held up a hand.

"You didn't like that kiss?" he asked.

"You're getting better with practice, but I think somebody's coming."

A couple of seconds later, he heard the low whine of a car engine and the chink of gravel kicking off a steel undercarriage. Loss of hearing came with the years, he supposed, but it still sucked mule eggs. Sounded like a big ride, maybe another Caddy full of Budget Bill's monkeys in neckties, but he decided to give the shotgun a pass for now. Pearl followed him out the front door.

The sheriff's beige-and-white cruiser slewed to a stop, its bubble-gum machine strobing blue on the roof. Frank Littlefield climbed out of the driver's seat, leaving the door open and engine running, meaning he was either hellbent for leather or else had a warrant burning a hole in his pocket.

Littlefield had gone a little soft in the belly and patches of gray marked his temples. His eyes were pouched and bloodshot, but that was only natural for a man who had lost a couple of detectives along the way, not to mention his kid brother. People gossiped about Littlefield, since freak accidents tended to dog his every step, but Hardy had pulled the lever for the man come every election day, Republican or no.

"Howdy, Sheriff, what can I do you for?" Hardy shouted, Pearl pressed close behind him and smelling of clean Ivory soap.

"Mind opening your cattle gate, Mr. Eggers?"

Ordinarily, Hardy would have made a joke about his cows being the law-abiding sort, but Littlefield's expression and clipped tone discouraged tomfoolery. This was a man on a mission. "Sure enough," he said, heading down the steps and breaking into a gimpy trot.

Littlefield got back behind the wheel and by the time Hardy swung the steel gate open, the sheriff had pulled the cruiser to the dusty twin tracks that led past a couple of hay barns and into the hills. Littlefield paused, his driver's-side window down.

"I'll need to go through the upper gate, too, but I'll close it behind me," the sheriff said.

"That one's stickier than a widow's honeypot," Hardy said. "You might need a hand with it."

Truth was, Hardy just wanted to poke his big snout into Littlefield's business, and they both knew it. But Littlefield nodded his head to the passenger door. "Let's roll."

Just before Hardy ducked into the car, he gave Pearl a reassuring wave, but it didn't diminish the deep worry lines on her forehead.

"Keep an eye on Donnie," he said.

"And you keep an eye on yourself," she shouted back before he closed the door.

The car bounced up the old roadbed that had once been used for logging, back before the timber clear-cutting of the early twentieth century. A lot of the access roads had been abandoned and gone back to saplings, and though Grandpappy Eggers had sold off logging rights, he'd kept open the main road across the mountain, even though it was now best navigated by four-wheel-drive vehicles. The sheriff seemed plenty determined, however, and Hardy didn't think a few dents to the oil pan would slow him any.

"Manhunt in progress?" Hardy ventured, a line he'd probably picked up from a TV show.

"I'm not sure yet," Littlefield said. "And I couldn't tell you if I knew."

The radio crackled. A laptop computer was fastened to the dashboard with Velcro, and a pump-action .20-gauge rested in the crotch between the two front seats. Littlefield picked up the handset and spoke into it. "Any word on Perriotte?"

"Nowhere in sight," came the reply, the sibilant lost in a spray of static.

"I heard two shots," Hardy said. "Is some nut up there with a gun?"

"Like I said, I can't say."

"Can't say, or can't tell?"

"Neither one."

The sheriff ditched the handset and locked both hands on the wheel. The October heat and stress were squeezing sweat from his scalp. As they gunned up the incline, the herd of cattle gazed with disinterest, as if figuring that even if the car were edible, it was moving way too fast to munch.

"Might be one of them hippies," Hardy said, enjoying his brief turn as an accidental deputy.

"What hippies?" Littlefield said, checking the digital readouts on the dashboard.

"Tree huggers. The ones trying to stop Budget Bill and the developers, claim Mulatto Mountain is an environmental treasure."

"They aren't the violent kind," Littlefield said. "They're more likely to pass out flyers and hold rallies on the library lawn, not pull an ecoterrorist number. They're too busy smoking pot to figure out which end of a firearm is which."

When they reached the upper gate, they found it as rusty as Hardy had promised. Littlefield pounded the sole of his boot against the latch until it finally broke free, and then the two men lifted the gate and shoved it against a reluctant tuft of blackberry briars until the opening was wide enough for the car.

"Thanks, Mr. Eggers," the sheriff said. "Sorry I've got to leave you here, but this is official police business."

"Go get 'em," Hardy said, slapping his palm on the roof. As the wide Buick cruiser weaved through the forest, branches slapping at the car's flanks, Hardy wrestled the gate back into place. He looked down at the farmhouse and outbuildings nearly half a mile below, where they were tucked in the valley like a child's alphabet blocks on a rumpled green rug. He imagined Pearl was still standing on the porch, hand shading her eyes, her thin lips pursed in worry. At a time like this, Hardy was glad his eyesight was as gone-to-shit as his hearing and his pecker.

He waved, on the long chance that she could see him, and started hoofing it up the roadbed in the wake of the cruiser. Sure, this constituted trespassing, as he was officially on property belonging to Budget Bill Willard and Elkridge Landcorp, and given his game legs and short wind, he probably wouldn't make it another hundred feet, but he hadn't had a thrill since the armed showdown with the developers and damned if he wasn't looking forward to some action. Besides, his one-eyed rattlesnake twitched a little in the moist den of his boxers, as if maybe it wasn't yet resigned to permanent hibernation.

Too bad he didn't have his shotgun. But no way in hell was he going to walk down to the house and get it. He'd just have to improvise, if worse came to worse.

Littlefield might be able to handle the drug addicts and petty crooks of Pickett County, but Mulatto Mountain was an entirely different story.

A whole *bunch* of stories, come to think of it.

Hardy just hoped, for the sake of all that was good, right, and holy, that he'd make it to the top in time to keep everybody away from The Jangling Hole.

He'd not been there for his own son, but maybe he could scare off the next bunch before the Hole spewed more of its wickedness into the world.

CHAPTER FOUR

*Shots fired. Officer down. Maybe.*
*I hate the unknown.*
*Too bad there's so damned much of it.*

Sheriff Frank Littlefield punished the cruiser, bouncing up the eroded twin ruts that passed for a road. Most of his counterparts in surrounding mountain counties drove

Humvees or oversize SUV's, but Littlefield's departmental budget had been stressed by the opening of a new jail and demands for beefed-up security at the courthouse. It seemed judges didn't like the rash of nutballs passing down their own sentences in court, punctuated with the bang of hot steel instead of a cool wooden gavel. Besides, Littlefield's self-image required he drive the most beat-up, high-mileage vehicle in the fleet, and the whining Buick had been ridden hard enough to earn a place on the scrap heap.

Some would put its driver in the same category. Littlefield had won the last election by 12 votes, and that was only after a recount. Pickett County hadn't endured a Democratic sheriff since the 1970s, but political unrest had trickled even into the most remote and conservative pockets of the South. And folks still whispered about the red church and how Littlefield's younger brother had died, as well as his chief deputy. Trouble cast a long shadow over the sheriff, not a good circumstance for someone in his line of work.

He didn't dwell on the past, because the past was mostly a string of failures. A less-arrogant man would have turned in his badge, or fail to campaign vigorously enough to win. Littlefield, approaching 47, figured he still had a few good years left, since modern police spent more time at the computer than chasing bad guys. The sad truth was, he didn't have anything else to do with his life, and the opportunity for redemption always hung before him like a sagging Christ on crooked dogwood.

Maybe this was the chance. The report of "Shots fired" had kicked his heart into high gear, especially since his deputies were involved. Morton and Perriotte were recent hires, both with criminal justice degrees, and the Saturday-afternoon shift was a good way to break them in. Domestic violence calls and drunk drivers were the most common log ledgers, but this was Pickett County, and Littlefield had been around long enough to know things could take a sudden turn into the strange, especially on Mulatto Mountain.

The radio had been spitting static for the last two minutes, and Littlefield had no idea of his location. Like most native males, he'd hunted the mountain as a youngster, but the terrain had changed a bit since then. The hardwood forest became more dense, slabs of granite shelves had given way in places, and the old logging roads were slowly reverting to their natural state. Leaves slapped the windshield, and a branch slammed the side mirror against the chassis, cracking the glass. The front wheels of the Buick dropped into a ditch, and Littlefield decided he'd better go the rest of the way on foot.

Littlefield called dispatch and ordered the other responding deputies to stake out the foot of the mountain. If there was a shooter on the loose, better to keep the stray bullets away from town. Two roads girded the mountain, but anybody with a half a lick of sense could slip through the woods and stay out of sight. Littlefield's order was designed to keep people out of the firing line, and he told himself it was smart strategy.

But the fringe benefit was that no witnesses would be around if things went weird.

Littlefield was out of the car and trying to get his bearings when a third shot rang out. Shouts arose from somewhere to his left, maybe a few hundred feet. His deputies must have tracked a suspect into the woods and now the parties were in a standoff near the ridge.

Good versus evil, right against wrong, light and dark in their eternal dance, all bleeding in a blind gray struggle that kept people like Littlefield motivated and employed. Littlefield cursed under his breath, wondering which side he truly served, and then eased between the trees, hunched low and stepping lightly.

*Why hadn't the boys used their field radios?*

The last transmission had been their standard 10-20 check,

reporting their response to the shoplifting call. Maybe they figured to perform a quick search and make the store owner happy, knowing shoplifters who left the premises were rarely apprehended. That didn't matter now. All that mattered was getting everybody off Mulatto Mountain in one piece.

"Over here," Morton shouted.

Littlefield drew his Glock, the first time he'd gripped the pistol in months, and risked giving away his location by answering. "You okay?"

"It's Perriotte."

"Is he down?"

"Sort of," Morton shouted.

Littlefield worked past trees and up the slope, breathing harder than he cared to acknowledge, his chest a little tight around his ribs. He eased around a boulder, bits of lichen breaking loose and tickling down his collar.

"Sort of? A man's either up or he's down."

"He's down, but he's not shot. Not that I can see."

Littlefield was now close enough to talk without shouting, though the deputies were still concealed from him by the evergreen growth. "Where's the gunman?"

"That's the odd part. I don't see one." Then, lower, "Hang on, J.R. It's going to be okay."

Littlefield skirted behind a low thicket of cedars, the Glock heavy in his hand. He hadn't shot anyone in years, not since Archer McFall, and he still wasn't sure whether McFall counted as "anyone" or not. The jury was still out on that one. When your victim up and drifted into the river, leaving only a pile of dry mud behind, you couldn't rightly carve a notch in your gun.

Winded, he leaned against an oak, bark scraping his cheek. From his new vantage point, he could look down on his officers, who were crouched behind a jumble of granite that jutted from the ground like the broken teeth of giants. Morton, the youngest, his chin red from a severe shave, peered over the stones and up the slope to Littlefield's left. Littlefield surveyed the foliage. He saw no movement.

"Psst," Littlefield called to Morton, figuring the element of surprise was shot to hell anyway. The distant sirens had surely tipped off the gunman that the cavalry was riding in, and not many roads led off Mulatto Mountain.

"Up there, Sheriff," Morton said, waving his own pistol toward the peak.

"Did you see anything?"

"Movement, nothing much. Could have been a deer for all I could tell."

"How's Perriotte?"

"Peculiar."

*Peculiar? What the hell kind of diagnosis was "peculiar"?*

Littlefield squinted into the forest, where gnarled limbs hugged the darkness and ancient things slept beneath the rotten crust. "Did he fire his weapon?"

"Three times. The last time, I was here, but I don't know what in hell he was shooting at."

"Hell with it," he muttered under his breath. "Guess it's always now or never."

Littlefield approached the ridge, edging out from cover enough to let the gunman see him without getting a clear shot. If Perriotte had fired three times, the gunman might not even be a gunman at all. The correct term was "suspect," but the target had not been identified by anyone but Perriotte. So that made it what they liked to call "a person of interest," the lingo lawmen fell back on when they didn't know their asses from a hole in the ground. And he was up-to-date on what constituted a hole in the ground, because The Jangling Hole was just such a creature.

*"Creature," shit. There I go personifying inanimate objects again. Should have checked into the loony bin the first time I ever saw a talking, shape-shifting stack of dirt. That would have spared lots of people lots of trouble, and maybe kept a couple of them alive.*

Littlefield looked down to see his pistol hand was shaking. So much for all those Louis L'Amour novels. The sheriff's only comfort was in knowing the Hole was on the far side of the mountain, hundreds of yards from the ridge and Perriotte's apparent target.

"Cover me," Littlefield said to Morton. The kid's eyes were wide and wet like oily olives, but he nodded in something approximating confidence. A sheriff's hiring practices rarely came down to a life-

and-death roll of the dice, but Littlefield hoped Morton lived up to
the bluff and bluster on his resume. Littlefield took three steps, then
lost his footing in the slick leaves and fell on his rump. A fart
escaped his clenched rectum.

He bit back a curse and rolled to his hands and knees. Keeping
low, he scuttled to Morton's and Perriotte's concealment. Perriotte's
eyes were wide and blank, staring through the canopy as if scanning
for angels against the high clouds. The downed officer was an Iraqi
war vet, had served two tours with a National Guard unit before
finishing his criminal justice training. Maybe he was suffering
delayed post-traumatic stress disorder and had lapsed into some
sort of bizarre episode, though the North Carolina ridges were far
removed from flat sand, crumbling mosques, and roadside bombers.

"You okay, J.R.?" The new generation of deputies went by
initials while on duty, an annoying habit that had migrated from the
ranks of the state highway patrol. Littlefield would have preferred to
call the man "Jimmy," which would have seemed a little more
humane. The deputy looked like he could use all the human
connection he could get, because his lips were stuttering soundlessly
and his eyelids twitched in broken focus.

"He's been like that ever since he fired the third shot," Morton
said.

"Did you see what he was shooting at?"

"No, he just yelled, 'See that?' and cut loose. He dropped his
gun and curled up in a ball, and he's been like this ever since."

Littlefield put two fingers to Perriotte's jugular. The pulse was
strong and rapid. No physical injury. But the deepest wounds were
invisible and a lot of soul juice could leak from them before the
protective scars formed.

"We were in pursuit of them kids," Morton said. "J.R. went after
the fastest brat, chased him around the ridge."

"Were you guys near the Hole?"

Morton's eyes narrowed and he rubbed at the raw skin of his
close-shaven neck. "We could see it, but we didn't go in. You think
somebody was hiding in there? A fugitive, maybe, who got spooked
when he saw cops?"

"Did he say anything after the first two shots?" Littlefield played his gaze along the ridge line but saw nothing. Even the crows had been startled into silence.

The ridge was like the backbone of a dinosaur, lined with boulders and spiky trees, the branches shorn and stunted by the endless winds. The Appalachian Mountain chain, the world's oldest, was worn by eons, but parts of it had resisted age, as if beholden to laws besides the natural. Mulatto Mountain was such a place, and Littlefield could have sworn the mountain throbbed. He checked his watch and saw the numbers hadn't changed since he'd stepped from the cruiser. He shook his left wrist and tapped the watch with the butt of his gun but the red numerals winked in a mockery of mortality: 5:53.

"When I reached him, he said what sounded like 'He's walking on nothing.' What do you think that means?"

Sounded to Littlefield like a quote from some book or movie, but Perriotte wasn't exactly among the culturally hip. He was more of a pork rinds-and-roller derby kind of guy. Though the deputy had a fondness for videogames, he mostly stuck to the shoot-'em-up kind where the line between the guilty and innocent often blurred and both were acceptable in piling up body counts. Perriotte was a registered Democrat, though you couldn't tell it by his shop talk, and he attended the big new Baptist Church in Whispering Pines. Littlefield wasn't one to meddle in his people's private lives, unless there were suggestions of behavior that might come back to haunt his department.

Right now, Perriotte looked to be suffering from a problem bigger than psycho girlfriends and party politics, and Littlefield wondered how he would spin this to keep the deputy's jacket clean. Anytime an officer fired shots in the line of duty, the State Bureau of Investigation stuck its beak into the situation and it became a race to see who could whip it out the fastest and measure it the longest. Under normal circumstances, Perriotte could defend the shoot. But this time there was no inciting action and no target.

Which probably meant Littlefield could cover it up. But he wasn't sure he could wipe the slate of Perriotte's memory as easily, because the man hadn't blinked since Littlefield's arrival two minutes before.

"He wasn't shooting at the kid, was he?" Littlefield asked Morton.

"No, sir. The brat was long gone by the time I caught up."

"Did you get a look at him?"

"All those brats are the same. Skater punks. There were a couple on the other side of the ridge but they took off when we heard the shots."

"We?"

"Me and Ammanahiya whatever. The store owner."

"So there's another witness to worry about." Though Littlefield wondered if it counted as "witnessing" if there had been nothing to see.

"I doubt it. He took off faster than the kids, squealing like a teenybopper at a Clay Aiken concert."

Littlefield looked down the slope, which was quiet, not even the breeze rustling the trees. He was glad now that he had ordered the deputies to stake out the main roads. The fewer who knew about this the better, at least until he came up with a good story.

He had more than just Perriotte to worry about. The suits of Elkridge Landcorp had a lot at stake on Mulatto Mountain, and the county commissioners were wetting their pants over the potential tax revenue that would roll in when the slopes were stacked with million-dollar summer homes. A little bad publicity might slow down the project, and three of the commissioners were coming up for reelection. They couldn't fire him, but they could jerk his chain and make him roll over and beg.

"Let's get him up," Littlefield said, pointing out the overgrown logging road. "My cruiser is closer than yours. About a hundred yards that way."

Perriotte swayed like a drunken sailor but stayed on his feet, flopping against Morton's shoulder. Littlefield got them balanced and wobbling in the right direction.

"Want me to call an ambulance?" Morton said.

"No, we'll deal with it at the office. I'll catch up in a second. I got to check out the ridge first. Can you handle him?"

"Hell, I've had dates groggier than this, and I got them to bed just fine."

"Well, treat him like a lady, not a woman."

Morton tried to crack a grin but the strain and uncertainty were evident on his face. "What do you think he was shooting at?"

"Don't worry, we'll come up with something. Bear, dog with rabies, hell, maybe even a wild, man-eating goat. Stranger things have walked this goddamned mountain."

As the two deputies negotiated the stumps, fallen trees, and jagged stones, Perriotte leaving long black strips of mud where his patent-leather shoes dragged, Littlefield climbed the last hundred feet to the slope. The pines, oak, and beech trees at the top of Mulatto Mountain were bleached by acid rain, the limbs jagged and broken from savage winds and ice storms. While the woods below were comforting, the kind that evoked images of cute little chipmunks and dewy-eyed deer, the ridge was raw and bristling, full of sharp edges and broken chunks of granite.

From the top, which was about a thousand feet in altitude above the valley floor, Littlefield took in the 360-degree view. Titusville spread out in a chaotic grid, the streets squeezed together to accommodate the uneven topography. The main strip was a four-lane boulevard that looked like Anywhere, USA, with a Walmart, Western Steer, Taco Bell, Burger King, Auto Zone and enough different banks to foreclose on half the county. When Littlefield was a boy, the town had been little more than a motel, general store, and a Greyhound bus terminal with a gas station attached. Now Titusville was the biggest town in three counties, evolving into a business park for Realtors, lending institutions, and lawyers, who were basically all hogs at the same trough sucking down the swill of vacation-home owners.

But not everything was new and glistening with white concrete, glass, and steel. Mulatto Mountain had stood watch over all of it, and its legends had seeped into the dirt and run down the gullies like spring freshets spawned by melting snow. The forest, despite having been logged heavily a century before and now squarely in the sights of a development group, still had a primal feel, as if extinct predators might emerge from cover at any moment and give a hungry grin. Though the town was an hour's hike away, it might as well have been a thousand miles.

Littlefield walked the ridge, looking for any signs of recent passage. He found a lump of animal spoor, most likely from a deer, but it was too dried and desiccated to have dropped from Perriotte's target.

*"He walked on nothing."*

That didn't sound much like a deer, either. Being dead didn't always account for much in Pickett County. The dead could rise up and walk, though not many people remembered the last time it had happened. And those who remembered tended to keep it to themselves.

He was about to give up and head back to the cruiser when he saw a series of long gouges in the soil. It looked like feet had dragged across the ground and kicked up small piles of leaves. The line of footprints tracked from a deadfall to a fern-pocked cluster of rocks. Littlefield followed the trail, one hand on his pistol, but when he reached the rocks, he saw only a mound of dirt. The footprints had abruptly ended, and no feet were in sight. Nor any face, body, or soul.

Littlefield knelt and rolled the cool, dark dirt in his hand. If it came to it, how could you fight a mountain and its most sacred and sick secrets?

CHAPTER FIVE

Bobby struck a match and held it aloft, the momentary stench of sulfur overpowering the fungal, wet-fur smell of the cave. "You hear that?"

Vernon Ray nodded, and then realized Bobby couldn't see his face. They were about twenty feet inside the Hole, and though they could still see the jagged opening and the forest beyond, daylight didn't penetrate to where they stood. The floor of the cave was uneven and peppered with tiny rocks that glinted in the bobbing flame. Vernon Ray wanted to grab Bobby's sleeve for comfort, but didn't want his best friend to think he was a sissy. That's why he'd entered the Jangling Hole in the first place, despite every cell in his body screaming at him to run.

The rattling snare had faded a little, as if the drummer were marching deep into the bowels of the mountain. "Maybe it's some geology thing," Vernon Ray said. "A settling of tectonic plates or something."

The explanation sounded feeble even as it left his lips, because as the world's oldest mountain range, the Appalachian chain had seen its earthquakes and volcanic activity epochs before. The upward thrust and breaking of mantle was ancient history, the Earth cracking its knuckles, and now all that remained was the slow sinking under the gentle persuasion of time. Besides, the cave had collapsed when Union troops blasted it with cannons. If you believed the stories.

"No, man, that's a drum," Bobby said.

"You think it's a ghost?" Vernon Ray wanted proof, something to tell his Dad—*You're right, Capt. Davis, the Civil War never ended*—and maybe there was nothing more to being a man than sticking your neck into unnecessary danger. If it would make him a man, he'd march down into the Jangling Hole until he came to the ass end of Hell.

Though he'd keep his eyes closed, just in case.

"Why would a ghost play a drum? *Ouch*." Bobby dropped the match, throwing them into near-pitch darkness. A pungent waft of burnt flesh teased Vernon Ray's nostrils.

"They got anything better to do?" Vernon Ray's false bravery failed as his voice cracked. "Light another match. Hurry."

"Shh."

The drumming had faded to a muted drone, the staccato beats blending together in the distance. A match *scritched* and as the yellow light flared, Vernon Ray glanced at the ceiling. Were symbols carved up there, or were the shapes just the flickering shadows cast by cracks in the stone?

"This is where the soldiers camped," Bobby said, kicking at a rock.

"My dad said they did an archaeological survey," Vernon Ray said. "No artifacts were found besides a few Cherokee tools and flint. If any troops were ever here, they must have been way down in the hole and got trapped."

"Who are you going to believe, a bunch of pencil pushers like Cornwad or your bestest bud?"

"Who do you expect me to believe?"

"I saw one of them."

"One of who?"

"Them. Why do you think I came in here?"

The second match went out and they stood in the dark, which pressed against Vernon Ray's flesh like stagnant water. The space was silent except for their breathing and the soft rustle of wind through the trees outside. Vernon Ray's heart was racing as fast as it did when he touched himself under the midnight covers of his bed, fueled by the same fearful anticipation of something that couldn't be missed, no matter the consequences.

"Don't dick with me, Bobby."

"Serious. One of them called me. Well, actually, he said 'Early,' but you know."

"I've heard of ghost whisperers, but I never heard of a ghost whispering back."

"I heard it, plain as day," Bobby said. "When I was running from the cops, he called again."

"Who called?"

"Nobody. I mean, he was barely there."

"Did you and Dex smoke a joint behind my back? Because you're acting like a freakozoid." Vernon Ray shivered. He didn't like having this conversation in the dark, and the cave seemed to be sucking down the sunshine and digesting it, because now the entrance looked forty feet away even though they hadn't moved.

"People say ghosts hide out in the Hole, but this person had flesh and bones," Bobby said in a flat tone, as if reciting a line from a half-remembered movie. "It moved around and talked and smelled like chewing tobacco and coffee."

"Hit another match."

"Asked me if Stoneman had passed through yet. Asked me if the war was over. Asked if he could go home."

Vernon Ray took another step closer, at the risk of being called a homo, until he bumped into Bobby. "Give me the matches."

Vernon Ray found Bobby's outstretched hand and took the matches, fired one up, and tore two more matches from the pack. Tiny twin flames reflected off Bobby's eyes, giving his face the appearance of a hell-spawned demon. As the match burned low, Vernon Ray lit another and bent low, looking for tracks. Though the light didn't penetrate much of the cave, the muddy floor appeared to show only their two sets of footprints.

"I don't see nothing now," Bobby said.

"Maybe you heard a fox or something. Or bats."

"It was a soldier."

"It's dark in here. Easy for your imagination to run wild."

*I'm trying to talk you out of it because I want to believe it so bad.*

Bobby turned away, toward the back of the cave. Vernon Ray looked over his shoulder, stepping closer, toward his friend's comforting body heat. A solid wall of murk stood before them, and somewhere beyond it lay the bones of soldiers. Vernon Ray could picture the pale skeletons, bones picked clean by vermin, mold and moss sinking spores into the dried marrow. Whatever Bobby had seen, it was best to let it rest in peace in this stifling tomb.

"Let's get out of here," Vernon Ray said, lighting a third match and holding it until it nearly burned his fingers. Despite his academic assessment of Appalachian tectonics, the walls looked fragile, rock stacked on a whim, glistening with the moist sweat of the world. He could imagine primordial reptiles slithering in its crevices, the first furry creatures huddling for cover.

Bobby pointed toward a dark stain on the wall, a splotch of faintly fluorescent indigo. "That looks like dinosaur crap."

The air was ripe with must and decomposition, as if the cave were in constant decay, the world rotting from the inside out. Stones were bones, after all, just dying at a different speed. It was all star stuff, and cosmic nonsense aside, the cave was a graveyard, a garbage hole, a place where light and life were sucked toward the inevitable. And maybe that consumption, the bottom of the hole, was the final resting place of all that walked and breathed and prayed.

Vernon Ray tossed the final match down, plunging them into darkness again, and glanced back at the entrance to the cave. He hadn't taken a single step, but now daylight appeared *fifty* feet away. He closed his eyes and saw lime-green flashes where the flame had imprinted his retinas. When he blinked several seconds later, the cave seemed darker, as if the sun were going down outside. But it was probably only six o'clock, an hour before dusk.

"Come on, the cops are probably gone by now," Vernon Ray said. The cops had become an abstraction. Even a jail cell would be better than the unseen but constricting walls of granite around them.

He was glad to feel Bobby's hand on his arm, though the fingers were cold and moist. He only wished his friend hadn't gone so silent. He could no longer hear Bobby's breathing.

A faint ticking filled the air. *Ratta-tat, ratta-tat.*

The snare drum became audible in the same way it had faded out, swelling as if the invisible, impossible drummer were marching toward them from the depths.

"Come on, Bobby!" Vernon Ray tugged his friend's hand, leading him toward the safety of the forest outside. But he lost traction in the mud and the air had grown heavy, and he fought against it as if wading through a receding tide. The mouth of the cave now appeared uphill and despite taking a dozen slow, straining steps he was no closer to safety. The drumming gained in volume, echoing off the wet walls.

*The cave is sealed off. Nobody can come up from the dark.*

*Especially not dead soldiers.*

Bobby's hand slipped off his arm and Vernon Ray was unmoored, drifting in a morass that pressed against him on all sides, a sour molasses that clogged his nose and throat. The cave mouth not only looked farther away but smaller, as if he were looking down the fat end of a telescope. The forest beyond, suggested only by swathes of green and gold, had taken on the aspect of fantasy, as if this cloaked realm were the reality and all else a dream. The snare drum rattled, the reverberation booming like a cannonade.

*Claustrophobia. Sure, that made sense.*

Anxiety was distorting his perception. The snare was nothing more than the pounding of his heart. The cave shut off all noise from outside, creating an isolation tank of almost total sensory deprivation.

"Bobby?" Vernon Ray took two steps toward the mouth of the cave, only he must have gotten turned around in the dark, because the mouth of the cave was now behind him. Had he gone deeper into the cave instead of leaving it?

He flailed his arms in the dark, reaching for Bobby. He didn't care if his friend thought he was a faggot, he didn't even care if he bumped into Bobby's butt, all he wanted to do was hug the only anchor of sanity left in the black and smothering abyss. His hand made contact and he clawed at Bobby's shirt.

Bobby clamped down on his wrist, squeezing hard, and Vernon Ray yelped. Bobby yanked him off balance—and *deeper* into the cave—and Vernon Ray tried to plant his feet, but the Earth beneath him was ebony butter and he skied forward, slapping and tearing at Bobby's hand. *When had Bobby gotten so strong?*

The ratta-tat rose and filled the cavity, penetrated Vernon Ray's ears and rolled around the arc of his skull. The thunderous drumming was so loud that it would surely trigger an avalanche. And Vernon Ray would be trapped in this sepulcher of stone and slime, buried with the soldiers, doomed to forever march to the beat of a deceased drummer.

But he wouldn't die alone. He would be with Bobby, and in the dark, with time against them and no one to ever find out, who knew what might happen?

Except Bobby's grip was fierce, like thick and cold handcuffs girding his flesh, roping him deeper into the bowels of the world and closer to the drummer.

"Bobby, the *other* way." Vernon Ray leaned back, throwing all his weight as resistance, but still Bobby dragged him forward into an unknown antechamber of hell. But the preachers said hell was hot, a place where sinners and homosexuals and liars and boys who had bad thoughts all burned for an eternity. If so, and surely plenty of others had been fed to the eternal flames over the centuries (he wasn't alone in *that*, too, was he?), then why was the cave so cold?

The drumming became a cacophony, roaring in a mad range of tones and timbres. Or maybe it was the winds of the underworld rushing through some unseen open door. Vernon Ray twisted his neck, yearning for a last glimpse of the safe and sunlit world.

The silhouette of a man was framed in the cave mouth. A cop had found them. They'd be safe after all.

"Help!" Vernon Ray shouted, competing with the drums, yanking against Bobby, the pack of matches damp and crumpled in his palm. They could blame it all on Dex. The cops would fall for that easy. It would all be okay now, sane and normal and brightly lit.

But the man showed no sign of entering the cave and Bobby wasn't letting loose. Vernon Ray slid another five feet deeper into darkness, digging his heels against the mud. Surely they'd reach the back of the cave soon, the place where the ceiling had collapsed and stacked the granite in an impossible jumble.

And then what would happen? Would Bobby continue dragging him down, through the narrow cracks in the rock, to the cavity where the bones of the soldiers lay?

*Ratta-tatta-tat.* What if the percussion was made by bones, skeletal fingers beating an insane rhythm against rock?

Where was the cop? Weren't they supposed to risk their lives to protect the innocent? Didn't the cop watch "NYPD Blue" or "T.J. Hooker" or even "The Andy Griffith Show"?

Vernon Ray, the last kid picked in sandlot football games, the part-time right fielder on his Little League team, the reigning chess champ of eighth grade, couldn't count on brute strength, and his brains were pummeled by the snare cadence. He was reduced to blubbering Bobby's name over and over until it came out as "Buh-buh-buh," and to his horror he found his syllables had fallen in synch with the snare.

In the fifth grade, Vernon Ray had gotten into a fight with Whizzer Buchanan, a goon from across the county. Well, it hadn't really been a fight, more of a Close Encounter of the Turd Kind. Whizzer had set aside his skateboard to go behind a tree and live up to his nickname, and Vernon Ray had picked up the abandoned skateboard and spun its wheels. He wasn't going to steal it or anything; he was too chicken to board even if he'd owned one.

Whizzer had snuck up behind him, grabbed him, and threatened to smack the skateboard across his lips. Vernon Ray had pretended to go slack for just an instant, in a sissy fainting spell, and when Whizzer relaxed his grip, Vernon Ray had wriggled and yanked at the same time. The movement had surprised the goon, whose strength-and-size advantage was not only negated but worked against him. As Vernon Ray pirouetted away, Whizzer fell to the ground, smacking his own face on the board. By the time Whizzer regained his wits (*both* of them, Vernon Ray had smirked in the aftermath), his quarry was long gone.

Vernon Ray tried the same maneuver now, flattening his feet so that he slid in the mud while simultaneously leaning forward, falling toward Bobby. It was like skating on owl grease. He lost his balance and slammed into the dank mud. Up close, the floor of the cave smelled like rainy-day dogs, black powder, and rotted canvas.

Bobby stayed right with him through the fall, the meat lasso tightening. Vernon Ray slapped at his friend's hand, and then clawed at it, the flesh peeling away like peach skin beneath his fingernails. Bobby didn't utter a peep, not that Vernon Ray could have heard him over the swelling *ratta-tatta-tat*.

When had Bobby gotten so goddamned *strong*?

Vernon Ray tried a variation of the Great-Whizzer-Escape, springing forward from his knees, but all he did was propel himself deeper in the cave, banging his shins against rocks. Bobby was playing him like a sport fish, reeling him not toward shore but into a drowning black lagoon.

*Where was that Christ-forsaken robocop?*

Whatever gleam of light had trickled down the kaleidoscopic tube of stone and dirt was now stifled, like a reptilian eye blinking shut. Had they turned a bend? Worked through the fallen stone of the cave-in? The drum line now roared to thunder, threatening another landslide.

And he'd be trapped in here with . . . .

Bobby? The dead troops, unsung heroes whose common grave bore no marker? Or the Little Drummer Boy from Hell, pounding pounding pounding until Vernon Ray's skull exploded and his brains scattered like grapeshot.

He had one more trick up his well-gripped sleeve, and it was less a conscious flop than a mild seizure of panic. He wriggled his elbows as if he were doing the funky chicken, at the same time driving his palms together in one smack of sick applause. The skin lasso loosened, and Vernon Ray scrambled backwards, bumping into something unseen and mushy, and a bat brushed his face—*not another hand, certainly not a third hand*—but by then Vernon Ray was clawing his way toward the warmer air, and now light suffused him, a bruised balm at first and then a solid gob of yellow-white.

And there was the silhouette, the cop at the mouth of the cave, and Vernon Ray was ready to confess to every unsolved crime in the Pickett County log book, just as long as the bars were thick and the cot warm and he could see each wall.

He stumbled, staggered, headless-funky-chicken-strutted his way toward the light, and he reached out his arms like a punk rocker diving into the front row, going for the cop. Faggot or not, he was ready to hug the hell out of the man, cling to the cop until they had to scrape him off with a shovel. Because the cop was solid, warm meat, not like the cold, dead things behind him . . . .

As he fell, he realized the *ratta-tatta-tat* had died, though its echo rolled around the curved bone of his skull like a metal ball on a roulette wheel.

"Dude, what were you doing in there?"

Didn't sound like a cop. Vernon looked up from the grass, squinting against the red death of day. "Bobby?"

"Been waiting here five minutes. Didn't you hear me yelling?"

"I was . . . ."

Vernon Ray looked at his hand. It clutched a scrap of ragged gray wool.

CHAPTER SIX

"What you boys doing on private property?" Hardy Eggers stepped from the concealment of the underbrush and tried to look like a crotchety bastard, the kind who would grab a nurse's ass at the old folks' home and pretend he had Alzheimer's to get away with it. After the uphill hike, he had the heavy-breathing part down cold.

He didn't recognize the boys, but they didn't bolt when he challenged them. The runty one had the vacant-eyed stare of a videogame addict, or maybe he'd been snorting model airplane glue or sucking on wacky weed. The other boy was a little taller and better built, and his face pinched in a sullen expression as if he were used to getting his ass chewed. They were both blond and could pass for brothers.

"Nothing," the tall one said.

"What's your names?"

"I'm Bobby and this is Vernon Ray."

"Don't he talk?"

Vernon Ray gazed off into the woods as if naked elephants were parading among the trees. Bobby put a hand on his friend's shoulder. "He just had a scare."

*Shit. They went into the goddamned hole. Stupid kids.*

*At least they made it back out.*

*But it looks like maybe the runt, like Donnie, left a little bit of himself in there.*

"You boys hear the shots?" Hardy didn't know how long he could pretend to be menacing. He wished he'd carried his shotgun, because the weapon would have added to the picture of the addled hillbilly, but he figured his white stubble and filthy long john shirt were enough of a prop if he played it right.

Bobby nodded. "The cops ran through the woods. We hid in the cave because we were afraid somebody would shoot us."

"You look familiar. Who's your daddy?"

"Elmer. Elmer Eldreth."

"Eldreth, huh? He work in construction?"

"Plumbing contractor." The boy's face tightened. "We need to be getting home. Our moms are going to be worried."

"I know your daddy," Hardy said. "If I see you boys snooping around up here again, he'll be hearing about it."

Bobby didn't blink. "Are you with the developers?"

"No. This land's been in my family since King George. Got it in a land grant."

"I heard some Florida dipwads bought it. You don't look like you're from Florida."

*Goddamned brats these days. Don't they teach 'em not to talk back to their elders?*

Vernon Ray wasn't doing any kind of talking, but for the first time he snapped out of his daze, looking at his hand. He was holding something Hardy couldn't make out.

"Don't get smart with me," Hardy said, approaching the pair. "I'm friends with the sheriff."

"You're trespassing the same as we are."

"You got no business messing around up here. You could break your necks and nobody would even hear you scream."

"Don't worry," Bobby said. "We know all the spooky stories. It's just a bunch of trees and rocks to me. I don't give a crap if they bulldoze it flat and paint 'Save Our Planet' in mile-long letters. Come on, Vernon Ray. Let's get out of here before this geezer has a stroke."

As Bobby led Vernon Ray down to the hill toward the trail, Hardy went to the edge of the Hole and peered inside. Even from ten feet away, the odor of old sulfur and sin oozed out like the belch of a long black snake. Maybe the boys had seen something they would tell their friends, and hopefully it wouldn't make the little turds dare each other to come back. Hardy felt an obligation to keep people away, sort of a self-appointed guardian of the gate. But the gate was about to be busted open by Bill Willard's big-money investment team and Hardy couldn't do a thing about it except pray.

Hardy cocked an ear. Sometimes it sounded like breathing, which he could chalk up to the wind slipping between cracks in the stone. Sometimes it sounded like a deep and faint heartbeat, like when the doctor put the stethoscope to Pearl's swollen belly and let him listen to the life inside. Other times, it was the rumble of a nightmare train rolling up from the depths of Hell. Now it resembled the drone of an International Harvester reaping hay, chugging black air and chewing up whatever the ground had to offer.

Except the noise wasn't coming from the Hole.

The kids were out of sight, so Hardy figured he'd put a little distance from himself and the oily throat of the cave. He'd been inside the place as a kid, several times, it was practically a rite of passage in these parts, but he'd never stayed for more than a minute and each time he'd emerged with the feeling that he'd donned a second skin, a black film that even a plunge in the creek couldn't wash clean.

Anyone who stood too long looking into that place, or listening to the mad music of the Earth's hidden secrets, would end up like Bennie Hartley, who'd been found lying half in the Hole, stone dead from a heart attack, his legs lying in the shadows as if he hadn't quite reached the sunlight in time.

Hardy circled the rocky knob that housed the cave, expecting to meet up with the sheriff. The rumbling engine grew louder, a thing of the real world and not some confabulation of a superstitious mountaineer. A vehicle was droning up the path on the west side of the mountain, moving through the woods where construction crews had carved the first dark stretch of road into the slope. The vehicle was big and slow, cracking saplings, the engine hiccupping as it powered over stumps and rocks.

Hardy moved between the tangles of rhododendron. The sheriff must have already cleared the scene, meaning Hardy would have to hoof it all the way back home without benefit of a lift. That meant nobody had been shot; otherwise, the place would have been crawling with rescue personnel and sirens would fill the valley below.

*Unless the monster climbing Mulatto Mountain is some newfangled kind of emergency vehicle, sucking down taxpayer diesel.*

It rolled out of a stand of underbrush 100 feet below Hardy, its black crash grill pocked with broken branches. The customized silver Humvee rode five feet off the ground, sitting on tires that were fatter than a killing-season sow. The SUV was girded with roll bars, looking more like a cage designed to hold a rabid rhinoceros than a mode of conveyance. The windshield was tinted, but there was only one man in Titusville who would dare operate such a shitty and showy hunk of rubber and steel.

The Humvee roared into a stretch of grassland, a bald where the high winds kept trees from taking root. In the vehicle's wake, the vegetation had been flattened and Hardy could see almost to the end of the newly graveled access road. Looked like Phase II of the Mulatto Mountain rehabilitation project was well underway.

Hardy raised a hand to the tinted driver's-side window. It descended and Bill Willard's round face broke into a grin. If his skin were shaded just a little more toward orange, he'd have made a dandy Halloween jack-o-lantern. As it was, he flashed jagged teeth that even the best in modern dental care couldn't shape up and set square. Though the teeth were white, the eyes above them were every bit as black as the inside of a pumpkin, or the Jangling Hole for that matter.

"You Eggerses are all the same," Bill said. "Can't let it go. You're all pissed because your property got chopped up and sold off over the years. But if your ancestors hadn't liked screwing so much, there wouldn't have been so many heirs."

Hardy didn't have an answer to that, because it was true. An Eggers male would stick his pecker into just about anything, as attested by his own Jewish-Cherokee bloodline. Some claimed it was a good thing that goats and sheep couldn't take human seed, or there might be some little four-legged Eggerses running around. But Hardy had nothing to say on that subject, either.

"I heard about the ruckus," Hardy said. "A man's got an obligation to keep an eye on his neighbor's property."

Bill gunned the engine once, as if in defiance of high gas prices compliments of gutless politicians and endless war, and killed the ignition. "That's more of Littlefield's talk," Bill said. "He's as jumpy as a frog on a hotplate."

Hardy nodded at Bill's contrived colloquialism, the kind of

backwoods buffoonery he considered folksy wisdom. Thought it made him one of the gang, but instead it only showed the man was trying way too hard. He'd buy Arveleta Perkins's chow chow at the farmer's market and pretend like he actually ate the mess, whereas only tourists and college hippies were dumb enough to buy the green mash of pickled onions, tomatillas, radishes, and cucumbers.

"The sheriff's a good man," Hardy said, keeping the defensiveness out of his voice. No use disputing Bill, because the baldheaded money-grabber never lost an argument. Like any man, he was wrong about half the time, but he mistook surrender for weakness, whereas any fool knew that sometimes it was better to run like hell and live to fight another day. Then again, Bill owned about five percent of Pickett County and it didn't look like the bank was foreclosing anytime soon.

"Sheriff out to be enforcing these 'No trespassing' signs," Bill said, the grin staying in place to add, "I'm just joking, but I don't have to be."

"Nobody wants any trouble up here."

"Yeah, I know. We did that dance. The North Carolina Historical Society didn't find one trace of Kirk's Raiders, and all the do-gooders at Westridge University didn't find a damned thing, either. Just some stories that make the rounds every Halloween when folks want to scare their kids into good behavior."

"Them names had some basis in history."

"There's no record that Earley Eggers joined the raiders, but I know you're little touchy about it."

"You would be, too, if your family's reputation was shot to hell."

"That was a century and a half ago."

"People bury the past, but some things stick around long after they ought to be forgot."

Bill opened the Humvee door and rolled out of it. Economic prosperity had spread to his waistline. Standing, the top of his balding head barely reached the door handle, but his belly was as inflated as his tires. He smacked his lips as if chewing sunflower seeds. "I know you were the only heir that fought against selling the family property, but I also noticed you didn't offer to give up your share after we cut the check."

Hardy swallowed hard. "Turns out people keep buying up property around here and building big homes, driving up their neighbors' taxes until they either have to sell out or go bust. I needed the money or I'd have lost my land."

Bill's grin widened, throwing wrinkles across his forehead and scrunching his bulbous nose. "Growth happens whether you're ready or not."

"Yeah, well, shit happens, too, but you don't see me diving in headfirst and telling everybody the water's fine."

"Titusville's not a secret anymore. It kept popping up on those national lists the magazines keep, the 'Top 20 best places to retire,' '50 best outdoor adventure towns,' and all that. After Westridge upset Duke in basketball, you could make it a reasonable question on a geography test."

"If I didn't know better, I'd say your pictures might have made a difference."

Pride made the grin shift into a smirk, the eyes growing even darker. Budget Bill swept his arm out to indicate the view of the mountains that rippled soft and blue-gray in the distance, evidence that the Earth was a work in progress, a shifting landscape that only appeared fixed and firm from a man's temporary perspective. "I've got the eye, my friend. But I had great material."

"I'm not your friend."

"Neighbor, then."

"Got your camera with you? Thought you might want to get a few shots of the knob before your bulldozers do their trick and knock it down forever."

"It's already well documented, neighbor."

"Or maybe you want a picture of my rosy red asshole." Hardy twisted his head and spat into the leaves, wishing he hadn't given up chewing tobacco so he could squirt a strand on the man's fancy and squeaky-clean Timberland hiking boots. "I don't got no legal cause to stop you. Them 'Save the Knob' hippies couldn't get anywhere with their long-haired Yankee lawyer, so what good could I do?"

"You sound just like them, making it 'Good versus evil.' But I'm providing a product and contributing to the community. Funny, in all the kiddie movies these days, developers are the bad guys. Why is that, Hardy?"

Hardy nodded toward the ridge that covered the cool, black tunnel of subterranean secrets. "I don't know what 'evil' is, but I know when something ain't right."

Bill took a couple of brisk steps forward and slapped Hardy on the shoulder. Hardy looked down on the beaming cherub in the catalog-ordered flannel shirt.

"Take it easy," Bill said. "I wouldn't subject a stranger to the sinister mysteries of The Jangling Hole. It wouldn't be neighborly. That's why I'm putting my house right there on top. Once I clear the trees so I can get the view."

"You mean, so everybody can see how big your house is."

Bill gave a laugh that sounded too big to have come from his belly. "If there are any Civil War ghosts, restless Cherokee spirits, hillbilly horrors, or tap-dancing babies of Satan, then they're welcome in my living room anytime. I might even rig up an infrared camera and see if I can get any of it on film. Those would fetch a pretty penny, don't you think?"

"Enough for you to buy another mountain."

"Hey, don't take it too hard. We won't have the road cut all the way to the top until next week. Plenty of time for all the wild turkey, rabbits, and deer to scamper off into the valley. Or maybe down to your pasture. You still hunt, don't you?"

Hardy didn't want to acknowledge that he'd given up hunting Mulatto Mountain one misty November morning after he'd gotten the feeling that something was hunting *him*. "Mountain's been here since the Book of Genesis."

"I tell you what," Bill said, pressing on Hardy's shoulder to guide him toward the Hole. "You find me a verse that says a man ought to ignore a calling. And it's not like I'm going to pave every square inch. We're working with a land trust to place a few acres under conservation easement."

"So you can get the tax breaks on land too steep to destroy and spread even more cost onto the shoulders of the working folk," Hardy said, shrugging off the man's hand and walking beside him.

Bill gave the irritating laugh again. "If I didn't know you were a registered Republican, I'd swear you're turning into a Commie. Come on, admit it. The truth of the matter is you don't want me to ruin your view. Within five years you'll be selling out and moving into one of my condominiums near the hospital."

"Over my dead body."

"That's one way of doing it. I'm sure the missus isn't quite as hard-headed as you. Not so opposed to change."

A hawk soared overhead, a dark silhouette against the high clouds. The maples had turned early this year, the leaves dark purple and brilliant red. The buckeyes and poplars were golden, and the oaks were in the first throes of going dark green. A squirrel darted along a hickory branch, then leaped into a pine and cut a candy-stripe route down the trunk. The traffic from the distant highway was softened to a distant whisper, and the wind played its own voice through the trees. Hardy wondered how much of his anger was due to his inability to stop the spinning hands of time.

*Change is fine with me, as long as it's not change for the worse. But some things are better left alone. Like whatever's sleeping in the Hole.*

Hardy followed the developer, wondering how many times the man had poked his head in the Hole. Maybe Budget Bill Willard didn't have enough imagination to get into trouble with it. Then again, Bill hadn't lost kin to it like Hardy had. Hardy feared the Hole for good reason: it had stolen his son from him.

They were within twenty feet of the Hole, near where the two boys were standing when Hardy had first arrived, when Sheriff Littlefield stepped out of the woods.

"Howdy, Bill," the sheriff said, nodding at Hardy and narrowing his eyes and giving a small shake of his head. *Nothing*, the look said.

"Big day for trespassers," Bill said.

"I checked out the property. We didn't find a trace."

"I heard one of your boys got a little loose with his pistol. Maybe he was shooting at one of Hardy's spooks?"

Littlefield stepped between the two men and the Jangling Hole, overtly avoiding glancing into the chilly depths. His hand rested on the butt of his sidearm as if he were guarding gold bullion. "A lot of funny stuff goes on in this place," Littlefield said.

"Yeah, like what happened in the red church in Whispering Pines? People are still snickering about that one."

"Nobody who lived through it is doing much laughing."

Bill looked at the sheriff, then at Hardy, and he gave his thigh an animated slap. "You fellows are serious about all this, aren't you? I can understand it from Hardy here, being a seventh-generation, pig-porking hillbilly. But you've got education, Sheriff. You know there's no such thing as boogeymen."

"I know what I see and I know what I know," the sheriff said, before pursing his lips into a stubborn line.

"Your chief deputy died in a car crash," Bill said. "Those other deaths were just what the coroner said: animal attacks. And, anyway, just because you've gone goosey in the head doesn't mean I have to change my plans any. I've got approval from the planning board and I've followed every line in the building code and subdivision ordinance. Hell, I practically know them by heart, since I helped draft them."

"Maybe there's a higher law," Hardy said.

"Don't thump the Bible on my head, Hardy. You haven't been to church much since the day your boy went squirrel-shit nutty."

The blood rage filled the backs of his eyelids. Hardy, who was two decades older, launched himself at Bill and wrestled him to the ground. The farmer's limbs were tough and leathery, like strips of beef jerky, but they bulged with muscle around the bone. He climbed on top of Bill, who squealed in surprise and tried to roll away. Hardy's arthritic knees sent blue lightning to his skull but he rode the developer as if the man were a wayward bronco in need of busting.

Hardy's hands were tightening around the man's throat when Littlefield reached down and yanked him away by his long john collar. The fabric stretched and the elastic snapped as Hardy clawed his way back toward Bill's face, but Littlefield got one of his arms in a wrestling lock and tried to restrain him. Hardy pulled free of the sheriff and was about to ram his knotty fist into Bill's fig of a nose when the voice wended low from the cave.

"*Earley.*"

The two combatants froze, and the sheriff stepped back from the fray. Bill rolled away and scampered to his feet.

"He . . . I'm filing on this one, Sheriff," Bill said between slobbering gulps of air. "You witnessed it. Assault."

"Didn't you hear it?" Littlefield said.

"All I heard was the wind."

"Something in there *talked*."

"Arrest him, Sheriff."

Hardy eased away from the Hole, wondering if his son had heard that same voice on a long-ago summer day. He looked down at his hands as if they belonged to a stranger. "I'm guilty," he said. "Of a lot of things."

Sheriff Littlefield picked up his hat and pulled the brim down so it threw his eyes in shadow. "Looked like you slipped to me, Bill. I don't see any probable cause."

"You're both crazy," Bill said, breaking into a jiggling jog back toward his Humvee. "See if I support your ass in the next election."

As the oversize engine gunned to life and the vehicle circled, smashing into a two-foot wild cherry in the process, the sheriff moved to Hardy's side. "Maybe he's right," Littlefield said. "Maybe we're both crazy."

"I wish," Hardy said. "That would make a whole lot more sense."

They shared a gaze into the silence of the Hole but looked away before whatever might be in there had a chance to look back.

CHAPTER SEVEN

Wood and lacquer exploded in a white cascade, a cannonball thundering through the ranks.

"Mother *fuck*," Elmer Eldreth said, balancing on one toe like a ballet dancer after two pitchers of Old Milwaukee. He squared and faced the 6 and 10 pins, which wobbled with just as much unsteadiness as the man who'd tried to knock them into the next county. Hands out, Elmer pointed his index fingers at the pins like a gunslinger in a street showdown.

"Split like a whore's legs on payday," Jeff Davis said. "Too bad Mac's gone high-tech redneck with those electronic scoreboards, or I'd cheat you a pin on the card."

Elmer holstered his fingers as the rack swept the fallen pins away and replaced the two outside pins. Only one way to play it, knock the 10 with a reverse spin and hope it kicked off the wall and across the lane to the other gutter. But that was a shot only a lefty could pull off, and only under the blessing of a blue moon, or by selling his soul to the Gutterball God. And damned if Elmer's soul wasn't already maxed out, run-to-the-red bankrupt.

He trailed Jeff by seven pins in the last frame, and unless he nailed the split, he wouldn't get that final bonus roll that might push him over the top. Tonight's bet was for tickets to the Lowe's Motor Speedway in Charlotte. The big NASCAR races were heading west and north, following the corporate money, and all the Southern tracks were stuck with the Tru Value Hardware Monster Truck Mash and rinky-dink shit like that.

Not that Elmer was opposed to watching mountains of steel and rubber pile up in a giant, smoking scrap heap, he just didn't feel like driving two hours to do it. He could get the same experience right at home in the trailer park and have a fridge full of beer at his fingertips to boot.

Still, a ticket was a ticket and a win was a win.

Not that a win was likely. Jeff had drilled two strikes in a row to come storming up from behind. That little jab about Mac McAllister's new computerized scoring system was pretty much dirty pool, except Jeff usually kicked his ass at pool, too. Elmer suspected Jeff had laid back and coasted in his draft, fell behind on purpose just to make a last-second run and blow Elmer's head gaskets while dashing for the checkered. Elmer was running on fumes but he was going to punch the pedal to the end. He realized he was mixing racing and bowling in his head but he figured one beer-drinking activity was as good as the next.

"I'll nail this one," Elmer said, licking his thumb as the ball rolled up the return and clacked against Jeff's in that macho ball-knocking ritual that no heterosexual male would ever acknowledge for what it was.

"You can't even nail Mac's wife," Jeff said, loud enough for their pal to hear over the clatter of pins, the rumble of wracking machinery, and a twangy, boozy Kenny Chesney blaring from the jukebox speakers.

Mac lifted the aerosol can he'd used to sanitize a row of rental shoes, pointed the nozzle at Jeff, and shot a pine-scented mist that mingled with the popcorn-and-pungent-pork stench from the concession stand. "That's about the best blow job you'll ever get, Captain," Mac said.

"Serious," Elmer said. "Let's make it double or nothing. If I get the split, you owe me four tickets."

"And if you miss?" Jeff said, his squirrel-gray eyes toting up the odds in his favor.

"You get game and I throw in a freebie at Dolly's Dollhouse." The dollhouse was a private club featuring what the tourist trade referred to as "exotic dancers," but Elmer and his friends called "titty wigglers." Because of the anti-porn sentiment of the Baptist South, the girls had to wear thongs, but anybody with half an imagination (and Elmer often used his imagination both during the visit and later on in bed, squeaking one off while Vernell snored and drooled beside him) could see enough to get his money's worth. Though Elmer's oral hygiene was limited to Slim Jims and toothpicks, he'd seen thicker dental floss than the moist fabrics that ran between the dancers' ass cheeks and up their clean-shaven diddies.

"Freebie, shit," Jeff said. "Looking's free but touching ain't."

"I'll get you one in the back room." Rumor had it a C-note would buy you a hand job in one of the private rooms that rented by the minute. Elmer never had enough bills to test the theory that a full menu was available from Chucky, the former Hell's Angel who served as bouncer, harem king, and part-owner of the gentlemen's club. Elmer wasn't getting much action from his wife, but he figured he was paying out more for it than if he'd stayed single and bought his companionship straight up.

Vernell kept bitching and whining about the two yard apes that always had strep throat or needed new shoes or some shit. Worst part was only one of the brats was for-sure his. The youngest, Bobby, a tow-headed, sleepy-eyed kid who looked like he'd been squirted from a Scandinavian, was no way in the world pumping Eldreth blood.

Could be worse, though. Poor Jeff's kid was a blooming faggot, sizing himself up for pantaloons and mascara before he was barely old enough to beat off. And Elmer tried not to bring it up, but sometimes when a good pal had an oozing scab, you couldn't resist scratching it a little.

Jeff held his arm straight, thumb up, sighting down the lane like an engineer building a bridge. "Considering your odds are maybe the same as a Democrat taking the courthouse, you're on," Jeff said, then hollered at Mac, "Hey, what's the mathematical probability of sparing out a six-ten?"

Mac slapped a pair of red-and-green clown shoes against the counter top. "Mathematical probability, my ass. If you roll perfect, odds is one in one. Roll bad and you got no odds."

Elmer hefted his ball, a royal blue 16-pounder with sparkles in its smooth finish. He gave one biceps curl, flexing his wrist. The backspin would be a bitch. Elmer had no intention of ever making good on the bet if he lost, but he needed to take at least one pin out or Jeff would rib him for the next three weeks. Bitch of it was, you could settle for the one but that would pretty much knock out all chance of getting the spare. This was one of those all-or-nothing rolls.

Plus he needed that extra roll or Jeff took the game and the tickets anyway.

In the next lane, a fat man whose gray jacket failed to bag the vanilla pudding of his gut sat like the Buddha of Bowling, a cigarillo in his slack mouth. Mac had not yet given in to the anti-smoking sissies, and though Elmer didn't smoke himself, he loved the poke in the eye to all those goddamned liberals who dared tell a man how to run his business. Elmer had an insane urge to rub the Buddha Dude's belly for luck, but the guy might sit on him and roll him out like the Pillsbury Doughboy in a laundry press.

"I've made a couple six-tens before," Elmer said. The lie tasted like the chalk on his fingers.

"This ain't before, it's right now," Jeff said.

Just because Jeff had a two-year certification in heating and air conditioning from the local community college, the bastard had to lord his book-learning over everybody else.

"Hey, better put that on a T-shirt," Mac said. "That's cosmic."

"You wouldn't know 'cosmic' if your balls turned the color of Mars," Elmer said. He blinked against the Buddha's gray smoke and stepped toward the lane. It was probably just his imagination, but it felt like the whole alley had gone into freeze frame and all eyes were on him. This was as close to the spotlight as folks like Elmer ever got. Too bad he was pretty much guaranteed to trip over his purple shoelaces and dick it up.

He closed his eyes, and the freeze-frame illusion passed, the cacophony of shellac and shouts rushing back at full volume, Chesney warbling about some old heartbreak or another, as if any guy actually had a heart. The ball hung in perfect balance above his wrist, his sweating palm a couple of inches off the surface, fingers hooked in the holes like they were a teenager's twat on a second date, when you drove them 10 miles out to Baity's Lake and told them to put out or get out.

He took a breath, testing his knees, and a spark of early-onset arthritis flared from his right joint. He'd have to compensate, bend with his back, make sure his wrist turned in counterweight. No excuses left, no prayers, no last-second reprieves, no upping the ante.

At least Elmer had scored himself a visit to Dolly's, even if he wouldn't have enough money to cram a twenty in one of the tiny waistbands, maybe getting a wet knuckle in the process. Sure, all the tits were inflatable, but he'd take a rubber ducky over his wife's sagging sacks of elephant hide any day. Not that he'd much chance for the taking lately. Seemed like the bitch was on the rag three weeks out of the month and rashed up the other week.

"You gonna roll or you gonna tie up my lane all night?" Mac shouted.

"You're breaking my flow," Elmer said.

"The only flow you got is the trickle down your two-inch pipe."

Elmer lowered the ball. Buddha smiled with all the wisdom a six-pack could deliver, teeth yellow around the plastic tip of the cigarillo. Elmer backed up until the shaft of blown air on the ball return drifted up the sweat line of his spine. "You want in on this, Mac?"

"I got nothing you want," he said, his Mario Brothers moustache wriggling as if it were packed with sneeze powder. "You already bowl for free, and you ain't banging my wife."

Elmer actually wouldn't mind a go at Mrs. McCallister. Mac had traded down for a younger model, a peroxide bimbo with dead-deer eyes and a rack that would spice up any man's trophy case. But she was church all the way, one of those three-times-a-weekers who passed out religious tracts featuring cartoon drunks burning in hell. No matter how many times Mac drilled her, Elmer doubted her husband ever reached as deep inside her as Jesus did.

"Okay, then," Elmer said, rubbing his fingers together as if itching for cash. "How about if we go for captain of the troop?"

Jeff, who had risen to the rank of captain of the imitation army in the same manner as those in the real military, shook his head. "No way. You don't know the drills, you don't know the protocol, and you don't know the history."

"All you gotta do is stand around saying 'Ten-hut' and 'At ease,' and throw in a couple of Stonewall Jacksons here and there."

"Stonewall Jackson was long dead by the time Stoneman's cavalry rode through Titusville," Jeff said, unconsciously twirling one end of his midget handlebar mustache. "This was late 1864, near the end of the war, the final refrain to 'Dixieland.'"

Elmer rested his bowling ball against his hip and chugged an amber swig of Old Milwaukee from a plastic cup. Jeff was about to go into one of his boring rants about Sherman's march, and how Stoneman split off to break Confederate supply lines through the mountains. As Stoneman found out, there weren't many supplies of any kind in the South by then, and certainly not in the remote Southern Appalachians.

Elmer didn't give a damn for history, but he'd been in the N.C. 26th Living History Society for eight years and had sat through Jeff's lecture a dozen times. As long as Jeff was buying the beer, Elmer could spare an ear.

"Home Guard met them up the valley," Jeff said, eyes getting that faraway glaze as if he were looking through the neon-lighted walls and back into time. "The boys in gray were outnumbered five to one but they gave as good as they got."

Which wasn't exactly true. For one thing, the boys didn't have uniforms, much less gray ones. For another, the Home Guard lost seven men and the Yankees suffered only one casualty, and that one occurred when a green private drank too much whiskey and was thrown by his horse, breaking a leg on the jailhouse steps. And Kirk's Raiders had split from the Yankee command and set up their own private little war, one where Rebel daughters got knocked up and livestock got stolen. So there was no cause for Rebel Pride in Pickett County. But damned if Jeff would admit a mistake, especially when he got rolling.

*Speaking of rolling, I better put the twist on this baby and nick it a cunt hair to the left.*

"All right, we'll stick to a ticket to Titty Palace," Elmer said, patting the ball. "You're the captain and the rest of us volunteers ain't nothing but cannon fodder. But that's on the field. Here in the alley, you don't give no orders."

"Unless it's for another pitcher of beer," Mac said.

"That mean one on the house?"

"You're going to drink me to the old folks' home," the bald man said.

"Mac, you'll be nickel-and-diming on the shuffleboard court,"

Elmer said. "Your basic situation won't change a bit."

Mac's eyes twinkled. The guy had a good air about him, never let crap stick. Maybe that's why he got a looker for a wife and Elmer was stuck with the saggy-tit version of the Elephant Man. Sure, Mac's kid Dex was a little hooligan, swiping his old man's rubbers and riding his skateboard in town without a helmet, but he was smarter than Elmer's oldest son, Jerrell, the genetic Eldreth. Bobby had them all beat on grades and looks and batting average, but then you got to that little problem of him maybe being somebody else's kid, so Elmer couldn't muster much pride in that.

"You bowling or jerking your roosterneck?" Jeff said. When the conversation had shifted to the upcoming Civil War event, he'd sat a little straighter and squared his shoulders. Jeff's posture remained ramrod at the scorer's table, his wavy hair a little like that Elmer had seen in pictures of General George Armstrong Custer, who had cut his teeth as a Yankee officer before riding to infamy in Sioux country. Blonde, almost-girlish hair. Blonde like Bobby's.

*Focus on nicking the ten.*

"Okay, maybe this will make you choke on your grits." Elmer backed to the lip of the wooden platform, sizing up his run. He rubbed his left forearm for luck and glanced down at the glossy finish. His distorted reflection stared back, the neon lights throwing an aurora borealis across the curved landscape. He tilted his head so he could see the Buddha Dude in the ball's surface. The chair was empty.

He looked over to the next scorer's table. The Buddha Dude was gone, probably headed for a chili dog and cheese fries. So much for sucking karma from somebody else.

Jeff tapped his 7-Up can against the scorer's table. "Stalling won't save you."

Elmer glanced at his shoes. The strings were neatly knotted. But the psychological edge was getting to him. You couldn't roll when you were hallucinating, and he hadn't done any hard drugs since high school. Still, he'd learned a lesson during those teen years, back when hope wasn't hopeless and the future stretched out like an eight-lane highway lined with cheap gas pumps and cheaper highway hookers.

When things got fuzzy, you focused right in front of your face. Which was what he did. The ball became his universe, its weight the solid evidence of reality, the straining fingers clutching the holes as if they were the clefts leading up out of a dark well. He had a bumper sticker on his truck that said, "When the going gets weird, the weird go bowling," a slogan Mac had printed up when the alley first opened five years back.

Now Mac was driving a Beamer and Elmer was driving a rusty-assed truck. Jeff was captain in the regiment and Elmer was a common private. Buddha Dude was off somewhere talking to a tree and Elmer was aiming for a thousand-to-one shot. Didn't get much weirder than real life.

He breathed, centering, letting his muscles tighten and relax. The ten-pin seemed larger now, bloated, as if it had taken on water. He felt eyes on him, several eyes, and he knew the bowlers in the next lane over had stopped to see the outcome. Somewhere, maybe from the other side of the tinted windows or the dark chaos of the videogame room, Buddha Dude was probably plotting Elmer's reincarnation as a toilet seat.

"Hell with 'em all," Elmer whispered, taking the first step and bending from the waist. His wrist curled in a slightly unnatural position, sweeping down so he could roll the ball off his fingers with a little reverse English. As he snapped his fingers free and kicked his right heel behind him, balancing on his left foot, he thought he had a chance.

A little one, maybe down to only five-hundred-to-one, but still a chance. The ball spun out as smoothly as if he were shooting a marble, fighting to get a bite on the slick wood of the alley. Halfway down, it began a gentle break and hooked toward the gutter.

A gutter ball was just as bad as a single pin. Both worthless.

Elmer planted his feet and stared after the ball as if he were a gunfighter about to draw. The alley had fallen silent during his roll, except for Chesney's crooning about a woman who should have treated him right.

"He's got it," Mac said, with the surety of someone who'd seen a few six-tens in his day.

"Bull run," Jeff said, just as the ball glanced off the edge of the pin. The pin whispered with the contact and kicked to the left, wobbling as it fell. It gave three pathetic spins, like a crippled break dancer at a high school prom, and then rolled across the lane into the six. The six staggered and fought gravity, then lost.

Elmer turned and wagged his fingers at Jeff as if they were hot pistols, then did a half pirouette and thrust his fat ass at his nemesis. "Got you, Possum Face. Smoke that shit for breakfast."

The metal sweeper descended as the last pin dropped, setting up a virgin rack for Elmer's last ball.

"Don't go singing to the fat lady," Jeff said, mangling the pet phrase of those who never gave up. "I'm still up by five."

"I can get five in my sleep," he said.

Mac had come from behind the counter to watch from the edge of the scorer's area. "Sleep's about all you're getting in bed these days. Nice roll, though."

Elmer removed his ball from the return queue, giving it first an affectionate pat, then a dry kiss. He usually blamed the ball for bad rolls and never gave it credit for the strikes, but after nailing his first-ever six-ten, he was in a generous mood. And he'd be in an even better mood after winning those race tickets.

He curled the ball, relaxed, and approached the line, falling into a smooth motion.

The man in gray appeared just in front of the lead pin. Elmer thought at first it was one of the alley employees, fishing out a stuck ball or unjamming a rack. Except when Mac was on duty, the cheap son of a bitch ran the show all by himself. And this guy wasn't messing with equipment, he was walking up the buffed and shining lane toward Elmer in dusty, cracked boots that had more holes than leather.

Elmer's fingers were already relaxing and he couldn't stop the momentum of the ball. He gave out a croak and lost his balance, the ball bouncing two feet in front of him with a bone-crunching *thwack*.

"Hey, no dribbling allowed," Mac snapped. "I'll sweep up the splinters with your ass if you do that again."

Elmer stared at the sudden man, seeing more of him, the ragged scratchy-looking clothes—*uniform?*—and a cap tilted over his face. And beneath the brim of the hat, nearly lost in shadows, was the gleaming bone of a fleshless grin.

The ball meandered another twenty feet before it slipped into the gutter and into the mysterious depths where pulleys and levers pushed the ball back uphill to the scorer's table.

The man in gray had disappeared.

"You see that?" Elmer said.

"Yeah, pretty damned pathetic," Jeff said.

"The man—he got in my way."

"Yeah, and the sun was in your eyes and the dog ate your homework and you forget to throw money in the plate at church." As the metal arm descended and swept the pins away, Jeff stood and grabbed his jacket. "I'll take a rain check on Titty Palace, but you can bring the race tickets Monday."

The end of the lane held only pins, not a bone-faced man in scarecrow battle gear, and an electronic banner on the scoreboard scrolled the words "Push for next game." Elmer wasn't going to do any pushing. Now that he'd had a moment to process the image, he realized the man had been wearing a ratty kepi, a Civil War cap. And the uniform had been wool, like the replica clothing Captain Jeff Davis insisted his men wear for the living-history re-enactments.

"I'm going to start charging if you're going to stink up the joint like that," Mac said as Jeff strutted away in his tight-assed officer's march.

"That guy was walking in the lane when I rolled."

"Some bastard steps on the parquet I spent all week polishing, I'll shoot his ass."

Elmer knew Mac kept a gun hidden behind the counter, but he wasn't sure bullets would do much good against the unknown soldier. "You didn't see him?"

"Hell, Elmer, you only had two pitchers. Not near enough to justify a hallucination."

Elmer finished his beer, hand shaking so much he spilled foam down his chin. If he drank enough, maybe he'd wash the vision of the soldier from his brain. If not, at least maybe Vernell and the brats wouldn't be so dog-ass ugly when he got home.

CHAPTER EIGHT

The Room.

His dad usually kept it locked, but Vernon Ray had checked out the Internet and learned a trick called "lock bumping" that had allowed him to snap open the flimsy hollow-core door without breaking anything. He saved his break-ins for special occasions when he knew his parents would be away for an hour or more. Mom was out shopping and it was Dad's bowling night, so he had some time.

Plus, since the weird incident in the Hole, he'd felt a calling to The Room as if some deep religious secrets lay behind the door. "The Room" had never been officially named; it was the spare bedroom in their three-bedroom mobile home, and Vernon Ray figured that was probably why his parents had never given him a sibling: Dad would have had to move his collection. Since Dad always referred to it as "The Room," that's how Vernon Ray thought of it.

The mobile home was quiet, and it seemed the whole trailer park had taken the night off. Usually Saturdays were an around-the-clock cacophony of stereos, drunken laughter, revving engines, and TV sets, punctuated with the occasional shattering glass or fistfight. A clock ticked in the kitchen, its rhythm recalling the *ratta-tat-tat* of the snare drum he'd heard in the Hole.

Vernon Ray bumped his hip into the door, twisting the knob as the wood yielded slightly and the tumblers rattled. The lock sprang and he swung the door open. Vernon Ray switched on a bedtime reading lamp that emitted a diffuse glow. The strange, bluish light made the contents of The Room even more unreal, like exhibits in a museum.

Books with leather-bound covers, many of them rare and fragile, lined shelves covering one side of the room. Among his dad's collection were one-of-a-kind personal items like diaries and letters, as well as history books and biographies with low print runs. An autographed copy of Gen. Ulysses S. Grant's memoir, one of the first tell-all celebrity bios ever published, was also in the collection, sealed behind a sheet of Plexiglas. The aging paper gave The Room an aroma of decay and must, much like what Vernon Ray imagined Grant's Tomb smelled like.

Vernon Ray had read many of the books. Not from Dad's collection, of course, but modern reprinted copies he'd found in the public library or public-domain scans posted on the Internet. Vernon Ray ran the soft light over the shelves, but he wasn't interested in two-dimensional history at the moment. He took a few steps deeper into The Room, careful not to step on anything fragile.

An obstacle course of period antiques covered the floor: hand-hewn chairs, a maple church pew, blacksmith's and furrier's benches. A saddle rode the blacksmith's bench, moth-eaten wool blankets and rusty cast-iron tools stacked beside it. The other furniture was parted to make way for a black cherry roll-top writing desk that his dad used for the sole purpose of penning out marching orders for the N.C. 26th Living History Regiment. It was as if his dad's fantasy life intersected with these solid relics only when vital to the mission, an act of discipline that proved Capt. Jefferson Davis was the only man fit to command the regiment.

The smell of old wood and leather blended with that of the paper, but it aroused nothing in Vernon Ray. Instead, he navigated between the pieces of furniture and reached the Grail. He tilted the light up so that it glinted off the muskets, revolvers, bugles, medals, insignia, and a cavalry sword with an ornate brass handle.

Several of the pieces were replica, but one of the medals bore the deep dent of a musket ball, suggesting it might have once saved the life of the wearer. Powder horns and sheathed Bowie knives dangled from rawhide strings. A tin canteen in a canvas satchel hung by a strap, and underneath it a mess kit, coffee pot, and other steel cookware were arrayed as if readied for breakfast.

A card table bore a *papier-mâché* diorama designed to mimic Titusville, complete with the surrounding mountains carefully labeled with their traditional names: Cracker Knob, Eggers Ridge, Calloway Mountain, Tater Hill, The Balds, and, rising over the valley like a tsunami wave, Mulatto Mountain. A tiny white flag, bearing a meticulously rendered image of the Home Guard's insignia and glued to a toothpick, was poked into the highest point of Mulatto Mountain, in the approximate location of The Jangling Hole. His dad had invested six silent months working on the diorama, alone with the door closed.

The last two months had been spent arranging lead-cast miniature soldiers, ordered through collector's catalogs. An HO-scale train track ran through the valley to mark the narrow-gauge tracks that had once carried Tweetsie into town. The real rails were still there, running along the foot of Mulatto and parallel with the back street of downtown and an old creek, but the last train had run in 1931, when the dwindling profits of timber clear-cutting collided with the Great Depression.

Vernon Ray had learned about that in the Pickett County history book his dad had written and self-published. All of Dad's remaining copies were tucked away on the top shelf of The Room, pages still pristine and spines intact. Vernon Ray had borrowed his reading copy from a school teacher. Dad had made a few grammatical errors but overall the prose was pretty solid.

In the diorama, the Home Guard was divided into two platoons. One small group of gray-painted soldiers was huddled in a camp in a field near the old courthouse, the building indicated only by a painted cardboard box. Other small boxes marked the downtown area, though Titusville during the war had been little more than a couple of banks, a mercantile, a tobacco warehouse, a train station, and a jail. The camp had been designed to protect the train station, and in that mission, the real troops had succeeded, though the courthouse had eventually been burned by Yankees and the jail used to secure their Confederate prisoners.

The second platoon of cast-lead Confederates was spread across the face of Mulatto Mountain, recreating the position the real troops had taken above the narrow pass that provided the easiest access into the valley from the West. From there, the troops had hoped to surprise Gen. Bill Stoneman and his marauding Bluebellies. They had obviously failed, though historians disagreed on the reasons.

Vernon Ray's dad said the troops had been poorly commanded, but most people believed the ragtag platoon had simply turned chicken and scattered in the woods without a fight. Some of the deserters had joined the renegade band led by Col. George Kirk, and Kirk's Raiders had hidden away in the Hole, waiting for Stoneman to leave so Kirk could impose his own law on Titusville. According to legend, the raiders had refused to surrender and Stoneman's cannon had blasted their cave into a tomb, but historians had never presented a convincing case for the unofficial court martial and death sentence.

Jefferson Jackson Davis, Captain of the 26th North Carolina Troops Living History Society, known to his friends as "Jeff" and his wife as "Hon" (except on those special occasions when she called him "a carpet-bagging asshole"), had arranged the toy Confederate troops in defense of a town lost in time.

And Vernon Ray had lost his father to that time, a casualty that bled as deeply as any victim of Bull Run or Gettysburg. The war's outcome would never change, only spawn more revisionist histories until the truth no longer mattered. And while winners usually wrote the history books, plenty of Southerners felt their side had never lost, merely run out of time, money, and men.

Vernon Ray was in the mood for a little revisionist history of his own. He touched the nearest of the toy soldiers on Mulatto Mountain and moved it closer to the road in the pass, near where Stoneman's mounted cavalry were poised for a make-believe ride into Titusville. No doubt Dad had memorized the positions in which he had placed the troops, but Vernon Ray had spent almost as much time himself studying the battle lines.

"Private Joshua Ames," Vernon Ray whispered, picking a name at random from the muster rolls. "This is Capt. Davis. Hold your position down by the road and don't let any Yankees in. You know what they'll do to your wife and kids if they get a chance."

The darkness seemed to press against the windows of the room, like black water kissing the side of an aquarium. A little bit of orange streetlight leaked between the curtains, just enough to give the impression of a false dawn. Vernon Ray propped his reading lamp over the tableau so he could maneuver the troops with both hands.

He dropped into a deep Southern accent, drawing in breath to hit the lowest registers of his adolescent bass. "Aye-aye, sir, them devils will even rape the sheep if they got the chance, and God help the guilty if they break through."

Vernon Ray went back to his normal Captain voice, almost unconsciously imitating his father. "I'll get Squire Taylor to cover your flank, and Dooley Eggers will take the other side of the road. Got it, men?"

He moved two more of the soldiers away from the Hole, placing them as sentries against the approaching cavalry troop. With nimble fingers, he positioned a line of the in-town platoon across Main Street, placing the rest on the tops of the buildings. The men were frozen in an assortment of poses, some of them poised in a bayonet charge while others stood at attention with their rifles on their shoulders.

Now Vernon Ray was falling into the fantasy, becoming as self-absorbed as his father, only dimly aware that this was both the closest emotionally he'd ever get to his father and, in an odd way, the best way to get revenge for the years of neglect—he was overriding his father's orders. He commanded three more soldiers off Mulatto Mountain, chiding them for nearly missing the action to come.

"Do you gentlemen want to live forever, or do you want to be laid out in glory with your brothers?" No good officer ever asked his men to tackle any danger or hardship he wouldn't face himself, and Vernon Ray knew when Gen. Stoneman came thundering through the pass, he'd be standing in the dirt road himself, pistol in hand, a wide-open target. Vernon Ray could almost smell the dust, the rot of the oak leaves, the horse manure, the sulfuric tang of fresh gunpowder, the faint coal smoke of the last steam locomotive.

"Sgt. Childers, take three men and cover the west side of the mountain so they don't dismount and follow Skin Creek into town," he said, snapping off the palm-up salute in response to his sergeant's salute. A few more orders and the remaining men had advanced down the slopes of the mountain and into harm's way.

"Capt. Davis," said Sgt. McGregor, his most trusted noncom. "If enemy troop strength matches the reconnoiters, we're set up for a slaughter."

Capt. Davis gave a grave nod of his head. "War is hell,

Sergeant."

"If we fall, we lose the town."

Vernon Ray nudged the toy sergeant toward the fence line, where he would die shortly after his captain. "We don't get to win this time. Our job is to slow them down."

"The men are sticking with you, sir. Even the conscripts."

"Good. That will be all, Sergeant."

"Aye-aye," the soldier said. He was Scottish, and such men were foolhardy and brave as long as you kept them sober. Leadership came with its own worries, and though Capt. Davis had already accepted his fate, the certainty of his followers' deaths weighed on him, making him feel much older than his 13 years.

The ground shook with the distant rumble of a hundred hoof beats. The Room fell away, and it was 1864, October, birds taking wing as they sensed the coming calamity. The dirt roads of Titusville would be stained red before this day was done. Capt. Davis was almost ready to take up his position in the pass.

But there was one more soldier, a special volunteer, who was awaiting orders.

"Vernon Ray, you can't sit out on the side forever," Capt. Davis said. "You've got to join the dance sooner or later."

He fondled the toy drummer boy, the one he'd touched so often that its lead was shinier and less tarnished than the other pieces. It was half the height of the other soldiers, his little kepi askew, head bent down to his instrument. The snare was cocked on his right thigh, angling the drumhead so his dull gray wrists could roll out the signals.

"I'm ready, Dad," the drummer boy said in a small voice.

"Might get dangerous, son. Keep your head low."

"I won't blink an eye, no matter what. I'll make you proud."

"I know you will. You already make me proud."

The drummer boy smiled at this, at least in that autumnal fantasy land, though the grim lead face stayed as set as it had been since the day it was cast. He'd drum even if he lost his sticks, even if a cannon blast took his hands. He'd beat his splintered bones against the leather head of the snare, pound until his sinews and ragged flesh fell off, he'd roll reveille until the gates of Hades opened up and the soldiers followed his cadence into the pits of Gen. Grant's infernal prison.

Because Daddy had given him a duty.

Vernon Ray was lost in the imaginary battle, the sun filtering through the yellow-and-red forest, the wind running soft through the meadows, the creek tinkling between slick stones, the hoof beats getting louder, the whinny of horses and the clanking of harness growing louder in the narrow pass. They'd be coming around the bend any minute, horses and riders alike breathing fire, red eyes promising a swift punishment for rebellion.

And Vernon Ray found himself before the open closet, where his dad's uniforms hung. The captain's crisp wool uniform with its braids and epaulets, the coarse tow-linen shirts for period civilization reenactments, the white cotton blouses, the regular gray buck private's outfit with its frayed cuffs and bullet holes. At the end of the row was the one that would soon be too small for Vernon Ray, the drummer boy's suit with its bone buttons and knickers. As he had many times before, he touched the scratchy fabric of its sleeve.

"I'll make you proud," he whispered, and it was neither the captain's nor the toy soldier's voice, but his own.

He slipped out of his Incredible Hulk T-shirt, the cool air of the room sharpening his nipples to tiny purple points. He kicked off his bedroom slippers and shucked down his pants. The underwear would have to go, because though the briefs were cotton, the waistband was a synthetic blend covering rubberized elastic, neither of which was extant during the War.

With trembling fingers, he wrested the uniform from its hanger. It smelled of campfire smoke and cobwebs. He slid his one bare arm into the woolen sleeve, enjoying the delicious scraping inflicted by the fabric. It was a little tight in the shoulders, but he shrugged into it until it rested comfortably. He was aware of his runaway heartbeat—

*ratta-tat-tat*

—as he buttoned up the front of the coat. Next he stepped into the matching knickers, sliding them up until the cloth tickled his penis. All the leather boots were adult size, and most rural children in those days wore no shoes anyway. He took the small kepi from its place on the rack, where it was tucked between a grandiose French cavalry hat and a felt fedora. He perched the slanted Rebel cap on his head, the brim tipped low just the way the toy soldier wore it.

Vernon Ray stood at attention for a moment, as if undergoing the captain's inspection. Then he gave the Confederate Army salute and opened the cedar cupboard.

The snare drum was on the middle shelf, the largest object in the collection. The horsehide head was girded in place by a steel band, which itself was attached to the wooden shell by neat rows of brass tacks. A series of pig-gut strings held the head tight and could be adjusted to change the tone of the snare. A bridge of woven steel ran just beneath the head, designed to give off the signature rattling sound as the drumhead vibrated.

He lifted the drum carefully by its canvas strap, slinging the strap around his neck and almost knocking off his cap in the process. The drum's weight felt comforting against his abdomen. He collected the hand-carved drumsticks and gave them an experimental twirl. He had his own drumsticks, rubber-tipped ones bought in the music store at the mall, but these had an entirely different balance and feel.

Like the bones of war.

"I'm ready, Dad," Vernon Ray whispered.

He turned toward the table and the mock battle. Capt. Jeff Davis would die this day, but he would die proud.

Vernon Ray turned his left wrist up and rested the tip of the stick against the snare head. He clenched the stick in his right hand and raised it several inches above the horsehide.

"Awaiting orders, sir," he said.

*Do it, Earley.*

Tears welled in his eyes, but soldiers didn't cry, only scared little boys. He wanted to blink, but he promised his dad he wouldn't. A freshet of salt water threaded down his left cheek and he licked it when it reached his lips.

Stoneman's unit was closer now, the horses hammering out their own cadence, static in the air as if the sky were holding its breath.

Vernon Ray drove the right stick solidly against the drum, following with a snap of the left, then again with each stick, letting the pattern roll into a flourish. He would sound the advance, encourage the troops against long odds, stand firm in his duty amid the cries of agony and rage and panic.

He slapped out the cadence —

*ratta-tat-tat*

— the drumsticks blurring, the air moving with the action of his hands, the beat echoing off the cheap paneling, punctuating the bravery of those who repelled the invaders who sought to destroy the homes and hearths the Home Guard stood united to defend. The tears flowed freely, cooling on his face, but he was smiling.

The toy soldiers on the table didn't hold their positions, though. They retreated, their stiff lead bases vibrating back away from the road and into the cover of the forest, winding up the slopes of Mulatto Mountain. Vernon Ray pounded harder, certain that if he stayed strong in the face of flying steel, the men would rally and return to their posts. But the soldiers turned tail in the face of Stoneman's superior force, or their fear of looming death, or their lack of faith in the Confederacy. They scrambled madly up Mulatto Mountain, scaling the *papier-mâché* until they huddled around the Jangling Hole, seeking entrance among the mouse-gray boulders.

They would hide today in the Hole and live through Stoneman's Raid, but their end would come soon enough.

The important thing was for Vernon Ray to hold his line, drum until the Grim Reaper harvested with his steel blade, stand tall, make his dad proud —

The Room exploded with the bright fury of a cannonade, and Vernon Ray blinked.

His dad stood in the doorway, hand on the light switch. "And just who do you think you are, you sorry little sack of civilian shit?"

CHAPTER NINE

"Look at this long list of environmental violations," Cindy Baumhower said, spreading the sheaf of papers on Littlefield's desk.

The sheriff sat back in his chair, the hinges squeaking and driving rusty nails into his skull. He rubbed his crew cut, hoping the headache would magically rise into the ceiling. Cindy Baumhower was normally more of a thorn in the side than nails in the palms, but tonight her crusading-journalist bit was merely annoying. If *The Titusville Times* wasn't such a convenient mouthpiece when he wanted to crack down on any type of public nuisance, he would show her the door and lock it behind her.

But besides her drooling desire for a Pulitzer, or at least a few state press association awards, Cindy wasn't so bad. At least she had ethics and when he gave her information off the record, it stayed off the record. In a small town, gossip could mean the difference between reelection and unemployment.

"You know that's not my jurisdiction," Littlefield said. "That's the state's problem."

"Christ, Frank, the Department of Environment and Natural Resources is just a rubber stamp for developers and industrialists. The lobbyists in Raleigh are practically blowing the governor. And who wants teeth when you're getting a good hummer?"

"You forget, Bill Willard is a Republican and the Democrats have had a hammerlock on the capitol since Reagan."

"This is about rich and richer, not right and left."

Cindy jutted out her chest, but Littlefield forced himself not to look at it. She wasn't much younger than Littlefield, but her freckles and sun-bleached hair, along with her ardor, gave the impression of a college co-ed. Her blue eyes were radiant and piercing, and Littlefield knew better than to meet them for too long at any one stretch. She reminded him of Sheila Story, and that hurt way too much.

"I'm sorry, Cindy," he said, regretting that he'd let their

relationship get on a first-name basis. As always, that made lying a lot more difficult.

Cindy swept up the papers and shoveled them into her hemp tote bag, which bore a pot leaf and the slogan "Legalize It." She claimed not to smoke the stuff herself, and Littlefield was inclined to believe her. He'd arrested more than one bong-huffing member of the Hemp Liberation Movement, but all things considered he'd much rather have ganja gangstas in his holding cells than meth junkies or dry drunks. Stoners tended to stay mellow and never complained about the food.

"Okay," Cindy said. "What about financial wrongdoing?"

The sheriff kicked his boots up on his desk and crossed his legs. "Depends. If it's interstate, it's federal, and these days practically every white-collar crime involves the Internet in some way."

Cindy snorted in derision. "So I should check with your fraud division?"

Littlefield's staff consisted of 12 officers, and between four and eight were on duty during any given shift. With J.R. looking like he'd be on a long leave of absence, there would be a gap in regular patrols, and drug investigations would have to be scaled back. While drug busts made for good photo ops, people generally were more concerned about their houses being broken into, the old "Hitting close to home" theory of law protection. No way could the department afford an extra shift or two devoted to Cindy's latest vendetta against Budget Bill, even if there had been some decent evidence.

"Bill Willard's never been accused of anything shady," Littlefield said. "Truth is, I think you don't like him just because his photographs have gotten more recognition than yours."

Like many small-town reporters, Cindy took her own photographs, and though she clearly had an eye for composition, Willard's equipment was thousands of dollars finer than what the *Times* could provide. "That's not fair, Sheriff."

The only thing worse than being on a first-name basis was when she shifted into that cold, professional demeanor. He tensed a little as she came around the desk, thinking he'd rather be anywhere else at the moment, even at The Jangling Hole after sundown.

"Are you in Budget Bill's pocket, too?" she asked, standing over him, hands on her hips.

"Why in the world would you say a thing like that?"

"You sure buried my sexual assault charge."

"Hell, Cindy, your own paper was afraid to run that incident report. There was just not enough evidence to make an arrest, much less get an indictment from the Grand Jury. He would have sued you and half the county."

"Well, I hope one day he squeezes *your* tit and see how you like it."

Littlefield let his gaze flick to her chest. Not that he had to do much letting. His eyes seemed to take off of their own free will, like other parts of him did whenever crazy women infected him with sweet madness. "Budget Bill's an upstanding citizen," Littlefield said. "He's got a right to develop Mulatto Moun tain. Maybe people like you think it's immoral—"

"People like me? And just what kind of people is that, Sheriff?"

The sheriff took his feet off the desk and sat forward, but she didn't back away as he'd expected. She was less than a foot from him, much too close for a professional relationship or to respect personal space.

The sheriff swallowed hard. "All I'm saying is he follows the law, and I follow the law. Check with the planning department. He has all his permits and he even took out a bond for the road."

"Can't you block the site in the interest of public safety?"

"What are you getting at?"

Cindy twisted her lips and sighed out one corner of her mouth, spreading fine tendrils of her hair. Maybe she knew how fetching the mannerism was and used it to keep him off guard. But the sheriff got the impression she wasn't as calculating as some women he'd known. She genuinely seemed not to notice the effect her simmering, subtle sex appeal had on men.

Or maybe Littlefield was just an old pervert. He'd been called worse.

"I monitor the scanner, remember?" Cindy said. "Crime beat? So how's Officer Perriotte?"

"Fine. He's under observation. But I guess you knew that

already."

Her smile would have made the Grinch proud. "Privacy laws kept the hospital from giving out his condition," she said. "But I have my sources."

*Bat your goddamned eyelashes and you could win over Marcus Welby, House, and Dr. Doolittle.* "No visible injuries."

"Just some head trauma. On the *inside*."

"That's undetermined at this point. Could be stress, epilepsy, hell, even low blood sugar."

"Three shots fired."

"That's undetermined, too."

"Doesn't that trigger an internal investigation? I'm assuming your officer was the one who fired the shots, since Sandy in records said no incident report had been filed."

Littlefield had not yet got around to filing an incident report simply because he wasn't sure which lie to put on it. He'd been hoping to avoid it altogether, even though Hardy Eggers, Mr. Ayinari the Pakistani store owner, and Willard all knew the police had been on the property responding to a complaint. And those three boys . . . .

He stood, towering a foot over Cindy, and she backed up half a step. "I'm looking into it," Littlefield said through tight lips.

"You looking into the Jangling Hole while you're at it?"

Littlefield forced a laugh that sounded like he was choking on a biscuit. "Not you, too, Cindy. Why don't you save that one for your Halloween feature? You know, where you crank out some cheesy local ghost story and pretend it's in the interest of serious paranormal research."

Her blue eyes sparked ice and then fire. "I do my job and you do yours."

"That's all I want."

"Just like you did in Whispering Pines in 2002," she said.

The sheriff's lips worked like a trout trying to learn French.

"I did some checking," she said. "You covered that one up pretty good, but I found a few people willing to go off the record. So is Archer McFall still considered a missing person?"

"That case is cold," he said, though in his heart it was as closed as a coffin lid on a rotten corpse. Not that McFall had been considerate enough to actually leave a body. Well, he'd left behind several bodies, but not his own, though Littlefield believed he didn't really own one, just borrowed them from time to time.

"You have a lot of holes, Sheriff. In your stories, and in your soul."

She turned and marched to the door, her tote bag pressed against her side.

*Please, God, don't let me look at her ass.*

Even though he didn't believe in God any longer, the prayer was answered. Or maybe he was just upset enough that whatever odd light she'd aroused in him had been darkened by the curtain of self-doubt and fear.

He rummaged around in the bottom drawer of his desk. His fingers brushed against the cool bottle with its greasy liquid. This would be a hell of a time to give in to the habit.

*No, not a habit. 'Habit' is for normal people and nuns. I'm a plain old garden-variety, C-grade drunk. For people like me, it's not a habit, it's an occupation.*

Littlefield shuffled some papers on top of the bottle and continued digging. The newspaper clippings on the McFall case were sparse and mostly centered on Sheila Story's accidental death in the line of duty. In fact, McFall was barely mentioned in connection with the death. The incident report said Littlefield and Story had been responding to a public disturbance call at McFall's church when Littlefield's patrol car plunged into the river. The newspaper and the incident report both contained the truth, but Littlefield had been around long enough to know the truth never told the entire story.

He glanced at the color photo of Sheila that had run on the front page of the *Times*. It had faded with the years, and the *Times* had never been known for its print quality, but those honest blue eyes seemed to appraise and taunt him from beyond the grave: "Come on, Frank. Something weird is going down and you're pretending everything's normal. But I know you too well. You'll just close me up in the drawer and leave the past in the dark where you think it belongs."

He dropped the clipping and slammed the drawer shut.

*Drop it, Frank. There's probably a perfectly reasonable explanation for a set of footprints that ends in the middle of nowhere.*

Yeah, and the Tooth Fairy was coming to steal everybody's Halloween candy, too. He put on his Stetson cowboy hat and pulled the brim down so it shaded his eyes. He'd donned the headgear during the last campaign and his popularity had swelled. Now he wore it on all but the most blustery day, and it didn't hurt that the stiff suede covered his ever-expanding bald spot. The hat also had the effect of improving his posture because he found himself holding his shoulders back so the headgear was better balanced.

He'd wanted to check on J.R. before turning in, but he had one more stop to make first. Two of the boys were unidentified, but the store owner had tabbed Dex McAllister from a mug shot. Of course, misdemeanor shoplifting rarely merited such a time-consuming investigation, but Littlefield wanted to get this little mystery under wraps and pray that Bill Willard and his silent partners blasted the Hole to hell and gone before anything went poking its head out.

"I'm on call tonight, Sherry," he said to his dispatcher as he headed for his cruiser.

Despite a smoking ban in all public facilities, Sherry kept the office in a menthol fog, compliments of Kool 100's. Since she'd been on the county payroll longer than the politicians who'd voted in the policy, no one had ever had the guts to take her on. The smoking had given her face a tough, leathery quality, and two brown acorn eyes stared back like those of a cigar-store Indian.

Sherry would gossip but only with people she could trust, and that particular circle was small. Fielding calls during 32 years of night shifts, she'd heard dirt on every family in Pickett County at one time or another. But Littlefield wasn't ready to share his theory that something supernatural was stirring on Mulatto Mountain. For real, not legend.

"Any word on J.R.?" she asked.

"No, but I'm going to check on him and pay a visit to the McAllisters."

"I never had no use for that Dexter," she said, taking a draw on her cigarette that left a good half-inch of ember. "The little twerp would just as soon skin a cat as pet it."

She let the ash dangle for a moment and watched the sheriff as if daring him to challenge her on either the civil violation or her unprofessional opinion of a juvenile delinquent.

Littlefield adjusted his hat. "The most we can get him for is trespassing and shoplifting. And the shoplifting charge probably wouldn't stick. He took a pack of smokes and that kind of evidence disappears fast."

She sucked again and now the ash was over an inch long and sagging. Her hand was poised over the computerized dispatch equipment. Littlefield didn't understand the technology, but it had to be upgraded every few years, when he practically had to get down and blow off the commissioners during budget season to secure the funding. A blizzard of gray flakes probably did little to enhance the equipment's longevity.

"Well, you tell J.R. I'm going to drop him by a sweet potato pie tomorrow," she said, managing one more draw before tapping her cigarette in a ceramic cat ashtray. Her hand was so steady, she probably would have made a decent surgeon, except her patients would turn up with high rates of lung cancer. As for J.R., if he consumed some of her award-winning pie, he was likely to see a cholesterol boost and a heart attack before he was discharged.

"10-4 that," he said. "Got five on the night shift?"

"Yeah, Wally's running late but he's got the hemorrhoids so he'll probably be doing a lot of standing around."

"That's comforting."

"Cindy Baumhower sure is a bitch, ain't she? What kind of name is that, anyway? She a German, or a Jew?"

Since Sherry had no use for the smoking ban, he figured there was little use in bringing up anti-discrimination policies. Besides, in Sherry's view, being a reporter trumped any shortcomings inflicted by race or religion.

"She's just doing her job."

"But does she have to do it so damn *loud*?" The cigarette was back in her mouth as punctuation.

"Call me if there's anything big, or anything to do with the Willard property," he said, reaching for the door.

"The Hole, you mean. Call if anything crawls out of the Hole."

He parted his lips, trying to grin, but instead spoke through stiff lips. "Halloween's still a couple of weeks away."

"The Hole don't wait for Halloween."

"Good night."

She stabbed out her cigarette and was firing up another by the time he entered the cool, clear air of Titusville. The town twinkled with green and orange light, the Main Street businesses long since closed but the display windows casting their commercial allure onto the pavement. The sheriff's office was on the edge of the municipal limits, and Titusville proper was the jurisdiction of Chief Rex "Boney" Maroney.

If only the town had annexed more land and expanded its borders, then Mulatto Mountain and the Hole would be Maroney's problem, not Littlefield's. Once the million-dollar homes in Bill Willard's development were constructed, no doubt the greedy town council would want to tap the tax base there, but whatever was hiding in the Hole would be stirred up by then.

And it would happen on Littlefield's watch.

The McCallisters lived on the west end of Titusville in a little community known as Greasy Corner because of the three gas stations and mechanic's garage that used to mark the intersection. Two of the gas stations had gone belly up and, after the expensive process of digging up leaky underground tanks and removing contaminated soil, the properties now featured a McDonald's and a Mitsubishi dealership. The mechanic's garage was still there, but the business had been converted to a quick-lube joint that changed your oil while you read crinkled sports magazines. The lone intact business had changed corporate overlords several times, and the pumps that had once sold gas for 19 cents cash on the barrel now took credit cards and offered a discount on Super Slurps.

As he turned onto Taylor Lake Road, Littlefield decided that Bill Willard had the right idea: take what you could and then catch the next stage out of Dodge. If he kept driving, he'd hit the Tennessee line in half an hour, and Tennessee was a long enough state that he'd put Mulatto Mountain and its weird tinkling noises far out of earshot. But he'd stuck it out through the death of his little brother and Sheila Story and a handful of other people over the years, and he figured that whatever was up there in the sky moving around the stage pieces was hungry for a showdown.

And Littlefield was one of the pawns on the board.

"Howdy, pilgrim, I'm the law around here," he drawled in a parody of Saturday-matinee actors who'd donned the tin star long ago.

But he wondered what would happen if he took his brand of law up to the dark peak of Mulatto Mountain and shouted a challenge into its cold cleft of stones. He kept the cruiser over the speed limit to burn off some adrenaline.

The bowling industry must be booming, because Mac McCallister's house was a good 3,000 square feet, with a three-car garage on one end, a neat row of rose bushes and oleander girding the brick walls, and a new bass boat tucked under a canvas cover in the back yard. But exterior order and value didn't always extend into the living room or family closets. Littlefield had knocked on many nice white doors and delivered bad news, court summonses, or arrest warrants.

Nan McCallister opened on the first knock, squinting due to her cheeky smile. "How are you, Sheriff? You come for a contribution to the Benevolence Society?"

The sheriff looked down, hat in his hands. It seemed Nan had been under the knife again, and her chest was up there around 44 or so. No way could he step inside without brushing against one of the inflatable marvels.

"Is Dexter here?"

The smile faltered only slightly. "He's playing videogames in his room."

Littlefield looked up at the second story, but all the windows there were dark. By the time he'd finished his visual reconnoiter, Mac had appeared behind his wife, signature bowling-ball belly stretching out a tank top, a sweat-beaded beer in his hand. "Howdy, Sheriff, got time for a tall cold one?"

"Not really."

"Not my wife," he said, swatting her on the ass and causing her to jump, though her smile stayed in place. "I'm talking about a beer."

Littlefield swallowed. "No, thanks. I don't drink."

Mac peered from under bushy eyebrows. "Since when?"

Littlefield saw no reason to go into his sobriety date and subsequent recovery, but damned if that beer didn't smell sweet and yeasty. "Can you get Dexter for me?"

"Dex? What's he done now?"

"I just want to talk to him."

"That's what you said the last three times, and once he left in the back seat of your patrol car and the other two bought my lawyer a new Harley-Davidson."

"He's suspected of shoplifting," Littlefield said. "A store owner ID'ed him. Since this is his first time, I can probably let it swing light, since I doubt we'll have any evidence besides one person's word. But there's something else."

Mac stepped in front of his wife. Neither had invited him in. "This ain't about the Hole, is it?"

"Pardon?"

"Dex said he and the boys were up there fiddle-farting around and all hell broke loose, cops with guns firing shots and such."

"We had...an incident."

"I thought he was pulling my leg," Mac said. "He's got his old man's sense of humor. Ain't that right, Nan?"

Nan smiled as if everything was always right. She fondled the golden cross that hung down onto her obscenely enhanced bosom. "He sure doesn't get it from his mother."

"If I could just have a word with him," Littlefield said.

"I don't know about that," Mac said. "Seems like I might have grounds for some sort of reckless endangerment or something. A civil suit. You can't just go around shooting at innocent boys."

"Police have immunity when in the legal pursuit of their duty."

"Well, you ain't talking with him until I've talked with my lawyer. Unless you got a warrant."

Littlefield could probably round up a magistrate and cobble together a warrant on the cigarette heist, but by then it would be after midnight. It wasn't like Dex McCallister was a flight risk.

"Can you bring him by my office tomorrow? I promise the

shoplifting will go on the scrap heap, but I would like to talk with him. He'll be in and out in time for ice cream."

"Sure, sure. And come by the alley sometime. Roll one on the house."

"I'll do that."

Nan beamed at that, as if anyone who enjoyed bowling was a child of God, goodness, and light. Then again, the sport had paid for the bowling balls behind her nipples, so Littlefield figured she'd done her time behind the counter. Bent over or not.

As Littlefield returned to his cruiser, he gave one more glance at the house. Dex was clearly silhouetted against a lighted upstairs window, nose pressed against the glass. The boy pointed his index finger at the sheriff, thumb raised in the universal symbol for a gun. He mouthed three popping noises and grinned as if he'd actually gotten his sense of humor from a serial killer instead of his father.

CHAPTER TEN

*Cue the midget and send in the clowns, let's get ready to rumble, the freak show is about to begin.*

Daddy was drunk again, and Mom had strapped on the battle ax and gone in like the female version of "Braveheart," and Bobby expected blood to flow as freely as it did in any Mel Gibson-directed epic. Bobby thought about sticking his head under the pillow or clamping on the headphones and turning up the stereo to Def Plus. But, like the sound of a cruise ship's bow scraping along the brutal edge of an iceberg or a car's braked wheels squealing before impact, the Eldreth warm-up act sparked that same compelling electricity. You could cash out your ticket for a ringside seat, but the show went on just the same.

Bobby pushed away the comic books piled on his desk. As creepy and weird as Neil Gaiman's Sandman was, it couldn't compete with the Elmer and Vernell Variety Hour, and the opening act had something to do with a pack of matches Mom had found in Daddy's jacket pocket. Which was even funnier because Daddy didn't smoke.

"Dolly's Dollhouse," Vernell shouted, loudly enough that it might have carried through the thin aluminum walls of the mobile home and out across the trailer park. Not that anyone would be shocked at the latest knock-down battle royale. There weren't many secrets in a trailer park.

Bobby knew what Dolly's was, of course. No kid could reach the eighth grade of Titusville Middle without hearing about the local boob joint. A few of the kids claimed to have witnessed exotic exposure of the flesh there, but Bobby was inclined to doubt the tales. He was less able to dismiss the thought that his dad had paid a visit there, since a not-so-secret stack of magazines in the tool shed gave testament to the man's taste for naked women.

"Jeff gave me those," Elmer said, mushy and growly enough to display some fight. "The pilot light went out on the gas grill when we were grilling dogs last week."

"Oh, yeah? Then how come none of the matches is struck? The book's full."

*Nice one, Mom. Colombo would be proud of your deductive reasoning, though you'd look fruity in a trench coat.*

Bobby pulled his ear away from the door. There was no need to eavesdrop now. The armies had sounded their trumpets and the cavalry had charged, and now the sides were fully engaged. His brother Jerrell was lucky enough to have a part-time gig at Taco Bell, and though his clothes stank of beans and that weird yellow goo that squirted from big caulking guns labeled "cheese food product," at least the job offered some escape from home. Bobby, meanwhile, had only school and football practice as an excuse to be gone.

The boys shared a room, with Jerrell taking the top bunk, which meant those oily bean farts oozed down during the night much like Bobby imagined chlorine gas drifted over the trenches during World War I. But what Jerrell lacked in fragrance, he made up for in generosity, having proclaimed his comic collection "kid's stuff" and passing it down to little bro' for nothing more than a well-placed lie or two when Jerrell felt like cruising or playing hooky. Jerrell could have turned some decent coin on eBay with the collection, which included complete runs of obscure curios like *Jonah Hex* and *Boris Karloff Tales of Mystery*. Now they belonged to Bobby, who had read them all at least twice before sealing them back in their archival-quality, acid-free plastic sleeves.

If only he could stow away his real life as easily, or close the pages when the cartoon got weird.

"So what if I did go to Dolly's?" his dad shouted in the living room. "It's not like I see much skin around *here* lately."

"Bastard," Mom responded, the word she went to when Daddy either drove home a valid point or she'd run the gamut of put-downs and had reached the bottom of the barrel. "How much did you throw at them whores?"

"Nothing. I just sat there and had a few."

Bobby knew from experience that "a few" probably meant a dozen. The way Daddy was slurring his words, he was lucky to wheel the pick-up home without getting blue-lighted for a DWI.

Daddy had been caught a couple of years ago, giving Mom the opportunity to rag him about high insurance premiums and having to haul his sorry fat ass around while his license was revoked. She hammered him on money despite the fact that she preferred to be unemployed and complain that Mexicans had taken all the good jobs.

"You probably pissed away a month's work of paychecks," Mom yelled, a quaver in her voice that was almost gleeful.

"I got more coming from the Collins job," Daddy said. He got defensive when his role as provider was challenged.

"You know Bobby's going to need some braces," she said, not dropping her volume despite Daddy's apparent surrender. She'd landed the right cross square on the jaw and they both knew it, but this dance was old. Daddy still needed to dangle on the ropes and take a few before he dropped to the canvas.

Bobby resented being dragged into the ring. Sure, he was self-conscious about his crooked teeth, especially when Karen Greene or Andrea Hill smiled at him in algebra and he couldn't smile back. All he could do was grimace a little, afraid his lips would pop open and advertise his white-trash status. If you wanted to see class division in action, you didn't study genealogy trees or stock portfolios. A visual dental inspection was all it took to separate the Haves from the Have-nots.

"I told you, I'll have the Collins job finished next week," Daddy continued, his voice raising just a notch. "The weasel-eyed son of a bitch put in a change order for half-inch PVC and that threw my bid off. Plus the carpenters put a wall in wrong and I've got to rearrange the fixtures in the master bath. That damned David Day, he couldn't nail Christ to the cross with an air gun."

"Blame blame blame. Always somebody else's fault."

Bobby knew some of the mistakes Daddy made were Mom's fault, and once in a while Daddy screwed up all by himself, but Bobby had a feeling Elmer Eldreth had made the decision to go to the skin joint all on his own. Well, the tag team of Anheuser and Busch probably had a little to do with it, too.

A flurry of verbal counterpunches followed. Then the television switched on, which meant there were two possible outcomes for tonight's battle. Either they'd sit in silence through a couple of hours of canned laughter, Mom going to bed early and Daddy polishing off a few more to guarantee a raging hangover in the morning, or Mom would scream over the TV and hostilities would escalate.

Bobby studied the latest graphic novel from Boom Studios, wondering if it was already under option for motion picture development. This one was about weird zombie astronauts and the vampire space pirates that hunted them down, which meant it was just stupid and cool enough to pass for "high concept" in an era when the lamest remake was heralded as "an instant classic."

Mom yelled over a toothpaste commercial and, for the first time ever, Bobby grasped the idea of entertainment as escapism. If a vampire space pirate had at that moment driven a titanium-tipped rocket through the spit-and-tin wall of the mobile home, Bobby would gladly have climbed the gangplank and set sail for the Andromeda Galaxy.

"Bobby's teeth are going to cost six grand," Mom said, "How many beers and titties does that add up to, Mr. Genius?"

"If you don't shut up about teeth, I'm going to knock some of yours right down your throat."

Daddy had never hit Mom, as far as Bobby knew, but volcanoes sometimes smoked and gurgled for years before they finally blew. The sparring continued, though it dropped down to mix with the sitcom dialogue so that Bobby could no longer keep score.

Bobby went to the window and turned the cheap crank, letting cool autumn air into the room. The screen had long since been ripped from the frame, and in the summer when the room got stuffy and Jerrell's anal expulsions reached critical mass, Bobby was faced with the choice of asphyxiation or exsanguination by hordes of mosquitoes. For some reason, the little vampires weren't the least bit repelled by Jerrell's personal brand of "Off." But cool weather sent them to wherever bloodsuckers went to die.

A 100-gallon oil drum stood on short metal stilts below the window. It made for easy escape, but getting back in was a lot harder. Bobby rolled his sleeping bag like a lumpy burrito and covered it with blankets on the lower bunk. The spontaneous effigy would pass inspection if one of his parents happened to glance in and check on him, but wouldn't stand up to the scrutiny of a caring guardian. Luckily, his parents were too wrapped up in their own civil war to notice an empty seat in the audience.

He slipped on jeans over his dorky boy-briefs, crawled across the desk, and skinnied out the window. He scraped his shin then he was perched on top of the barrel, squinting past the streetlights and their swirling moths to the faint stars beyond. The October air was crisp, tinged with distant wood smoke and the exhaust from the sputtering muscle car Ned Dieters was tuning a few trailers down. Dieters changed spark plugs like he changed girlfriends, tossing them at the first sign of fouling.

Bobby scooted off the barrel and hit the ground running. The menu of destinations was limited. He could hop his bicycle and pedal to the mall, but it would be closing in half an hour and his pocketful of coins would barely get him one round in the game arcade. Planet Zero Comics would probably let him hang around until closing time since he frequently traded there, but it was a good three miles away and he'd have to ride the railroad tracks in the dark. He could go to the shed and get some of Daddy's magazines and go play with himself in the strip of woods that separated the trailer park from the highway, but the thought of naked breasts made his stomach hurt.

*Maybe Vernon Ray's awake and up for an adventure.*

The Davises lived four trailers down, their mobile home set at the end of the park, turned perpendicular to the two rows of trailers that lined the gravel drive. Vernon Ray's folks acted like what Daddy called "the High Lord and Lady of Manufactured Housing." Theirs was a double-wide modular home, built on the spot, which gave it a slight cachet over the ones that had been wheeled in, and it had a fake brick skirt on the bottom. Mrs. Davis put a lot of energy into a flower garden out front, but stray dogs and poor soil made for a losing proposition.

Bobby made his way around the back ends of the trailers, eager to talk with Vernon Ray about what had happened in the Hole. His memory of the events had taken on a surreal quality, as if they'd been CGI tricks of the Dreamworks film team: the nicotine rush of the cigarette, the adrenaline jolt of the cop chase, the shock of gunshots, and those weird few moments hiding in the Hole that had somehow felt like days. He rubbed his arms as he recalled the way the darkness had covered his skin as if he were submerged in oil, grateful that the mountaintop was hidden in the night.

The lights were on in the Davis house, and both cars were parked in front, the Jeep Wagoneer closest to the low porch. A flagpole on the railing sported the famous Confederate battle flag, a symbol of either heritage or hate, depending on which political or social wind seemed to blow most favorably at any given moment. Elmer stuck a Rebel flag decal in his window just to piss off armchair liberals, but Vernon Ray said most Appalachian Mountain families had been Union loyalists because the Confederacy had conscripted soldiers against their will. As much as mountain settlers hated the idea of licking dust from boots that had walked in from Washington, D.C., they resented it even more when the bossing came from their own neighbors.

Bobby didn't think it was that simple, and even if it was, it sure as heck didn't matter beans in the Twenty-First Century, when half the residents of Pickett County had New York accents or Florida license plates, and a good portion of the rest sported green cards and brown skin.

Vernon Ray gave such matters grave import, as if he'd memorized his dad's lectures or history books. When all the normal kids at school were reading *Sports Illustrated*, *Teen*, Spiderman, or Harry Potter, Vernon Ray had his nose in books by Bruce Caton or Ken Burns. Bobby wondered for the hundredth time why he had to pick the weirdest possible kid for a best friend, but maybe best friends, like premeditated murders, had more to do with motive and opportunity than free will.

The scrubby stretch of forest came nearly to the back of the Davis home, providing superb cover. Vernon Ray's light was on, which didn't mean much, since he slept with his light on. Bobby climbed a familiar young dogwood and peeked through Vernon Ray's window.

There the dweeb was, belly-down on his bed, thumbing through a thick book. Vernon Ray had a cell phone, another one of the Davis status symbols, but Bobby couldn't text him because the Eldreth computer was right next to the television and currently part of a free-fire zone.

Bobby climbed back down and chucked a pine cone against the glass. He tossed two more before the window opened.

"What are you doing here?" Vernon Ray whispered.

"What does it look like? I'm standing in the woods throwing pine cones."

"Smartass. You know what I mean."

"Can you get out?"

"I don't know. My dad's pretty pissed at me."

"That's a switch."

"You're sure funny tonight. Your dad must be pissed, too."

Bobby shrugged, even though he wasn't sure the motion was visible in the shadow of the trees. "I was just restless. I mean, this is our lives, ticking away second by second. Before you know it, we'll wake up one day and be eleventh graders, with jobs and SAT tests and girlfri—I mean, whatever—and the good times will be over."

"Saturday night fever. Yeah, I know."

"So, you coming or not?"

"I don't think I can get permission. It's after curfew."

"Christ, you didn't *enlist*, you were born to him. And last I heard, the War Between the States settled that little issue of slavery."

Vernon Ray looked around, mostly at his bedroom door, and then nodded. "Okay, but if I get busted you owe me your Fantastic Four movie poster."

"Sure. That one was lame anyway."

"Comic-book movies are always lame because they treat them like kids' stuff instead of serious art."

"Whatever, Bookworm. Save it for your term paper. Now come on."

Vernon Ray's screen was intact but could be removed from the inside. Bobby stood under the window so Vernon Ray could straddle his shoulders and prop the screen back in place. Once they were safely moving through the woods, Bobby raised his voice to a normal level and said, "Did you put a dummy in your bed?"

"Nothing as dumb as the one that usually sleeps there, but I've got a good one. The life-sized inflatable vampire my parents got me last Halloween."

Bobby stopped. "Wouldn't it be cool if vampires were real and one stopped by your bed to suck your blood but then found it was an inflatable vampire?"

"That, my friend, is the very definition of 'irony.'"

"Yeah. Blood is irony. Get it?"

"Put that pun on the scrap heap."

"Hey, that was a good one."

"Okay, two points for trying. So, what do you want to do?"

They had been pushing through the trees, the soft night glow of Titusville casting its suffused light around them. Bobby noted that, with neither of them saying anything, their feet were carrying them toward the creek that skirted the highway.

Running alongside Norman Creek was the dead railroad and then the trail that wound up Mulatto Mountain. The Jangling Hole was too far to reach without flashlights, and Bobby was pretty sure he didn't want to go there ever again, much less when midnight was lurking and the woods would be full of mysterious chattering and fluttering.

"Looks like something is summoning us to the Hole," Vernon Ray said.

"I thought we agreed not to talk about it."

They came out of the woods but followed the shadows so headlights of passing cars wouldn't sweep over them. Motorists were unlikely to pull over, but the local cops might be on the lookout for kids wanted for questioning in a shooting. Not that anybody had actually been shot, as far as Bobby could tell. The TV news hadn't mentioned it, and his mom was part of the trailer-park party line that helped good news travel fast and bad news travel faster.

"You think Dex ratted us out?" Vernon Ray said as they came to a concrete pipe that carried the narrow creek under the highway.

"No, he's golden," Bobby said, and adopting a James Cagney wise-guy accent, he added out one side of his clenched mouth, "He's a tough nut to crack, shee, and the cops ain't got no nuts."

"I wouldn't know what to tell the cops, anyway," Vernon Ray said.

Bobby imagined his friend in a small concrete holding cell, the harsh light on his face, deputies hitting him with the Good Cop-Bad Cop routine. He could easily see Vernon Ray breaking down, weeping, wetting his pants, confessing to the murders of Jimmy Hoffa and JFK and Anna Nicole Smith and whatever other crimes had gone unsolved during the last century.

And after all the cold cases were closed, the coldest of all would come up. Some kindly, paternal plainclothes detective would put his hand on Vernon Ray's shoulder and say, "Okay, kid, now tell us what happened at the Hole."

Bobby had a feeling the truth wouldn't be good enough, because it would sound like a kid making up goofy stories to bug the cops. Bobby hopped into the drainage pipe and straddled the water that sluiced through it. "You know where we're headed, right?"

Vernon followed, his voice echoing above the soft lapping of the creek. "Into hell?"

They stooped to keep from banging their heads, then duck-walked into the black depths of the pipe.

"Going to ask the devil for a match," Bobby said.

"Shh, I heard something," Vernon Ray said.

"Hell-ooooooooooo," came a disguised voice from the other end, the word reverberating through the tube. A flashlight switched on, blinding them, and Bobby raised his elbow over his eyes.

"You girls going somewhere without me?" the voice added.

"Dex!" Bobby said. "Who let the monkey out of its cage?"

"I'm clean, no thanks to you two losers," Dex said, dipping the beam down so that it sent yellow snakes of light up the creek.

"We were afraid the cops got you," Vernon Ray said. "Or shot you."

"I can tell you're in mourning, V-Ray. I bet you're wearing your black dress and everything."

"Something freaky happened at the Hole," Bobby said.

"Yeah," Dex said, beckoning with the light. "Just wait until you hear what happened after you chickens ran like your heads were cut off."

CHAPTER ELEVEN

Hardy put down the portrait when Pearl entered the bedroom. He thought about shoving it under the stack of farm bulletins on the night stand, but Pearl didn't miss much and would make a bigger deal out of the face than it deserved. Besides, memories were one of the few salves of age, a balm when tendons creaked and eyesight was failed and the years shrank like the skin around clouded eyes.

*Looking at an old family portrait is normal, especially when you're as old as Methuselah's grave dirt yourself. But what happens when the memories go, too? When it's nothing but adult diapers and horse pills? What's the measure of a man then?*

"How's Donnie?" he asked.

"Asleep. He barely touched his dinner."

"At least he ate some."

"The doctor said if he stopped eating on his own, they might have to put him on a feeding tube," Pearl said, wiping her thick hands on her apron.

"And you know what that means."

"We'll keep him here as long as we can."

"Probably longer," Hardy said.

"What you looking at?" Pearl said.

"Just some pictures. I guess we ought to hang them up one day, since we seem to be settled in here pretty good."

She reached for the old daguerreotype in its round frame. The silvery photo finish had faded to sepia over the century-and-a-half since the portrait had been taken, and the subject wore the sober, frozen expression typical of the era. Beetle-black eyes stared up at Hardy, and as his wife took the frame from him, the picture tilted and for a moment the light refracted Hardy's image over the face. Not much difference he could see, besides the man's mustache and sideburns.

Pearl held it in her hands, wiping dust from the rim of the frame. She took pride in her homemaking, and she always grew fidgety after dark anyway. Hardy had begun leaving his socks and underwear on the floor so she'd have something to do. "Corporal Earley Eggers of the Pickett Home Guard. What brought this on?"

"I'm just getting sentimental in my golden years."

"Golden, my foot. If anything, these years are brassy. Or maybe pewter. I go in for pewter, since it's a little duller and doesn't take as much polishing."

"He'll be all right," Hardy said. "God gives us these trials to see how much we set store by Him."

"I guess they don't have any more gizmos to stick our boy's head in," she said. "No more shots, no more medicine, no more high-dollar therapists from the health department."

She sat on the bed and laid the portrait on the quilt she'd stitched with her own hands. Hardy was relieved she hadn't pressed him about Earley, but on the other hand, she could have used a distraction. Her resentment went around and around like a waterwheel at an old grist mill, grinding and creaking even after the grain was long gone. Worst of all, she'd lost the glimmer of faith, and that troubled Hardy. Sure, things were bad now, but how would she shoulder the even-heavier burdens piled just ahead?

"It's in the Lord's hands," Hardy said.

"I wish the Lord would lift a little," she said.

He got out of the wicker chair, his back flaring with the effort, and sat beside her. The bed gave a rusty squeak that might have mirrored the fainter sound of his knee joints. He took her hand in his, noting the blue veins that had swollen to subterranean rivers over the years and the freckles that age had mapped.

*If hands could talk, these would spin a yarn or two.*

"Honey, we've been blessed beyond measure," he said, knowing it sounded lame the moment he spoke. He took his own comfort in the Lord, but he'd never been much for words. All he could do was spout Preacher Staymore's tidings, feeling like the gaudy, overgrown parakeet he'd seen at Animal Alley downtown that begged for crackers and sported a $295 price tag. Hardy figured the parakeet probably put as much feeling into its memorized lines as Hardy did, and was probably just a tad more warm-blooded, too.

"I guess I should give thanks that it ain't a brain tumor," she said. "Except it would almost be better to *know*, even if it was something terrible, than to go on like this for years."

"He might get better," Hardy said. "The doctors said since they can't find nothing wrong, it might—what's that word they use?— 'resolve' itself."

"Nothing wrong, my foot. Not speaking, barely able to blink, drooling, scratching at the walls until he's bleeding from under his fingernails...yeah, not a thing wrong with that."

Hardy squeezed her hand again, ashamed that his palm was sweating. So much for standing strong in his faith. Since hoofing it up Mulatto Mountain and back, his feet pulsed as if they had nails driven in them. He could barely toe the line, much less walk it.

Maybe he should tell her the truth. She probably wouldn't believe him, but at least it might help spread the blame around a little. After all, the secret had bent his spine these last two decades, and the Lord hadn't lifted that particular sack any, not even to shift its weight.

"I reckon it's time," he said.

"You know you don't want to sell."

"Bill Willard already put a decent offer on the table. Once Elkridge gets rolling, the taxes will go through the roof, and we never chipped in much to Social Security."

"Oh, Hardy," she said, sliding the portrait away from between them so she could rest her head on his shoulder. She smelled of Ivory soap and woodstove smoke.

"We got our third of the Elkridge money," Hardy said. "Even after we pay down the doctor bills, that can get us a place in town, maybe one of them spanking new condos Willard built. Walking distance to the motion picture show and the grocery and the feed store and—"

"You won't need the feed store if you sell the farm," Pearl said.

"Yeah," he said. His throat was dry as November corn.

"We don't have to decide that yet."

"Well, I ain't looking forward to having a bunch of strangers for neighbors."

"People are only strangers until you get to know them. And nothing could be much stranger than what's already up there."

He stroked her hair and put his mouth near her ear. In happier, younger days he might have nipped on the lobe and set off a round of lovemaking, but his teeth were in a jar on the dresser and love seemed to have withered like the arteries in his heart. "I best tend to the critters," he whispered.

She lifted her head and nodded, eyes already searching the room for a new way to kill time. She straightened up, making the bed squeak. "Mr. Eggers. I thought I had you broke in good. I'm sure those socks didn't walk off and plop down in the floor all by themselves."

As she stooped to sweep them up, Hardy walked barefoot to the dresser to get a fresh pair. She fussed with something in the bathroom while he wrestled into his boots. As he was heading to the door, she hollered, "Look in on Donnie, will you?"

She knew he would, but it was one of those habits of language that came with constant companionship.

Donnie's room was right across the hall. A simple latch bolted the door from the outside, hardware made necessary when Donnie had started sleepwalking, or what Dr. Mendelson had called "presenting somnambulism," and Hardy had mimicked that diagnosis over and over in his head like a parakeet until it lost all meaning. Even familiarity had not changed the oddness of the phrase, nor the accompanying "sleep terrors" that Mendelson had added to the chart.

Hardy slipped back the bolt, swallowing hard. *Locking my son up at night like he's livestock.*

Preacher Staymore had gone on about starvation and hardship one Sunday, dipping into verses from the King James Bible to give people inspiration in lean times. One in particular had stuck out, and Hardy had asked about it after the handshaking at the end of service. Staymore, pleased as a peacock that someone had actually paid attention and not drowsed off or flashed forward to images of the Redskins-Cowboys kickoff, had written the verse down on the back of a tract.

"From the Book of Joel," the preacher had said, pride evident on his red face. "Anybody can cite from Psalms or Ecclesiastes, but God gave us the miracle of the Internet so we might know Him better."

Hardy had read that verse until he'd memorized it as well as he had the word "somnambulism": *How do the beasts groan! the herds of cattle are perplexed, because they have no pasture; yea, the flocks of sheep are made desolate.*

His son was a desolate sheep, and Hardy was a grim shepherd.

The door opened with a squeak, letting light spill into the room. Since Donnie had developed what Mendelson had called "photophobia," the shades were usually drawn in Donnie's room, unless the day was overcast. Night was no real problem, since there were no lamps in the room, only a single overhead light sunk in the ceiling and sporting a 20-watt bulb. Hardy had moved the switch so that it was in the hall, not that Donnie had enough muscle control to grab the switch on purpose. However, he might go into one of his flailing spells and bump into it, and the sudden cascade of light would send him even farther off the edge.

Because of the strange epilepsy, the room had little furniture: a thick wooden desk whose corners were rounded and padded, a mattress on a low wooden frame, and plenty of papers and crayons. For some reason, Donnie only seemed calm when he was doodling, and since he could never see well enough to finish and his fingers were nearly as useless as sausages, his black stick figures, box houses, blue clouds, and big orange suns resembled the work of a five-year-old.

Donnie was 27.

Hardy wondered if Mendelson had any fancy-assed, twenty-dollar words for "livermush head."

But you loved your son no matter what, through adult diapers and rain, tears and expensive medical tests. Since the day Hardy had found his teenaged son on the side of Mulatto Mountain, shuddering under a tree near the Hole as if frozen by the balmy July air, Donnie had been stuck with needles, strapped down and placed in big hollow tubes that hummed and glowed, poked with glass instruments and gauges, and generally treated like the prized pig at a 4-H livestock competition. And the doctors just shook their heads and came up with "somnambulism" and "photophobia," or Mendelson's favorite, "catatonia," until Hardy's head was maybe spinning faster than his unresponsive son's.

After nearly a decade, Hardy had pretty much lost faith in miracles, no matter what he told Pearl. As he nudged the door open, he was ready for anything, because Donnie was as likely to be standing on his hands and leaning against the wall as he was to twist himself in the blankets. Hardy squinted into the gloom.

He heard a soft tapping sound, almost like a rat running behind the walls. When Donnie was pitching a fit, he usually hammered and clawed at the pine paneling like a man awakening from a coma to find himself sealed inside a coffin. Donnie's vocal chords had given up on language, and instead he projected a staccato series of barks, grunts, and clucks, all of which amused him greatly and led to parakeetish squawks of laughter.

But tonight there was only the tapping.

Hardy eased into the room, careful not to startle his son. Donnie was hunched over the desk, and though his mental level had regressed to that of a kindergartner, his physique was that of a young man raised on a farm, muscles bunching on his shoulders. Sitting on the bed so that his back was to the door, Donnie seemed intent on whatever lay on the desk. He could be coloring, but that usually made a scratching sound as he held the crayons in his fist and scraped their tips along the paper.

Papers were scattered all over the floor, maybe a dozen pages. Given Pearl's neatness, the drawings must be newly rendered, because she'd been in half an hour before to get him ready for bed and she would have cleaned the floor.

"Donnie?" Hardy said in a low voice.

Donnie kept tapping. Hardy came around the bed and looked at the desk and his son's head tilted down to stare at the dull cherry surface. Donnie was tapping the wood with the pads of his fingers, rolling them in a coordinated pattern that seemed beyond his abilities.

His first instinct was to call Pearl, but she'd suffered through so much false hope that Hardy couldn't bear to bring her more. He knelt on cranky knees and looked across the desk at his son, but the man-child might as well have been on the surface of the moon for all the attention he paid his father.

*Tap tap tap. Tappa tap.*

Too repetitive to be a random muscle twitch. Donnie's lips moved as if trying to provide vocal accompaniment to his cadence.

The Lord promised miracles, and though Preacher Staymore said miracles were often hard to recognize while they were happening, Hardy figured this one qualified as much as the turning of water into wine.

"Donnie?" Hardy kept his voice low and even, though his heart was racing in tandem with the offbeat rhythm of Donnie's fingertips.

Donnie shuddered and lifted his head, as if jerked back from a happy dream to the claustrophobic box where he spent most of his day. His mouth pursed as if aware of his return to misery, but his eyes stared ahead as dead as polished coal. Eggers eyes, the same as those in his Confederate ancestor's portrait.

Donnie's fingers tapped once more and then flopped against the surface of the desk. His face went slack and his body slouched like a marionette whose strings had been clipped. Any sign of concentration or awareness was gone, if indeed it had really been there and not just a wishful projection.

"Muh-wak," Donnie said, and then gave his parakeet chuckle.

*At least he's not slamming himself against the wall. That little* tappa-tap *could have just as easily been his skull saying 'Howdy' to the desk.*

And it would give Mendelson yet another reason to push for Donnie's going into a group home. "He'll get the care he needs," the doctor would say for the thirtieth time, and Pearl would glare as if her own nursing skills, attention, and love were under criticism.

Hardy reached a hand to his son and touched his cool cheek. The black eyes flicked over his face, but there was no joy or recognition in them. Maybe he and Pearl were being selfish after all, the way some had suggested. They were keeping Donnie a prisoner here out of their own guilt and shame.

And Hardy ate a double helping of guilt, because he hadn't told Pearl about Donnie's trip to Mulatto Mountain. He'd told her he'd found Donnie lying by the fence, suffering an apparent seizure. And though Hardy had no proof that the Jangling Hole had sent out a messenger to recruit Donnie into the army of the lost, Hardy took some comfort in the notion that he could shift some of the blame to a thing he couldn't see or know. Better than blaming the Lord, and better than letting the pain eat him from the inside out.

He helped Donnie into bed, making sure his pajamas were still clean. Donnie was pretty good about the potty, even though he had the occasional accident. He was able to sit at the dinner table, but he often had to be spoon fed.

Hardy sometimes walked him to the barn and back, but once in a while Donnie would launch into a floppy spell, as if his limbs had turned to rubber, and Hardy was getting too old to haul him back to the house. But sleeping was pretty straightforward, and though Donnie was apt to rise up and walk while his eyes were closed, he was usually safest and calmest in the night.

Hardy bent and picked the loose papers off the floor, glancing at the swirls of blue and gray. The scrawls looked like tangled skeins of loose yarn. He stacked them on the desk, then decided Pearl might like to see them, make a fuss over them, and maybe even put one on the refrigerator with a big cow magnet.

"Good night, son," Hardy said as he paused by the door. "Hope you have yourself a good dream."

*Dream you're a normal man and can walk and talk and breed and spit like a man instead of letting it drool down your chin. Dream you can run and jump and tap your fingers like you're beating the drums. Dream you can play the fiddle and whittle and —*

Hardy glanced at the top page. The random squiggles made his brain itch. The patterns whispered of a recognizable shape, but he didn't think Donnie had suddenly turned into Leonardo da Vinci. The drumming had been a flight of fancy, and there seemed no room for miracles tonight.

He switched off Donnie's light as he closed and bolted the door.

As he eased down the stairs, boot leather and wooden treads creaking, he wonder if maybe he and Pearl should move their bedroom to the bottom floor. It would mean moving Donnie, too, which would require a little renovation. Hardy wasn't in the mood to make extra work, so he figured as long as he was still able to make it up and down the stairs, things were better left alone.

Alone, the way Donnie was.

Alone, the way he was with his shame and his knowledge of the Hole and what it might have done to his son.

Hardy tossed the drawings on the kitchen table, where the pink pig salt-and-pepper shakers danced with each other in a celebration of seasoning. Their cherubic faces, like those of the happy porkers that adorned signs for barbecue joints, seemed oblivious to their ultimate destiny.

The end always cut to the bone, and under the blade you died alone.

He stopped at the back door, put on his jacket, and rummaged a flashlight from the closet. He had livestock to feed.

CHAPTER TWELVE

Sheriff Littlefield stood in the bay lights of the ER exit and dashed the remains of his cold coffee into the gutter. The brown liquid looked like blood in the reflection of the red exit lights.

*My cup sure runneth the helleth over with that. And the more innocent the blood, the better.*

The hospital was one of the fastest-growing enterprises in Pickett County, spreading like a malignant tumor, and currently a parking deck was under construction behind the west wing, a spindly derrick standing in silhouette over it like a witch guarding a stack of bones. A few spaces near the emergency room were reserved for police, since sudden trauma was often accompanied by illegal activity. Littlefield had technically been off duty, but he figured visiting an officer was good enough justification for hogging one. Besides, the hike around Mulatto Mountain had cramped up his legs.

He was sliding behind the wheel when the radio sputtered and hissed, then sputtered again. Sherry's voice came out amid a spray of static, as if she were exhaling cigarette smoke over the dispatch microphone.

"Sheriff, we've got a 10-32 on Water Street," Sherry said.

He picked up the mike and thumbed the button. "'Suspicious person'? I'm on my way home. I told you I didn't want any routine calls."

"I don't think this is routine," the dispatcher responded. "And how many suspicious people do we get around here, anyway?"

"That's downtown, isn't it? It's Maroney's jurisdiction."

"Yeah, but I got a feeling he wouldn't know how to handle it."

Though Water Street was in the opposite direction from the cabin he'd bought near the gas-station-and-post-office community of Simms, it was only four blocks from the hospital, and besides, Sherry would keep bugging him until he checked it out.

"What did Morton report?"

"That's the thing. He said he was checking it out but didn't request backup."

"He left his cruiser?"

"Either that or he's fast asleep in the back seat and not answering. Harrington and Greer are patrolling Taylor Lake and Markowitz is doing the paperwork on a drunk and disorderly."

"Where's Wally?"

"He had a flare-up so he's on foot patrol at the high school. His rump's so swollen he can't sit down in a patrol car."

That was about as much as Littlefield cared to know about one of his officer's rectal tissues. "I'll swing by, but I told you not to bother me unless something crawled out of the Hole."

"If Wally gets any worse, might be something crawling out of a hole that none of us wants to see."

"Thanks for that visual, Sherry." Littlefield eased out of the parking lot, amazed at how much it had expanded and at the dozens of cars that filled it. Dying was a growth industry, and since the hospital had tacked on a cancer wing, business was booming. Littlefield figured there was a joke hiding somewhere in that observation, but he was too weary to parse it out.

After a pause, the radio static cut out and Sherry's voice came on. "How's J.R.?"

"He was in and out, not much new. The doctors said there was no sign of serious injury but they wanted to keep him under observation for a few days."

"Did you tell him about the pie?"

Littlefield had forgotten, but he said, "Sure. He perked up and I swear there was some drool running out the corner of his mouth."

At least he hadn't lied about the drool.

"Good thing I'm around or this department would fall to pieces."

"You got that right, Sherry. I'm switching channels to see if I can raise Morton. What's that 10-20?"

"Between the lumber yard and the old depot. Where the hippies opened that coffee shop with all the books in the windows. What's it called?"

"The Depot."

"Damned smart-aleck hippies."

"10-10, I'll check back later. Keep monitoring."

"Aye-aye, boss."

Littlefield saw no reason to turn on his flashers, especially since he was invading another department's bailiwick. No doubt Sherry was jittery because of all those legends about the Jangling Hole, and because one of the hen's chicks had been injured, but it was unlike her to send Littlefield on minor calls. Littlefield had never asked for special treatment, but he felt his officers should be trusted to use their own discretion in their duties.

Morton, despite the incident at the Jangling Hole, had been scheduled to work a double shift. Though Littlefield had offered him the chance to skip out, Morton said they might be shorthanded for a while since J.R. was down. The department was under a tight budget ever since the Democrats had retaken the county commission in the last election. Calling in an extra officer would have padded the overtime line item.

Even though it was Saturday night, traffic was dead downtown. Titusville was in the middle of an identity crisis, with the banks, the hardware store, and the general store that had sprung up during the railroad heyday finally closing or moving out to the boulevard strip that linked the town with Barkersville, Westridge University, Hickory, and then on down to Charlotte.

Now the town was revitalizing as a series of craft shops and art galleries, with three coffee houses to keep the clientele juiced. Though town voters had approved beer-and-wine sales, most of the drinking was done in Beef O'Brady's and the other chain restaurants clustered around Walmart. The downtown had been inherited by business owners, even those with sandwich shops, who liked to be home in time for dinner.

Littlefield turned onto Water Street, conducting casual surveillance. The abandoned railroad bed ran parallel to the street, which featured the backsides of old brick buildings. The depot stood by a bridge, its rough-cut porch timbers still blackened from the coal smoke of long-gone steam locomotives.

Morton's cruiser was wedged off the road and against the chain-link fence that girded the lumber yard. Though the wood business had shriveled up with the railroad's demise, long dark sheds still dotted the property. Dunes of gray sawdust made the shadowed lot resemble the surface of an inhospitable alien planet.

Littlefield parked behind Morton's car and tucked a long flashlight in his belt. Though Morton's bar lights were off, his engine was running, which meant he either didn't expect the errand would take long or he'd made an abrupt exit from his vehicle. Littlefield checked the padlock at the main gate. It was rusted shut.

Littlefield circumvented the fence, passing behind the depot and its smell of scorched Folgers and bran muffins. The streetlights didn't reach beyond the bridge, so Littlefield switched on his flashlight and headed for the back of the lot. He found a rip in the seam of wire fence and ducked through. Once inside the lot, he played the light around the stacks of warped lumber.

A darker shadow stood beside a rusted hulk of milling machinery.

"Morton?"

The shadow was still. Annoyed, Littlefield headed toward it. A vagrant or trespasser would at least have had the decency to flee and let Littlefield know he should give chase.

He raised the light and though the shadow didn't move, couldn't have moved, the beam revealed only the metal skeleton of dead equipment, its wheels, gears, and bands frozen in time.

*Shit, where did he go? Just what I need, another goddamned invisible suspect.*

He wanted to wrap up the 10-32 and get to bed before it became a more serious set of numbers. He doubted if he'd get any sleep—memories of Sheila Story and Archer McFall would erase any hope of that, not to mention whatever stirred in the Hole—but he was a man of habit, and six hours spent restlessly wrinkling the sheets seemed like the best way to cap off the day. Mulatto Mountain was miles away, and though its solid black form dominated the western horizon, whatever mysteries it harbored had no reason to touch the town.

Littlefield circled the shed, the decaying sawdust muting his footsteps. Anyone fleeing wouldn't have made a giveaway sound.

Assuming they fled by foot.

The flashlight beam dodged over dented sheet metal. The wind picked up and as it cut through the shed, it whined and moaned, carrying the scent of the creek and rotted wood and the pungency of rust. The bandsaw blade was still on its pulley, straddled by a flat steel table where logs once slid into the jagged teeth. Littlefield came to a steel ladder that led up to a glassed-in cab where operators could run the big bandsaw with minimal risk.

The cab would offer a good vantage point to survey the grounds. If Morton were in the lumber yard, Littlefield would be able to see him, assuming the deputy carried a flashlight. The steel rungs were cold under his palms as he climbed. A flutter of motion erupted to his left and brushed his cheek, nearly causing him to fall.

Littlefield regained his balance and leaned against the rungs, catching his breath. The creature flapped into the night then dipped into the glow of a security light where moths swarmed in random patterns.

*A son-of-a-bitching bat.*

He studied the backs of the buildings on Water Street, some of the windows glowing yellow but most boarded up or covered by curtains. Many of the upper floors had been converted to apartments, with slum lords doing a booming business in rodent reproduction.

Littlefield surveyed the lot, though the scattered stacks of lumber shielded his view of some sections. Nothing.

Littlefield finished his ascent, now 20 feet above the ground. He steadied himself with the light tucked under his arm as he reached for the cab door. The latch was either locked or rusted shut. He yanked once more, the light bobbing up.

A face pressed against the glass.

Littlefield almost fell a second time. He braced his legs and directed the beam toward the face, but it was gone, just like the shadow earlier.

"Screw this cat-and-mouse crap," he said.

Whoever was in the cab had no other way down, so it was simply a matter of waiting until the perp came down. If it was indeed a perp. By now, Littlefield was determined to slap a charge on the person, out of annoyance if nothing else. Besides trespassing and loitering, he could probably tack on obstruction of justice and delaying an officer. Those charges were usually dropped by the District Attorney during plea negotiations, but they sure were satisfying to write on the arrest report.

Littlefield banged the glass with the bottom of his fist. "Come on out," Littlefield said. "I just want to ask you some questions."

*Like "Where in the hell is my deputy?" and "How did you get in there through a locked door?" and "By the way, have you seen any invisible people?"*

He tried to reform the face in his mind. It was haggard and pale, with a sparse brush of beard, but the glimpse had been too brief to offer much more. Certainly nothing a sketch artist could work with, if it came to that.

*Jeez, Sheriff, a little melodramatic, don't you think? Morton's probably sitting in the coffee house right now, talking up some college coed and hoping she digs a man in a uniform. Pushing his luck. But the biggest risk he's facing is a lap full of warm coffee at four bucks a cup.*

Littlefield peered through the bottom pane on the cab door, shining his light into the dim interior. It featured a seat like that of a tractor, and a series of gear levers protruded from the floor. An instrument panel featured a few dials and buttons, but obviously predated the era of microelectronics. Dirty rags littered the floor, and a length of rusty chain was coiled in the floorboard like a sleeping snake.

Otherwise, the cab was empty.

Littlefield fought an urge to ram the butt of his flashlight into the glass. Before the McFall incident and his latest failure, he would have figured himself for a head case on the verge of a breakdown. The shrinks would say it was only natural, a delayed post-traumatic reaction to the death of his younger brother when they were children.

Just a little guilt trip catching up with him, nothing to worry about, take a few weeks off and it should clear up on its own. With a little intensive therapy, of course, and possibly a little medication to keep the brain wires firing toward a desired result. All in the name of returning to normal.

But there was something shrinks would never acknowledge:

once you've peered into the black heart of hell, once you'd ridden the nightmare rainbow all the way down, "normal" no longer existed.

And disappearing faces no longer were mere figments of his imagination.

Just like the footprints on Mulatto Mountain that had faded into thin air...

He glanced down into the milling area, where large steel claws arched upward. Years ago, they had sunk their jagged tips into oak and poplar and cherry, pushing their prey into the grinding, chewing jaws of the saw blade. Now they flexed open like the upturned palms of a metal martyr. Chains dangled from the rough-cut rafters, clinking softly as they swayed in the October breeze.

A pile of slabs, covered in ragged gray bark, lay to one side of the sawmill bench. Littlefield ran his light over them. He spotted a pair of eyes and steadied his beam, only to find a couple of knots protruding from a warped hardwood burl.

Then one of the slabs separated from the pile and moved into the orange circle of his beam. It approached him.

"Morton!" Littlefield scrambled down the ladder, feeling a little silly at his relief. He was able to dispel the vision of the face a little more with each rung, and by the time he reached the bottom he had convinced himself the incident had never happened.

As he jogged toward the end of the long steel saw table, he called to his deputy. "Did you see anybody?"

Littlefield stopped short, almost losing his balance and pitching into the raw teeth of the saw blade. It wasn't Morton after all, not with those black eyes that soaked up the light and the scruffy beard that swayed in the wind like dried corn stalks. It was the man from the cab, probably the one who'd cast the silhouette he'd seen as he'd entered the lumber yard. The man was undeniably solid, though he was gaunt, checks sunken, ragged clothes draped on his body as if someone had hastily dressed a scarecrow.

"Who are you?" Littlefield said. *Thank God for vagrants and trespassers, safe, normal, everyday bums and creeps.*

The gaunt-faced man stood at the end of the saw table, looking around as if not recognizing his surroundings. Littlefield had a chance to study him in profile now that he was relatively motionless. He had the drawn cheeks of a meth addict and looked like he'd missed a few turns at the soup kitchen. His dark brown hair ran just past his collar, and when he grimaced, there were black gaps between his yellow teeth.

His clothes appeared to be natural fiber, dusty and stained, the cuffs of his shirt frayed. He wore a vest that was pocked with holes, and his gray cotton trousers had a rip in one knee. The leather boots were dusty and cracked, the heels coming loose and the toe of the right one lolling open like the mouth of an exhausted hound.

On his head was a peculiar cap that seemed two sizes too small and looked as if it had been mashed lopsided.

Since the man had not acknowledged Littlefield's challenge, the sheriff took three steps toward him and spoke again. "This is private property."

"Churr," the man said, and it was almost like a question.

"You been drinking?" The encounter was moving back onto familiar footing and Littlefield gained confidence. His right hand, which had reached to the butt of the pistol holstered on his belt, now relaxed.

The man finally stared into the burning glare of the flashlight, not squinting or blinking. The eyes appeared to swell with darkness, and the light didn't glint off them, as if they were bone dry and as dusty as his boots.

*Where the hell is Morton?*

Littlefield was not just concerned about his deputy, he didn't like the idea of being alone with this weather-beaten scarecrow of a man. If it weren't for Sherry's dispatch record of the call, Littlefield would have been tempted to just mosey back through the gash in the fence and drive away.

The lumber yard offered little satisfaction for vandalism, and as a decent sleeping quarters for Titusville's scattered homeless, it rivaled the Living Waters Mission's stiff steel cots. And, the sheriff reasoned, if the department made a precedent of rousting one wino, Sherry's 9-1-1 hotline might be flooded with reports of other emaciated and hollow-eyed wanderers.

Chickenshit rationalization. The same justifications that had led him to past mistakes, some that ended with a shovel, flowers, and a preacher's solemn eulogy.

"Churr," the man repeated, turning and walking toward the back of the lot.

"Stop, or I'll..." Littlefield let the threat trail off because he didn't know exactly what to say. He certainly wasn't going to shoot, and he didn't think the suspect was making what could be called a high-speed attempt at escape. In fact, Littlefield wasn't even sure the man had heard or seen him. His reaction to the light might have been the instinctive response of a mindless animal.

The man walked with the stiffness of a scarecrow, as if his limbs had been long unused. He moved between two dunes of decaying sawdust, clothes swathed against a skeletal frame.

"Churrrrr," the man said then rolled the syllable into "rrrrain" as if learning a new language.

The sound was as slow as everything else about the strange man, and Littlefield followed, slogging through the mix of wood chips and mud. That's when he noticed the man's boots left no prints.

"Stop!" Littlefield shouted, and now he wasn't even sure he wanted the man to stop or if he'd simply fallen back on professional protocol when faced with the extraordinary.

The gray scarecrow didn't heed, if it had heard in the first place, and just kept flopping its broken boots toward the fence.

Littlefield drew his gun and steadied the flashlight beam against the Glock until the circle of light was centered on the man's back. The vagrant was carrying a haversack, slung low and dangling with old equipment.

"Churr-rain," the man said, a little faster this time, as if a termite-riddled tongue had learned to speak.

*Train?*

Littlefield's finger tickled the trigger, but he knew he wouldn't shoot. For one thing, his hands were shaking and the light bobbed up and down, and a stray bullet might zing through the chain-link fence and ricochet toward the run-down section of Titusville, where houselights and flickering televisions glowed behind the kudzu-draped trees. The town's few Mexicans, employed in the Christmas-tree fields because of their willingness to work hard and ignore warning labels on pesticide containers, were clustered in the clapboard shotgun shacks, and a random shooting promised a flood of Charlotte news crews. On the other hand, one more non-arrest on a suspicious-persons call would flush into the ocean of forgotten paperwork.

Thank God Morton was still nowhere to be seen, because Littlefield didn't want to explain why he holstered his weapon. Unable to totally neglect his duty, he gave half-hearted pursuit, maintaining a distance of 30 feet.

When the man approached the chain-link fence, where the rusty and abandoned railroad track ran parallel to Norman's Creek, Littlefield was left with a skipped heartbeat at the thought of the man's turning and staring into the flashlight.

But, as might be expected of something that had probably tromped across Mulatto Mountain and eventually given up the need for footprints, the man didn't pause when he reached the steel fence. Instead, he passed through it and stopped in the middle of the tracks, looking both ways as if listening for a distant steam whistle.

Then the wind blew and he was gone.

CHAPTER THIRTEEN

Vernon Ray had to stretch his legs and take unnatural steps to walk the crumbling creosote crossties. Railroads were made for the travel of big steel monsters and not boys, though Dex seemed to be doing fine with his hopping motion. But Dex was a jock, a linebacker who could already bench press 10 reps of his body weight, and owner of enough bowling trophies to melt down and cast as a statue of a general on horseback. So he could hop and get away with it.

If Vernon Ray tried to hop, it would probably look like some prissy little ballet move, so he settled for what felt like a manly stride, even though the motion strained the backs of his knees.

Bobby somehow floated along with an easy grace, but then Bobby made every action look cool. And though Dex could probably beat up both of them with one hand tied behind his back, Bobby was in the lead, moving down the track like a locomotive that was right on schedule. Dex followed, fanning the light along the rails and crossties ahead. Vernon Ray, the caboose, could come uncoupled and the train would keep rolling. Except, probably, Bobby would feel the loss of weight and the new ease of acceleration.

As if everything had to be a metaphor . . . .

"And then that doofus Deputy Dawg shot at me and I heard the bullet whistling through the trees over my head," Dex said.

"Bet you about crapped your pants," Bobby said.

"Hell, I was too scared to be scared, if you know what I mean. I was running like I was going in for the winning touchdown and Kitty Hawkins was waiting at the goalpost with her legs spread."

"How do you know he shot at you?" Vernon Ray asked.

Dex stopped and Vernon Ray had to brace himself and get his balance to keep from pitching forward into Dex's back. Bobby continued down the track, even though he must have noticed their shoes had stopped flapping behind him in that rollicking train rhythm. Vernon Ray would have to deal with this one alone.

"Because I was the one they were chasing," Dex said without

turning. "I was the only one who had enough balls to go for it. You sissy-boys sat there whining for mercy. You ain't figured out yet that the system don't allow no mercy."

Though Dex had meant it as a challenge for Bobby as well, Bobby kept right on motoring. The lights of Titusville cast a gray gauze against the black ceiling of night sky. The creek clinked and gurgled, sounding merry despite the runoff from the town's parking lots and gutters. The wind was soft in the trees and Vernon Ray spun a metaphor of gently beating wings until Dex yanked him back to reality.

"So he shot at me because I'm worth shooting," Dex said. "But the second time, I don't think he shot at me."

Bobby, now 50 feet ahead, stopped and yelled back at them. "Come on, guys, we can make it to Planet Zero before it closes."

Bobby tossed rocks from the gravel rail bed into the tide of encroaching kudzu until the two boys caught up. Dex said, "I was just telling V-Girl here about getting shot at. It was a better rush than sniffing glue, I can tell you that."

"If he had hit you, you'd probably be singing a different tune," Bobby said.

"Yeah," Vernon Ray said, emboldened. "Like 'Precious Memories' or whatever else they do at a funeral."

"Big deal," Dex said. "I ain't scared of dying. The preacher saved me so I got a free ride from here on out."

Vernon Ray was about to dispute Dex's theological justification, but it was hard to argue with a true believer. And Vernon Ray was jealous, because Dex had a destination after death, a shimmering, pillowy heaven where everyone was happy and nobody was different.

Plus he got to commit all the sins he could pack into a lifetime and not alter the eternal outcome one tiny bit. Vernon Ray had nothing waiting after death, no peaceful rest that he could anticipate, and his soul was a train rolling into a strange, misty tunnel that—

"What was he shooting at, then?" Bobby asked, spinning a rock into the trees that lined the creek. Lights from passing cars on the highway blinked amid the dying foliage. The smell of roadkill skunk drifted over.

"Nearest I can figure, it was that weird wino dude," Dex said.

"Wino?"

"Yeah. Kinda makes you wonder why cops get to carry guns and normal folks don't. If they're that freaking loopy, they ought to join the Army where they can kill all the people they want."

"As long as they're brown," Vernon Ray said.

"You don't know nothing," Dex countered. "Them ragheads attacked us on our own soil and—"

"What about the wino?" Bobby said, cutting off Dex's favorite jingoistic rant, no doubt learned from his father and endlessly recited down at the bowling alley.

"Well, after that first shot, I ducked under a big shelf of rock," Dex said. "You know how up on the ridge the boulders poke out of the ground. I figured, barring a ricochet, I'd be safe until the cops got tired of looking. I mean, I can outrun any cop in the county, but I haven't figured out how to outrun a bullet yet."

"Keep training," Bobby said. "Maybe you got muscles somewhere besides your head."

"Hey," Dex said. "I'd rather run than try to talk my way out of it. Vernon Ray can use them big words and do okay in front of a juvie judge, but I been down that road before. Daddy's lawyer is smart, but at the end of the day those pig porkers all kneel down at the same trough."

"What's that got to do with the wino?" Vernon Ray asked.

Dex gave him a shove, and Vernon Ray's ankle caught on the rail. He nearly tumbled backwards off the bank and toward the creek, but Bobby grabbed his shirt sleeve.

"Come on, Dex," Bobby said. "Don't be a dickhead. Just tell us the story."

"This creepy old guy was walking around on the ridge," Dex said. "Probably been hanging out in the Hole and knocking back bottles of MD 20/20 and malt liquor 40's."

"That's dumb," Bobby said. "The place is two miles from the nearest package store and there's plenty of places to tip a bottle downtown."

"Well, he's white, and only niggers and Mexicans can get away with loitering downtown."

Vernon Ray wondered what would happen when Dex got to heaven and realized that blacks and Hispanics had been saved as well, and that the blood of Jesus had also washed away the sins of people who didn't bowl 230 or listen to Toby Keith. God's unconditional love extended to everyone except the homosexuals, that much was clear.

"Okay, so how do you know it was a wino?" Bobby asked, obviously trying to change the subject.

"His clothes looked like junk you'd pick out of a dumpster at a thrift shop," Dex said. "All raggedy and dirty, like he'd been sleeping in them for a hundred years."

*Or maybe 150?* Vernon Ray wasn't sure exactly what he'd encountered in the Hole, but if the mountain was coughing out whatever dead things it had swallowed during the war, then maybe one of the deserters was walking loose. Or floating, or whatever ghosts did.

*Which obviously messes up any Earth-based theology. Because if the soldier was dead, then he should have gone on to whatever afterlife had been promised by his faith. Unless he had no faith, and his was the fate of all who didn't believe. Unless the dead soldier was a homosexual, then . . . .*

Vernon Ray was still confused by all the contradictions, but he was getting the feeling that the eternal afterlife was going to be a lonely place. He moved closer to Bobby. The fall night had suddenly grown chillier.

"That don't explain why the cop shot at him," Bobby said.

"Didn't you hear what I've been saying?" Dex said. "Those guys are nuttier than a corn turd. Anyway, the wino kept on hoofing it over the ridge, and then the cops were yelling at each other and I waited about 10 minutes and hustled my ass down the back side of the mountain and headed home. What happened to you guys?"

In the dim light, Vernon Ray couldn't see Bobby's face but could feel that ocean-eyed gaze on him. Bobby was waiting for Vernon Ray to spill whatever had happened in the Hole. Bobby hadn't bought the story that Vernon Ray had bumped his head and gotten a little dizzy and confused.

Well, the "confused" part had been no lie, but babbling about being dragged into the dark depths by an unseen force might have cemented Vernon Ray's reputation as the sole occupant of La La Land, a fairy spud in his own private Idaho.

"When they fired the shots, the other cop went running into the woods and the shopkeeper guy freaked out and ran in the opposite direction," Vernon Ray said. "We dicked around a little until the coast was clear and then beat it out of there."

"The only beating you do is your own meat," Dex said.

"Dex, you're the only guy on the planet who would eat a bullet over a pack of smokes, then brag about it at his own funeral," Bobby said.

"All I'm saying is I'm going for it," Dex said. "You guys can pansy-pwance around the edges but I'm walking right through the front door."

"Come on," Bobby said, taking the lead again. "I want to get to the comic shop before it closes. There's a new Hulk I want to get."

"Fine," Dex said. "Give Vernon Ray something to look at besides his mom's panties."

"And no stealing this time," Bobby called back over his shoulder.

Their feet crunched on gravel for a minute before Dex stopped again. "Sheriff came out to my house," he said, with evident pride.

"You get charged?" Vernon Ray said, knowing Mac McCallister let some of the town's top attorneys bowl on the house. Cops occasionally got a freebie, too, but only lawyers got the beer to go with it.

"Hell, no," Dex said. "My old man read him the riot act."

"He ask you about Mulatto Mountain?"

"I never even talked to him. But I'm supposed to go down to the office tomorrow. I wouldn't be surprised if Sheriff Fiddlefart wants to pin a few charges on me just for old time's sake."

"Shh," Bobby hissed. "Somebody's coming."

The railroad tracks were the boys' usual route into town, unless they braved the highway on their bikes. More often, Bobby and Vernon Ray went without Dex, heading for comics, ice cream, mall loitering, or other buddy activity.

They rarely encountered anyone on the tracks, and in Twenty-First Century America, any adults conveyed by their legs instead of a fossil-fuel vehicle were considered odd and somehow subversive. Namely, cons and dregs, people too poor for cars, or those nabbed for multiple DWI's. People to be avoided if you were a kid with a little money in your pocket.

Bobby stepped off the tracks and skidded down the bank to the vines and shrubs bordering the creek. Vernon Ray followed, sensing no real anxiety in his friend, but making the safe move nonetheless. Dex flicked off the flashlight and stood for a moment with his hands on his hips, as if welcoming a chance to prove himself king of the road.

"Come on, Dex," Bobby said, as Vernon Ray crouched beside him in the weedy concealment.

"We got a right to be on the track," he said.

"What if it's a cop?" Vernon Ray said, though the notion of any officer straying half a mile from the cushy front seat of his cruiser was a little ludicrous.

"No flashlight," Dex said. "Plus he already saw ours."

"He won't know where we are," Bobby said, confirming Vernon Ray's belief that only an adult male would be brave, foolish, or drunk enough to wander down the tracks after dark. "You can't judge distance for crap in the dark."

Dex paused for another moment, as if to let Bobby know that he wasn't about to follow orders, as if Vernon Ray could be a whipped little puppy dog but Dex by God was top dog in a pack of one. Then he stepped over the rail and eased down the bank. He slipped once and landed on his rear in the damp grass, and his "Shee-it!" hissed out loudly enough to tip off whoever was coming.

As Dex wiped at the back of his jeans and stood in the kudzu and briars, Vernon Ray spun a fantasy that they were three Rebel scouts, waiting for a locomotive to come barreling down the tracks so they could get an idea of Grant's numbers and strategy. Or, better yet, they could be spies, risking death by hanging in order to foul up Sherman's March and Gen. Stoneman's incursion into the North Carolina mountains. Daddy would be proud.

Vernon Ray strained to hear the approaching footsteps over the gurgling of the creek. Maybe Bobby had misjudged and it was a platoon, Union infantry rooting out rebel rabble. If so, they were dead meat for sure. But Vernon Ray wasn't about to let his comrades swing at the business end of a hemp rope. No, he would dash right up to the platoon, yell, "Come and get me, you Lincoln-loving Johnny Yank!" and flee into the woods. Sure, they'd catch him, and he'd dance on air with his eyeballs bugging, but his buddies would have a chance to escape.

He didn't realize he was actually about to bolt up the bank until he felt Bobby's hand on his shoulder. "Easy, V-Ray," Bobby whispered.

A stand of thin pines lined each side of the tracks, swallowing the approaching man in the shadows. Despite a weak grimace of moon overhead and the fuzzy glow cast by Titusville's various storefronts and streetlights, they wouldn't be able to see him until he reached the spot where the boys had left the tracks. The rushing creek covered any sound of footfalls.

Thirty seconds passed, with Bobby's breath near Vernon Ray's ear, and even the distant highway fell silent. Vernon Ray felt a surge of warmth at the closeness of his friend, and a feather tickled the inside of his stomach. The man must have stopped in the concealment of darkness and Vernon Ray imagined him waiting just as they were, perhaps also wondering who was sharing the tracks in the night. Maybe the man was afraid, too. It was easy to imagine a group of boys as a gang of hooligans out to rob and plunder.

Then the edge of the shadow swelled and a piece of it broke off. The man stepped into the graylight and moved down the tracks, his head tilted forward in determination. The hollow eyes were hard to see, but they were as black as the shadows that had spawned them, and the pale jaw was clenched into a creased dimple. This was a dude with a destination, and he wasn't about to let anyone stop him.

"Holy freak-a-holey," Dex said, a rare note of reverence in his voice.

"What?" Bobby whispered.

"It's *him*."

"Him?"

"The wino from Mulatto Mountain."

"He doesn't look drunk," Vernon Ray said. The man's shabby clothes hung as if they had rotted for years on a clothesline. The jacket appeared to be wool, and the cotton trousers were wrinkled and soiled. Though the jacket was open, it still had a couple of brass buttons gone green with age. A strap was slung over one shoulder, and a rounded object bounced off his right hip.

The man was close enough now that they could have hit him with a rock, but even if Dex had been in a frolicking, rabble-rousing mood, the man's odd gait would have given him pause. The man's feet were not visible from their low vantage point, but his legs appeared to be out of synch with his rate of motion, as if he were walking on ice and was being pushed forward by a strong, cold wind.

Then the man's jaw hinged downward, the thin lips parted, and a black maw opened. *"Churr-rainnnnnnn."*

"The hell was that?" Dex said.

"He said something," Bobby said.

"That wasn't a word. That didn't even come from his mouth."

Vernon Ray had the same impression. The sound had not been directional, and if Dex hadn't also noted it, Vernon Ray would have assumed he'd imagined it. The man continued his peculiar locomotion, and was nearly out of sight when Vernon Ray noticed the dented tin canteen slung over the man's pack. It glowed silver in the moonlight. A symbol was stamped into the dull tin. The distance was too great to discern the letters, but their shape suggested a familiar acronym.

C.S.A.

Confederate States of America.

Then the man was gone, and the silence that had descended in his wake gave way to night noises, the merry creek, the hiss of distant tires against asphalt, the wind in the dying leaves.

"The hell was that?" Dex repeated.

"Something from the Hole," Vernon Ray said. "He was wearing a kepi. A Rebel cap."

"Come on," Dex said, raising his voice. "You ain't pulling that noise, are you?"

"He's headed toward Mulatto," Bobby said.

"You taking this shrimp's side?" Dex said. "Trying to scare me with your stupid little ghost stories?"

"I'm not trying anything," Bobby said. "I'm just saying."

"He was wearing a Civil War uniform," Vernon Ray said. "Natural fiber. That looked like an army-issued canteen, and those are pretty rare."

"Yeah, right," Dex said. "He's probably some loser that came in early for the reenactment. A rebel without a clue."

"Okay," Bobby said. "Suppose he is. Let's follow him."

Vernon Ray recalled the man's weird steps and how he'd moved faster than his legs should have carried him. Dex must have been thinking the same thing, because he said, "I don't want to waste my Saturday night tailing a wino. He's probably up there puking a rainbow of Kountry Kwencher."

"V-Ray?" Bobby asked, and Vernon Ray felt a sudden rush of warmth and appreciation. Bobby was giving equal weight to both opinions and letting his vote count as much as Dex's. Vernon Ray wasn't sure what would happen if he voted against Dex, but in truth he didn't *want* to know if the man was a long-dead soldier who had crawled out of the Hole and gotten lost and was now wandering the Earth in search of a place to belong.

"Dex is right," Vernon Ray said. "The comic store's more fun."

"Damn straight," Dex said, emboldened. "Those comic-book chicks got some gazongas you could play water volleyball with and never come up for air. Plus Whizzer might be hanging around and we can score a joint."

Vernon Ray had resisted his friends' attempts to lure him into trying marijuana, but tonight might be different. Since reality was becoming increasingly unreliable, an altered state suggested comfort, though he was afraid that if he indulged in a trip to the outer limits of fantasy, he might not return.

Then again, he had little worth returning to: a bastard of a dad, few friends, and strange changes below his waist that didn't seem to know in which direction to point. Vernon Ray was as lost as the Churr-rain man, whether he was a wino or a Civil War ghost.

"I'm with Dex," Vernon Ray said.

"This don't mean we're going steady, sweetheart," Dex taunted.

"Okay," Bobby said. "Majority rules."

Bobby stood aside and let Dex lead them back onto the tracks and toward town. Vernon Ray wasn't sure whether Bobby was secretly disappointed or not, and he was too afraid to ask.

CHAPTER FOURTEEN

The morning was crisp and its breath held the threat of frost. Hardy was braced by the chill and always found the sunrise a glorious miracle that only the Lord could concoct. The only thing cockeyed about it, at least from his flesh-and-blood perspective in the opening of the barn, was that the sun made its virgin appearance each day over Mulatto Mountain, painting the peak in red and gold like it was getting licked with hellfire.

Since it was Sunday morning, the developers' bulldozers were silent. Even the roosters seemed sleepy, crowing like they didn't give a darn whether they impressed the hens or not. The cattle were scattered across the sloping pasture, working the sweet fall grass. Wood smoke from the chimney whisked across his face, momentarily masking the aroma of manure and the rotting tomatoes in the garden.

Donnie was playing in a stall, the one where Hardy kept clean straw. Whether inside the house or in the barn, he had to keep his son penned up. And he wasn't sure whether the headshrinking doctors at health department were right when they said Donnie would be better off in a state hospital. Couldn't be much worse than pacing around in a stall like a blind horse.

Hardy peered over the stall door at his son. Donnie wore overalls, a father-and-son match, though Donnie's were two sizes larger. Pearl had secured a straw hat on his head so Donnie could pretend he was a normal boy going to help his dad with chores. But Hardy couldn't trust him with pitchforks, milk buckets, or horseshoes. Maybe he was doing wrong, as overprotective as he accused Pearl of being, but he didn't want to allow any more pain in his heart by allowing his son to get hurt.

"All right, Donnie," Hardy said. "I got to go into the loft and throw down a few bales."

Donnie looked up and grinned, lips wet with drool. He tossed some straw into the air and it spun in the sunlight that leaked between the siding planks. A piece of chaff stuck to his chin. He looked happier than any of the kids Hardy had seen hanging around down at the bowling alley or the shopping mall. Then again, Donnie was probably the world's oldest kid.

Hardy gave a wave and Donnie raised both arms as if mimicking the gesture.

*I'll take it. Hell, better than a trained monkey, and this one gets the Eggers name and birthright.*

"Someday, son, all this will be yours," Hardy said.

"*Gwek,*" Donnie said.

"That's right. With the price of beef going up, you might have yourself a future."

Donnie's lips fluttered as if imitating the sound of a tractor engine.

"You just stay here and hold down the fort and I'll be right back," Hardy said.

In the loft, he shoved bales to the south end so he could throw them down a feeding chute. Though the cows didn't mind short grass, the two horses were particular, and the three goats were big fans of fiber, though they were so picky they only ate the seed heads.

Hardy had purchased the goats over in Solom to rid the pastures of briars, and they were so troublesome he'd wanted to get rid of them, but Donnie's face had lit up when he'd first seen them. He'd clapped his hands and went "*Gwa, gwa.*" Most likely he'd only been suffering indigestion, not showing joy, but then Donnie wasn't the only one grasping at straws these days.

Hardy tumbled a few bales down and got busy rearranging a few stacks to make room for the fall's tobacco crop. Since the Great American Cigarette Settlement, most small growers had sold out their quotas, the latest version of farm welfare. But Hardy continued to maintain the half-acre patch his own father had once reaped.

He wasn't sure it was due to habit, tradition, or a finger in the eye to all those liberal do-gooders who made smoking seem like the crime of the century. Whatever the reason, the income barely covered the property taxes for the dirt it grew on.

*Another reason to sell out to Budget Bill and head for greener pastures. I couldn't make that much if I grew tobacco here for the next 200 years, but at least I'd help put a few nails in a few coffins before then.*

Hardy gathered the oak tobacco stakes, which were warped and gray with age. The tobacco stalks would be speared on the stakes and allowed to dry golden-brown in the sun, and then the crop would be hung from the barn rafters until it was the color of chewing tobacco spit. Long after the first frost, Hardy and Pearl would sit on buckets and crates and twist the leaves into bundles, talking over old times, swapping Bible verses, and doing everything they could to pretend they were happy and their son was normal.

The tied bundles would be hauled to the warehouse auction in Winston-Salem, Hardy making the trip alone in the two-ton flatbed Ford. The Ford was so slow that the payment check would probably beat him back to the farm, where a stack of bills would be waiting for them both.

A winter of split firewood, potatoes, and cabbage, and then they might be lucky enough to do it all again, with Donnie cooped up in his upstairs room with crayons and pillows as the blue happiness in Pearl's eyes continued its glacial melt to gray.

Hardy tumbled some stakes through the loft door, enjoying the knocking as he played an oversize game of tiddlywinks. He was about to toss down the next armful when he saw Donnie halfway across the pasture, climbing the slope.

Headed for Mulatto Mountain and the Hole.

"Donnie!" Hardy almost tripped as he tried to run before he'd tossed the stakes out of the way, and one of them rebounded off the wall and glanced him across the side of the head. Dizzy, he wobbled to the stairs.

*Donnie never tried to climb out of the stall before.*

Donnie barely expressed the coordination to walk to the bathroom, much less go hand-over-hand and place his feet in the right notches to escape. But now he moved like an athlete, still a little hunched and swinging his arms low, but motoring just the same. Hardy reached the ground floor and broke into a jog, his worn lungs wheezing, wishing he'd quit the smokes himself before they'd painted a permanent skin of tar inside him.

Hardy wasn't sure what would be worse, Donnie reaching the woods and maybe getting lost, or Pearl stepping out on the porch or looking through the kitchen window and seeing her 27-year-old baby boy escaping from the zoo.

And the one question Hardy didn't want to ask: Why was his catatonic son heading straight for the Hole, like a migrating bird picking up the magnetic currents of the Earth?

And another question Hardy didn't want to ask: What would happen when Donnie got there?

Hardy pushed himself as hard as he could, sweat beading on his forehead despite the cool weather. He reached to brush it from his eyes and came away with blood on his fingers. Hardy was gaining on him, but Donnie was just a few hundred feet from the fence.

"Donnie!" Hardy yelled, wasting a precious gulp of air.

Donnie's head juddered up and down as if he acknowledged his name, but he didn't slow a bit. A few of the cows lifted from their grazing and looked at them. Hardy dared a glance back at the house and it was still and peaceful, a thread of smoke rising from the chimney and stitching itself into the shredded clouds. Hardy wondered if he'd have been better off with the tractor instead of boot power, but it was too late for second-guessing.

As if there were any other kind of guessing.

Donnie was almost to the fence when the primrose shrubs and blackberry vines along the fence line shook as if rushed by a sudden wind. Hardy saw shapes among the undergrowth but chalked them up to lightheadedness.

*Surely those ain't people in them briars?*

Then Donnie reached the fence and went up and over with the ease of a chimpanzee, barely causing the split locust posts to shiver. Even amid the fear, Hardy felt a surge of pride. His son was finally a man. Or at least a boy again.

Then Donnie disappeared into the maple saplings, silver birch, and jack pine, and the shapes along the fence solidified.

Men. Six or seven of them.

Except they weren't quite men. More like man-sized balls of fuzz, indistinct, though they stood and appeared to monitor Hardy's approach. Then they grew a little more solid, and Hardy noted those familiar gray uniforms and the kepis on several of the heads. Just like Earley in the portrait.

*The things from the Hole.*

It wasn't bad enough that they'd beckoned his son through some kind of invisible signal, they had to come down and meet him. Like a welcome party.

A couple of the men were armed, bearing long muskets rubbed shiny with cloth. Hardy wondered what happened to you when you were hit with ghost bullets. Did they only kill ghosts, or could they work on the living, too?

The way Hardy's heart was beating against his scrawny rib cage—

*ratta-tat, ratta-tat*

—he didn't think he'd have to worry about which way he died.

The big sky squeezed.

He fell to his knees as his chest muscles clamped down hard, and though his ears clanged with that goddamned metal drumbeat and he couldn't suck in a breath, he forced himself to crawl toward the fence.

The dead soldiers watched him with dead faces, their strange pale skin pocked with filth and their beards knotty and mottled.

Hardy put one hand in a fresh cap of cow manure and shoved forward, making it a few more feet before he collapsed. Then he dragged himself forward by wriggling like a cold serpent fresh out of hibernation, crushed clover sweet in his nostrils. He found he could breathe again, and the grip behind his ribs gave way to the punch of a dozen glowing spikes.

This was the part where he expected to hear trumpets and open his eyes to see a heavenly host of pillow-breasted angels, but all he heard was that confounded *ratta-tat ratta-tat*. He rolled onto his back and saw the world upside down, and the bearded soldier in the broad slouch hat floated through the fence.

*Funny, the things you see when you're dying. I always thought it would be liquid sunshine and sweet Jesus Christ driving a golf cart.*

The officer moved toward Hardy, legs not moving, scuffed boots dangling inches above the ground. The man grew more solid as he approached, as if Hardy's life force was being sucked from his heart and charging up the batteries of the long-dead spirit. He stood over Hardy and knelt down as if tending a fallen comrade.

The officer's eyes were deep and cold, and that same bottomless chill was mirrored inside Hardy's throat. The man reached for Hardy's face, and Hardy felt it was safe to go ahead and surrender if the war was already lost.

Just before he closed his eyes, two sounds battled for storage space in the sodden silo of his brain.

Pearl, yelling his name.

And *ratta-tat, ratta-tat,* fading, fading, along with the soldiers, the October trees, the bearded officer's face, the soft-clouded heaven that was now below, the dream of being a man.

CHAPTER FIFTEEN

"We should have brought Dex," Vernon Ray said.

"Nah, I'm tired of his pissing and moaning," Bobby said. "Besides, he doesn't believe in any of this."

"I'm not sure I believe it, either."

"Keep watching."

Bobby was lethargic, groggy from an extra hour of sleep. The laziness of Sunday morning had infected the woods as well. A church bell gave its soft toll in the valley below. If not for Vernon Ray's obsession with whatever had happened inside the Hole–and his own memory of the whispered words from the cave–he'd be lying in bed touching himself or flipping through some Spawn comics while Mom burnt the bacon. Instead, he was on a ghost-hunting patrol.

They had staked out a position on the ridge, in a stand of laurels where they couldn't be seen, cushioned by galax and fern. Bobby wasn't sure whether concealment did any good if you were trying to hide from ghosts. If they could float right through tons of granite, then they could probably see through trees. Vernon Ray peered through a pair of binoculars he'd swiped from his dad's collection, and Bobby had a digital zoom camera he'd checked out from school.

He was supposed to use the camera for a nature project, creating a slide show of fall flowers, but he figured if he nailed a ghost for "Show and Tell," he could probably impress even Karen Greene. He'd been sniffing around Karen all semester, but she was currently hot for Josh Brannon, son of Titusville's biggest car dealer. Bobby figured, as the son of a drunken plumber, he was barely on her Top 10 list, so any publicity was good publicity.

Vernon Ray was sprawled on a North Face sleeping bag, a Boy Scout special, while Bobby had a ratty blanket. If Dex were along, he'd have brought an entire camping outfit, with tent, Coleman stove, and probably a global-positioning compass. Bobby wasn't really resentful of his wealthier friends, because he'd never really known his family was poor until he'd gotten into the middle grades and the division between trash and treasure grew more stark.

The trailer-park kids got free lunch at school, and Bobby was so embarrassed at getting his ticket punched that he'd stopped eating at school. Sure, the other boys hung with him because he was a pretty decent halfback and could drain three-pointers on the hoops court, but when his dad picked him up after practice in the rusty truck with scrap pipes hanging all over it, Bobby slunk away as fast as he could.

But a digital photo of the creeps from the Jangling Hole would even things up. Bobby would be featured on the front page of *The Titusville Times*, maybe with a headline of "Legend Buster" and a mug shot that would moisten Karen's panties, assuming she'd passed puberty, and she sure had the look of it judging from what she was sporting upstairs.

"V-Ray, do you think a camera can see a ghost?"

"Well, sometimes digitals capture orb phenomena, balls of milky ether that represent paranormal activity. Skeptics say it's just lens flare or the flash illuminating specks of dust."

"You're really into this."

"I don't have any friends, remember? If it wasn't for the Internet, I wouldn't exist."

"Just like our imaginary friends in the Hole."

"Oh, they exist, all right. One of them tried to grab me yesterday and drag me in."

"Bull."

Vernon Ray laid down his binoculars and rolled up his right sleeve. "My wrist is still bruised. See?"

Bobby didn't think bruises were such a rare commodity. His dad roughed him up a bit, usually when drunk, and Bobby figured that stuff went on in every household, not just the poor ones. Dad had made an art of playful abuse, making sure the evidence wasn't visible enough to be noticed by nosy neighbors or do-gooders in the public education system. But Vernon Ray's marks were pretty ripe and impressive, the purple blotches spread out as if made by big, strong fingertips.

"That don't make any sense," Bobby said. "If ghosts aren't solid, how can they grab you?"

"Manifestation."

"Do what?"

"Manifesting into physical form. Sometimes they're invisible, sometimes you can see them a little bit. So why couldn't they make themselves real if they wanted? It's not exactly like they have to follow the rules of physics. They're obeying a different set of laws, learning as they go."

"Right. And you want to go back *in* there?"

"I just feel some sort of connection. The Hole's has been around forever, but nobody has ever offered any real proof of the supernatural. Mostly it's just been urban legends dressed up in overalls and corncob pipes, with the Civil War flavor thrown in to play better to the audience. So why should the Hole become active all of a sudden?"

"The bulldozers ripping the mountain to pieces?"

"Maybe. Ghosts are sensitive to disturbances of their resting place."

"Think it has anything to do with the Stoneman's Raid re-enactment?"

"Who knows? Maybe the ghosts have been walled inside the mountain listening to those bugle calls and shouts of muster and it triggered some sort of memory. If they get energy from the things around them, they get stronger the more they get pestered. Maybe they get a charge just from us sitting out here thinking about them."

"Man, this sounds pretty damned loopy, you know?"

"Hey, all you got to do is tell this to a grown-up, and I'm sure you'll get a rational explanation, a warning not to trespass, and a weekly session with the school shrink. Only kids can be trusted with this kind of knowledge."

Bobby took a sip from his Gatorade bottle and peered through the tree trunks at the grassy entrance to the Hole. "I reckon. But if we don't see anything, this never happened, right?"

Vernon Ray looked through the binoculars for a moment, then lowered them and turned to Bobby, red rings impressed around his eyes. The brown irises and thick lashes again reminded Bobby of Bambi, and he hoped his friend wouldn't say anything stupid and sensitive. Why couldn't he just be a *guy*, for Christ's sake?

"Thanks for coming along," Vernon Ray said, though it looked like he wanted to say more.

"Well, I'm a sucker for anything weird," Bobby said, hoping Vernon Ray wouldn't translate it into an invitation of some kind. "I mean, beats hell out of sitting around watching the race or doing homework."

"Think you'll get in trouble?"

"I was born in trouble."

Vernon Ray was about to respond when Bobby heard a pattering like rain on leaves. He squinted at the sky, and though some gray clouds had gathered, there was more than enough blue to patch a pair of jeans. The wind had picked up a little and the sun-speckled canopy was whispering in a parched autumn voice, limbs creaking slightly. "Shh," Bobby said.

"I hear it, too," Vernon Ray said.

"Ratta-tatta-tat?"

"You got it."

Bobby lifted the camera, ready for action. "Showtime."

The rolling thunder of drumbeats was muffled at first, echoing from deep within the Hole, oozing forward as if testing the resistance of air.

"Rolling out reveille," Vernon Ray said, sweeping the clearing with the binoculars. "Time for the troops to fall in."

Bobby heard the scuffing of fallen leaves before he saw the man. At least, he was big enough to be a man, a few inches over six feet and filled out, though his arms seemed a little scrawny. Maybe the overalls exaggerated the effect, but there was a childlike quality to the man's movements, as if he had only recently learned to walk.

"It's one of them," Vernon Ray whispered.

"No, I don't think so. He looks a little too *real*."

"Something's off about him."

Bobby wanted say that *everybody* was a little off, especially V-Ray, but he was too intent on following the man's movements. His wobbly steps were carrying him straight toward the Hole, though the way he cocked his head made it appear he was listening for instead of looking for his destination.

"Dude, that's Hardy Egger's boy," Bobby said. Donnie Eggers had attained some urban-legend status himself, as few people had ever actually seen him. The story of a mute, senile, drooling lunatic locked away in the old farmhouse was juicy enough to launch a hundred variations.

Some told it that Donnie was the lone survivor of a summer-camp serial killer and didn't have enough marbles left to tell the cops the killer's identity. Others chalked it up to a weird red church over in Whispering Pines where some people had died. Vernon Ray had looked on the Internet but a Google search for "Donnie Eggers" had yielded hundreds of Web pages about Donnie Osmond, chicken hatcheries, and genealogical records of people who had died long before George Washington had dropped his trousers to the King.

"I thought they never let him out of the house."

"Look how he's walking. Like a spaz."

"He's following the sound of the drum."

"Creepy." Bobby clicked a picture of Donnie, figuring he would get a little attention for providing proof of the man's existence. He checked the photo and found it was blurred, but before he could aim the camera again, Vernon Ray elbowed him.

"Holy molars, Batman," Vernon Ray said.

Coming through the trees behind Donnie, marching in a ragged line, were a half-dozen soldiers. They reminded Bobby of the re-enactments his dad participated in, except these guys looked worn and haggard, as if they had been in a real war for years instead of a pretend one for a weekend. Bringing up the rear was a man in an overgrown felt cowboy hat, a scabbard dangling from his belt.

"They don't look like ghosts," Bobby said.

"Of course not. They're actualized."

"Do what?"

"They've become real."

Bobby clicked a couple of pictures, not stopping to check them lest he miss a good shot. Donnie was nearly to the Hole now, and the drum roll swelled into a cavernous echo. "Then they should show up on the digital, right?"

"Something should. Ectopic matter, maybe, or ether."

"They're headed for the Hole."

"And taking the Eggers boy with them. Just like they tried to take me."

It sounded weird to call Donnie Eggers a "boy," but despite his size there was a definite boyish innocence about him. Or maybe his imbecility brought a lack of motor control that made him appear vulnerable and fragile.

Bobby lowered the camera. "Damn. Think we ought to save him? He probably doesn't know what he's doing if he's out of his mind."

"What can we do? These are *ghosts*, for Christsakes."

"Go get the cops."

"And then what?"

Donnie's halting steps led him to the mouth of the cave, where he stood swaying and blinking into the darkness. The snare reveille rattled out of the stone tunnel and filled the forest. The weary, slump-shouldered troops narrowed the distance and were approaching Donnie when the drum fell silent. The soldiers stood hunched in place, at raggedy parade rest, with only the bearded man with the scabbard moving, taking brisk but discordant steps to the front of the line.

"I don't think the cops will do a damn bit of good," Vernon Ray said.

"Well, if they're solid, they can be shot and killed," Bobby said.

"I don't think it works like that. They're already dead, remember?"

"So we just watch while they do a ghost version of throwing a virgin sacrifice into a volcano?"

"Well, there's one other option. That bearded creep must be the colonel."

"Colonel Kirk?"

"The leader."

The man with the scabbard—*Colonel Creep*, Bobby decided—stopped in front of Donnie, but Donnie stared at the ground, swaying back and forth as if the snare were still rattling out its rhythm. Through the zoom of the lens, the colonel's eyes looked like black, miniature versions of the Jangling Hole.

Bobby looked at his friend, running down the many other

options besides the one he knew Vernon Ray would offer. "We can shut our mouths and pretend nothing ever happened. We can say we got photos but have no idea what happened to the Eggers boy. We can say we thought they were Civil War re-enactors."

"I know what it's like in the Hole. If they take him in there, he'll never come out."

"Christ."

"Yeah. We can't let that happen."

Bobby sighed, reluctant to lose the Karen Greene hero-worship fantasy. Or possibly his life, for that matter. "Well, at least we won't have to worry about becoming grown-ups."

"You want to do it, or me?"

"Which way you running?"

"You're faster than me, so you head across the ridge. When they follow, I'll grab Donnie and drag him away."

"What if they don't all chase me, or if more of them come out of the Hole?"

"Nobody lives forever."

"Except *them*."

Donnie still hadn't looked at Colonel Creep. The other soldiers sagged like handless puppets, waiting to be snapped into action. The air was charged with expectation, as if the static were building for a thunderbolt. Bobby let the camera dangle from the strap around his neck and stood up, emerging from the concealment of the laurels.

He cupped his hands to his mouth. "Up here, you dirty Connecticut Yankee dogs."

Donnie was the first to turn his head, followed by the bearded colonel. Shaking, Bobby lifted his middle finger and shot the ghost a bird, wondering if the universal hand signal for "Screw you" had been in vogue in the 1860s.

Vernon Ray waited in the thicket, peering through the binoculars.

"What's he doing?" Bobby asked.

"Darn. Better duck."

The soldiers, without speaking, had turned their attention toward Bobby, some of them raising their rifles. Bobby wondered if the ghostly musket balls and minis had any power in the real world, and decided despite his bravado about not growing up, he was in no rush to get killed.

For one thing, he still had a few gaps in his Spiderman collection to fill, and for another, he was going to kiss Karen Greene before the eighth grade was over. And one more notion ran under the others: if he died, then maybe his ghost would be stuck on Mulatto Mountain, too, conscripted to an endless darkness with the cold company of Colonel Creep's Raiders.

He dodged behind a massive gnarled oak just as thunder erupted. Lead balls ripped though the leaves over his head, answering his question about the reality of ghost bullets. The soldiers scattered and headed up the slope toward him, their feet making no noise as they passed over the carpet of dead, dry leaves.

Bobby cupped his hands and yelled. "What now, Ghostbuster?"

"Run for it," Vernon Ray said.

"Which way?"

"Both."

"Great plan." Another volley sounded, and Bobby peered around the oak to check the positions of the approaching soldiers. Two stood in the clearing by the cave, smoke rising from their rifles. One was reloading.

*Good thing they're using breech loaders instead of semiautomatics, or I'd be Swiss cheese.*

Donnie finally looked up, though Bobby couldn't make out his expression, and the colonel drew his sword from its dull brass scabbard and pointed it toward Bobby in another universal "Screw you" signal.

*So much for Vernon Ray's plan of "Divide and conquer." Time for Plan B: Get the hell out of Dodge.*

Bobby broke from cover and scrambled across the ridge, the protruding granite boulders giving him cover. He wondered if the sheriff's deputy had known he was shooting at ghosts yesterday. Since cops were trained to be good shots, it probably proved that ghosts couldn't be killed. On the other hand, ghosts seemed not only able and willing to kill the living, but took the mission pretty seriously. After all, Kirk's Raiders had spent a century and a half stewing on their resentments.

An explosion of powder sounded. Something pinged off a nearby boulder, throwing rock chips in the air.

Bobby stayed low and kept running, dancing between rocks and trees the way he dodged tacklers on the gridiron, the camera bouncing off his rib cage, the dying green smell of autumn forest mixed with the rot of loam. Another shot echoed through the trees. He wondered if Vernon Ray had enough sense to run away, then realized they were almost recreating yesterday's chase, only this time it was dead soldiers and not the law that was after them.

Breathing hard, he reached the highest point of the ridge, where storm-sheared hickory trees stood in jagged brown lines. A low branch thwacked him across the cheek, nearly knocking him off his feet. He rubbed the stinging flesh and hurried onward. He was about to descend the slope, figuring to curl around the rocky promontory and wait for Vernon Ray at the bottom of the mountain, when he heard a loud, low rumble.

Too loud for rifles.

Cannon? A hundred snare drums?

He slowed and squinted at the sky. Cloudy, but not dark enough for thunder.

Bobby found a rocky, rain-cut gully and scooted down it, sliding in the black mud. The mechanical chugging grew louder. The gulley opened onto a clearing of cut trees and an open, level gash of brown soil.

Two dump trucks and a logging truck were parked along one edge of a rough dirt road, and a bulldozer was parked in the clearing, black smoke rising from its smokestack. Bobby waved his arms and ran toward the man in the baseball cap who was revving the noisy, stinky diesel engine.

The man didn't see Bobby at first, and Bobby climbed onto the dozer's thick steel tread. He grabbed the dozer operator's shirt and the man spun in surprise, nearly knocking Bobby from the bulldozer. "What?" the man shouted.

"Ghosts," Bobby said, knowing it sounded like a bratty prank, but too shocked to tell anything but the simplest truth.

"Go?" the man yelled.

"They got somebody," Bobby said, pointing toward the ridge.

The man's face was blotched and his eyes bloodshot. His breath smelled of beer and onions. His eyebrows furrowed in anger and he yanked down the throttle, quieting the engine to a deep throb. "What you talking about?"

"They got my friend."

"Who got him?"

"Ghosts. From the Jangling Hole."

The man's face scrunched again, but he must have seen the fear and panic in Bobby's eyes. "Who are you?"

Bobby was again too shaken to lie. "Bobby Eldreth."

"The plumber's kid?"

Bobby nodded.

"What you doing out here? Don't you know this is private land?"

"We came to see the ghosts."

"That's just stories they make up for kids on Halloween."

"I saw them. And they're taking away the Eggers boy. They're taking him into the Hole."

The man fidgeted with the throttle. "You been smoking something?"

"No, sir. You got to help."

"I don't know what you seen. But the Eggers boy ain't got enough letters in his soup bowl to spell 'C-A-T,' much less wander this far from home. I got work to do."

"Please."

The man's mouth twisted in a "Hell with it" mime then he shut the engine down. The diesel engine chugged, chuffed, and died, acrid exhaust hanging in the air. Bobby hopped off the dozer and waited for the man to climb down.

Bobby turned and found the soldiers had tracked him down. Or maybe they'd simply materialized in the clearing.

*Because this is their mountain and they don't like trespassers.*

They circled Bobby and the bulldozer operator, their rifles leveled. They were close enough that Bobby could see the tarnished insignia on their uniforms and the moth holes in their filthy jackets.

"What in God's name?" the man whispered.

"Like I said."

"It's them dress-up boys for Stoneman's."

The man stepped toward the closest soldier, who sighted down his barrel and thumbed back the flintlock.

"I think they want you to stop," Bobby said.

"No way," he said, continuing. "Nobody points a gun at me and gets away with it. Even if it's a pretend gun."

The soldier pulled the trigger and the flintlock struck, igniting the powder charge and propelling a lead ball into the man's face. Bone crunched and a red spray jumped from the back of the man's head, his cap flying off from the blow. A few drops of blood hit Bobby, and he saw other soldiers were aiming their weapons.

The bulldozer operator's head, which had snapped backward on impact, now lolled forward as his knees collapsed. He flopped face-first as if making a snow angel in the mud of the road bed.

Bobby put his hands over his eyes, figuring the next volley would rip him to shreds, expecting his life to flash before his eyes. But all he saw was Karen Greene and his sneering dad and Vernon Ray's Bambi eyes and a scene from *Shrek* where Donkey first realizes he can fly. Some life. He listened for the click of a trigger, wondering if he would die before he heard the shot.

He wondered how his dad would take it, and whether Will would sell his comic collection. Would Karen cry? He was wondering about the photos on his camera–maybe a little fame after his death–when he realized he'd been wondering for too many seconds.

*What's taking so long?*

He uncovered one eye and blinked.

Nothing.

The soldiers were gone.

The man from the bulldozer lay on his belly, a pool of thick red spreading from his shattered skull.

After a minute, the birds began chirping again in the high treetops.

## CHAPTER SIXTEEN

"Come give me a hand, squirt," Elmer said, knocking on the door to his sons' room.

The Schlitz 40s had clubbed his head but good and the last thing he needed was little Bobby adding to the headache. Sunday afternoons were for sitting on the couch and watching NASCAR, but Vernell had ragged him so hard about Dolly's Dollhouse that he'd promised to fix the leaking sewer pipe under the trailer.

It wasn't like he'd even copped a feel, and the closest dancer to his table was a used-up warhorse whose tits drooped like cold balloons. He could have sworn that when she clamped her thighs around the brass pole and spun, dust had floated into the air and her skin had chafed like rusty brakes. So even if he didn't feel any particular need to make amends for that sin, he'd rather wallow in shit under the trailer than put up with shit inside the house.

The space beneath the trailer was only three feet high, and while Elmer could slither through the septic mud and find the leak, he needed Bobby to fetch the proper lengths of pipe, carry tools, and do all the wriggling in and out.

Elmer pounded on the door harder. He wasn't surprised Jerrell was nowhere around, because Jerrell had a job and his own wheels and was banging babes all over town. His real son, a real man. While Bobby, the bastard blonde, was probably polishing the old bone to pictures of those big-titted superbabes in the comic books.

*Could be worse, could be a flaming fag like Jeff's boy.*

His face broke into a triumphant grin. Jeff could kick his ass in bowling, boss him around in the Civil War games, and draw twice the income, but when it came to raising them right, Elmer had the heating-and-AC man beat all to hell.

Elmer gave the door one more hard blow with the bottom fist. "Bobby, get your ass out here."

He tried the door handle. Locked. Elmer could shove the flimsy door in, but then Vernell would give him shit about that, too, and he'd spend the rest of the evening replacing it, and the money would come out of his beer kitty.

Elmer went down the hall and through the living room, where Vernell sat on a sofa drying her fingernail polish. Elmer never understood how a woman could fix on one thing and block out everything else in the world. When Vernell dried her fingernails, that was all she did. If some corporation could figure out how to channel that empty happiness on her face, then preachers, barkeeps, and shrinks would all go out of business.

"Where's Bobby?" she asked, as if she'd missed the tom-tom job he'd done on the bedroom door.

"Little idiot didn't answer," Elmer said.

"Stubborn," she said. "Gets it from your side of the family."

Elmer ducked his head back in the door, but didn't catch her face in time to see if she was jerking him around. Pushing the little secret in his face. If he had the damned money to spare, he'd send the cuckold-spawn for DNA testing and then Vernell could bounce her ass out onto the street and start walking. "At least my side can cook."

"He might have sneaked off with Vernon Ray," she offered.

"Well, he didn't come through the house."

"Maybe he got up before we did. You was snoring so loud an elephant parade could have wandered down the hall without us knowing."

Elmer didn't want to get into it, not right now. He brawled better with a few tall ones under his belt. There were a couple under the truck seat and it would give him a head start on the afternoon and make crawling in shit a little more bearable.

He slammed the trailer door hard enough to cause Vernell to yip and then got his tools from the truck. Like most in vocational trades, Elmer didn't like to take his work home with him. Carpenters couldn't be troubled to so much as hang a picture hook, painters wouldn't color a toenail, and plumbers were pissed off if they had to *slorp* a plunger around in a blocked toilet to jam out some cooze's bloody Tampax.

As he went around the trailer, he saw the open window in the boys' bedroom. He braced himself on the oil-tank rack and stretched up to look in the room. It looked like Bobby was still asleep, curled up in the blankets on the bottom bunk. He watched for a moment, figuring if Bobby was tickling the one-handed puppet then the bunk would be shaking.

Nothing. Not a thing. Not even the slow rise and fall of breathing.

Elmer was about to punch the glass hard enough to break it when he saw a crevice in the blankets, right where they met the pillow. He peered through the window at the place where Bobby's head should be. The skin was smooth and white, and a stitched patch of black met it.

*Soccer ball. The bastard pulled the old sleeping-dummy trick.*

Elmer stifled a surge of pride. Though he'd played a version of that stunt on his own folks plenty of times, sneaking out on Friday nights to knock down whiskey that his friends paid winos to purchase, he couldn't rightly claim a genetic link. Bobby was just a drain on the wallet and another pain in the ass, and if Elmer couldn't even get a little labor out of him, then he might as well send the brat's medical and grocery bills to the real father, whoever that was.

Bobby was probably down at the Davis trailer, dorking around with Vernon Ray. Elmer had no idea why his inherited son would want to hang around with a blooming fruit, but Bobby had always been a little too sensitive for his own good. He read too many books, for one thing.

Elmer would have worried about Bobby maybe having a little sugar in his britches, but Bobby was a jock and the little chickies seemed to dig him just fine. Too bad he spent all his time hanging around with his guy friends. He was probably missing out on a ton of stinky finger.

*Well, even a bitch like Vernell can't expect me to fix the busted pipe all by myself. I'll go round up Bobby and maybe even get Vernon Ray to help out, too. About time Bobby learned the family trade, anyway.*

Elmer walked to the Davis trailer, making sure he kicked over one of the little flagstones that girded the flower garden around the porch. *Yes, suh, Captain Davis. The officer's quarters are always a mite finer than what the troops get. Privilege of rank and all that happy horseshit.*

Elmer pounded on the door, his hangover gripping his skull in the bright sun. Maybe he'd hit Jeff up for a cold one, even though it was barely past noon. Chat him about the Civil War and Elmer might even get two or three freebies, plenty of lubrication for wallowing in shitty water and fixing a pipe. Just like a regular workday.

Jeff opened the door a crack, his mustache twitching. "Hey, Elmer. You not in church?"

"I already been saved. After that, I didn't see much point."

"Got your golden ticket, huh? Want a beer?"

"Does the Pope shit in the woods?"

"Come on in. Martha's gone to Barkersville to get her hair done."

Elmer stepped inside. The trailer, as usual, smelled like mothballs and Clorox. Framed portraits of Jeff's Civil War ancestors covered the walls, and a print of the *C.S.S. Neuse*, an ill-fated ironclad, dominated the wall behind the couch. Jeff's wife had made a few decorative overtures like a basket of potpourri and doilies on the armchairs, but this was clearly Jeff's house. It made Elmer resent him even more, because Elmer busted his ass to pay rent, but that lazy-assed Vernell called the shots.

*Hell with it.* He followed Jeff to the kitchen, his parched tongue licking his lips in anticipation.

As Jeff handed him a Budweiser, Elmer nodded thanks and said, "Say, did Bobby come over?"

"Bobby? I thought he was at your house. Vernon Ray said he was spending the night over there."

"I ain't seen either of them."

"You mean they were out all night?"

Elmer didn't want to think about the boys' sleeping together. Bad enough to be raising the creation of another man's sperm, but raising a fag would be 10 times worse. "Probably nothing. Boys will be boys. Remember when we was kids?"

Jeff gazed out the window at the trailer park, chin up in that prissy little officer's stance he used, and Elmer doubted if the guy remembered much of anything that didn't feed his little Civil War fantasy. "Yeah. We had some good times. Playing army, hiding in the woods, building forts."

Come to think of it, Jeff had been a mad general even back then, always giving orders and making sure they all died dramatic fake deaths. Then he'd command them to stand up and do it all again, the outnumbered Rebs against the blue-bellied hordes of the devil. He'd even refused to play with Lincoln logs because of their connection to the Union's leader.

Elmer took a sip of his beer, which washed down the resentment. "Yeah. Kids nowadays with their goddamned videogames."

"They don't know how to use their imaginations anymore," Jeff said, twirling one end of his mustache.

*Right-o, Cap'n. And some of us still live in the land of make-believe.*

"Well, I got to fix a busted sewer pipe or I'll have to listen to Vernell bitch for the rest of the day," Elmer said.

"You going to watch the race later?"

"If I get done in time."

"I got a new cap-and-ball pistol to try out. Want to do some shooting?"

"You bring the beer and I'll be there."

"Okay. I'll pick you up after the race. We can go up Mulatto Mountain."

Elmer blinked redness from his eyes. "That ain't game land anymore. It's private development."

"We won't hurt anything. Besides, it's Budget Bill. He never had any problem with people hunting his land."

Elmer had no desire to go anywhere near the Jangling Hole, but he wasn't about to admit it. Jeff had practically built his life on notions of honor, glory, and courage, and while Elmer couldn't give two shits about any of that, he wasn't about to show his spinelessness. "Pistol, eh?"

"Remington .44 replica. Got a nice kick to it."

"Set you back a bit?"

"A couple hundred."

"I don't see how Martha lets you get away with that. Vernell would shit a squealing worm if I dumped any more money into the hobby."

Jeff reached up to his forehead as if to adjust the brim of his Stetson, then realized his head was bare. He touched his hair instead. "It's all in making enough to keep her happy. Send her to Old Navy with the credit card once a month, keep her satisfied in the sack, and let her win all the arguments except the ones that matter."

Elmer didn't even have a credit card, and he couldn't remember the last time Vernell had even bothered to fake an orgasm. And Vernell won every argument, whether important or not. He was beginning to hate Jeff even more than before. But another sip of cold suds washed down a little bitterness. A few more cans of Bud and good ol' Cap'n Davis would be as worthy of worship as Stonewall Jackson and General Lee.

"Vernell's a bitch," Elmer said.

"You just haven't figured out what makes her happy."

Elmer studied the man's eyes. They held a gleam of secret triumph. Elmer noticed for the first time they were blue-gray, the color of a gun barrel. The same color as Bobby's, now that he thought about it.

"Why would I want her to be happy?" Elmer drained the Bud can, tilting it so the flat foam in the bottom tickled his tonsils. In his trailer, he'd throw empty cans across the room, trying to bank them off the wall and into the trash. Jeff's house was regimented and orderly and smelled like one of those specialty gift shops in the mall, the kind that made you sneeze about as fast as it made you bored. Elmer set the can on an imitation, catalog-ordered antique tea table. "Well, time to eat some shit," he said with exaggerated good cheer.

Jeff, still gazing out the window, held up a hand as if signaling troops to be quiet. Elmer went to the window, figuring either the 19-year-old tart Shawna Hicks was strutting around the trailer park in cut-off jeans and no bra or else the cops had driven up to the Baker double-wide with another warrant. Something worth seeing, in other words.

Instead, it was just another drunk staggering off from what was likely a sleepless night of porking Louise Templeton at 50 bucks a pop. Elmer had dipped his bucket in that well a couple of times himself, but the last time he'd reeled it back in with a dose of the clap, and he was worried what else she might have picked up in the meantime. Plus, 50 bucks was 50 bucks, and Vernell was cheaper, and his hand was free.

"You know him?" Elmer said.

"Check out that tunic."

"Tunic? Looks like a coat that the squirrels have been sleeping in."

"Wool. And the canteen."

*Canteen?* Nobody carried canteens anymore. Even hunters had gone to bottled water. The last time Elmer had actually seen somebody sip from a canteen, they'd all been dressed up in Civil War costumes and gathering for a bivouac in Charlottesville. "He's walking a mite wobbly."

"Man on a mission."

Elmer didn't want to add that the guy's boots didn't appear to be touching the ground. Jeff left the window for a minute, rummaging in the broom closet, and Elmer licked his lips, wondering if it was too soon to cadge another beer. Jeff returned with some field binoculars and squinted into them.

He whistled low. "I thought it was a replica, but damned if it doesn't look authentic. Even has the C.S.A. stamp in the tin."

There were plenty of counterfeiters skilled at taking a replica, beating the hell out of it, then cramming a century-and-a-half's worth of grime into the crevices until it could pass for the real thing. And the weekend soldiers who collected such items couldn't tell the real from the fake, and they didn't really care that much as long as they had bragging rights. But Jeff was pretty hard to fool, even from a distance.

"Maybe he's come for the Stoneman re-enactment," Elmer said, punctuating with a belch that mocked the contrived elegance of the Davis living room.

"This early? I know the 37th is coming in, but they won't be here until Friday."

"Well, if he's not in the troop, I guess we ought to recruit him."

Jeff smiled and lowered the binoculars. "Saddle up, soldier."

Elmer gave a wistful glance at the kitchen but Jeff was already out the door, so Elmer followed. The wobbly wino was a good 100 yards ahead, nearing the trailer park's entrance, where a walking path veered off to a strip mall and gas station.

Jeff broke into a jog, a benefit of Titusville Total Fitness and its $40-a-month membership. Elmer padded along in Jeff's wake as best he could, embarrassed by the jiggle in his belly. He half expected Vernell to shriek at him from a window, but he actually would have welcomed it, because it would have given him an excuse to drop the pursuit.

Because the wino creeped him out big-time and made him think of the disappearing man in the bowling alley.

For one thing, the man's legs were moving like he was hellbent for home and nothing would stand in his way, but his feet skimmed over the ground as if he were ice skating. Like he was moving forward faster than his steps should have carried him. And, Elmer wasn't a nature freak by any means, but he'd noticed the birds in the neighboring trees had fallen silent. The shithead Baker pit bull, staked to a clothesline post and ready to bark every time a gnat farted, had not even uttered a growl.

Jeff was now a good 20 paces ahead of Elmer, and that was just fine by him. Elmer slowed down a little, breathing hard, acid from the rising beer gas scorching his throat.

A tractor trailer rumbled down the highway, air horn blaring because the wino was nearly to the road and didn't follow the standard rule of looking both ways before crossing. The wino didn't slow a step and the buffeting force of the passing trailer didn't shake him in the slightest.

"Hey," Jeff shouted, breaking into a jerky middle-aged sprint.

Elmer stopped and waited for Jeff to catch the man. The wino stepped onto the asphalt and kept hoofing it, and a Honda screeched its brakes to avoid him. Then he was on the other side, into the scrub vegetation bordering the creek, and he disappeared into the tangled growth with barely a rustle of leaves to mark his passage. Jeff was delayed by a string of traffic, and by the time he crossed the road, the trail was cold.

Elmer reached the creek by the time Jeff had given up. "Too bad you couldn't recruit him," Elmer said. "The guy had the makings of a good soldier."

"Yeah, too bad," Jeff said.

As Jeff turned and headed back to the trailer park, Elmer looked down at the muddy creek bank where the man had vanished in the brush.

No footprints.

CHAPTER SEVENTEEN

"Why couldn't you wait six more months before you brought me another hard-to-figure corpse?" said Perry Hoyle, Pickett County's white-haired medical examiner of record. "Then I'd be retired and a younger idiot would be around to clean up your messes."

"It's not much of a mess," Sheriff Littlefield said. "Looks like a cut-and-dried bullet hole to the head."

"Ain't all the way dried yet, but it's plenty cut," Hoyle said, motioning to the spray of blood-stained hair and brains that were scattered across the dirty leaves. "Looks like a high-caliber bullet, but something is a little off."

"What's that?"

"The back of his skull is blown out like you'd expect from a close-range shot, but his forehead is cracked, too. Almost like he was struck with a blunt object instead of a bullet."

Littlefield knelt and peered at the corpse, which now lay on its back on a stretcher. The man's eyes stared up as if communicating his shock to the heavens. Hoyle had wiped around the wound, but it still resembled a tarry third eye that had wept mud. The edges of bone that showed were chipped and broken.

"I don't guess there's much chance of finding the bullet," Littlefield said. Morton was surveying the area behind the bulldozer, checking the tree trunks for signs of an imbedded fragment, but it could just as easily have ricocheted off the bulldozer and disappeared into the leaves. That would almost literally make the task like looking for a needle in a haystack.

"I'd say you got bigger problems than that," Hoyle said. He brushed back his wild Einstein hair and pointed to the yellow crime-scene tape that cordoned off the clearing.

"One set of footprints besides the guest of honor's. Sneakers."

"And they're little, a size eight maybe. Not much of an impression in the mud, so you figure somebody lightweight."

"A woman or a kid."

"Why can't you just have a normal murder once in a while?"

"Because you'd get bored."

Hoyle waved to the ambulance attendants who stood waiting at the scene's perimeter. Bill Willard, who had been sitting in his pickup, rolled down his window and shouted at Littlefield. "Hey, can I come in now?"

"We got to get some plaster casts of these footprints first."

Budget Bill exited the truck and joined the attendants at the yellow tape. "Good thing he wasn't on payroll. That would have sent my workman's comp through the roof."

"You're a man of compassion, Bill."

"Hey, it's not like I'm the one who shot him. Carter was the best damned dozer man in the county. This will set me three days behind schedule."

"If Christ rose from the dead in three days, I'm sure you can find another dozer operator in that time."

A vehicle engine wound up the rough-cut road through the forest below. "Dadgum," Bill said. "May as well set up a circus tent and sell tickets."

Hoyle said, "I've got all the photos I need. May as well get this one back to the morgue and dig around in his head."

He motioned the attendants to the body and they dragged the stretcher, its wheels miring in the mud. Littlefield checked the bulldozer's engine and noticed it was a little warm. He was about to ask Morton if any evidence had turned up when a rusty, primer-spotted Honda sedan emerged from the trees, an "I Brake For Unicorns" bumper sticker flanking one that supported Ralph Nader for president.

"Wonderful," Littlefield said aloud.

"Can she just drive up like that?" Bill said, his cherubic cheeks reddening. "Isn't it trespassing?"

"Technically, this is private property, but it's also a public crime scene," Littlefield said. "So it's a gray area, and I'm sure she could sic the state press association, the American Civil Liberties Union, and an army of liberal legislators on both of us if we tried to stop her."

Cindy Baumhower got out of her car, dangling a camera with a telephoto lens, a small steno pad tucked in her armpit. "Howdy, gentlemen," she said, her face bright enough that it looked like she might start whistling like a lark.

"You look pretty happy about a dead man," Littlefield said.

"I don't make the news, I just report it," she said. "Hello, Mr. Willard. Do you have any comment for the record about the first fatality in your planned development?"

"First?" Bill was wary, heeding the unwritten rule that it was bad strategy to piss off anybody whose company bought ink by the barrel. "You say that like there's going to be more."

"Depends on how I spin it," she said, bringing the camera to her eye as the attendants began loading the corpse.

"Come on, Cindy," Littlefield said. "Have a little respect for Carter's family."

"Shucks, Sheriff, you know I won't run anything red on the front page. But I have to give my editor something to prove to readers we were here."

"Okay, then. I won't check your images. I'll trust you."

"Sheriff, you touch my camera and I promise I'll pull every public-records request in the book and tie up your staff for the next two years on paperwork. Push your solve rate way down and kill your reelection bid."

Littlefield turned to Budget Bill. "And they say the liberal media has no heart these days."

Cindy clicked a few photos of the attendants struggling to ferry the corpse to the back of Hoyle's station wagon, then Littlefield affected a somber study of the crime scene as Cindy took his picture. Bill Willard put his hand over his face when she pointed the camera at him.

"So, what do you have, Sheriff?" she asked. "Hunting accident? Suicide? Maybe a crime of passion or a dispute with his boss?"

"Hey!" Bill said, raising his voice enough to cause both the attendants and Morton to stop what they were doing and look. "I don't give a hoot about your Green Party, Green Peace, lesbian-ecoterrorist act, because I've got a legal right to rip this mountain down to pebbles and sawdust if I want. But a smart little reporter like you surely knows slander and libel law."

She shrugged in feigned innocence. "I'm just generically speculating. Are you confirming that Mr. Carter was employed by you at the time of his demise?"

Bill's face twisted as if wanted to spit out whatever poison was sitting on his tongue. He moved over to inspect the bulldozer.

Littlefield kept his face neutral, though half of him wanted to laugh despite the grimness of the death. The spilled blood had soaked into the mud and turned brown, and the next rain would erase it forever, drawing nutrients to the worms and beginning Carter's slow return to dust. He focused on the footprints and realized what had troubled him.

Judging from the way the body had fallen, the person in the sneakers—and Littlefield was leaning toward "kid" instead of "woman"—couldn't have been the killer. The wound was from the front, and the sneaker prints were beside or behind Carter's prints. They were slightly deeper and more smeared where the kid had apparently dashed toward the woods, possibly after the gunshot, though there was no easy way to tell if the sneaker prints had been made before or after Carter's death.

Cindy started to duck under the yellow tape, but Littlefield yelled at her. "We got evidence to collect still. This scene isn't cleared."

"I can get a better picture of you standing over here."

Littlefield debated the value of giving her a little ground. Bill Willard was glaring at him as if promising to never contribute another dime to his campaign coffers, but with the low contribution thresholds, Willard's money meant nothing. He faced more damage from an antagonistic reporter. Plus, despite his proclaimed devotion to bachelorhood, she was still way cuter than Budget Bill Willard.

Morton came from the woods shaking his head, carefully circumventing the footprints. "Nothing out there I could find," he said. "We can come back with a metal detector and go over it."

"Let Perry Hoyle dig around in the skull a little first. Sometimes bullets bounce around in there and do their damage without ever leaving. What do you think of these footprints? Maybe one of the kids you and Perriotte chased yesterday?"

"We can go over to the Hole and make some plaster casts, assuming the footprints are still there. But lots of kids come up here to party, fool around, do all the things we did when we were kids."

Littlefield gave a terse nod toward Cindy. "That was off the record."

She gave her grave-robber smile. "Sure, Sheriff. Anything you say."

"Well, I know one of the kids. Dexter McAllister. His dad's supposed to bring him by the office today for questioning."

"Be easy to run a match on his shoes, or pull a warrant and go clean out his closet."

"Nah. Even a homer judge like Bleucus needs a little more evidence than this to issue paper, especially with a juvenile suspect."

"So you already have a suspect?" Cindy asked. She'd eased closer, pretending to focus her camera, and Littlefield had seen through the ploy and let it slide. He was annoyed at himself for so obviously playing her game.

"He's only a person of interest at this point."

The attendants had loaded Carter into Hoyle's big Chrysler station wagon, where the man would be taking his last ride until the undertakers came to drain him and dress him for his going-away party. Littlefield didn't know the man, but a search of his pick-up had turned up a copy of "Guns & Ammo" under the front seat, a six-pack of RC cola, a box of clean and well-oiled tools, and a plastic crucifix hanging from the rear-view mirror. No drugs, no firearms, no pornography, nothing to suggest a seedy character that would have lots of enemies.

Hoyle was right: Littlefield had a lousy record of serving up sensible corpses. At least this one had died from a bullet. Or so it seemed. This was Mulatto Mountain, and all bets were off.

"I think I'll take a walk over to the Hole," Littlefield said.

Morton was about to open his mouth and note the obvious, that the Hole was a quarter-mile from the crime scene and even without the trees and ridges in between, the shooter couldn't have pegged a perfect forehead shot from such a distance. But Morton also realized this was Mulatto Mountain, and his eyes went to the leaf-covered floor of the forest.

"What about my bulldozer?" Bill Willard said. "Can I run it tomorrow morning or are you going to keep the scene clean? Besides reporters mucking around in it, I mean?"

"I thought you couldn't find another dozer man."

"I can run it myself if I have to. I got a schedule and a heavy bank note. The interest is eating me alive and I have to get these lots sold before the damned Democrats get us in another recession."

"Maybe you should go back to photography," Cindy said. "I'm sure the world could use another few hundred limited-edition prints featuring fallen-down barns and white farmhouses. Rural nostalgia for people who don't want to leave their condominiums."

"As soon as the sheriff clears the scene, I'm asking him to arrest you for trespassing."

"Hold on, Bill," Littlefield said. "You'll get your roads carved soon enough, and it won't hurt you to lose a nickel or two."

Hoyle called from beside his station wagon. "I'm getting this guy back to town before he gets stiff on me. Give me a call later this evening."

Littlefield waved and turned to Cindy, figuring he could defuse the situation by getting her away from Bill Willard. "Morton, you take over the scene. Cindy, you're welcome to come with me and check out the Hole."

Morton's mouth twitched as if he wanted to snicker at the unintended double *entendre*. But Littlefield's warning glance reminded him this was serious business and that somebody might have lost a husband, father, brother, fellow parishioner. He ventured into the woods, Cindy right behind him.

"So this is connected to the 'Shots fired' report from yesterday?" she said, struggling to keep up with his long, purposeful strides.

"I never said that."

"Damn it, Sheriff, everything you say, you say you didn't say. When are you going to dish me something straight?"

"I'll give you the incident report as required by public-records law. I'll have a statement after the next-of-kin is informed."

"I could already write your statement, blindfolded and without fingers. Let me guess. It goes, 'We are diligently pursuing every avenue to solve this incident and bring the suspect to justice. Since this is an ongoing investigation, I can make no further comment at this time.'"

"Not bad. If we had the budget for a P.R. person, you'd be a natural."

"I couldn't work P.R. I'd never be happy telling only one side of the story."

Littlefield held back a briar vine to allow Cindy to pass. He released it too soon and it tangled in her hair. He fumbled with it, not caring that the thorns pricked his fingers. Her hair was soft and smelled like a summer meadow, and his heart felt funny, as if it had spooled loose from its arteries and was floating around the cage of his chest. By the time he'd freed her, the golden hair was streaked with his blood.

"Sorry about that," he said.

"You got a soft touch for such a hard-ass," she said.

He swallowed, aware that she was playing him, working him over with a feminine magic spell so she could elicit enough inside information for a good scoop. But, like any man caught in a spell, being aware of it didn't matter one damned bit. All he could do was gape and try not to drool.

"Well, I've had some practice," he said.

"Sheila Story, right?"

He felt the clouds collide and block the sunshine that no doubt had radiated from his face. "That was a long time ago."

"The newspaper's records go back to the early 1900s. And urban legends have a way of hitting the Internet."

"None of that ever happened."

She started walking again, obviously aware of the Hole's location, and Littlefield wondered how many times she'd trespassed onto Bill Willard's property seeking environmental violations. Or ghosts.

"Death by drowning, due to a car accident in which you were the driver," she said. "Could have happened to anyone, right?"

"There was way more to it than what made the papers."

"Isn't there always?"

He followed after her, tempted for a moment to tell her the whole truth about Archer McFall and the red church, but he wasn't sure what the truth was. That was all in the past, the dead had made their peace the best way they knew how, and the living learned to forget. "Okay. There was nothing to it. I killed her. I should have faced manslaughter charges, or at least reckless endangerment."

"And your little brother? Dying in that tragic hanging accident?"

Littlefield stopped and let her walk ahead, over a rise that would give them a view of the Hole. "What kind of a heartless bitch are you?" he said. "You enjoy other people's pain?"

She spun, kicking up leaves in her anger. "No, I just have a thing for the truth. And I have no respect for people who hide themselves away and sleepwalk through life. Especially when other people are counting on them."

"Like I don't swallow my guilt every waking minute and get a double helping when I'm asleep? You think I haven't noticed that people around me keep dying in weird ways? I can taste it. You don't have to shove it down my throat."

Cindy looked down then her eyes flicked to the ridge. "Sorry, Sheriff. I guess I want to believe in something magical so much that I'll even take ghosts and boogeymen if that's the best I can get."

"Well, there's always the Baptist Church."

"That's not magical to me. Religion has little to do with spirituality."

Littlefield didn't have an answer to that one. Two years ago, he'd started attending intermittent services again, though he felt nothing inside the church except the vibrations of the pipe organ and the heat of too many perfumed bodies crammed into such a small space. "You want to believe the Hole is haunted?"

"I've read the clippings and I talked to Arvel down at the history society," she said. "I've been in the cave with my tape recorder and digital camera and all I got was a sinus infection."

Littlefield considered telling her about the vanishing man he'd encountered the night before, but she would either laugh in his face or else make him remember every detail, and it was just another incident he was learning to forget. Besides, he had no proof that the man—"*ghost*," *if you want to call it that*—had any connection to the Hole.

For all he knew, Pickett County coughed up its dead on a

regular basis, which only affirmed his plan to move to Florida after his retirement. He had no desire to be buried here because he didn't know how permanent the eternal rest would be.

"Well, let's check it out and get you off Willard's land before he has a stroke," the sheriff said, continuing over the wooded rise. "Two deaths on Mulatto Mountain in one day would get people talking more than they already will."

"Don't worry, Sheriff. I won't play it up. I have to report the shooting death, but I'll go oatmeal. But you have to promise me the scoop if there are any breaks. The Charlotte and Winston-Salem papers will be up here, maybe even the television vans, once the word trickles out."

"We've got the body scraped up, so there won't be much for them to shoot. And I'll give you the best quotes."

She moved ahead of him again, in better shape and scarcely breathing hard. The streak of his blood in her hair had dried to brown. She reached the ridge and stood among the laurels, looking through the trees. Littlefield was about to join her when he saw the pair of binoculars lying in a bed of waxy green galax.

He slipped his shirt sleeve down over his fingers and picked them up. He peered through them. The field of vision was adjusted so that it was focused on the Hole. Somebody had been watching it.

Littlefield looked around. The leaves had been ruffled but the forest carpet was too thick to yield footprints. That didn't necessarily mean the binoculars had belonged to Carter's killer, but it was too much of a coincidence to consider a coincidence. Since Perriotte's mind-blowing experience of the day before, a lot of people had become interested in Mulatto Mountain. Littlefield looped the binoculars strap around his neck and headed for the Hole.

Cindy grabbed his arm. "Hear that?"

Littlefield tilted his head. He'd lost some of his high range and the doctors were threatening to plug him with hearing aids. He'd resisted them so far but soon he wouldn't be able to pass his physical without them. Despite his aural limitations, he made out a hollow tapping from inside the cave.

"What's that?" he asked.

"I don't know. But somebody's in there."

"You might have your scoop. But you better stay here."

Littlefield wasn't sure why the killer would be dumb enough to hang around near the scene of the crime, but criminals were usually just plain stupid. That's why gunmen held up the neighborhood liquor store, where they knew the lay of the land, instead of robbing a liquor store in the next town or state.

He eased down the slope, hand on the butt of his sidearm. He wished he'd carried his radio so he could call Morton for back-up. It would be safer to scout the surrounding area in case the killer hadn't acted alone, but Littlefield didn't want to give the suspect a chance to slip away.

Maybe this would solve a lot of mysteries, and that was worth a little risk. Littlefield was fed up with footprints ending in the middle of nowhere, raggedy men fading in the dead of night, and preachers who rose from the boneyard and led their dead congregations into the river. Even if it was a kid hiding out in there, an accidental killer, Littlefield would finally be able to wrap one up.

He drew his revolver and eased across the clearing, the tapping sound swelling inside the cave and taking on a rhythmic beat. He scanned the woods and saw no movement, hoping Cindy was sharp enough to serve as sentinel.

When he reached the mouth of the cave, he knelt by a jutting crag of granite and squinted into the shadowy opening.

A man sat in the dirt, beating on a rock with a crooked stick. His movements were spastic and uncoordinated, elbow flying one way and wrist flexing another, but somehow the stick fell in a steady motion.

The man's hair was unkempt and he was pale, as if he'd spent most of his time indoors. He was wearing jean overalls, a farmer's outfit. His mouth moved silently as if echoing the tapping of the stick.

"Donnie," Littlefield said.

The man played on.

"Donnie Eggers."

Littlefield didn't like the scene that would play out once people learned Donnie was a murder suspect. Pickett County residents were civilized enough to be beyond lynching him, but plenty would grumble about the moron who should have been sent off to the state nuthouse before "something like this happened, just like we knew it would."

"Hardy Eggers's boy," Cindy said from behind him, and Littlefield wasn't even annoyed that she'd disobeyed his order to stay back.

"This will plumb break Hardy's heart," Littlefield said. "And Pearl's, too."

He called Donnie's name several times, but the vacant-eyed man only swung the stick harder, rocking awkwardly back and forth, staring into the inky depths of the cave where the rockslide had sealed it shut.

Littlefield bent and touched Donnie on the shoulder, flinching in expectation of sudden violence. But Donnie stood, swaying and quivering, still flailing the stick in the air like a stoned orchestra conductor.

"Let's go, Donnie," the sheriff said.

Donnie lifted a palsied hand to his forehead, touching his stringy hairline, and it took Littlefield a moment to realize Donnie was saluting.

## CHAPTER EIGHTEEN

Bobby expected to get his ass kicked, or at least endure a good, old-fashioned cussing, but Dad was as docile as a lamb when Bobby got home just before sundown. Dad was sitting on the couch, a small pile of empty cans at his feet, trash his dad often called "dead soldiers." He stared blankly at the television as the clock ticked away "Sixty Minutes," and Bobby knew something was wrong, because Dad was about as interested in current events as he was in the Dewey Decimal system. Even Mom's high-pitched pestering barely roused him from his stupor.

"Where you been?" Dad asked without looking at him.

"Over at Vernon Ray's."

Dad nodded and gulped his Bud.

"Why don't you try sipping for a change?" Mom said.

Dad took another swig in response, glassy eyes fixed on Andy Rooney's doughy face as Andy launched into another old-fart rant. Bobby tried to slip to his room, but Mom stepped in front of him in the kitchen.

"You had any dinner?" she asked, moving close enough to sniff at him. She'd caught him raiding Dad's beer stash over the summer, and since then she'd been on him like a bottlefly on fresh dookie. Luckily, she didn't know what marijuana smelled like, so he could huff rope all day and she'd think it was dirty laundry. Not that he cared to get stoned at the moment. After watching the bulldozer guy get shot by the ghostly soldiers, he wasn't sure he wanted to edge any further away from reality.

"I ate at the Davises's," he said.

"Roast beef? Martha always has roast beef on Sundays." Mom said it with the frustrated air of a homemaker who had nothing more than hamburger and tuna fish to work with.

"Yeah. Mashed potatoes. That kind of stuff."

"Well, you ought to invite Vernon Ray over here to eat once in a while. They'll think we're sending you over to sponge off them." She smoothed a greasy strand of hair over her ear. The kitchen smelled like old mushroom soup.

"Sure, Mom."

The microwave dinged and Bobby took advantage of her distraction to beat it to his room. The door was still locked, meaning Dad hadn't gotten pissed and kicked in the handle. Bobby retrieved the key from its hiding place under the washing machine and unlocked the door, securing it behind him.

Jerrell would probably come dragging in around midnight, but Bobby hoped to be asleep before then. He wanted to rid himself of the image of the bulldozer guy's brains exploding out the back of his skull and figured a dream, even a nightmare, would scrub some of the freshness from the memory. He tossed, thinking of Karen Greene, Vernon Ray, Col. Creep's Jangling-Hole eyes, the sudden red spray, and finally the red blended to black.

He awoke sweating and tangled in sheets, Jerrell snoring on the bunk above him. Bobby got up and dressed in the dark. He grabbed a couple of slices of white bread, squeezed them into balls the size of marbles, and popped them like pills. He decided to walk instead of waiting for the bus, because Dad might drive by on his way to a job. And Dad probably would want to ride his ass extra hard to make up for lost time.

Bobby jogged the last quarter-mile to school, making home room just as the bell rang. The sweat made him self-conscious, especially when Karen Greene gave him the once-over and rolled her eyes away.

He made it through algebra okay, not even batting an eye when the P.A. system clicked on and the principal beckoned a list of students to the gym for honors photographs. The students were mostly the same old rich kids that won everything and caught all the breaks, and of course Karen was among them. Bobby smiled when he heard Vernon Ray's name called.

*Assuming V-Ray escaped from the Hole . . . .*

Mikey Pitts in the next aisle snickered and said, "Vernon Gay." Bobby was tempted to give Mikey a little tweak, but he bit his tongue and focused on figuring out whatever the hell $x$ equaled.

It didn't help his concentration when Karen sashayed down the aisle with a twist of her small hips, giving off a faint smell of soap and flowers. Bobby pressed his pencil hard against the paper until the lead tip snapped. He wondered how anybody survived the eighth grade, much less made it through high school, where the girls filled out more and their tight tops drove guys like Bobby wild.

"Look but don't touch," was the message radiating from between their eyeliner and mascara, and trailer-park guys were doomed to dumpy, dull girls of their own social class. It wasn't much of a consolation that such girls typically had low self-esteem and parted their legs for any guy that grinned and bought them a Big Mac, showing their gratitude by getting pregnant at 15.

The great thing about adolescent sex was, despite the fact that it was mostly nothing but daydreams, it helped you forget about ghostly killers, haunted caves, and a home life that was right out of FOX television.

Bobby rode out the frustration until lunch time, when he saw Vernon Ray sitting alone in the cafeteria, reading a book as he shoveled mystery meat into his mouth.

Bobby slid into the plastic chair beside him. "What you eating? Looks like pterodactyl turds."

"Beef stew. You eating today?"

"Not hungry," Bobby lied. In truth, the stew smelled good, despite its brown, watery appearance.

"You should have called me."

"I figured you bailed."

"Never. What happened?"

Bobby ran down the list of possible lies and decided maybe being a coward wasn't so bad, at least when compared to the truth. Even superheroes took off an issue once in a while, when saving the world became way more trouble than it was worth and some special guest star had to step in.

"I freaked," he said. "When those ghosts were chasing me, I just kept running. I didn't know how far they'd go. I mean, maybe they're tied to the mountain or something. And their charge would drain down if they got too far away."

"So you left me there by myself?"

"Dang, V-Ray, I figured you hoofed it, too."

"And leave Donnie there to whatever is hiding in the cave?"

"What *is* hiding in the cave? Now I'm not so sure we even saw anything." Bobby reached over to Vernon Ray's plate, snagged a roll, and shoved it in his mouth, figuring the food would give him a chance to think before he spoke again.

"Dude, I thought the plan was to get some evidence so people would have to believe us."

Bobby chewed and nodded, nearly choking on the dry bread. Just his luck, he'd strangle on dough not 30 feet from where Karen was holding court with half the cheerleading squad.

"Okay, chill out," Vernon Ray said. "Here's what happened: Right after you ran away, most of the ghosts chased you. I was about to go down to the Hole and get Donnie, but then that weird officer in the big hat was standing right in front of me, like he didn't even take a step, just zapped himself up the ridge."

Bobby swallowed, wishing he could take a sip of Vernon Ray's milk. "Christ. You got Col. Creep and I got the rest of the gang."

"It fits the transubstantiation theory. You gave off energy by running from them. Your fear fed them."

"Then they should be fat as Julie Houck, because I about crapped my pants. But what about you?"

"I wasn't really that afraid. More like curious, because I'm not sure these guys want to hurt anybody."

"Umm, dude. They were *shooting*."

"In quantum physics, reality is an ever-shifting set of illusions. It's energy changing form. Nothing to be afraid of, when you think about it."

"My head hurts," Bobby said. *But not as much as the bulldozer man's.*

"Forget all that for now. Col. Creep looked me in the eyes, I was as frozen as polar bear poop, and his lips moved under that gnarly mustache. He didn't make any sound but I swear I heard his words in my head. They said, 'This ain't your war.'"

"Ain't your war?"

"My first thought was that this creep was just like my dad. Keeping me out of the game. Out of sight, out of mind, like I didn't matter. Like I was a nuisance."

"Jesus, Vee. You need to see Gerhart." Bobby wouldn't have wished a visit to the sour school counselor on his worst enemy, but Vernon Ray had so many issues that even Dr. Phil would need an entire broadcast season to solve them.

"It ticked me off," Vernon Ray said, his grimace revealing a strand of beef caught between his teeth. "Here was some 200-year-old dead man giving me hell, like *he* had any more right to be on Mulatto Mountain than me. I'd say I had more right, since I'm alive and he's not."

"What was Donnie doing while this was going on?"

"What do you think he was doing? He's a moron. Drooling, spazzing, probably wetting his pants."

"Did you try to save him?"

"You kidding? I tried to run past Col. Creep when he reached out with one hand and touched my head. I mean, his fingers went *into* my skull and it felt like he was tickling me. I sort of spaced out for a while—it could have been seconds or minutes, it was like swirling down a Twilight Zone toilet. Then I heard a shot on the other side of the mountain and I snapped out of it."

"Yeah, I heard it, too," Bobby said, which was about all he wanted to give up at the moment. "I thought the bullet was headed my way."

"Well, you're still alive."

"Barely." He glanced over at Karen and the table of twittering, giggling honeys.

"When I came back around, Donnie was gone, and I knew they had him. I could see into the Hole and figured Col. Creep had either recruited him already and he was down in there behind the cave-in or he'd wandered off. So I grabbed our blankets and got the hell out of there."

"You weren't worried about me?"

"No, you're like a weasel, quick and sneaky. I figured I was easy meat."

"Easy meat?" Dex cut in, approaching their table with his bagged lunch. "Vern, you might want to keep that kind of thing to yourself. People are already starting to talk, if you know what I mean."

Dex smirked. Bobby flipped him a bird and pulled out the next chair so Dex could sit down.

"Speaking of talking," Bobby said. "How did your little meeting with the sheriff go?"

"He was just putting on a show. He gave me the standard line about trespassing and how even juveniles could get in big trouble for it, especially if they already had a record. 'Course, my dad was sitting there the whole time so I'm sure the sheriff toned it down a little. A couple of times he squinted at me like he wanted to grab me by the collar and shake the crap out of me."

"That would take a lot of shaking, you're so full of it," Vernon Ray said.

"Bite me," Dex said. "On second thought, never mind. You might like it too much."

Bobby looked at Vernon Ray. "Should we tell him?"

"Nah."

"What?" Dex said. "You guys got some action going on?"

Bobby brought out his digital camera. He powered it up and flipped through the thumbnails, tilting it forward so the two boys could see the images.

"So?" Dex said. "Looks like nothing but woods to me."

"They didn't show up," Vernon Ray said.

"What didn't?" Dex said.

"We went back to the Hole yesterday," Bobby said. "And we saw them."

"Saw who?" Dex was already bored and had turned his attention to the table full of cute girls. "Who's the redhead sitting next to Karen? She got nice knockers."

"Ghosts," Bobby said. "The dead soldiers at the Hole."

"You guys still into that?" Dex ripped open a Lunchables pack and shoved sandwich meat into his mouth. "The only hole I'm interested in right now is the one inside that redhead's panties."

"They're getting active," Vernon Ray said. "Undergoing some sort of transformation. Juicing up."

"You guys need to get out a little more," Dex said. "Look, I don't mind hanging around. You're both kind of weird, and that packs some entertainment value. But if you start taking this Jangling Hole stuff seriously, I might have to keep my distance for a while."

"Yeah," Vernon Ray said. "Wouldn't want you to be judged by the company you keep. Guilt by association."

"Whatever that means, yeah," Dex said. "If your I.Q. is higher than your bowling average, you ain't worth a turd."

"Give him a break," Bobby said. "Something weird is going on but you're too cool for Fool School."

Dex paused with a fruit roll-up dangling from his mouth. He looked around to see if anyone had heard Bobby raise his voice, which might have required a response that would confirm Dex's bad-assness. Everyone was too busy with their own adolescent identity crises to notice. Dex chewed for a moment, eyes narrowed.

"You guys can diddle each other to your Ghostbuster fantasies all you want, but don't drag me into it." Dex began shoving his leftovers into a paper bag. "Now, if you ladies will excuse me, I got business to attend to."

Dex sauntered over to the table where Karen sat, gave his money smile, and the redhead slid over to make room for him. Bobby's neck grew warm when Karen laughed at something Dex said.

Vernon Ray gave an exaggerated roll of his Bambi eyes. "He's an asshole but he knows how to work a crowd."

"Yeah," Bobby said. "So what's going on with the re-enactment?"

"Dad's polishing his brass, as usual."

"Big deal, huh?"

"Well, they're too old for video games, so what can you do?"

"You get to be in it this year?"

"Nah. Who wants to dress up funny and march around in the sun all day? Besides, Dad bosses me around enough as it is."

"He gets off on being the captain, doesn't he? And all that memorabilia and stuff must have cost a fortune."

"Yeah, Mom would give him hell except he deals some of the duplicates and makes pretty good money. Enough to pay for his hobby, anyway."

Bobby glanced over at the crowded table, hoping Karen would ignore Dex, but she was as enthralled as the rest of the girls. The redhead appeared to be brushing shoulders with him.

"Think that has something to do with it?" Vernon Ray asked.

"Dex being an ass-wipe?"

"No, the re-enactment. Like there's some kind of weird vibe that's waking them up. Maybe an echo of their war or something."

"Where do you come up with this stuff?"

"Comic books, TV, the Internet. It's not that weird. What's a ghost, after all? Why do they hang out in the places where they suffered some kind of pain? What's so strange about ghost soldiers waking up when they hear the drums of war?"

"Or maybe they don't like the fake soldiers pretending to be them."

"Well, who's real? The living or the dead?"

"I wish I'd never heard of Kirk's Raiders," Bobby said, again thinking of the bulldozer man and the geyser of red and gray as the back of his skull exploded.

"They let Donnie escape, so they must be under orders to take no prisoners."

"Yeah," Bobby murmured. "Take no prisoners."

"So we might just have to wait until the armies suit up for battle and see what happens."

"You sound like you're going to enjoy it." Bobby thought of his dad in a scratchy wool uniform, marching with a replica Springfield on his shoulder, sweating beer. Dad had served four years in the Marine Corps after high school, marrying Mom the summer his furlough came through. Dad often made smart-assed comments about "Captain Jeffie," but when the pretend battles started, Dad fell back into his buck-private days and ate whatever crap the officers dished out.

"We ought to go see the reporter," Vernon Ray said. "She writes those local ghost stories for the paper every Halloween. Maybe she knows something."

"Like you can trust a grown-up with this stuff?"

"We can pretend we're doing research. For class."

"Maybe."

The bell rang. Time for English. Dex and the redhead left together, and Karen was surrounded by her cutie-pie consorts. Bobby eyed the last three French fries on Vernon Ray's tray.

"You going to eat those?" Bobby asked.

"Knock yourself out."

Bobby ate them, though they tasted as cold and greasy as the waxy fingers of a decaying corpse.

CHAPTER NINETEEN

"You about scared the life out of me," Pearl said. "Both of you."

Hardy nodded and rubbed his chest, recalling the piercing pain and the desperate sucking for a breath that would not come. The bearded man—*GHOST, you old fool, it was a ghost as plain as day*—had touched him and sent him into darkness, but Hardy had awakened when the shot was fired.

He'd opened his eyes to Pearl's worried face looming over him, and he'd smiled at her, seeing her the way she was as a virginal teenager. He'd felt young himself, invigorated, as full of milk sap as a March dandelion.

Then he'd remembered Donnie, and he brushed aside Pearl's concerns and pleas, climbed over the fence, and staggered to the Hole, where he'd found Donnie with the sheriff and the newspaper reporter.

The sheriff had said there had been "an incident" and Donnie may have been involved, but when Hardy had figured out it was about the shooting, he'd asked the sheriff to sniff Donnie's hands for signs of gunpowder and made the sheriff look at his son's fingers, which flexed and twitched too spasmodically to ever be able to work a trigger.

"We're both fine and dandy," Hardy said to Pearl with fake bluster, winking at Donnie, who was huddled over his papers and crayons. Donnie grunted and gave a peacock's squawk.

"Well, I don't know how I'll ever be able to trust you with him outside again," Pearl said. She was rolling out some scratch biscuits and had a dot of flour on her nose that, despite her serious tone and mournful eyes, made her almost unbearably cute.

"We can't keep him in a cage all his life," Hardy said. "Might as well turn him over to the state if we're going to do that."

Though Donnie's strange autism gave the impression that words had no meaning to him, Hardy was uncomfortable talking about Donnie's fate within his earshot. But something had changed Donnie the day before, from the mad dash up the mountain to whatever had happened to him before the sheriff found him in the Hole.

His eyes held a peculiar light, and when Pearl had dropped the rolling pin and it rattled across the wooden floor, Donnie had snapped alert and grinned, tapping on the table with his fingers. Donnie's scribbles had also exploded with color, though the patterns seemed as random as always.

Pearl pounded her fist on the dough a little harder than was necessary. "I ain't the only one protecting him," she said.

"He's my son," Hardy said. "What do you expect?"

"I expect you to keep a better eye on him and not let him wander off like that. Who knows what might have happened if the sheriff hadn't found him?"

Hardy didn't want to explain that Donnie hadn't wandered. He'd made a direct line for the Jangling Hole, as if the path were laid with golden bricks lit by the sun. And Hardy was afraid the road was still open. "Well, we best keep him inside for a while," he said.

Inside. That meant either the special little hog pen Hardy had built for him or the kitchen with its gas stove and onions hanging from a string over the window. Steam from bacon grease had coated the ceiling yellow and a single bare bulb descended over the chipped cherry-top table.

The room smelled of coffee and cabbage, and as prisons went, Hardy supposed it could be worse. At least the windows had no bars and the fridge was open for business around the clock.

"*Snurk,*" Donnie said, joy splitting his face. He grabbed a crayon and worked his elbow in a dramatic flourish. He tossed the crayon aside and it rolled off the table, and before it hit the floor Donnie had another one, gashing at the page. He replaced the crayon again, and he was so aggressive with his scrawling that Pearl put aside her rolling pin and came to peer over his shoulder.

"What's that?" she said.

Pearl had been to the Hole several times, including once when they were young and Hardy had put the moves on her, which was expected behavior for teens of his generation. "Going to the Hole" was local slang for intercourse, and though Pearl had turned him down that day and stayed a maiden until their wedding night,

Hardy had made only a half-hearted attempt at lifting her skirt. He'd been too anxious about getting her away from there. So Pearl, despite knowing the ghost stories, had no real reason to ascribe any particular meaning to Donnie's drawing.

The black crevice wedged between gray stones and red-tinted trees was a clear reproduction of the Jangling Hole, and for the first time Hardy saw its resemblance to a woman's mysterious opening.

Donnie's newfound skill wasn't the only startling aspect of the artwork. Inside the waxy darkness, yellow splotches were suspended like stars against a night sky. Candles, maybe. Or the same shapes Hardy had seen flitting between the trees over the years.

"I need some eggs," Pearl said.

Hardy swallowed hard. Pearl didn't make out the geometry of the drawing, or else she was willfully ignoring the evidence of her own eyes. Pearl wasn't one for flights of fancy, but neither was she one to deny the signs that God shoved right in front of her face.

"That's a right good drawing, Donnie," Hardy said.

His son, apparently spent from his burst of creativity, sagged in his chair, mouth open, a strand of drool hanging from his lower lip. His face had gone slack again, the brief burst of light in his eyes now extinguished.

Pearl kissed the top of Donnie's ruffled head. "You just rest up now," she said, reaching over him and pushing the crayons away. She picked up the drawing, crumpled the paper with her flour-dusted hands, and carried it to the cast-iron woodstove. She tossed it inside and clanked the door closed, then turned as if a dead memory had been shelved in the root cellar and was nobody's business but the Lord's.

"How about them eggs?" she said.

Hardy knew that marriage was a long dance without music, and sometimes the toes of one spouse or the other were stepped on. Sometimes one of them even broke a foot or got crippled, or sometimes the partners each heard a different tune. But even when the steps were off kilter, you stayed on the floor and didn't walk out. And he couldn't walk out and leave a lie on the table.

"Ignoring it won't make it go away," he said.

"The Good Lord doesn't allow such shenanigans," she said. "Dead is dead except for them that dwell in the bosom of Heaven."

"The Good Lord gave us eyes to see with, and a tongue to call evil by its name," he said.

"Don't go giving me your kitchen-table sermons," Pearl said. "If the Lord was so wise and mighty and merciful, why did He do this to my Donnie?"

Hardy had asked that same question himself, both on his knees in the Baptist church and in the dark, wee hours of the night when only solitude and sweat filled the space between heartbeats. Despite all the cockiness of the preachers who claimed to speak on behalf of God, the Bible pretty much set everything down as a mystery, and even Jesus seemed befuddled by it all.

The sick, the halt, and the lame accepted their misery and sought solace in the promise of peace everlasting. But first they had to drag their pain over a long road to death's gate before they could cash in on the promise.

"This ain't just about Donnie," Hardy said.

"It is to me," she said. She folded her arms and Hardy knew the argument was over. He'd known the outcome before it had even begun. Pearl was that best kind of wife, one who brooked no bull manure in her mate but knew when to allow him to salvage a little pride, but when she made up her mind, even a divine thunderbolt would hardly shake her.

Donnie tapped on the table, tongue wagging. Hardy knew the rhythm. He'd heard it a few times too many lately.

"How many eggs you need?" he asked. "The guinea's been laying those blue eggs but they're kind of on the smallish side."

"Six, maybe. I'll make enough biscuits to last a few days so we won't have to run to the grocery store."

Hardy stopped by the back door to shrug into his jacket. He planned on spending a little time in the barn. The kitchen was getting a mite cramped.

"Set the latch," Pearl called after him, and Hardy was happy to oblige.

The early-evening air was crisp with autumn, and the smoke from the woodstove whisked in the breeze. The grass was sweet, its sugar breaking down under the chemistry of the first frosts. Cows grazed with their heads pointed toward the west, where the sun made its slow crawl over the Blue Ridge. The sky was bruised and brooding with clouds.

Hardy gathered seed corn and shoved a few dry ears into the grinder, turning the metal crank so the kernels spit out onto the packed-dirt floor of the barn. Chickens scurried out of their hidey holes at the familiar sound, and Hardy looked over the flock to see if any were healthy enough to serve up for Sunday dinner.

A rooster looked up, exposing its neck before strutting into the thick of the feeding frenzy. Hardy sized it up for an ax blade and decided the rooster was a good fit for the frying pan.

He was raiding the wooden boxes for eggs when a shadow separated from the corner of the barn and walked.

Hardy's heart sputtered and he was afraid he'd have another spell, maybe a full-blown coronary, and this time there was no healing touch around to restore his breath. He dropped the basket, breaking the four eggs he'd collected.

The shadow shifted toward shape, until the raggedy man stepped more or less whole onto the dirt floor. The man's eyes were black as roofing tar, empty and devoid of light. His clothes were threadbare, made of coarse material–a soldier's uniform so filthy it would never pass muster.

He moved toward Hardy without a sound, and Hardy knew enough of ghosts to stand aside and hope the dead man's business would take him off the farm. The man stopped in the center of the barn and stood in the swirling yellow dust as hay chaff appeared to float right through him. The face formed more fully and reflected back like a mirror spitting out a lost time.

"Get on, Earley," Hardy said, voice cracking. "You got no business here."

Earley Eggers turned toward Hardy, and Hardy backed up and fumbled along the wall for a sharp tool. No pitchfork, but he found a length of chain used to hang hogs for slaughter. He pulled it from its nail and let it clink.

*Time for some jangling of my own. Oh, Lord, grant me the strength to kill what's rightly already dead.*

He let a few feet of steel links slide between his hands, the hooked end swinging back and forth like the brass tongue of a grandfather clock. Earley's scruffy head tilted to one side as if listening to the wind leaking between the cracks in the siding. Hardy was about to offer up another prayer when the colonel came through the open barn door.

"Get on back to the Hole where you belong," Hardy said, but the colonel didn't even look at Hardy. If "look" was even the right word for what those midnight eyes did.

The colonel strode toward Earley, and Hardy sensed an air of odd familiarity, as if these two had shared the same dance floor in some distant past. The colonel's legs moved but his boots scuffed up no dry manure or straw. Earley retreated, except he didn't use his feet, he drifted as if he were sliding on a meat hook down a well-oiled cable.

The soldier had no weaponry that Hardy could see, and the colonel–*Kirk, you know it's Kirk, he was a bastard back then and he's a worse bastard now*–carried a sword tucked in its sheath. Hardy figured if it came to a throwdown, he'd put his money on the colonel, but you stayed on the side of blood kin even when it was the losing side. Through some peculiar witchery, the officer had probably saved him from a heart attack, but Hardy wasn't willing to contemplate the motive. Better to just thank the Lord for mercy.

And he wasn't even sure Earley qualified as "blood kin" anymore since his blood should have long since gone to dust. At any rate, the chain felt cold and limp in his hands, and Hardy felt foolish, like he'd brought a knife to a gunfight.

As the colonel closed in on Earley, other soldiers stitched themselves together from cobwebs and slivers of shadow, encircling their apparent quarry. Hardy recognized them from the fence line, the toothless man whose jaws twisted a plug of dark chaw, the gaunt teenager who looked far too young for service, the fat man with the red kerchief around his pale neck. They all wielded rifles, rusty muzzle-loaders from the looks of them but suggesting they could deliver some damage if necessary.

Earley turned in a slow circle like a lamb surrounded by wolves. *Well, you don't have to outrun them, Earley. You can just up and disappear. And that would be fine by me.*

But Hardy knew this showdown wasn't just North versus South, slave versus free, state's rights versus federal say-so. This was about territory, heritage, and family pride. It was bad enough when the spirits had stuck to their old haunts up on the ridge, but now they were tromping all over the proper boundaries.

Maybe no war ever really ended, not while its ghosts and echoes still hung like smoke over the land. Hardy rattled his chain, but no one noticed, so he let it drop to the dirt.

Earley's bony head swiveled as he took in the armed troop that surrounded him, then settled his gaze on Hardy. Though the dead eyes remained stovepipe black, the face around settled in an expression that might have been confusion.

*Don't blame you none. Life is supposed to be a one-night barn dance and there you are acting like you don't know where the door is.*

The soldier with the red kerchief leveled his rifle barrel, a blunt bayonet fixed on its tip. His eyes were as blank as Earley's but there was menace in his movement. Kirk nodded in silent command and the soldier charged Earley.

Chickens squawked and scattered, confirming that the soldiers were now solid and part of the same world that held Hardy trembling against the rough-sawn pine.

Hardy wanted to look away, knowing the images would paint his dreams for the rest of his life. But he stared transfixed as his barn became a bull run for the dead, the bayonet aimed for Earley's heart.

"Run, Earley," Hardy said, throat choked with chaff and fear.

Kirk drew his sword, and Hardy heard–or imagined–the snick of steel against leather. The bayonet soldier rushed forward, bent at the waist as if still beholden to gravity. Earley dived toward the horse stall, metal canteen bouncing against his hip, the toe of one boot flopping against packed manure.

The colonel moved forward with those weird, airy steps and swung his blade in a graceful arc. A swath appeared in Earley's wool tunic and the gap gave way to the dark substance of a sick galaxy, as if the man's form were stuffed with star crumbs and moon dust.

A howl erupted inside the barn, rattling off the support timbers, causing the hog to squeal in unease. The sound rose in pitch until Hardy thought his eardrums would pop. Then, when it seemed the stifling air could hold no more vibration, the howl ended, giving way to silence as Earley swayed in place for a moment, mere feet from the gate of the stall that likely would have afforded no escape anyway.

*The only escape for the dead is to get on the Golden Road and follow where God intended, and these Jangling Hole hideaways have defied their call to duty long enough.*

*Die proper this time, Earley. Please God, learn how to die proper.*

Earley's face was twisted not in pain, but in the sadness borne by the lost and the lurking. His flesh faded and the dirty clothes fell, leaving the dented tin canteen lying on top of the pile. The colonel stood over the now-vacant uniform, pale lips pursed amid his beard as if toting up another war casualty.

The revenant soldiers, now at ease, faded into the gloom until at last only Kirk stood, tugging at his matted facial hair. He nodded at Hardy in dismissal. Then he, too, joined the dusk and was gone, and Hardy stood in the dying cracks of leaking sundown until the canteen and uniform vanished, too.

Hardy went back to the house empty handed. Pearl's biscuits would just have to get by without eggs.

CHAPTER TWENTY

The newspaper office smelled like old comic books and even older coffee grounds.

Vernon Ray sat on a ratty sofa that looked like dogs and bums had shared it for a few decades. He'd never been in the *Times* office, at least not the section behind the classifieds counter where the typing and printing went on. He'd imagined stacks of mail, mountains of computer equipment, and rusty filing cabinets, and while he was not disappointed on those counts, the rest of the place was simply drab and cramped.

Crusading journalism was apparently a long way from Twain, Hemingway, Woodward, and Bernstein these days, with the corporate money shifting to sexier media. Cindy's cubicle was the only occupied one of the four that were tucked away in a corner of the warehouse. The rest of the space was filled with advertising slicks stacked on pallets, broken-down vending racks, and tall spools of leftover newsprint.

Cindy Baumhower had ushered the boys to her cubicle, which was adorned with pin-ups of press awards, kindergarten art, and Carolina Panthers photographs. "I couldn't resist an anonymous news tip from a couple of eighth graders," Cindy said, giving a pleasant smile with slightly crooked teeth that put Vernon Ray at ease.

Bobby appeared to be eyeing her breasts, and Vernon Ray gave them a glance, too. The shapes suggested beneath the taut cotton blouse were artistically pleasing, but they didn't give him a zing of electricity. They might as well have been decked-out party balloons for all the thrill it gave him. He felt like he was missing out on something, but he wasn't sure what, or if he should be upset about it.

"I guess it wasn't anonymous once we gave our names," Bobby said.

"Well, I'm good at protecting my sources," Cindy said. She

nodded toward the glassed-in office across the room, where a bald man with a janitor-broom mustache fidgeted with a page-layout program. On the window was a sign printed in large block type that said, "Don't Feed The Editor," and under that, someone had scribbled with a marker "dirty copy!!!"

"We trust you," Vernon Ray said, though he wasn't sure they could. She was a grown-up, after all, and she seemed like the no-nonsense type, despite the collection of fast-food Harry Potter figurines lining the top of her computer monitor and her Halloween articles on local haunted hot spots,.

"Fine, then, let's get to it," she said. "I've got a deadline in two hours."

"This might take longer than that," Bobby said. "This might take forever."

Vernon Ray figured it was Bobby's way of flirting, but his best friend was too vacant-eyed and unfocused. Vernon Ray put his camera on the reporter's desk. The thumbnail setting showed the Jangling Hole and a vague wisp of white fuzz against the dark opening. "We took this up at Mulatto Mountain," he said.

Her eyebrows arched as she brought the camera view screen for a closer look.

"Bill Willard's property?"

"The Hole," Vernon Ray said, noticing Bobby was still zoned out. "You wrote about it a couple of Halloweens ago."

"Kirk's Raiders, yeah," she said, peering at the photo. "Unfortunately, there's never been any solid evidence to support the legend."

"We've got plenty of unsolid evidence," Bobby said.

"'Unsolid' isn't a word," Vernon Ray said. "I think in ghost-hunting nomenclature it's 'insubstantial.'"

"So you fellows are ghost hunters?" Cindy said, her smile displaying no hint of a smirk.

"I don't think we hunt so much as get hunted by," Vernon Ray said. "We saw Col. Kirk and his Raiders yesterday, and the night before that, we encountered a soldier we believe must have escaped from the Hole."

"Let me download this so I can blow it up." Cindy poked a cable into the digital camera's port. After clicking her mouse, she said, "Assuming I believe you guys, why do you think the ghosts exist? What are they after?"

Vernon Ray and Bobby shared a glance. "We were hoping you'd tell us," Vernon Ray said. "We read comic books and watch *Ghost TV* like everyone else, but we're basically grasping air on this thing."

Cindy clicked until the photo filled her screen. Enlarged, the wisp took on the indefinite shape of a man, though no features stood out that would have suggested he was a long-dead soldier.

"Looks like he's trying to power up," Cindy said. "Like he doesn't quite have enough juice to grow meat."

*Jeez Louise, she believes us.*

Vernon Ray had almost hoped she would have laughed them out of the office. Because now they had to explain what was happening, and neither of them was sure what was real and what was the work of comic-book-geek fantasy. Vernon Ray described his experience in the Hole, when he thought he was being dragged into the cold darkness while Bobby waited outside.

Then Bobby told her the story of the soldier on the tracks whose feet didn't touch the ground—"And he had an authentic Confederate canteen," Vernon Ray threw in—and then Bobby said someone in the cave, or maybe the Hole itself, had whispered "Early."

They then took turns telling about their stake-out of the Hole and how Donnie Eggers had wandered up crazy-eyed and spastic, with the ghosts solidifying around him. Through it all, Cindy sat soberly, occasionally glancing at the digital image.

"And then they shot the bulldozer guy," Bobby said, staring past Cindy at an Audubon calendar featuring the saw-whet owl.

"*Do what?*" Vernon Ray said, unconsciously picking up one of Bobby's pet phrases.

"They popped out of thin air and shot him," Bobby said. "I thought they were shooting at me, and he got in the way or something."

"Dang it, Bobby," Vernon Ray said. "Why didn't you tell me?"

Bobby's eyes looked sunken and glassy, as if he'd aged two decades in a heartbeat. "I was scared Col. Creep would come after me."

"You're saying the ghosts shot Carter Harrison?" Cindy said.

"I saw it with my own eyes, but don't ask me for no proof," Bobby said. "Because the proof vanished into thin air."

"Why didn't you report it to the cops?" Cindy said.

"I couldn't even tell my best friend, much less sit in front of Littlefield and his goon squad," Bobby said, defensive.

Cindy nodded. "Can't say I blame you."

Vernon Ray, however, *could* blame him. After all, the shooting proved that ghost bullets could become solid, and Vernon Ray could have been killed, too. Except—

*Except I sort of think they LIKE me.*

He stomped that thought down and offered up his and Bobby's theory of transubstantiation. "Maybe they got something in the Hole charging them up," he said. "Underground volcano, uranium, something weird like that."

"Some say ghosts get solid by drawing on energy around them," Cindy said. "That's why you get cold spots—they take heat from the air."

"But that still doesn't explain why the bullets got real, or why they shot the bulldozer dude," Bobby said, sagging with relief.

"Or what they want in the first place," Vernon Ray added. Vernon Ray wanted to punch him on the arm for holding out, but it would only hurt his fingers and Bobby wouldn't even get a bruise.

"This ghost you saw on the tracks," Cindy said. "Was it near town?"

"In between town and the Hole," Vernon Ray said.

"Okay, try this," Cindy said. "Your railroad ghost escaped from the Hole somehow, and he has more energy than the others. This Col. Creep, as you call him, wants him back. Military desertion carries a death sentence, and I don't see why that would change just because they all happen to be ghosts."

Cindy was interrupted as a warehouse door rose in a screech of tortured metal, and a forklift motored in and took away a pallet of circulars. Vernon Ray and Bobby leaned forward as she continued.

"Now, the problem with that theory is we'd have to figure out why the deserter is able to get away from the mountain while the others can't," she said. "Otherwise, we'd have a rash of sightings in town."

"The other problem is that these ghosts can kill you," Bobby said, his face blanching a little as he recalled Carter's death by supernatural firing squad.

Cindy gave a grim nod. "We'll get to that later."

"We might not have much 'later' if these things start spilling out all over the place with guns," Vernon Ray said. "If people thought Kirk's Raiders were a pain in the rump back in 1864, just wait until they get a load of this bunch."

Cindy bent over and slid open a bottom drawer of her desk. Vernon Ray glanced at Bobby and saw that his eyes had widened and focused on the neckline of her blouse. Vernon Ray followed his gaze and observed the soft, pale swell of Cindy's breast straining against the hem of a peach pastel bra. Bobby's tongue unconsciously protruded a little, settling on his lower lip like Cleopatra's asp on a warm Nile rock.

Vernon Ray swallowed a sting of bitterness and watched Cindy pull out a sheaf of yellowed papers and curled magazines. She spread them on the desk and thumbed through them.

They were local Civil War records, many of them duplicates of material tucked away in The Room. Vernon Ray had read them during his incursions into Dad's hallowed bivouac, and though he was no expert on Kirk's Raiders and Stoneman's Raid, he recognized some of the faces in the old portraits.

"You said the Hole whispered 'Early,'" Cindy said, turning her intense gaze to Bobby, who visibly flinched.

"Yeah."

"It wasn't 'Early' like 'late,'" she said. "It's a name. E-a-r-l-e-y.'"

She slid a document to the edge of the desk. The face with the severe eyes glared up at Vernon Ray.

"It's him," Bobby said.

"Corporal Earley Eggers," Vernon Ray said. "Now I remember the name from dad's muster rolls."

"Member of the Pickett Home Guard," Cindy said, reading from the records. "Reported missing in action during Stoneman's Raid."

They turned as a throat cleared and the editor stood at the

cubicle opening, idly rubbing his hand over his protruding belly. His eyes were pooched out and bloodshot, face pinched as if he'd been deciphering hieroglyphics by candlelight. He nodded at the boys, and Vernon Ray smelled a mix of fried chicken and sweat beneath musky cologne.

"I've got to send this to plates in fifteen minutes," he said to Cindy. "Anything breaking on the Harrison shooting?"

Vernon Ray glanced at Cindy, sensing Bobby's held breath. Cindy's face lost some of its animation and grew almost placid. "Nothing. Sheriff still has no comment."

The editor stared past her as if imagining a bland banner headline. "'The investigation is continuing,'" he said in a monotone.

"You got it."

"I got nothing, you mean."

"I'll stay on it."

"What's that on your screen? Looks out of focus."

"More nothing. A whole bunch of nothing."

The editor settled his bleary, diffuse gaze on Vernon Ray. "So, you fellows win a Boy Scout badge or did I get lucky and you're outing a perverted principal?"

"Boy Scouts," Vernon Ray said.

"Safe as milk," Bobby said.

The editor nodded, already drifting toward tomorrow's front page and consigning them to community news on page 12. After he wobbled away, Cindy held up the portrait of Earley Eggers.

"The Eggers family was among the original European settlers here," she said. "Migrated down from Pennsylvania in the late 1700's. They used to own a thousand acres, reaching from the valley to the top of Mulatto Mountain. They named the mountain after a mulatto—that's a half-white and half-black, in case you didn't know—runaway slave who hid out on the mountain."

"So maybe Earley's spirit has a stronger connection to the land," Vernon Ray said. "You always haunt the places you love or hate the most."

"That's dorky," Bobby said.

"I think he's tired of the war," Cindy said. "He's ready to go home."

"Laying down his weapons," Vernon Ray said.

Bobby shook his head, his mouth twisted to one side. "And run up the white flag? I don't think Kirk and the boys will go for that. The question is 'What are we going to do about it?'"

"Prove it, for one thing," Cindy said. "I admit, I'm a sucker for this kind of stuff, but most people would dose you with some serious medications if you sold them this kind of supernatural fairy tale."

"We've got the photos," Vernon Ray said.

"I could fake that in Photoshop in 30 seconds," she said.

"Then how do you know we aren't spinning a whopper?" Bobby said.

Cindy gave a grim smile. "Your eyes. They're war-torn, like you've both seen some stuff you wish you hadn't."

"Okay, we're on the same page, even if it's a page from *Freakly Weekly*," Vernon Ray said. "What next?"

"I'm sure you guys heard in science class that matter and energy can't be created or destroyed, it only changes form," she said.

"Yeah," Bobby said. "Einstein and that crap."

"So how do we prove that this energy has become matter? Spirit made flesh?"

"Well, I don't know what counts as solid evidence," Vernon Ray said, fishing in his pocket. After a moment's struggle, he tossed the filthy scrap of gray wool on Cindy's desk.

She poked it with a pencil as if it were a rattlesnake skin, then picked it up.

"Found it in the Hole," Vernon Ray said.

"Fabric from the war would be long rotted by now," Cindy said.

"Along with the meat that wore it," Bobby added.

"So something's making them real again," Vernon Ray said.

"If we agree that these ghosts are somehow powered by emotional energy, whether it's love or hate or pain or fear, then we need to restore balance."

"Balance?" Vernon Ray said. He was picturing some kind of Star Wars machine, a monster-sized electronic zapper that could scramble the ghosts' electromagnetic field and blast Col. Creep and his Raiders back to ether, where they could be sucked into a cosmic vacuum cleaner and stored until the end of time.

"If one escapes, they need to draw another soul back to the Jangling Hole," Cindy said.

Shivers crawled up Vernon Ray's neck as he recalled the cold hand gripping his wrist and tugging him toward the black bowels of the Hole.

"No escape," Bobby said. "Even when you're dead, you got to belong somewhere."

*Belong.* Vernon Ray wondered if he'd ever belong anywhere, on either side of the cemetery fence.

"So we've somehow got to lure Earley Eggers back to the Hole," Vernon Ray said.

"Or they'll take a replacement," Cindy said.

The ensuing silence was broken by a mechanical whirring and clatter as the presses kicked in behind the cubicle wall, rolling out the afternoon's edition.

*Great,* Vernon Ray thought. *The good news just keeps getting better.*

CHAPTER TWENTY-ONE

*The Titusville Times* had downplayed the shooting death, just as Cindy had promised. The article had suggested a hunting accident, with Littlefield quoted as believing the shooter could have been miles away and not even been aware of the accidental target. He'd issued the usual call for anyone with more information to step forward, and besides the victim's family ringing his phone off the hook, the public seemed content with the explanation.

As for the family, Littlefield had alluded to the possibility of suicide, and despite the shame he'd felt over the tactic, it worked: The survivors gathered among themselves and whispered about the possible shortcomings, debts, affairs, or mental defects Carter Harrison had hidden for all those years.

"The incident is still under investigation," the sheriff said, quoting himself before tossing the paper on his desk.

Because Cindy had scooped the regional dailies, they took her story for the Associated Press wire and the mystery was safely blanketed. Littlefield was getting good at cover-ups, and he wondered what other lies he'd have to spin before he retired and how many more corpses he'd leave behind. He sipped his coffee and it was as cold and bitter as the hole in his chest.

Sherry waded through the door, making a rare sojourn from her dispatch desk. Movement was unnatural for her, as if her gelatinous flesh had never quite connected to her skeleton. Littlefield wondered how her husband handled her in bed, and turned his thoughts away before he got to the point of a Sherry-in-the-buff visual.

"Jeff Davis is here," Sherry said. "The Living History group needs a permit for this weekend."

Littlefield wondered why Sherry hadn't simply pressed the intercom button as she usually did. As she made her way past his desk to the little refrigerator, he understood. Morton had left some Girl Scout cookies in the freezer and Sherry liked to raid the stash, taking two or three in the belief that nobody would notice.

She trusted Littlefield not to rat her out, and the sheriff liked to tease Morton about his inability to solve the crime. At least he had back in the days when cookie crumbs were the most important business of the day.

"I thought they got that through the town," the sheriff said.

"That's for use of public property," Sherry said, stuffing a coconut cookie in her mouth.

The re-enactment events were usually held at Aldridge Park, a piece of donated land at the base of Mulatto Mountain. Littlefield wasn't sure he wanted a few hundred people piled up within spitting distance of the Jangling Hole, and wondered if he could concoct some sort of problem that would allow him to change the location.

Maybe an anonymous threat of violence, somebody protesting the Confederate flag, or a Homeland Security alert. Feed people the image of a brown man with a bomb and you could pretty much get them to do anything you wanted.

"You got all the paperwork?" he said.

"Yeah, but he needs a permit for the guns. They use real guns in the event."

"All right, send him in," he said. "And thanks for keeping Morton's weight down. He's got his physical coming up."

"My pleasure," Sherry said, and Littlefield got the sense that cookies were one of her few pleasures besides crankiness. "I got some cherry jubilee for you to take to Perriotte."

"Will do." The deputy had made no progress, though his physical signs were stable and normal. Perriotte still manifested a strange form of waking coma, and though his eyes were open and he responded to some stimuli, he had not spoken since his admission.

The doctors were calling it a delayed form of post-traumatic stress disorder, probably caused by Perriotte's tour of duty in Iraq. Littlefield hadn't bothered to add his own theories to mix, but the discovery of Donnie Eggers at the Jangling Hole had caused him to form his own diagnosis.

Jeff Davis was wearing work clothes but he topped it off with a felt cavalier's hat, a dandy peacock feather dancing from the headband.

"Don't tell me they wore that in the Civil War," Littlefield said. "Seems like the feather would make it easy for sharpshooters to pick off the officers."

Jeff adjusted the hat. "Those were different times. Officers usually were at the front of the charge, sometimes carrying nothing but a sword. The days of paper-pushing captains didn't come until later, when the military became a tool of the industrialists."

Littlefield gave a salute and indicated an empty chair before Jeff could launch into a lecture. "You fellows are using Aldridge Park, I hear."

"Yeah. We bivouac on Thursday, have open camp on Friday, and conduct the battle on Saturday."

"And Sunday is for nursing hangovers and cleaning up?"

"This isn't a party, Sheriff. It's an educational event, and a chance to remember."

"Sorry. Whenever I think about men, campfires, and tents, I form assumptions based on my personal experience."

"I hope your drinking didn't include firearms."

"Right. I assume you guys are firing blanks, right?" Even though the guns were mostly replicas, they functioned and their powder charges simulated the noise of actual battle. State law and courtesy required advance notification, both to head off E-911 calls and make sure the horseless cowboys weren't too reckless.

"Safety is our most important concern, and we're fully insured. Every participant has a permit to carry, even though technically it's not required if the weapons aren't concealed."

Littlefield had no doubt Jeff Davis knew the gun laws better than Littlefield himself did, and he wasn't particularly concerned about the fine print. "You heard about the shooting Sunday?"

"Yeah. That's a shame. Carter was a real decent guy. We were hoping to enlist him."

"Well, don't you think it might seem a little inconsiderate to hold a bang-up battle near the site of his accidental death?"

Jeff's eyebrows lifted at the word "accidental," and Littlefield wondered what sorts of rumors were circulating despite Cindy's snow job. "The Civil War is still the bloodiest conflict in American history," Jeff said, and Littlefield braced for the inner professor to emerge. "Hardly a square mile of territory was untouched by blood, misery, and sorrow, whether on the battlefield or the home front. When Stoneman and Kirk swept through here, there were plenty of atrocities that never made it into the books. Theft, looting, foolery with the women. Kirk had a stockade at Aldridge, and plenty of Confederate prisoners died there, whether from dysentery or the pistol of that crazy Union colonel."

"I heard a few escaped, with the help of some guards who deserted and fled with them."

Jeff smoothed his moustache. "The Jangling Hole, Sheriff. Quit pussyfooting."

"Yeah. The Hole."

"I focus on 'living history,' not the other kind."

"Well, you got to admit, we're all living history one way or another. Even if we make it up as we go along, it's still getting made."

"Legends get made, too. But I've never found any records to verify the legend. The Union Army kept diligent records most of the time, but the North Carolina mountains were largely rough frontier, and the Union soldiers were mostly bushwhackers and goons who were locally recruited. Kirk was a rogue from the Tennessee line who was only too happy to rile up his neighbors. Making him a colonel was like giving him a license to kill."

Littlefield wondered how the colonel would view his license if he were dead and beyond punishment. "Well, my job is to keep the county safe and uphold the laws," he said.

"We're not breaking any laws. We've been doing this every year for a decade."

"Yeah, but people are a little fidgety right now. A lot of peculiar things are going on."

"We have a permit to assemble and we've got a standing agreement to hire off-duty deputies as security. We pride ourselves on running a family event."

Littlefield glanced at the paperwork on his desk. "Real guns with fake ammo. Plenty of folks have been killed by guns they didn't think were loaded'"

"I'll tell you what, Sheriff. Why don't you come on out for the bivouac and take a look around for yourself? I'll be out there tomorrow with a few of the boys getting the grounds ready."

Littlefield nodded. He would likely find something wrong that would give him authority to shut down the event in the interest of public safety. The re-enactors would piss and moan, the local business owners would bang their empty tin cups, and somebody would write cranky letter to the editor, but the action would buy him enough time to figure out what was going on at the Hole. And, whether the fake soldiers ever knew it or not, Littlefield might just be protecting them from an accident or two.

"Okay, then, come out tomorrow." Jeff Davis stood, shoulders erect, chin tilted up. "The permit?"

The sheriff scrawled his signature and slid the paper to Davis, who carried it out the door. His hearty "So long, Honey" to Sherry was the last sound besides the slamming of the front door.

He reread Cindy's article. He was three paragraphs into it when the phone rang. Expecting Perry Hoyle's report, Littlefield snatched up the phone.

"Sheriff, it's Barclay."

Chairman of the county commission, a property lawyer with a hand in practically every square inch of disturbed dirt in Pickett County, and boyhood best buddy of Bill Willard. Just what Littlefield needed. "What can I do for you?"

"I heard from the Chamber of Commerce that you're trying to shut down the Living History event."

"That's a slight exaggeration."

"Do you know how many hundreds of people the re-enactment brings to town, and how many thousands of dollars they spend? They fill up the hotels, eat in the restaurants, and buy souvenirs in the shops. Some of them even look around, like the look and feel of the place, and decide to buy a mountain getaway, and that helps the local economy all the way down the line."

*All the way into your pocket.* "I can't worry about profit margin. I've sworn to protect the public."

"Don't forget you hold elected office. The same people who put you in can take you back out."

The next election was over a year away, and voters could drop old grudges and form new ones by then. "I like to think people put their trust in me because I always did what was best for the county," Littlefield said.

"You don't hear the talk," Barclay said, his silver-tongued delivery as persuasive on the phone as in the courtroom. "Ever since what happened at the church in Whispering Pines, you've been damaged goods. I've been working behind the scenes to prop you up because I know you're a good man. But don't push your luck."

First Willard and now Barclay. He resented being viewed as a puppet for Pickett County's rich and powerful. "I only push when I get pushed," he said.

In the ensuing silence, the scanner crackled and Littlefield missed the first few words. He moved the phone from his ear so he could hear Sherry speaking into the dispatch mike.

"10-32 at McAllister's Bowling Alley," Sherry said. "Suspicious person."

"Got to go," Littlefield said into the phone. "There's a voter in trouble."

"The chamber carries a lot of clout—"

Littlefield clicked Barclay cold and jogged through Sherry's office, wincing as his knees creaked. "What's the deal?" he said, not slowing.

"Some weird guy in rags, carrying a gun."

Littlefield stopped at the door. "Weird guy?"

"That's what Mac said, but you know how Mac is. He gets a little paranoid."

As Littlefield headed for his cruiser, he hoped the weird guy didn't arouse Mac's suspicious streak. For one thing, Mac had a licensed handgun on the premises and had used it two years ago to ward off a robber. For another, Mac might actually put a hole in the guy, and then the whole town would be left to figure out why the victim not only walked away without a scratch, but left no blood on the floor.

He kicked on the strobe and siren, getting across Titusville in four minutes by ignoring red lights and forcing traffic to the shoulder. By the time he'd reached the bowling alley, Morton was already on the scene and rubberneckers were lined up outside, peering through the front doors.

Old Loretta Mains wobbled out of the neighboring drug store, pecking along the sidewalk with her cane, but when she saw the gathering and Littlefield's cruiser, she straightened the hunch out of her spine and hustled to the action. A young man in a leather jacket obstructed Littlefield's entry, noisily berating someone through a cell phone. Littlefield nudged past but the guy swung his elbow without looking.

"Hey, watch what you're—" The guy's mouth froze open when he saw he'd just committed what might pass for assault on an officer, and Littlefield counted three gold fillings in his molars.

"Step aside," the sheriff said, and the guy rubbed a hand over his moussed hair and made room. Littlefield entered the alley, the smell of lacquer, hot dog chili, beer, and floor wax combining into a heady mix punctuated by the sweat of the working class.

Littlefield was not much of a bowler, though he'd taken a few of his less-sophisticated dates to the lanes and spent one desultory season on "The Tin Stars," the departmental team. However, he'd responded to more than one fracas at Mac's, and it was a popular spot for drug activity, despite Mac's cheery marketing of the sport as "Fun for the entire family."

Three years ago, a Mexican had been knifed and seriously injured behind the alley. Fortunately, the man was a migrant worker with a temporary green card for the Christmas tree harvesting season, or Titusville would have embraced the attack as a sign of the Apocalypse.

About half the lanes were in use, so any disturbance had since settled. The sound system was playing "Flirting With Disaster" by Molly Hatchet, the Southern rock pounding the walls. Morton was interviewing Mac, but most of the bowlers found their half-empty pitchers of beer more compelling than police paperwork.

"He had a pistol," Mac was telling Morton when Littlefield approached. Mac was waving his pointy finger around to punctuate the description. Mac's son Dex slouched behind the counter, wearing a sullen smirk.

Morton shot Littlefield a glance before returning to his clipboard. "So you've never seen this fellow before?"

"No, I would have remembered him, because he stood out in a crowd. Skinny guy, scruffy sideburns and mustache, eyes black as coal."

"And a gun?" Morton said.

"Sure," Mac said, shifting his gaze between Morton and Littlefield. "Hey, you guys think I'm making this up?"

"Nobody's saying that," Littlefield said. "Given the situation with your son, though, it seems mighty coincidental."

Dex took a swig of his Dr. Pepper and broadcast a liquid belch. "Give me a break, Johnny Law. What's the matter, too busy trying to pin charges on kids to go solve a real crime?"

Littlefield fought the urge to reach over the counter and slap the soft drink out of the brat's hand. He let his face go soft and blank. "Did you happen to witness the incident?" he said to Dex.

"Yeah, I seen him. Just like Dad said. Rough goon, looked like he wandered out of a Dumpster somewhere."

"Okay. Morton, finish up the report and I'll go have a look out back."

"Watch out for the other one," Dex said.

"Other one?"

"Guy dressed sort of like him. Same kind of raggedy-assed clothes. Except this one didn't have no gun."

"He was here, too?"

Dex waved his drink and grinned. "Nah, saw him the other night on the railroad tracks."

"What time of night?"

"Can't say, or you might try to nail me for a probation violation."

Mac smiled, showing polished teeth. "That a boy. All that lawyer talk is finally getting through that thick skull of yours."

Littlefield directed Morton to interview some of the bowlers, and then focused his gaze on Mac. The studied blankness fell away and was replaced by eyes that flinted sparks.

"Listen, Mr. McAllister. You can talk turkey baloney all day, and your son can sit here and learn to gobble. But I have the authority to shut down this place in the interest of public safety. Sure, you can hit the speed dial and get your attorney in under a minute, but by the time your challenge made it to a hearing, you'd be out a few weeks of income. Maybe even months, if I can sweet talk the D.A. better than your suit can."

Mac's upper lip curled. "I'm the victim here."

"Without a crime, there's no victim." Littlefield didn't exactly believe that, especially given all the innocent people who'd died on his watch. But he was talking property crime, not crimes against nature. And Pickett County seemed to be coughing up enough supernatural trespassers to keep the jail full until Rapture, if Littlefield ever found a way to bring them to justice.

Dex dropped his Dr. Pepper and the brown can rolled across the counter, spilling foam. The boy was staring at the far end of the alley, and Littlefield turned in the same direction.

"There he is," Mac shouted.

Dex ducked behind the counter. Littlefield braced himself against the expected vision of the haggard man in gray. He saw nothing but the oversize business logo on the wall.

Then an explosion slapped against his right ear, followed by the tang of gunpowder and the shrieks and shouts of bowlers, who scattered like pins in a dead-on strike. Littlefield clapped a hand over his ear before the next shot rang out, then whirled and chopped Mac's wrist against the counter, causing the revolver to clatter to the floor.

"Damn it, Mac," Littlefield said. "Have you gone nuts?"

Mac's face was purple with surprise and rage. "He was aiming right at me!"

"I didn't see a gun," Littlefield said. "And I didn't see the suspect, either."

Dex's head poked over the counter, just enough for him to glance around. "Yo, man, are you blind?"

Morton tried to calm what little crowd was left, though most of the bowlers had already fled through the front exit. "Shots fired," Morton shouted into his handheld radio. "Request backup."

"You see the suspect?" Littlefield asked Morton.

Morton shook his head. "Lucky nobody got hit."

"Guess we'll be shutting you down for a while after all," Littlefield said to Mac, who rubbed his swollen hand.

"Yeah, but the personal injury lawsuit will make back my money and then some."

Dex grinned, and Littlefield wanted to shove a fist down the kid's throat in hopes of teaching him some respect before he grew up into a big-league criminal.

He couldn't risk losing his temper. If Littlefield was suspended, Pickett County would be short one more officer, and there were already too many leaks in the dike and not enough fingers. Just when he thought the situation couldn't get any worse, Cindy Baumhower walked through the door.

CHAPTER TWENTY-TWO

"The old man's been hitting the sauce pretty hard lately," Bobby said.

"Hey, at least he's not hitting *you*," Vernon Ray replied.

"Not much, anyways."

They were in the woods on the hill above the trailer park, in a falling-down garden shed that had once been part of the Eggers farm. Virginia creeper and honeysuckle vines snaked though the gaps in the chestnut planks, and the rusted tin roofing was pocked with enough holes to let the evening sunlight waft through the dusty confines. Muddy spats of dirt dauber nests clung to the rafters and cobwebs sagged under their own tired weight.

The shed had become an occasional hangout when both boys wanted to dodge their parents. Sometimes Dex joined them, cracking jokes about Bobby and Vernon Ray "playing house." They kept stacks of comic books and magazines on the shelf where a bunch of glass jars stood in rows, their lids tight with grime and puffing from the pressure of their contaminated contents.

Vernon Ray sat on a wooden crate, flipping through a Wolverine comic. Bobby had started with Green Lantern, but he wasn't really in the mood for superhero fare. He tossed the book back on the shelf and thumbed through the stack of glossy magazines he'd filched from his dad's secret collection.

Bobby opened a *Penthouse* and turned to the centerfold. Photos of naked women made his heart beat faster, and he'd often played with himself while looking at what Jerrell called "stroke books." But these women scared him—they were painfully inflated, their breasts looked like they could explode any moment, and their faces were vacant and bored.

He often wondered if the naughtiness of the voyeurism turned him on more than the women did, with their unblemished skin and their finely trimmed patches of pubic hair. He'd glimpsed Karen's panties once as her skirt had lifted in a sudden autumn wind, and when his self-inflicted passion was peaking, he often closed his eyes to the magazine and let the image of her pink lace come to mind.

Once he'd whispered her name as he'd ejaculated, and it made him feel embarrassed and sick, as if he'd taken something from her without her permission.

"Hey, check this out," Bobby said, showing Vernon Ray the blond with the oversize rack. "Those nipples are as big as silver dollars."

Vernon Ray glanced up from his comic and grunted. "You seen one, you seen them all."

"No, V-Ray, these are like the Taj Mahal of titties."

"Whatever." Vernon Ray slapped at a fly.

"I'll bet she could make you howl at the moon and quack backwards like a headless duck," Bobby said.

Vernon Ray stood and slapped his comic to the ground. Bobby stood frozen, stunned by the sacrilege. Both boys were serious collectors who kept their books in mint condition, not just because of future appreciation in value but out of respect for the creators, the stories, the art, and the colorful magic of the medium.

"Why are you pulling that crap?" Vernon Ray said. "It's not like Dex is around for you to impress."

The magazine felt as heavy as soggy newsprint in Bobby's hand. "It's just a titty rag."

"What's next? Tell me not to get my panties in a twist?"

"V-Ray, I—"

Before Bobby could utter some lame comeback, tears welled in Vernon Ray's eyes and a sob broke from somewhere within his rib cage. All Bobby could do was look at the Wolverine on the packed dirt floor, one corner of its cover crinkled. Since it was a relatively recent issue, a damaged copy was worthless. He'd have to dig through the back issues at Planet Zero to buy a replacement and keep intact his sequential run, which dated to the year he was born.

He was grasping for something, anything, to avoid noticing that his best friend was crying. Guys had a rule: you could squeeze off a drop or two once in a while, if something really bad happened, like your dog got run over or your grandma died.

But you would wipe it away fast and everyone would pretend it never happened. The problem here was that Vernon Ray had launched into waterworks for no good reason.

If Vernon Ray couldn't clean it up on his own, Bobby had an obligation under the Unwritten Guy Code to change the subject. "Look, I know this Jangling Hole business has got us all a little shook up."

Vernon Ray moved his hands from his face, and to make matters worse, he looked directly at Bobby with dewy, bloodshot Bambi eyes. "The dead are the lucky ones," he said, sniffing.

Bobby let the magazine fall closed, though the flap of the centerfold still dangled, Miss September's bare legs framed against crushed black velvet. He didn't know what to do with his hands.

The air in the shed had grown thicker, as if the ancient chicken manure and sawdust had coalesced into composted spirits and risen from the floor to haunt his lungs. Vernon Ray's eyes were gray, the color of a warship on a roiling sea.

*Funny, you know a guy for years and can't remember the color of his eyes. But damned if they ain't a lot like mine.*

"Why do you shove that crap in my face?" Vernon Ray said. Bobby was relieved to note the sobs had subsided enough for his friend to complete a sentence.

"What crap?"

"Titties. Naked women. Macho crap."

"That's just what guys do. I mean, art is art and meat is meat, right?"

"I thought you'd be different, Bobby. I *know* you're different. Dex, he's a gorilla in training, he'll be getting girls pregnant in a couple of years and laughing while he drives them to the abortion clinic. Dorkus Dan and your football buddies, they have to put on a show. You know, the warrior thing. But you have feelings. That's why you stick by me when everybody else is snickering and lisping behind my back."

"Dude, you're my pal, and pals stick—"

"Drop the Owen Wilson stoner clown act. You know what I mean."

Bobby turned and set the magazine on the stack, taking more care than usual, pushing the pile around until all the corners were aligned. Little black dots of mouse turds covered the shelf and he wondered if rodents would chew Miss September's golden flesh to line their nests.

"I know your dad is a little distant," Bobby said to the wall. "We're alike that way. We don't know what real affection is, and it's kind of scary to think about. Me, at least I've got a brother, even if he's a lot older."

"That's not what I'm talking about."

Whatever Vernon Ray was talking about, Bobby didn't want to know. He'd rather hum some Coldplay or gossip about quarterback Eli Manning's hot new girlfriend. Hell, he'd rather talk about the war on terror, which was so removed from his daily life that it might as well be taking place in the Andromeda Galaxy with the Silver Surfer kicking suicide-bomber ass.

"I better be getting home," Bobby said, still afraid to turn and meet those red-rimmed, doe-like eyes with their thick curling lashes.

"Yeah, wouldn't want you to miss out on all the joyful warmth and love of the Eldreth home," Vernon Ray said with a sneer in his voice.

Bobby started for the rotted, gaping door, but his friend moved faster and blocked his way. They were several feet apart, and Vernon Ray's breath rushed in and out, the liquidity gone. Bobby looked at him.

Mistake.

Vernon Ray's head tilted forward, eyes flaring, eyebrows lifting, as if he were staring deep inside Bobby to a place hidden from everyone, a hollow cave Bobby had glimpsed in the mirror once in a while but so fleetingly that he could shrug it off as an illusion.

"V-Ray, this is weird."

"It's been weird for me since we were 10."

"I mean, weird like *weird*, you know?" Those gray irises were smoldering with mad yellow flecks, the red veins streaking against the white like lightning made of fire.

Vernon Ray stepped forward and grabbed Bobby's shoulders, pulling him forward with a strength that his scrawny 85 pounds shouldn't possess. Vernon Ray's head tilted up and his breath was hot against Bobby's lips and—

*Holy crap, he's trying to KISS me.*

Bobby shoved hard, his forearms up and elbows back like he was assaulting the tackling dummy in football practice. Vernon Ray flew backwards against the wall, shaking the shed with the impact, and a dried-out husk of harness fell from its nail and rolled across the dirt. The tin roofing squeaked in protest then settled. In the silence, Bobby's breath came fast and frantic and he waited for V-Ray's whimper.

Instead, his best friend looked at him from his crumpled collapse, a thin line of blood leaking from his nose. The corner of his mouth lifted. He was smiling.

"I've known it ever since we were down by the creek catching crawdads that day," Vernon Ray said. "You were on that big flat rock, your shirt off, glowing in the sun, your face so alive and happy."

Bobby had no idea which day Vernon Ray was talking about. They'd hunted crawdads many times, and goofing off at the creek was way better than hanging around inside the hot trailer, especially if Mom was around bitching for him to clean up the bedroom. "I don't remember—"

"July 7, three years ago."

"You're freaking me out, Vee."

Vernon Ray straightened himself until he was on his knees and bent before Bobby like a penitent before a stone idol. A shaft of sunlight angled so that it suffused his face. His eyes were shining again, but not with tears. "I love you, Bobby."

Bobby backed up a step. The path to the door was clear now, but he didn't trust his knees. Bobbing and weaving toward the end zone between 160-pound linebackers was no problem, but those five yards to freedom now seemed a hundred miles of toxic swamp. He cleared his throat but it felt like a corncob was rammed in his windpipe, dry and abrasive.

"I know you feel something, too," Vernon Ray said. "I've seen it in your eyes."

Anger cleared his air passage. "You ain't seen shit. You know how hard it is when everybody thinks you're a faggot? I hear the whispers, too. Hell, they drag me into it half the time, call me your

'Little butt buddy' and 'Tinkerbell.'"

Vernon Ray's eyes shut briefly, those long lashes curling up in delicate swoops. Closed, his eyes looked a lot like Karen's, and his mouth did, too, at least his full lower lip. Bobby's stomach fluttered as if a pack of moths had been let loose. This was getting confusing.

"I know, and you still stick by me," Vernon Ray said. "That says a lot."

"That don't say nothing. You're my pal. Read comic books, shoplift once in a while, sneak the old man's beer, cheat on school tests together. Guy stuff."

"You're afraid, and I don't blame you. I've been afraid ever since I knew I was different."

"That's the trouble, Davis. You're a different kind of different." He hoped using Vernon Ray's last name would move things back to solid ground, a normal footing that would allow them both to walk away and pretend this had never happened.

Vernon Ray put his palms on the ground and leaned toward Bobby, then slid his knees forward, jeans rasping in the dirt. He was crawling like an animal, and his eyes radiated a strange gleam that was nothing like Bobby had ever seen in Karen's.

"Stay away, V-Ray," Bobby said. "Don't make me have to punch you."

Vernon Ray moved forward, *rasp rasp rasp*, breathing evenly, while Bobby's heart knocked against his ribs like a broken crankshaft in a tractor.

"Don't deny it," Vernon Ray said. "It's just you and me and God. Dex isn't around to catch you and God doesn't care."

Bobby backed up another two steps, glancing toward the door, almost afraid to let his eyes leave Vernon Ray. A shadow fell across the opening, and Bobby just knew it was Dex.

*Great, he'll tell everybody he caught me with my "boyfriend" on his knees. I'm frigging doomed.*

But at least Dex would kill the scene, disturb the private moment that was making Bobby nauseated, lightheaded, and off kilter. Ghosts were one thing, he'd come to accept them because he trusted his own eyes, and in a strange sort of way, they made sense. You died and you didn't want to leave, so you hung around a while and checked things out, maybe engaged in a little vandalism for entertainment. No biggie.

But *this* —

As the shadow grew, moving closer to the shed, Bobby wondered if his reaction would be the same if it were Karen at his feet, getting ready to worship him in whatever sublime fashion his mind and body could concoct.

Would he be sick and nervous, or would he be the cool jock stud he'd imagined?

And, worse, was there really any difference, when you got down to it?

The shadow crept, swelling larger, too tall to be Dex. Jeff Davis? One of the Eggerses? Or, Christ, his drunken *dad*?

In the hush punctuated only by Vernon Ray's rasping jeans, Bobby should have heard footsteps. Instead, all he heard was the roar of blood in his ears.

"I told you I love Karen," he said, extra loud, so whomever was approaching could hear. "I've been nailing it all semester."

He would have been thrilled to hear Jerrell, Dex, or anyone come back with, "The only thing you've been nailing is your own five fingers." But there was only the silent, encroaching shadow.

"We both know the truth," Vernon Ray whispered. "You and I are the same."

"No, we're not the same. I *like* looking at titties and some sweet pink. I don't love guys. And I don't love *you*."

Bobby didn't realize he'd been shouting, nearly screaming, until his mouth fell shut and the echo died away among the tin and timbers. The doorway was filled now and he looked away from his kneeling friend, who was now scarcely three feet away, his head uncomfortably close to Bobby's crotch and the electric warmth that had collected there.

The heat turned to needles of ice.

Col. Creep stood in the doorway.

He looked more solid than he had two days ago, when he'd issued the silent command that led to the bulldozer guy's death. As if racking up a body count did wonders for the spirit.

*He's real again, and I'll have to run right through him to get out the door.*

Bobby shivered at the thought of penetrating that cold ethereal flesh.

The dead officer's eyes glared out from beneath the brim of his slouch hat, glinting as if backlit by the hearths of hell. The hairs of the bushy beard seemed to writhe and twist like thin serpents. The man's pale skin was stretched tight around the bones of his face, and his lips pursed as if he were amused at the tableau before him.

Then again, when you were released from the bottomless pit of the grave, maybe the living were nothing but entertainment.

"Vuh—vuh—," Bobby stuttered. "V-Ray?"

The officer rubbed his beard with his left hand while his right stole to his scabbard and fondled the hilt of his sword.

Vernon Ray looked up at Bobby, palms pressed flat on the ground. His eyes were glazed and faraway, his mouth open and the tip of his tongue poking through. His friend was under some kind of weird spell, and Bobby wondered if a ghost who could order dead soldiers to shoot invisible rifles using real bullets had the power to make somebody do things they didn't want to do.

Because Bobby didn't want to stand there a second longer, but his legs wouldn't work, the wiring between his muscles and brain short-circuiting.

Col. Creep drew his sword with a metallic *snick*, the first sound he'd made.

Vernon Ray turned at the sound and almost nodded, as if he'd expected company. An audience for his coming-out party.

The officer stepped into the shed and pointed his sword at Bobby's chest. Bobby swallowed and it felt like chunks of brick and broken glass worked their way down his gullet and into his gut.

The sword didn't look invisible at all, and the polished metal caught the sunlight.

Bobby wondered how it would go down with his friends. Would he get a funeral and everything? Would he be the first of his class to die in a freak accident? How would the sheriff and the newspaper write this one up?

Even more importantly, where would he end up? Trapped in a casket for eternity, or was his hasty and enforced acceptance of Jesus in Barkersville Baptist enough to get him a ticket on the Big Elevator?

Or maybe he'd wind up in the Hole, the newest member of a troop destined to haunt the chilly hollows of Mulatto Mountain until the end of time.

The officer flexed his wrist and made three waves of the sword.

*Motioning me to the door?*

Vernon Ray nodded up at Bobby, telling him it was okay, that at least one of them would live. And Bobby's cheeks were hot and wet, and he realized it was his turn to cry, and he wondered if V-Ray was right. He didn't love the guy, not in *that* way, but maybe Bobby was different, too.

As he stumbled near-blind to daylight and freedom, Vernon Ray called out. "I'll be okay, Bobby. Don't worry."

Bobby paused at the door. Vernon Ray was now standing near Col. Creep, whose sword was lowered. The ghost looked almost paternal, not at all like the mean freaky phantom that would have sliced off his head moments before.

Bobby turned his face to the golden sunshine, the blurred forest, and an escape whose only price was the betrayal of his best friend. As he ran, his feet hardly touched the ground.

CHAPTER TWENTY-THREE

The saber hovered in the air, licked with the flames of dying sunlight.

Vernon Ray stared at it, transfixed by the dance. It lifted, came closer, swayed, grew larger in his vision until it filled the shed. It was real, he knew, as solid as anything this world had ever hugged to its gravity. And it could cleave him, lop off his head, remove his heart.

Yet he couldn't move.

The saber came closer, the shadows somehow growing deeper in the skewed corners of the lean-to. Vernon Ray settled on his folded legs, knees chafed from the crumbling dirt. His pulse rattled out a syncopated reveille, one that screamed "Retreat!" But his muscles were jelly clinging to icy bones.

The sharp steel hung motionless for a long moment. Branches brushed against the tin eaves and the old planks creaked against the Halloween breeze. Vernon Ray forced his gaze away from the killing blade and along the arm that wielded it, up the crinkled cloth of the sleeve to the terrible face.

Kirk's skin rippled like linen on a line, shades of light and dark interweaving and stitching gossamer flesh. Dark beard and eyes swam in the shifting shadows, and Vernon Ray felt the temperature in the room drop. Goose bumps rose on his neck and arms.

*He's sucking me. Taking my heat.*

The colonel tilted his head back, mouth open as if exhaling a long sigh of the grave. Amid the stained enamel of teeth, things squirmed and writhed. Vernon Ray expected something to spill from that mouth, moans or marching orders, but if anything came, it was lost in the wind that stole between cracks.

The saber lifted, higher and closer, pointed toward heaven as if gathering its strength from some distant and magical source. But Vernon Ray knew any power the colonel had was power that Vernon Ray offered. Willingly or not.

"Go ahead and kill me, so it will be over," Vernon Ray whispered through parched lips.

At least Bobby would escape, and probably cry at his funeral, and his dad would stand there in his formal best, Mom dabbing her damp mascara with a cotton hanky, all the kids from school squirming in pews, the First Baptist Choir singing "Amazing Grace" and Preacher Staymore dishing up a eulogy that sought more to save any heathens in attendance than to celebrate Vernon Ray's deliverance.

And as the casket was lowered into the cold red ground and the mourners filed away, Dad might linger a moment as the diggers sat on their tractors at the edge of the burial lawn like vultures. And Dad might frown at his lost little soldier, maybe secretly toss a valued relic the way others laid flowers. Perhaps a canteen, a cap, a dull brass medal, a mini ball, something to seal a connection that had never been forged on the Earth. A piece of history to carry on the endless journey, a history from some other time and not the recent one they had barely shared.

It didn't matter if the hole were jangling or whether it was six feet deep and trimmed to rectangular precision. When you went in, it was forever.

Col. Kirk held the saber aloft as if celebrating its profane menace.

And Vernon Ray waited for it to fall.

*Close your eyes. You don't want to watch your own head bouncing in the dirt.*

But he couldn't look away from that face and those eyes that were long, black roads of misery and sin. Kirk was said to have been a cold-blooded murderer, a horse thief, a rapist who would burn churches and piss out the embers. But those eyes held none of that rage, only a vast emptiness, the ethereal flesh around them swirling like star mist into unquenchable black holes.

Then the eyes glimmered, bits of hellfire or stray sundown.

In the stillness of the shed, at that moment of surrender, Vernon Ray felt a peace descend and settle on him, wrapping him in a protective warmth that would repel any blade or bullet or hateful words. His heartbeat, which had jumped to jackrabbit speed when he'd professed his love for Bobby and then kicked a gear higher when the colonel had appeared, slowed to a steady thud and he was aware of his blood flowing through his body, the pulse pushing life to his limbs. For the first time in thirteen years, he felt *alive*, and he laughed aloud at the irony that only impending death could have triggered the feeling.

*I surrender, but you take no prisoners.*

The saber poised.

And then lowered.

Slowly.

Down, down, arcing into its scabbed sheath.

It slid home with a war-weary whisper.

Vernon Ray waited, not sure if the man would speak—*could* speak—and the silence stretched like a glistening spider web. He wondered if Bobby would tell anybody, then decided the colonel's glowering eyes had contained enough threat to keep Bobby shivering under his blankets for a month. Vernon Ray finally looked up and the colonel reached into a bulging pocket of his tunic. He came away with a wad of gray fabric and thrust it toward Vernon Ray.

The boy studied those Jangling-Hole eyes for any sign of sleeping humanity. Only the long promise of night resided there. But the man nodded, in much the same way he'd motioned Bobby toward a hasty retreat, with a fluidity that was more liquid than muscle.

Vernon Ray reached for the fabric, his fingers brushing the icy ethereal mist of the officer's hand. It was a kepi, topped with frayed wool and banded with brown leather, the canvas bill creased and stained. The colonel's coal-black eyes narrowed, somehow no longer menacing, but strange and chilling all the same.

The eyes were almost kind. Almost fatherly.

But Vernon Ray shook that illusion away—this man had killed, captured, and maimed, he'd carved a red swath through these mountains, and the old settling families still used "Kirked" as a verb for wrongdoing. Sin could burn and embers cool to ash, and the dead could be forgiven but never forgotten.

Vernon Ray swallowed corncob dust and, with a trembling

hand, placed the kepi on his head. It had been made for a boy and fit perfectly.

The colonel floated forward, looming over Vernon Ray, whose head tilted down to stare at dusty, stained boots. Then the cold fingers were on his chin, lifting his face, and Vernon Ray wondered wildly if the colonel wanted what Bobby hadn't, if the cold company of the Jangling Hole had left Kirk as lost and alone on the other side as Vernon Ray was on the side of the living.

But the bearded mouth and wedge of cheeks and forehead visible beneath the broad hat's brim showed no hunger or passion. The fingers, as soft and cool as salamanders in a muddy spring, slid along the curve of Vernon Ray's jaw and stroked his hair. Then the hand gripped his shoulder with a strength that could have crushed granite and clawed its way out of any cave-in.

Words wended through the air, or maybe it was only the creak of rafters, or language leaking into him from the medium of necromantic connection:

*We don't belong together.*

The words made no sense, but Vernon Ray wasn't sure if they'd fallen properly in the carousel of his thoughts.

The hand lifted Vernon Ray, peculiar electricity shooting through the boy's chest, and he thought again of battery charges and energy transformation. Vernon Ray now stood chest-high to the dead man, legs weak and quavering

*He's draining my juice, just like the reporter said . . . .*

It was almost like an obscene dance of dust and air, Vernon Ray's partner literally light on his feet, swaying to an invisible music.

Then Vernon Ray heard it: the distant cadence of the snare drum, rolling over the ghost hills, insinuating itself in the currents of shiftless air, riding the dying autumn sky as if marching an exhausted battalion home.

The colonel's head lifted. heeding a call to arms, then his frigid fingers fell from Vernon Ray's body, going to mist, and the juice flowed backwards, the connection severed. Strength and vitality surged through Vernon Ray's limbs in a rush of warm blood.

Then the colonel paled, giving up the ghost yet again, the

threads of his illusive form fading. The officer's saber, sheath, and uniform with its dull brass insignia disappeared along with him, but the kepi remained, solid as the shed walls.

Vernon Ray reached up and adjusted the cap until the brim was perched over his forehead, shading his eyes against the death of day. The snare's soft rattle fell away to silence, and only the wind remained, pushing October on past so winter could bare its icy teeth and feed.

When twilight came, Vernon Ray left the shed, picking through trees, careful not to snag the kepi on any low-hanging branches.

CHAPTER TWENTY-FOUR

The uneasiness crept in like a rooster on crippled drumsticks.

Hardy stirred in bed under the heavy quilts. Pearl's snores were like the bleating of a lamb. She'd popped one of those blue pills Doc Sanderson had prescribed for her nerves, and those usually knocked her out pretty good.

The onions she'd cooked with the fried potatoes had tainted the room with oily air, but Hardy was nearly used to it by now. He couldn't blame the odor for his restlessness. After all, his old flannel longhandles were nearly stiff enough to stand in his boots and walk to the door by themselves.

The wind was flapping under the eaves, rattling the wooden shutters and causing the old farmhouse to shift and creak. The moon was up, its sick light sliding between the curtains and painting a green rectangle on the floorboards. Hardy strained his ears against the groaning of wood, listening for sounds from Donnie's room. As he rolled over, a quill poked through his feather pillow and stuck his cheek.

The thin hands of the dial clock on the night stand were pushing past twelve and beginning their slow drop into the wee hours. Hardy sat up with a creak of bedsprings. He could almost feel the sloping weight of Mulatto Mountain, its ancient swell of rock and soil crawling into the valley.

The mountain and its damnable inhabitants could fall into the sea, for all Hardy cared. Even without the ghosts, the mountain would soon be wrecked by security lights, vacation homes for rich folks, and paved highways winding across its face.

Just like when the Yankee raiders rolled through in 1864, the invasion was inevitable, and guns would do little to change the outcome. When the Yanks had done their dirty business and moved on, their lawyers sailed in on the wake and got themselves elected to local office, then proceeded to develop land-use ordinances that favored them and their friends.

The Eggers family had been lucky because their property was so steep and hard to farm that its value on the deed books was low. But the new breed of Yankee invaders put a premium on mountain views, so the steepest terrain had become the most expensive. Never mind that the wind hammered at those high houses and the well drillers had to go a quarter-mile deep in some places; the rich idiots were only there for a few weeks in the summer anyway.

Hardy moved to the window, his joints burning with arthritis. Since the incident in the barn, he'd kept to the house, and he wondered how long it would be before the whole mess blew over.

In his youth, back when Mulatto Mountain was in the hands of the Eggers family, the ghosts had been spotted here and there on occasion. Hardy had even glimpsed them a few times himself, faint wisps of mist cavorting through the trees. But he'd never seen them so up-close-and-personal—and as *real*—as he'd seen them when Earley had danced to the music of the colonel's sword.

As he peeked through the curtains, Pearl's snoring stopped. He half expected to see campfires on the mountain, as if the dead had decided to bivouac in the woods instead of the eternal dampness of the Hole. But the woods were dark and still, even near the turnaround where Budget Bill's bulldozers and trucks were parked. The air carried a cold weight, as if the killing frost was ready to descend from the North.

"You see anything strange?" Pearl said, her voice creaky with sleep.

He'd not told her about the incident in the barn. Lately, he'd kept a lot of things to himself, and he wondered if that was how marriages faded away until they went bust. "Nah," he said. "Just a mountain."

She got out of bed and Hardy heard the soft rustle of her slippers. "I'll go check on Donnie."

"He's all right," Hardy said without turning.

The shuffle of footsteps stopped. "You just keep watch and let me take care of my son."

Hardy nodded in the dark until the door closed. He switched on the bedside lamp and got his black-powder musket out of the closet. He'd seen an old episode of "The Twilight Zone" where a priest had killed a vampire by putting a silver cross on his bullets and shooting the creature through the heart.

Hardy didn't hold with the existence of vampires, but he figured if he was going to put his faith anywhere, it would be the Lord. That evening, he'd crept to the basement and melted down Pearl's silver chain and cross and fashioned the metal into three balls of shot. Three wouldn't be near enough, even if the silver had any effect on the dead, but their weight gave him comfort.

He opened the Eggers family bible, which had been passed down through four generations. Preachers had talked of the Holy Ghost, and Hardy wasn't sure how he'd feel about Jesus Christ's spirit drifting through the wall at any moment. But if the Good Book acknowledged the existence of ghosts, and resurrection was one of the juiciest parts of the entire tale, then maybe its pages packed a little bit of magical punch.

Hardy tilted his powder horn to sift some of the explosive substance into the barrel, then rolled in one of the silver balls. He ripped out a page from the Book of Acts and used his brass rod to pack it down for wadding to hold the shot in place.

"God, make me an instrument of your peace," he said.

The door squeaked open and Pearl padded into the room. "Is that thing loaded?"

"Just getting ready for trespassers."

"You ought not keep loaded guns where Donnie might get at them."

"Our son died ten years ago. He ain't nothing now but your 195-pound baby doll."

"Talk like that and you'll be sleeping in the wood shed."

"Fine way to talk to the man who put this roof over your head."

Pearl moved behind him, her reflection distorted in the glass. Her face was aged and sad, the lines deepened by the late hour and too-little sleep. He tried hard to see his young bride in those bloodshot blue eyes, but only pain looked back at him.

"What's happened to us?" she whispered.

Hardy laid the musket over his lap and waved toward the mountain. "The Jangling Hole happened."

She put her trembling hands on his shoulders. "Hardy, our

problem is in here, not out there. Our house has become a worse hell than anything a legend could stir up."

"I seen them. And look what they done to Donnie."

"Whatever it was Sunday—*if* there was anything—Donnie didn't get hurt."

"They didn't need to hurt him. They already took everything that mattered when they got ahold of him last time. They took his soul."

"And you call yourself a Christian. Donnie's soul was bound for heaven since he got saved and baptized. Ever since he was 6, his soul was set."

"Even if he don't know no better? At that age, you don't know what death's like. All you're doing is mocking back the words somebody put in your ear."

"Saved is saved. The Good Lord wouldn't have it any other way."

"I took many a comfort from the Bible," Hardy said, tapping the book. "But now I got to go with what I see with my own eyes and feel in my gut."

"Don't go turning your—"

*Ratta tatta tat.*

They stared at each other.

"Possum must have got in the attic," Pearl said, her hushed words barely audible even in the sudden silence.

*Tatta tatta.*

"Yep," Hardy said. "And it learned to carry a beat. Reckon we ought to catch it and put it in a circus."

"They're coming for him, aren't they?" Pearl pulled her bed robe tighter over her chest and held it with one trembling hand, as if somehow that would ward off invading spirits.

"They'll come sooner or later. But this time they ain't getting him without a fight."

The drumming rose from across the pasture, its origin difficult to pinpoint. Hardy peered out the window, expecting to see flickering campfires or a line of marching white wisps. Instead there was only darkness and the distant trees fighting off the autumn wind.

"How can you fight them, Hardy? You already turned your back on the one power in all the world that might beat them."

"There's two ways to look at it. Either the Lord has a reason for them to be here, meaning it's some kind of test, or the Lord has no power over them and we got to draw on what we can muster. Jesus is sitting on the sidelines for this one."

"It don't hurt none to pray."

*Ratta tatta tat.*

The drumming was closer now, between the house and the barn, and its percussion trailed off in an eerie reverberation. It was joined by another pounding, a deeper, hollow, less-rhythmic pulse. Coming from across the hall.

Pearl moved first but Hardy, his arthritis screaming like salty lime in an open sore, reached the door before she did. As he stepped in the hall, the room to Donnie's door shook in its frame.

"Donnie!" Hardy yelled, leaning the musket against the wall. His son threw himself against the door again, the wood around the hinges splintering with the force of the blow. Another meaty thud sounded as the snare drumming grew louder.

*They're on the porch.*

"Open the door before he hurts himself," Pearl yelled.

Hardy touched the sliding bolt that would allow the door to swing open. He hesitated just long enough for Pearl to push past him. She reached for the hardware and froze.

*RATTA TATTA TATTA TATTA.*

The drumming was beneath them now, coming from the kitchen, headed for the stairs. Donnie had stopped throwing himself against the door and now answered the snare drum with his own cadence, hammering the wood with what sounded like the balls of his fists.

The percussion rose up the stairwell, accompanied by the footfalls of boots. Hardy wondered why floaty things made of air and nightmares would need to march, but figured dead folks had no reason to follow sensible rules. When the dead got on a mission, they would hoof it through hell and back if that's what the job required. That was as true of Kirk's lost raiders as it was with Jesus of Nazareth.

When the time came for action, you dragged your ass off the cross and did your duty.

"They're coming, whatever they are," Pearl said, pressed against the door as if motherly love alone could turn back the tide. Donnie kept on with his rhythmic pounding, and the wind had risen so that the house creaked and shook on its stacked-stone foundation.

Hardy swayed on aching, bowed legs, flush with the fever of fear, his heart threatening to gallop off into a painful stretch run toward the finish line.

But he was still a man, despite his 63 hard years and his bad eyes, and he was the last line of defense between his son and the things that wanted a new recruit.

No, they didn't want tired, used-up old men—or else the colonel would have taken him the other day at the fence line or out in the barn—but Hardy had no doubt that some fresh meat would soothe them on their long vigil of darkness, make that crack in the mountain known as the Jangling Hole a little less lonesome for a while.

They'd take the rest of his son. And Hardy would live out his days at the foot of the mountain, feeling the weight of helplessness and the guilt of failure pressing on him until it finally collapsed his chest.

*No. Last time they took him without a fight. But I ain't down for the count yet, and this battle's just starting.*

Without taking his eyes from the stairs, where the phantom platoon continued its climb, he reached behind him for the musket leaning against the wall.

His fingers came away empty.

"Hardy, look!" Pearl shouted.

The musket hovered in midair at the other end of the hall, moving away from them.

Hardy suspected that particular maneuver had never been taught on the grounds of West Point, where the great military minds sat down at their charts and maps and moved paper around as if those shifting lines didn't cost the blood of thousands.

*If you want to beat the enemy, just take the weapon out of his hands.*

The musket floated a few more feet, as if it were made of dust instead of wood and steel. Then the motes around it swirled and thickened, collecting into a cottony shape.

It was the soldier from the barn, the mutineer who had been treated to the bayonet and sword at the hands of his brothers in arms. The man who had died again at the command and behest of his former leader, the dishonorable Col. Kirk.

Corporal Earley Eggers materialized, moving away from Hardy, the saber wound visible in his back. He carried the musket before him as if pushing unseen cobwebs out of the way. Maybe he was pushing through obstacles in *his* world, wading through something on the other side that Hardy couldn't see. It was a land that prayers never touched and that God had seen fit to leave alone, and though Hardy felt the comfort of faith give way to the deep chill of utter solitude, he also steeled himself because he had nothing left but his own spare strength and will.

"Soldier," he yelled, loudly enough to drown out the thrumming boots on the stairs. His commanding tone probably wasn't as forceful as the orders the young recruit had heard at Bull Run or Chancellorsville, but the dead man hesitated all the same.

"You deserted once and you see where it got you," Hardy said, knowing he was riding the greased rails of madness but finding no turnabout or detour. "It got you dead."

Pearl touched Hardy's shoulder but he gently shrugged her off. "Get in there with Donnie. I'll take care of this."

He was glad she didn't question him, because he would have had no answer for her this time. The deadbolt slid from its sheath and the door creaked open, Donnie's hammering interrupted. Earley Eggers waited, frozen in place, that gash in his old gray tunic oozing starstuff and darkness. Hardy waited for the door to close, ignoring the rattling snare drum that echoed toward the top of the stairs.

"When you going to stand and fight?" Hardy shouted at his ancestor's back, and he could as easily have directed the words at himself. He'd always known the Hole was there and had sensed its potential to spew out plenty of damage and disaster. And yet he'd sat back and ignored it while it gobbled his son's soul and took others along the way.

"You can't fight what you can't see," he said. "But you can't see the inside of your own heart, either."

The drummer was on the second floor now and Hardy could sense the massed platoon coming up behind him, but he kept his gaze on Earley.

The corporal turned, those forlorn, weary eyes pouring out darkness with all their lifeless might. They were Eggers eyes, dark and flecked with gold, but the glint was more of hellfire than the spark of animation. His bony fingers clutched the musket, face set in grim determination. Earley raised the gun and pointed the barrel at Hardy, who could do nothing but stare back down the sight at the man who was readying to kill his own kin.

The barrel shifted to the right and the musket roared, the percussion hammering between the wooden walls of the narrow hallway, sulfur-rich blue smoke boiling from the end of the gun.

A cry erupted behind Hardy, the snare drum fell silent, and finally his limbs broke from their rigor and he fell with his back against the wall, sliding until he was half sitting.

At the end of the hallway stood a boy of about 12, a small kepi perched on his head in imitation of the rag-tag bunch of soldiers who gathered on the stairs behind him. A strap descended the boy's shoulders, a snare drum against his hip. The drummer boy looked down at his chest, where a small hole appeared in the cloth just below the top brass button.

Hardy knew the boy was dead—*Christ, PLEASE let him be already dead*—but his flesh looked so solid that Hardy expected blood to bloom from the wound. Surprise and confusion battled on the kid's smooth face, as if the thought of death had never crossed his mind, though surely he'd witnessed all manner of death and mayhem on those long-ago battlefields.

"What's going on?" Pearl screeched from behind Donnie's door, but Hardy wouldn't have been able to describe it even if he could make his lips and windpipe work.

The boy looked first at Earley, then at Hardy, as if acknowledging the family resemblance, and toppled forward, his kepi rolling off the side of his tousled blond head.

Now Hardy recognized him.

It was one of the boys who'd been messing around the Jangling

Hole the other day—only he'd been alive and well at the time.

A soldier standing behind the drummer boy opened his mouth, and though no sound came out, the name "Earley" bounced around the inside of Hardy's concussed head. Hardy recognized his haggard face and possum-colored beard from the barn and Col. Kirk's execution squad.

The soldier dropped his weapon and reached with one arm to catch the boy. But when flesh met flesh, there was no resistance, and the boy continued falling until his rusted snare drum banged on the floor of the hall.

Other soldiers crowded the stairwell, silent and grim, leveling their rifles down the hallway, and at such close range, none of the bullets would miss. They wouldn't care whether the bullets ripped the flesh of the dead or the living.

Hardy wasn't sure he cared, either. As long as Donnie was safe behind that thick wooden door, Hardy could go in peace, knowing he'd fought to the end. But spirits didn't obey the rules of doors and deadbolts, and Pearl would be left alone in Donnie's defense.

Since she had nothing but prayers as a weapon, Hardy didn't hold out much hope. He glanced at his musket, knowing Earley wouldn't have time to reload before the platoon's fusillade sent him to the grave for the third time.

"Cease fire," came a deep command from below, and in the sudden silence Hardy heard his own throat working as he fought to expel the thick, acrid gun-smoke from his lungs.

The soldiers stood poised in firing position, teeth gritted and hollow eyes cold, as boots strode across the kitchen floor and climbed the stairs.

Hardy couldn't help hearing the boots as a drumbeat—*tatta tatta.*

The soldiers parted, allowing the colonel to squeeze through. The man gave one slow tug of his beard as he gazed down at the latest casualty in a war that never ended.

Then Kirk stooped and rolled the limp boy into his arms, standing with a creak of wood and hugging the boy to his chest.

"Retreat," he whispered, or maybe the wind hit the tin eaves, or maybe the word was only a hallucination that flitted across Hardy's ringing eardrums.

The soldiers followed their leader, but not before the possum-bearded soldier gave Earley a look that promised revenge.

After the soft parade back across the kitchen was over, Hardy dropped to his knees and sought out the corporal.

Earley Eggers was gone, the musket lying on the floor.

Pearl called out, but Hardy ignored her. He crawled to the musket and checked the magazine. The powder charge was intact. The gun had not been fired.

CHAPTER TWENTY-FIVE

*Goddamned mosquitoes. Can't wait until the frost wipes your pointy asses out.*

Elmer swatted at one of the bloodsuckers, but he missed, and a moment later it was whining against his ear again.

"Atten-*chun*," Jeff Davis barked.

*Yassuh, Cap'n, suh.*

Elmer would have said it aloud in search of a laugh, but his fellow soldiers standing erect on both sides had let their faces go to granite. They swallowed up this make-believe shit, and Elmer played along. Truth was, he'd just as soon stand around sweating yesterday's beer as crawl around laying pipe on the Collins job. The wool get-up was scratchy and trapped the morning heat against his skin, but all in all it wasn't a bad way to spend a Thursday.

If only he didn't have to lick his neighbor's boots to earn his day off.

Wally Hampton, to Elmer's left, didn't seem to mind being a buck private, especially since he'd poured a little Jack Daniels in his thermos to spice up his coffee. Hampton, a carpenter who was riding a disability claim for all it was worth, was used to idle weekdays. Flanking Elmer's other side was Darren Anderson, a teenager who had joined the Living History Society because he was dating a college girl and was trying to impress her with the uniform.

*The trouble a guy went to for some squeeze. Well, it won't be long until he's hanging out with guys to get away from squeeze, because it doesn't take long for the squeeze between their legs to start squeezing your head.*

The park was quiet in the morning, a few grosbeaks and cardinals working the branches of the big hardwoods. A Confederate battle flag dangled from a skinned locust post, as limp as a used handkerchief. The mountains sloped up from the creek that bordered the park, Mulatto the steepest and tallest, its autumn trees a little deeper in color than the rest. Pick-up trucks in the gravel lot were still packed with equipment, though Jeff and a couple of others had been up before dawn, erecting their tents and setting the stage for the re-enactment.

Jeff strutted like a peacock in front of the line of soldiers, his uniform so clean and starched that it looked like steel wool. He'd brought out his insignia for the occasion, pinned enough brass to his chest to stop a cannonball. Jeff was so spit-and-polish that he'd even held a mock enlistment, checking the recruits' teeth to see if they had enough enamel to bite the paper off a powder charge. Elmer had nipped the officer's finger.

Elmer grinned at the dregs of the memory, causing Jeff to stop his inspection and get in Elmer's face.

"And what's so funny, soldier?" Jeff said.

"Nothing," Elmer answered.

"Nothing what?"

"Huh?"

"You're speaking to a superior officer."

Elmer wanted to grin bigger and slap Darren on the shoulder, let him in on the big joke, but Darren gulped and stood a little straighter. Wally Hampton also stood erect, though he swayed slightly from the booze.

*Damn, these boys are taking it serious. And Jefferson Davis certainly got the role down pat, sausage breath and all.*

It was too early to get into character. A few civilians were gathered in the gravel parking lot on the edge of the park, and the woman from the newspaper was there with her camera, getting ready to make a big fuss. A couple of the wives, wearing their bonnets and hoop skirts, were setting up iron kettles, spinning wheels, and other homestead displays.

But the unwritten rule of re-enactments, at least during Elmer's service, was you goofed off during the warm-ups and didn't get serious until the first fake shot was fired. But Jeff seemed to have a bug up his ass this year, as if he had something to prove and Pickett County's future hinged on the outcome of a make-believe battle.

"Nothing what?" Jeff repeated.

"Nothing, sir," Elmer said.

"Good," Jeff said, slapping his pair of riding gloves against his sleeve as if to shake off the dust of a long furlough. "When Kirk and his bunch of blue-bellied demons ride through, you better not be doing much laughing, or else you'll be picking grapeshot from between your teeth. If you're head's still attached, that is."

"Sir?" Darren said, looking straight ahead.

Jeff stepped away from Elmer and stopped in front of Darren, adjusting the teenager's kepi so that it tilted down over his forehead. "Yes, Private?"

"I thought it was General Stoneman that would be riding through here. Like in the history books."

"Stoneman was the man in charge, but it was Kirk who did the hard riding and the hard killing. But I admire your research. Adds to the appreciation of the event."

"Thank you, sir."

Jeff stepped away so that he could face the entire troop, or at least those who'd been able to skip work. A bead of sweat ran down Elmer's forehead, riding the slope between his eyes until a drop dangled at the end of his nose, tickling him. He didn't dare reach up to wipe it away, though, because Jeff's eyes had gone as hard and gray as a saber's steel.

"Gentlemen, history is about to come alive, but it's not just the past we're about to honor," Jeff said, his voice somehow becoming half an octave deeper. "It's also the future. Because the Civil War truly pitted neighbor against neighbor, and the battle never ended in these parts."

*What the hell is he droning on about?* Elmer figured Jeff had been reading some of the newer, revisionist books on the war, which skewed toward bizarre social and psychological theory because the nuts-and-bolts history had been examined from every possible angle. Because there were plenty of collectors like Jeff who'd snatch up anything even remotely linked to the war, writers had plenty of incentive to slap books together and roll them out in expensive leather-bound editions, even if the grammar was so crappy that Elmer, a D student in English, found mistakes. At least on those occasions when he was able to get past the third page.

"Tonight you'll be defending your homes, your families, and your country," Jeff said, delivering the lines with a flourish as if he were channeling Honest Abe Lincoln minus the stovepipe hat and goofy sideburns. "I can't rightly declare that God is on our side, because it's God's duty to be on all sides at the same time. But it's our duty to fight for the blessings He's bestowed upon us, lest we bring dishonor on ourselves and our forefathers."

Elmer heard a snuffle and a choked intake of breath. He shifted his eyes to the right. It looked for all the world like Wally was weeping.

The woman from the newspaper, who had a badge that read "Press" over her left tit as if nobody could tell by her foot-long camera lens and pocket notepad, was zeroing in on Jeff, who sensed his moment in the spotlight and let his chest swell even bigger.

The drop of sweat danced on the end of Elmer's nose, taunting him, trying to get him to sneeze and break ranks.

*Not on your goddamned life. This is honor we're talking about here, not a turn on "American Idol."*

"Some of us will not make it through the campaign," Jeff said. "As your officer, I would not ask you to take on any risk that I wouldn't face myself. I've got a family—"

As Jeff paused, Elmer wondered if his own boys would make it out to the bivouac tonight. Jerrell would probably be out boning one of his blondes in the back seat of his Mustang, but Bobby had been hanging around his bedroom since last night, barely even coming out long enough to take a piss. The boy was probably rubbing himself raw the way any normal 13-year-old boy would. And, praise the Sweet Lord in Heaven Above, Bobby had turned out normal, unlike Jeff's little offspring.

"I've got a family and I'm willing to make sacrifices for it," Jeff continued. "And they have to make sacrifices as well."

Jeff nodded toward the civilian camp, where a fire was now jumping and water boiling. His wife Martha, a scrawny woman whose complexion and thin-necked, top-heavy head gave her the appearance of a buzzard, stirred the water in the kettle as if preparing to wash laundry or make a stew. Jeff probably wouldn't be dipping the old noodle in that tonight, considering they'd be bedded in a tent where every little sigh and moan would be heard by the whole camp. Jeff probably wasn't doing much dipping of any kind lately.

*Not since he'd planted a little blond seed inside Vernell.*

Maybe Martha had wondered the same thing Elmer had: Bobby looked a hell of a lot more like Jeff than he did anything from the Eldreth gene pool. And considering the one reproductive bullet Jeff had fired between her thighs had turned out a dud, she'd probably put the little muff pie off limits for good.

No big surprise that Vernon Ray was nowhere to be seen. The little sweetboy was a constant reminder of the sissy-girl hiding inside Jeff, the one he covered with macho commando horseshit and a child-molester mustache.

*Family sacrifices, my ass.*

The drop of sweat swelled a little bigger on the end of Elmer's nose and he crossed his eyes trying to look at it, as if concentration would make it evaporate.

"Sacrifices," Jeff said, pacing up and down in front of the assembled soldiers. He was putting on a show for the photographer, who knelt in the grass and took one of those upward-angle shots intended to make the subject look 10 feet tall and full of vinegar.

Wally belched, and another acid-tinged fog of coffee and whiskey seeped across Elmer's face. The sound stood out in the hushed morning, and the golden-topped poplars and red maples quit their flapping, as if Jeff's message was meant for the whole world.

"The definition of sacrifice is making an offering to something bigger than yourself, whether it's your God, your tribe, your comrades, your flag," Jeff said, pausing long enough so the photographer could frame Capt. Davis, with the line of troops in the background, against the colorful trees and the Stars and Bars.

*The worm wants to be the star of his own history book.*

"We're a living history society," the captain continued, the photographer clicking away. "But history is about dying. What we commemorate—what we *celebrate*—in these next few days is the very real blood that spilled on this mountain soil. That's our heritage, gentlemen. That's the debt we have to repay."

Elmer wondered how much of the goosed-up coffee remained in Wally's thermos. The drop of sweat seemed to have swelled even bigger, defying gravity and clinging to Elmer's snot-leaker like a frog to a wet log. He wiggled his head, trying to shake it free before he sneezed.

Jeff noted the movement and took three powerful strides forward, until Elmer could smell cheese grits on the captain's breath to accompany the sausage. Jeff moved his hand to the brass hilt of his saber, fondling the tassel.

"You're at attention, soldier," Jeff said.

"Damn it, Jeff, crank it down a notch," Elmer said, letting his shoulders slump as he reached to wipe away the sweat. "The crowd's not even here yet."

So smoothly that Elmer was sure the little worm had practiced it over and over in the privacy of his double-wide, Jeff *snicked* the saber from its scabbard and arced it, bringing the rounded tip forward until it pressed against Elmer's breastbone.

"The Confederate States of America can brook no insubordination in the ranks," the captain said, and his eyes were a color that Elmer had never seen, a smoky gray rimmed with red that looked for all the world like the haze over a wasted battlefield.

The tip of the saber pressed harder, and Elmer was relieved it was a cavalier's sword, made for slashing instead of skewering, or the steel would have worked through the fabric to his skin.

Elmer flicked his eyes to the photographer, hoping she'd get a shot in case Elmer decided to press charges. The dyke's hands were on her hips, and she glared as if she were disappointed by a coward's betrayal. The women of the civilian attachment had paused in their chores, awaiting the disciplinary action to come. The other soldiers continued to stare straight ahead, and a glance at Wally's ruddy face told Elmer that the walrus-assed drunk was glad that it was Elmer instead of him getting the verbal corn-holing.

Despite the increased pressure of the saber, Elmer was mulling whether to call Jeff's bluff and tell him at least his kid wasn't a little Swisher Sweet in a pink velvet wrapper. Then he saw the actors coming through the woods, heading for the creek from the direction of Mulatto Mountain.

It must have been the boys from the Eighth Tennessee Regiment, because they were decked out in gear that looked so authentic that it might have been dragged through Manassas and back. But the uniforms were filthy and not all of it standard, which added to the realism but didn't really fit the spirit of modern re-enactors, who were prodded by men like Jeff until they spent all their money on approved replicas. Plus, these uniforms were a mix of Union blue and Homeland gray.

"What do you have to say for yourself, Private?" Jeff said, chicory now joining the odors that rode his words.

Elmer decided to let Jeff play his little game, but that didn't mean the whole world would play along. He nodded toward the camp's perimeter. "Looks like we got company."

Without lowering the saber, Jeff craned his neck around, almost sniffing the air like a groundhog testing for danger. "Company?"

"The guys from Bristol," Elmer said, and then he remembered the Tennessee History Brigade wasn't due to arrive until tomorrow. They must have camped before dawn, maybe parking on the logging roads that wound around Mulatto, getting dressed and planning a surprise attack.

Not a bad strategy, except for the fact that the audience hadn't arrived, the battle was supposed to be scripted, and these guys looked like they'd been shitting in the woods for a decade instead of fresh off a sit-down breakfast at Denny's.

"Don't count on reinforcements in this battle," Jeff said. Smoke roiled in his eyes, and the narrow shape of them resembled the way Bobby's got when he was pissed off or paranoid. "Out here, we're on our own, the only thing standing between the devil and the folks back home."

"Okay, Jeff, I get it," Elmer said, quiet enough that even Wally and Darren would have had to strain to hear. "You got a hard-on for brass tacks, maybe you had a hard-on for Vernell, and you got a hard-on for this little make-believe world because your real life is crap. And I couldn't give two hairy rats fucking in a sock. Play your little game, but leave me out of it."

Elmer was reaching for the blade of the saber, telling himself it was only a toy, kept dull so that no one got hurt in the heat of pretend war. The Tennessee regiment was still advancing, but they were fading to smoke themselves, blending with the morning haze that hung over the creek.

Elmer thought his eyes were going, fuzzing out from a stroke.

He reached out as if to wipe away the gauze that hovered before him. His hand wrapped around the cold steel of the sword, grateful for its solidity, his heart ticking like a sick clock.

"No insubordination," Jeff said, stepping back and flicking his wrist, withdrawing the blade so that Elmer's hand became a sheath. The fleshy pads around Elmer's palm grew wet, but he couldn't tear his eyes away from the stacks of gray mist marching through the trees, and as the soldiers' bodies melted into the air, those haunted, weary faces hung around a little bit longer, floating like echoes of lost screams.

"The Tennessee boys," Elmer said, lifting his throbbing hand to point.

Red rain leaked from his palm, spattering on the dead leaves and dying grass. The shapes had dissolved, and now the sounds of the forest were back, mockingbirds warbling in the high branches, the creek tinkling like the tools of a thousand mess kits, the sugar-weighted maples flapping a gentle goodbye as they slid toward winter's sleep.

Pain flared up Elmer's arm, electric fire shrieking for attention, consuming all thoughts of invisible soldiers and his insane neighbor and the buddies beside him who must have chugged from the same coo-coo juice as Jeff. He looked at his wound, where yellow wells of fat protruded from the surgical splits in his skin.

*Say what you want about Jeff, but the crazy asshole knows how to handle a whetstone.*

"Nothing there, soldier," Jeff said.

The newspaper photographer put the camera to her eye, balancing the long lens and scanning the forest. Elmer pitched forward, falling to his knees. None of his comrades moved a muscle.

"Company!" Jeff bellowed, and the soldiers tensed and straightened. "Dismissed."

The soldiers relaxed and scattered, breaking into conversation. Wally slapped Elmer on the back. "Hey, this is going to be a hoot, ain't it?"

Elmer gripped his wound, trying to stanch the flow of blood.

"Yeah, a real wing ding. Say, did you see those soldiers in the woods?"

Wally blinked his bloodshot eyes, his replica musket leaning at parade rest. "The soldiers won't get here till tomorrow."

"That's what I figured," Elmer said, standing on wobbly legs.

"You're looking a mite pale," Wally said. "Heat getting to you? These wool clothes are a bitch."

"Yeah," Elmer said. "How about a cup of coffee?"

"Sure, come on over to the truck."

"Got any of that Jack left? I could use a little lift."

"Yeah. What happened to your hand?"

"It's nothing. Just an old war wound."

"Hilarious," Wally said, belching the word. "Come on, before Jeff makes us set up camp."

They passed Jeff, Wally snapping off an open-handed Confederate salute. Elmer imitated it, making sure Jeff saw the blood. Jeff didn't smile or smirk, merely returned the salute as if they were miles from the front lines and settling into the routine of a weekend bivouac. Elmer heard the distant rattling of a snare drum from the forest, but figured it was another trick of his imagination, so he tucked the bill of his kepi over his eyes and followed Wally to the canteen.

He didn't look back at the shadows beneath the freckled October canopy, nor the shapes that might have moved amid the low-lying gloom.

CHAPTER TWENTY-SIX

The morning sun poured its voyeuristic light through the trailer window.

Vernon Ray fingering the ragged opening in the wool just above the kepi's bill. The hole was ringed by a rust-colored stain and it could only have been made by a musket ball. The original wearer of the kepi had undoubtedly died from the wound. Surgery of any kind during the Civil War almost invariably ended in gangrene or staph infection, if typhus didn't get you first.

Vernon Ray tried on the cap for the tenth time. He'd slept with it under his pillow, afraid his dad would see it. Dad's memorabilia and replicas were carefully catalogued, so Vernon Ray couldn't be accused of stealing the kepi from The Room, but he didn't know how to explain where he'd gotten it.

But he shouldn't have worried; Capt. Davis was far too busy dressing for Stoneman's Raid to notice that his son had been late for dinner and sick enough to miss school.

Vernon Ray stood before his dresser mirror, tilting the bill forward so he had to peer out from under the oiled canvas.

*Soldier material. Battle fit and ready for action.*

His reflection snapped off an open-palmed Rebel salute and he marched four brisk steps until he reached his bed then spun on one heel and marched smartly back to the dresser. He let his feet hammer the vinyl flooring, making as much noise as he wanted. Dad was already at Aldridge Park for the re-enactment and Mom had tagged along as part of the civilian attachment, probably brewing up some gritty coffee and trying to keep the hem of her hoop skirt out of the fire.

Vernon Ray should have been in school, but he'd pretended to be sick. Good old belly ache, his folks were used to it, his dad saying he was born with a "weak stomach, probably got it from Martha Faye's side of the family."

The emptiness of the house gave him a tingle inside, so in a way, the reported ache wasn't a lie. He'd not been nauseated, just aching for something he couldn't name.

He thought about breaking into The Room to try on some gear, but Dad had added an extra lock after last week's little adventure and Vernon Ray couldn't gain access without damaging the wood. Besides, he had his own uniform now, or at least a piece of it.

"Private Davis reporting for duty, sir," he said to the mirror, half expecting the colonel's face to appear in the silvered glass and give him his marching orders. He'd dreamed of the colonel, though the events had been diffuse and broken up in bits of restless sleep. All he remembered was darkness, a cold campfire, and the whispers of voices from hidden quarters.

He cocked the cap to one side in a jaunty pose, goofing off around camp to entertain the soldiers. They deserved a little break from the grim duty of legalized murder. He reached up to adjust it back—

*Tak tak tak.*

Someone was tapping on the window.

Vernon Ray flung the kepi under his bed and thought about jumping onto the covers. He was pale and shaky enough to fake a fever. But only one person ever knocked on his window. Vernon Ray went to it, and there was Bobby's gorgeous, worried face. Vernon Ray cranked the window open.

"Jeez, I thought you were a goner," Bobby said.

"Nah, I'm okay. Just got a belly ache."

"Sorry I ran out on you. I was—"

"Forget it."

"It was black hat, total bad guy."

"It was the only thing you could do. And I told you to, remember?"

"Still . . . ."

"Forget it," Vernon Ray said, his gaze crawling back to the space under the bed where the kepi lay in shadows.

"What happened?"

"Why aren't you in school?"

"I skipped after first period. It's just gym."

"You like gym."

"I thought he was going to slice you like liver mush, Vee."

Vernon Ray released the tabs on the window screen and pushed it out, where Bobby caught it and set it against the trailer's aluminum skirt. Bobby launched himself up and inside the room. Vernon Ray sat on the bed while Bobby slouched at the computer desk and stared at a chess board where Vernon Ray was in the middle of a solo game.

"He just disappeared after you left," Vernon Ray said. "You know how those theories of transubstantiation go. It probably took all his energy to materialize enough to scare you away."

"Yeah, I felt all tingly and weird, like static electricity was crackling on the tips of my hair."

"Drawing juice from us, like a car draining a battery."

"So he didn't do anything?"

"Nah," Vernon Ray said, wondering if Bobby would mention their near kiss. He doubted it, since the bedroom would be about the most uncomfortable place to bring it up.

"What are we going to do about the ghosts?"

"Why do you think we have to do anything? They're not good or evil, they're just *there*."

"Except for what happened to Carter, you mean? And I got a feeling I'm on their hit list and I'm not even a Yankee."

"Kirk's Raiders were rejects from both sides," Vernon Ray said. "They were equal-opportunity haters. If you believe the history books, but I'm not so sure of the truth anymore."

"I don't get it. They let you go twice now. They could have got you when we were spying on them from the Hole. Now Col. Creep has you cornered and just disappears?"

"Maybe I was born lucky. But he let you go, too."

"They must want something," Bobby said.

"Certainly not prisoners."

"Maybe just casualties." Bobby reached across the desk and moved one of the chess pieces. "Check."

Vernon Ray crossed the room to the chess board. "You're making two dangerous assumptions, Bobby. You assume we can actually have an effect on the ghosts and you assume whatever we do will be in their best interests."

"Sure, 'Go toward the light' and all that crap. They probably have another level of heaven to move on to, or whatever."

Vernon Ray moved a knight, his favorite piece due to its deceptive nature, blocking Bobby's threat to the king. "What if that's the worst possible thing for them? What if you're sending them to heaven instead of the hell where they belong?"

*Let's not belong together. Maybe Kirk knows something we don't.*

"That's not the point. They don't belong here. When it's over, it's over, and you just bury the past and move on."

"And who made Bobby Eldreth lord and master of the universe?"

"Hey, at least I'm trying to do something." Bobby slid a pawn forward.

"Maybe we should just leave them alone."

"And hope they go away?"

"And hope they do whatever they're meant to do." Vernon Ray angled his bishop forward. "Checkmate."

Bobby leaned over the board and flicked his king with one finger so that it fell and rolled across the board, scattering other pieces. "I'm going to the battlefield. You can sit around and wait for them to take over the town if you want."

"What in the world would they want with the town?"

"That one ghost soldier, the one we saw on the railroad tracks? Earley Eggers? He's like an outcast, a deserter or something. They were shooting at him when they killed Carter. You heard the reporter. Earley Eggers lived in Titusville, and maybe he's bound for home and the others don't like it."

"Like that guy in *Cold Mountain*," Vernon Ray said. His dad not only possessed an autographed copy of the Charles Frazier novel, he'd made the family watch the Nicole Kidman movie every night during its entire two-week run at the Regal Cineplex.

"Maybe they're hunting him."

"But that doesn't make sense, because if they can get out of the Hole, they can escape, too."

"Maybe Deserter Boy has found another way to transubstantiate. A portable power source. Or maybe he finally heeded the call of hearth of home."

"V-Ray, if we could prove all this, we'd be rich and famous, like what's-his-name on that paranormal show."

"We couldn't even snag a decent picture of a ghost. What, you expect to get one in the guest chair on 'Oprah'?"

"Well, let's go check out the war. Maybe Kirk will come down to scout out the enemy. If nothing else, we'll get to see our dads make fools of themselves."

"Sounds like an adventure. Beats the hell out of algebra."

They stood at the same time, bringing them closer together than they'd been since Bobby had climbed in the window. Vernon Ray realized they'd deliberately put distance between themselves the entire time and now they shared a collective breath.

"Uh, about that thing in the shed," Bobby said.

"I told you, he disappeared right after you left."

"No, the other thing."

"Nothing happened, remember?"

"Yeah. I just want you to know it's okay. I mean, if I liked guys—you know, in *that* way . . . ."

Vernon Ray lowered his eyes, bit his lip to rein in a pout, and nodded, willing himself not to cry. *Christ, first I try to kiss him and now I'm about to open the floodgates like a goddamned little girl.*

He shifted his gaze to the bed and the kepi, whose brim was just visible at the dusty edge of darkness. He recalled the comfort and security the hat gave him, the sense of belonging, as if he'd finally discovered himself and that he was okay.

It didn't matter what Bobby or anyone else—any *living* person— thought of him, because the colonel found him worthy.

"It was nothing," Vernon Ray said.

Bobby blurted his words in a rush, as if letting them linger might leave him vulnerable and exposed in the bits of silence between. "You're my best friend and I love you like a brother, and whatever you do is fine with me, but I love Karen Greene and not guys and I don't think you're sick or anything—"

"Don't." Vernon Ray raised his hand, gaining self-confidence through the memory of the colonel's understanding-but-hollow gaze. "Don't try too hard. That's worse than not trying at all."

Bobby moved to the window and poised like a superhero about

to fly to somebody's rescue. "I'm cool with whatever."

Then Bobby was gone, slipping out with an athletic grace that caused a mild flutter in Vernon Ray's stomach.

The colonel's phantom words echoed again: *We don't belong together.*

He grabbed his backpack, retrieved the kepi, brushed it over his head just long enough to savor its comfort, and then squirreled it away. Tossing the backpack over his shoulder, he followed his best friend through the window and into a world where being queer was weirder than being supernatural.

CHAPTER TWENTY-SEVEN

Sheriff Frank Littlefield wove his cruiser between the horse trailers that were lined up along the edge of the parking lot. The Living History Society had set up a fledgling camp, and a few of the soldiers were sitting on logs and eating from tin plates. Women in bonnets and dresses bustled around tending fires and carrying water from the creek.

A couple of kids in wool britches and loose cotton shirts were playing army, using tree branches as make-believe rifles. As the sheriff got out of the car, he heard one yell, "Bang! You're dead."

The intended target, a red-headed boy whose floppy hat nearly covered his eyes, said, "Am not!"

Which Littlefield believed could just about sum up the situation for a lot of folks in Titusville lately.

The clouds were high and fine, promising a cool, dry October day. Mist wreathed the faces of the mountains, the vapor rising from dewy valleys to burn away under the sun. Laughter and birdsong filled Aldridge Park, and the sheriff relaxed a little.

*Just a normal day in the war.*

Cindy Baumhower was interviewing one of the uniformed men, camera slung over one shoulder. The incident at the bowling alley would be the headline, but a feature story on the local tourist event would get some good play to stroke the business community. Littlefield had cited Mac McAllister with discharging a firearm in a public building and disturbing the peace, but the bowling mogul had made bail before the ink had dried on the processing papers.

If Littlefield didn't somehow plug the Hole and find a way to exterminate this little supernatural infestation, then Pickett County might become the Disneyland of the Dead, with ghosts pouring in from every crack in the Appalachian Mountains. And that would draw national media attention, which in turn would bring investigative reporters who would want to know more about The Red Church, Littlefield's dead chief deputy, and the whereabouts of

Rev. Archer McFall.

The past should stay in the past and the dead should stay dead, and the living deserved to rest in peace far more than did those who had gone before.

Littlefield walked to the camp as a couple of dress-up soldiers mounted horses at the end of the field. The air was ripe with the odors of creek mud, horse manure, and wood smoke. A dozen or so locals had stopped by during their coffee breaks to get an early glimpse of the coming battle, and a handful were gathered around Cindy as if watching the media coverage of the event was more exciting than the event itself.

A line of locust fencing marked one end of the park and a dense row of hardwoods bordered the other two sides. The shaded woods seemed a little menacing in their closeness, especially since they were part of the same living-and-breathing ecosystem that covered Mulatto Mountain.

*Christ, now you're even giving trees the power of the paranormal. What next, Casper the Friendly Ghost in tap-dancing shoes?*

Jeff Davis was drinking coffee under a raised tent flap that was held up with skinned birch branches. A wooden table had his papers spread across it, and Littlefield assumed they contained maps and details of the re-enactment.

As the sheriff passed through the camp, he felt a strange kinship with the uniformed men, even though he'd arrested a couple of them. Elmer, who had once gone down for a drunk and disorderly during an explosive Fourth of July, waved at him with a bandaged hand and drank from a canvas-covered canteen.

"How's it going, Jeff?" Littlefield said when he reached the tent.

"It's 'Captain' out here," Jeff said. His hat was off and his dark hair was slicked back with some sort of gel.

*Or maybe possum fat, if he's gone Southern for the duration.*

"I just dropped by to check on things," Littlefield said, wondering whether Jeff now considered himself of higher rank than sheriff. "People are a mite antsy after the McAllister incident."

"Mac's no longer in the regiment," Jeff said.

"No, but he was shooting at invisible people, and there's a little too much of that going around lately. Not to mention the real people who are getting shot."

"War is hell," Jeff said, his eyes cold and strange. He seemed a different man than the one who'd been sitting in Littlefield's office the day before, somber and weighted with duty. "Whether it's real or not."

"The permit allows me the right to inspect any firearms on the premises," Littlefield said.

Jeff smiled and fished the revolver from his holster. He set the pistol on the table as if daring the sheriff to spin it for a game of Russian roulette. "Go ahead. Colt revolver, a period piece. Only 4,000 issued."

Littlefield, who appreciated firearms but was no historian, picked it up and opened the chamber. He shucked out one of the bullets and looked at it. The jacket was packed with tissue paper. Blanks had been known to kill people, most notably the actor Brandon Lee, who was shot by a prop pistol on set. A permit had not done a bit of good in stopping the concussion from propelling a lodged slug into Lee's abdomen.

"What about your soldiers?" Littlefield asked, replacing the bullet and clicking the chamber closed.

"They're a little rough around the edges but we'll be ready when Stoneman and his boys roll through," Jeff said. "Not much on spit and polish, but plenty of grit and backbone."

Littlefield gave a smile, his first in days. "I meant their safety habits, not their fighting spirit."

Jeff's eyes remained distant. "They know how to handle their weapons. We've been training all year for this battle."

"I'm sure the Confederacy will sleep better tonight, knowing you're standing sentry." Littlefield handed the revolver back to Jeff, butt first. The two mounted cavalry units thundered across the field, sod flying from the horses' hooves.

"It's not just about defending the home front," Jeff said. "It's a matter of principle."

Littlefield flinched in anticipation of a lecture in which state's rights and not slavery was to blame for the Civil War. It had been boring in the seventh grade and had not grown a bit more compelling in the years since. Instead, the erstwhile captain rolled the right tip of his moustache between his fingers and stared off toward Mulatto Mountain and slipped into a monotone, as if not aware of his words.

"The real enemy's waiting up there. The ones who won't do the honorable thing and give their lives for their beliefs. No, they make a mockery of all that is noble and sacred, all that's worth fighting for."

"Who?"

"You know who."

"Howdy, Sheriff," a woman's voice called, and Littlefield welcomed the distraction, though Cindy's greetings were usually followed by criticism, questions, or plain old pestering.

"Hi, Cindy, you getting some good copy?"

"Maybe," she said, giving her journalism-school smile. "The way trouble follows you around, I'm sure the best is yet to come."

"You got it backwards. Trouble doesn't follow me, I follow it. That's my job."

"I guess that explains all those ghosts rattling chains in your attic."

"She gets it, even if you don't," Jeff said.

*KER-chewwww.*

The gunshot rolled across the valley. One of the horses whinnied and reared and its rider slumped against the horse's neck, trying to hold on.

The sheriff glanced around, seeing if any of the soldiers were testing their weapons or holding mock drills.

Jeff rose from his chair, slipping on his hat and giving the crown a tap to paste it against his greasy hair. He glanced at a pocket watch that hung from a silver chain and gave a little nod. "A bit early, but then, who ever expected Kirk's Raiders to fight fair?"

The captain tugged down his tunic and shrugged his shoulders, squaring his epaulets as his passed between Cindy and Littlefield.

"That's a man on a mission," Cindy said after he was gone.

"More like a man jerking off to his own private wet dream," Littlefield said.

"Is that off the record?"

"It's just plain off."

Another shot rang out with its percussive echo. Jeff Davis broke into a jog, headed for the camp and the seated men. The rider clinging to the restless horse pitched forward and fell to the ground, where he lay without moving.

"Man, that looked like it hurt," Cindy said. "Good acting."

"That's nothing. We played dead all the time when I was a kid. Me and my brother—"

Cindy's eyes flicked to his face so rapidly that her penetrating gaze stopped him before regret had a chance. "What?"

"Nothing," Littlefield said, brushing past her. "I'm going to see if that guy's okay."

The second rider was wheeling his horse around, scouting the woods beyond the creek. Jeff yelled at the men, making dramatic motions with his arms. They were gathering their weapons and adjusting their gear when another shot rang out.

*KER-cheww. ZeeeeEEEEEP.*

Littlefield heard something whistling past his head. It had accelerated far too fast for an insect and carried a peculiar, violent quality, as if ripping the sky in half.

The rider slapped his horse on the flank and galloped toward camp. Half a dozen horses, tethered under a tall maple, whinnied and tugged against their leather restraints. Jeff reached the tents and stirred the men, rousing them into formation.

"He takes his make-believe seriously," Cindy said, following Littlefield across the pasture.

The sheriff didn't answer. He was watching the rider who had fallen to the grass. The man lay as limp as a bag of wet cotton.

Another shot rang out, and one of the women gave a high-pitched yelp.

"Now he's got everybody following the script," Cindy said.

A woman in a green dress and white bonnet held her arm, moaning in pain. Blood poured down to her elbow, staining the cloth.

"Somebody's shooting!" Littlefield shouted. "Stay low."

He ducked, fishing his Glock from its holster as he ran toward the prone rider. He reached the man and crouched, glancing around at the edge of the woods. Seeing no one, he checked the man's pulse. Nothing.

He rolled the body over. A blossom of rich blood oozed from the man's chest, an apparent shot to the heart. There had been no wound in the back, meaning the bullet must have lodged in the flesh and was likely of a low caliber.

*Figures that this event would attract some lunatic sniper who never met a war he didn't like, even a fake one.*

He mentally flicked through the roster of potential nutcases in the county–Weejun Li, the Korean peacenik; Laney Curtis, the income-tax protestor and resident rabid libertarian; and Sam Wakeman, the alcoholic Vietnam veteran who had suffered a breakdown in the Walmart one Christmas and slugged the hell out of Santa Claus.

But none of them seemed to possess the type of hair trigger that would kill a man. Besides, Wakeman was in the camp, one hand tugging up his too-large trousers as he scrambled for his equipment.

The camp was in chaos now, despite Jeff's bellowing attempts to restore order. "In line, soldiers!" he screamed, his face as purple as a plum.

The soldiers, some of them with their gray tunics undone or missing their hats, wrestled with their replica weapons, confused by the commotion. Elmer Eldreth had the butt of his rifle against his shoulder, peering down the barrel as if sighting an unseen enemy. Cindy, who had been startled at the sheriff's revelation of live fire, was now in full swing, pressing the button on her digital camera as fast as the machinery could process the information.

Two shots sounded almost simultaneously, then a third, and Littlefield realized this attack wasn't the work of a lone nut job. The shots appeared to be coming from the woods near the creek, though he still saw no movement or smoke in that direction.

"Here we go, boys," Jeff yelled, yanking out his saber and waving it in the air. "Time to give those heathen devils a taste of Confederate steel. Charge!"

The squadron of soldiers—maybe 10 in all—stood in loose formation and moved ahead in unison at Jeff's command. The civilian attachment hovered around the wounded woman in the camp. Martha Davis had ripped a strip of ruffled cloth from the hem of her dress and was winding it around the wound in a makeshift bandage. If not for the cooling corpse that lay beside him, Littlefield would have thought it was just a well-acted scene, carefully rehearsed and delivered for maximum dramatic effect.

"Sheriff," Cindy called, waving to get his attention. She pointed toward the creek.

Littlefield blinked, blinked again.

Shapes moved against the trees, flimsy as late fog.

*Like the man in the lumber yard . . . .*

He didn't know which was more surreal: the wafting, sinuous shapes or the flesh-and-blood men in replica military uniforms who approached in battle formation, muskets lowered and bayonets fixed.

He had no idea if real bullets would have any affect on ghost soldiers, but there was no doubt supernatural bullets could cut through human meat. The proof was cooling at his feet.

"Keep low," he yelled at Cindy, knowing she would ignore him and do her best to document the bizarre encounter. He duck-walked after Jeff Davis and his squad, keeping his head down, thighs aching from the unnatural movement.

A shout came from the woods, the voice hollow as if emanating from deep within the Earth. "Commence *fire!*"

A volley exploded from the forest, slugs zipping through the air. One of Jeff's men groaned and fell to his knees, and he perched there with his head bowed forward like a penitent in prayer. Littlefield doubted there was any god around to hear the begging, because if God existed, then the dead and living would stay on their respective sides. The line of soldiers pressed on in the face of the unholy fusillade, and Jeff waved his sword and urged the men toward their barely visible enemy.

The ghost soldiers solidified a little more, as if interacting with the material world had given them sustenance and form. They were little more than the suggestion of shapes, but Littlefield pieced together glimpses of Kirk's Raiders. They were a ragtag bunch, their frayed uniforms a mix of gray and blue, stained cotton showing in the rips.

Littlefield guessed there were a dozen of them, but it was difficult to determine numbers because of their constant shifting.

The gun smoke that issued from their rifle barrels was whisked away on the breeze, the muffled sound of their powder charges rumbling under the autumn canopy. Littlefield felt foolish holding his Glock, but it gave him a dose of courage and kept him from turning and running for the safety of his cruiser.

*Except why would the cruiser be any safer in a world that allows its dead to rise up and kill?*

Jeff ordered his men to fire, and the soldiers put their weapons to their shoulders. They'd be firing blanks, loose paper wadding and a few grains of black powder. Jeff Davis was sending his men into the lion's den without so much as a thimble of catnip.

The Home Guard fired in a staccato rhythm, the shot peppering the trees.

*Real bullets. Damned if Jeff didn't defy the terms of the permit after all. Maybe he knew something I didn't . . . not that I'd have believed him if he told me the war was about to pick up where it had left off a century-and-a-half ago.*

One of the otherworldly warriors eased from the cover of a thick maple and took three wobbling steps toward the creek, clutching his neck. Littlefield instinctively lifted his Glock, though the target was at least 50 yards away and beyond range. The ghost soldier dropped his rifle, then pitched forward and began crawling for the water.

*Christ, now I'm part of the horror show,* he thought, lowering his weapon. Behind him, Cindy was twisting the focus on her camera lens, standing up, legs parted to steady her visual aim. Littlefield continued his stooped, awkward jog until he caught up with Jeff.

A projectile whined past his head as he grabbed Jeff's arm. "Don't you know the word 'retreat,' you hard-headed son of a bitch?"

Jeff gave him that vacant gaze with eyes as dead as the amorphous men in the forest. "There's glory waiting," he said. "And revenge."

"Revenge for what?"

"This time, we get to win."

Littlefield fought the urge to punch the man in his weak chin and smear blood all over the carefully trimmed mustache. The erstwhile captain was clearly caught up in whatever mass hysteria had taken over Pickett County. Littlefield wished he had a rational explanation, such as contaminated food, a terrorist drugging of the water supply, an Army laboratory leak, or even an old-fashioned alien infection.

He'd prefer any of those over the possibility that his home county and his constituency were beyond the laws of physics and religion. At the moment, he'd even welcome back Rev. Archer McFall and his demented cult of flesh eaters.

*Better the devil you know . . . .*

The Home Guard was now 30 yards from the edge of the forest, and several of Jeff's men were reloading their muskets, skinnying long metal poles down the barrels to pack in more shot. Littlefield saw they were cramming hunks of dull gray metal among the paper wadding. Elmer Eldreth had a red ragged tear in his shoulder, but he ignored the wound as he lifted his rifle and squinted into the trees for dead prey.

"You were ready for this," Littlefield shouted at Jeff, but the captain was intent on waving his men forward.

"A soldier is ready for anything," Jeff said, breaking into a run and sending a Rebel yell into the sky that turned Littlefield's blood to ice water.

He realized he wouldn't be able to dissuade Jeff or rescue the soldiers who were determined to follow their crazed commander to the grave and possibly beyond, so he decided to turn his attention to the women and children who had taken cover in the parking lot, hiding among the trucks and horse trailers. They appeared unaffected by whatever insanity afflicted the menfolk, though they likely didn't know the "enemy" in the woods had risen from the grave.

Cindy was helping the wounded man up from his knees and Littlefield ran to them, bracing against the murderous projectiles whizzing across the field.

"You should have plugged the Hole while you had a chance," Cindy said to him when he arrived.

"Like my crystal ball showed a pack of ghosts waiting to come out and play 'Peek-a-boo'?"

"You knew something was up and you just pretended it would

go away," she said. "Just like the red church."

The wounded man—Littlefield now recognized him as Chalky Watkins, a member of the Titusville Volunteer Fire Department— moaned and Littlefield checked him for damage. Chalky had taken a shot to the hip, a crease wound from the looks of it.

"Just like them Yanks to pull a sneak attack," Chalky said, as if he'd have been invincible if the ghosts had only stood eye-to-eye and fought fair.

"You're going to be okay," the sheriff said, his words nearly drowned by the reverberation of charged powder. He slid his Glock into its holster so he could drag the man to safety.

"Patch me up and get me back out there," Chalky said. "Looks like the boys are going to need me."

Chalky had a point; at least three other men had fallen and the Home Guard's ranks were visibly thinner. Jeff had moved well ahead of his unit and Littlefield wondered if his frantic recklessness made him a difficult target. Jeff seemed to be almost daring the ghosts to kill him, as if he'd been denied his chance to die in battle and now was making the most of opportunity.

"When they said the South would rise again, I don't think this is what they had in mind," the sheriff said.

"It's not just the South," Cindy said. "That's Kirk's Raiders, men from both sides, which you'd have known if you'd taken your job seriously."

"Spare me the lecture," he said, propping Chalky against his hip and dragging him toward the parking lot.

"Looks like you've got the situation under control," she said, relinquishing her share of Chalky's weight to punctuate her sarcasm. The sheriff nearly lost his balance, but braced himself and continued his mission. Cindy was right. He couldn't stop this supernatural battle, so he focused on one small act that he could claim was "good."

*And conveniently get myself out of the firing line at the same time . . . .*

*Yeah, just like old times.*

"Sorry, Chalky, you're just going to have to grin and bear it," he said, letting the middle-aged man slide to the ground. Chalky grunted and called Littlefield something that sounded like "yellow-bellied traitorous scuppernong," but the sheriff was already racing after Cindy, the bullets still whizzing overhead but their frequency diminished.

Jeff's troops had reached the edge of the woods, and the enemy must have broken ranks and retreated under the suicide charge.

That's when a man stepped from the woods and stared down the assault, holding his own saber to match Jeff's. He was bearded, wearing a cavalry hat, and his breast was decorated with medals. "Fall back," he shouted, his voice echoing out as if from a cold, rocky cave.

Except Littlefield couldn't have sworn in a court of law that the words had been shouted; they may have merely fallen from the sky or crawled up through the ground from his feet to his skull.

The man looked so solid that Littlefield wondered if he were one of the re-enactors, but then he noticed the man's dusty boots were several inches off the ground. Littlefield realized the bearded man was the officer of the dead, the Big Cheese of the buried brigade, Kirk himself. Littlefield drew his Glock, thinking that if he somehow killed the leader, the others would dissolve and drift back to whatever netherland they had escaped from.

*The Hole...back to the Hole...*

He steadied himself, leveled his arm, and fired.

The bullet whizzed through the empty space where the colonel had been standing moments before, not even a thread of mist to mark his passing.

CHAPTER TWENTY-EIGHT

They were on the railroad tracks when the first shot sounded, and Bobby figured somebody down at the camp was popping one off early, probably showing off a new gun. It's not like the fake soldiers needed target practice, since they were shooting blanks.

When the next few shots up echoed from Aldridge Park, Vernon Ray said, "They weren't supposed to start until tomorrow."

"Maybe the other side isn't playing by the rules," Bobby said.

"Lame," Vernon Ray said. "If you're going to employ gallows humor, at least try to be funny."

"Should we go down and check it out?"

"Think the reporter's there?"

"Well, she could either cover the re-enactment or sit around the office waiting for two dorks to walk in with another bizarre tale of occult encounters."

"I'm not a dork. You're the dork."

"Nah, I'm more like a geek," Vernon Ray said.

Bobby wasn't sure homosexuals could be geeks. Neither of them had pimples yet, and Vernon Ray was skinny and Bobby was a jock, but they both read comic books.

Maybe the only difference was Vernon Ray hated Star Wars and Bobby had seen all the movies at least twice and owned a busty action figure of Princess Leia.

*Except Vernon Ray would rather kiss Han Solo . . . .*

They increased their pace, juiced by the adrenaline of the unknown. The staccato volley of shots was louder now, and Bobby guessed there were dozens of guns going off. "Sounds like a war."

"If Dad has anything to do with it, the sooner, the better."

"He's getting his jollies, then."

"I don't want to think about Dad's jollies."

Bobby was about to blurt out a comeback, but figured it might hit too close to home. Half of all eighth-grade jokes centered on guys giving blowjobs. Bobby wondered if he'd ever be able to tell a "queer joke" again. Even before he'd begun wondering about Vernon Ray, he'd never found them all that funny, but in the locker room, you had to laugh at them just the same.

Something crackled overhead, making a sudden beeline through the treetops. A yellow leaf fluttered down against the dizzying sunshine. Bobby recognized the sound from the incident with the bulldozer man.

"Crap, that was a real bullet," Bobby said, instinctively hunching.

"Think somebody's hunting this close to town?"

"No, I think your buddies from the Hole—"

Bobby swallowed the rest of his sentence. On the tracks ahead of them, three soldiers materialized, running at full speed.

*Except their boots aren't touching the ground.*

"It's them," Vernon Ray said, his voice flat.

They were 50 yards away. Vernon Ray had told Bobby about the inaccuracy of Civil War-era weaponry. Still, the image of the bulldozer man's shattering skull was vivid, and Bobby wasn't willing to bet his life that these dudes' rifles followed rules of any sort.

"Come on," Bobby said, grabbing Vernon Ray and jerking him toward the woods.

One of the soldiers shouted—except Bobby couldn't be sure if the noise was audible or just in his head—and the nearest soldier was slowing enough to raise his rifle butt to his shoulder.

And though Bobby stood near Vernon Ray, it was clear the soldier was targeting Bobby alone.

*He either thinks I'm the "leader," or—*

The *pock* of the powder charge echoed up the forested alley of the tracks. The shot nicked off the gravel in front of Bobby, kicking up a rock and skittering it against his shoe. If not for the canvas Nikes he wore, the stone would have cut into his flesh.

"Move it, or your disco days are done," Vernon Ray said, pushing Bobby toward cover. Bobby reached the edge of the gravel railroad bed and slipped on the loose stone, flopping onto his butt and sliding into the brown bristle of briars and locust. A second shot zipped overhead, and Bobby rolled to his hands and feet, crawling deeper into the scrub brush. Damp leaves soaked his pants and thorns bit into his palms, but he scurried forward toward the gurgling creek, wrestling doghobble and honeysuckle vines.

The tracks were now out of sight, along with Vernon Ray. Bobby was afraid to call out lest he attract unwanted attention, but if he reached the creek he'd be exposed.

*Great, I've thrown my best friend to the wolves again.*

Except that didn't quite jibe, either. Vernon Ray had not only survived his encounter with Col. Creep, he'd come out of it with his chin up and a little strut. And the troops on the tracks had not aimed at Vernon Ray at all. Maybe they'd picked Bobby because he was a moving target and the most likely to escape, but if the dead really were at war with the living, then any victim should have done the job.

Before Bobby could dwell on the puzzle, other shouts erupted from the woods. He recognized his dad's voice among them: "They're on the tracks!"

Bobby wanted to warn them that their quarry wasn't real, but he didn't know how many ghosts were around. About a dozen had surrounded him on the mountain just before killing the bulldozer guy, and who knew whether the dead could summon reinforcements? For all he knew, they could have dug up a Confederate graveyard somewhere and raised an entire army.

He held his breath, but his heartbeat pounded in his ears, muffling the creek that splashed between cold stones. The sulfur smell of ghost gunpowder hung in the air. Branches snapped as men plowed through the woods.

*Ghosts shouldn't make noise, right? But they can shoot real bullets. Why can't these bastards play fair?*

Vernon Ray's dad yelled something Bobby couldn't make out. No shots had been fired in the last minute or so, but Bobby's heart had probably drummed a thousand beats in that time. The Living History soldiers were moving up the tracks, which meant the ghost soldiers must have moseyed the hell back up the mountain.

*But where was Vernon Ray?*

Bobby crawled out of concealment, accompanied by the pungent tang of broken milkweed. Briars tugged at his clothes but he fought through, afraid he'd be left behind.

As he crawled out of the woods, several of the re-enactors ran along the tracks. He recognized Stony Hampton and Whizzer Buchanan, two well-diggers who sometimes worked with his dad. They were out of breath, legs pumping, gravel flying from beneath their boots. Whizzer's dented tin canteen bounced against his bony ass, making a pinging sound.

Ahead on the tracks, Vernon Ray's dad was leading the way, his revolver pointed at the sky. The ghost soldiers had either vanished or had kicked into some sort of supernatural gear and choo-chooed away.

And Vernon Ray had vanished with them.

"What the hell you doing here?"

Bobby turned to see his dad limping up the track, a bloody handkerchief wrapped around his bowling hand, a red wound blooming in his shoulder. "Me and Vernon Ray—"

"I told you not to hang around with that little faggot."

"The ghosts took him."

"The enemy, you mean."

"Dad?" Bobby sniffed the air, wondering if his old man was drunk. A hint of bourbon, nothing more, and Dad could always hold his booze. His eyes were not bloodshot, but they were glazed, the pupils engorged.

"Your dad's up yonder," Dad said, nodding up the tracks.

"Huh?"

Dad's face scrunched into a sneer. "Captain Jeffie Davis. The man who planted your seed."

Dad brushed past him, tottering up the tracks. The rest of the Home Guard had rounded the curve and were lost among the trees. Bobby took two steps after them then realized he was heading toward the mountain and the ghost soldiers instead of away, to the sane safety of town.

"Are you okay, Dad?" Bobby was almost afraid to ask, because it was the sort of question that answered itself.

"Gone around the bend," Dad said, gripping his musket so tightly his knuckles were white. A thick drop of blood welled at the end of his ragged bandage and his other wound looked like raw hamburger.

Dad took off, heading toward the shouts of his fellow soldiers. A shot fired somewhere on the slope above, then came an answering report from behind. Bobby debated crawling back into the obscurity of the weeds, pondering sitting out the war. But Vernon Ray was his best friend.

*Who cares if he has Bambi eyelashes and a little extra wiggle in his walk? He's the closest thing to normal I've known in this life.*

And Dad had suggested an even tighter kinship between Vernon Ray and Bobby, but Bobby didn't have time to figure that one out at the moment. His forehead hurt as if a wire were stretched around his skull. Dad was nearly to the curve in the tracks. In a moment, Bobby would be alone.

He glanced around for some kind of weapon, but the nearby branches were flimsy. He stuffed some rocks in his pocket, the way he did when they passed the mean dogs at the Stillwell house. Rocks didn't intimidate the dogs one little bit, and Bobby didn't expect they'd scare the ghosts, either, but the gesture made him feel better.

*Th'ow it, doof.*

If he'd stayed away from the Hole in the first place, all this never would have happened. But maybe the Hole was bigger than all of them, the inside-out darkness that was barely hidden by the thin painted illusion of life that lay over it.

He dashed after Dad, expecting to round the bend and find the entire Home Guard gone, Dad included, and the rest of the world giving way to a blank netherworld, the tracks dangling into the vast white void of space like a comic book page that had been partially erased.

Instead, he saw the battle lines drawn as if the stakes were not merely life and death, but past and future as well.

The ghost patrol stood in a loose formation behind Col. Creep, their weapons glinting dully as if they'd been salvaged from an underground cache. One of the men had a slanted face, his left eye frozen open, a jagged scar over one eyebrow. The colonel stood with his shoulders square, eyes blazing from beneath the brim of his cavalier's hat. Kirk's gloved hands were folded across his chest as if he'd been laid to rest that way, but Bobby didn't think the colonel had gotten much sleep in the 150 years he'd been dead.

Behind the colonel was Vernon Ray, standing among the ghost soldiers as if he'd been recruited into their ranks. He was a little pale but appeared unhurt. A ragged, stained kepi was tucked down on his head.

Cindy's words came back to Bobby: *Or they'll take a replacement . . . .*

Jeff Davis and his men stood spread across the tracks, weapons at ready. The rounded tip of Jeff's saber was pointed at the heavens, the polished edge gilded by the sun. Stony and Whizzer knelt in the gravel, muskets leveled. Five Home Guard troops stood behind them, Dad among them.

Dad aimed his gun and his cheek was pressed against the butt of his rifle as if he were sighting down the barrel. The battle cries had died away, along with the gun smoke, and leaves flapped in the hushed wind. The air carried the funereal taste of October, clouds brushing their slow shadows across the mountainsides and tinting the trees gray.

The two sides faced off, awaiting orders from above or below. Bobby couldn't be sure because of the woolly beard, but Kirk appeared to be smiling, though the eyes were as black as rotted sin.

*They're making their stand. Which doesn't make a bit of sense, because even a dummy like me knows they'd be better off defending higher ground.*

*But maybe they already occupy the high ground, because I sure can't tell good from evil anymore.*

"Looks like you're done running, Kirk," Capt. Davis said, as calm as if he were playing a video game. "I'd give you a chance to surrender, but I don't think we make garrisons that can hold such as you."

Bobby crouched behind Whizzer and Dad, peering through the gap in the firing line. The copper stink of Dad's wound blended with the mustiness of the old uniforms and the acrid tang of gunpowder

Capt. Davis raised his saber toward the sky and leveled his pistol. "Ready!" he shouted.

The boys of the Home Guard tensed, though across the way their undead adversaries were blank faced and as stoic as Spartans.

"Aim . . . ."

"Damn, Jeff, your boy's in there," Stony Hampton said. "He might get hit."

"There's no such thing as innocent blood," the captain said.

Col. Creep stepped protectively—*floated*, Bobby thought, still not used to the unnatural, liquid motion—in front of Vernon Ray, as if his amorphous flesh could shield the boy from real bullets. Bobby's and Vernon Ray's eyes met and Vernon Ray gave a small nod and silently moved his lips.

Bobby couldn't be sure, because he'd rarely seen the words formed, but he thought they might have shaped "I love you."

"Fire!" the crazed captain bellowed, and all hell broke loose in a cannonade of thunder, smoke, and screams.

CHAPTER TWENTY-NINE

Littlefield arrived on the scene just as the smoke cleared.

Jeff Davis was poking around on the gravel bed with his saber, chinking up rocks and tapping as if checking for escape hatches. The Home Guard looked as if the soldiers were fighting off a long hangover instead of a renegade pack of ghosts. Where Littlefield had expected carnage, bloodshed, and the moans of the dying, he found only the weekend warriors collapsed about the railroad tracks, wiping sweaty hair with their caps and rising unsteadily to their feet.

"What happened?" Cindy asked Whizzer Buchanan, who in civilian life had been busted for selling weed the year before. Littlefield wished this was a hallucination from the bottom of a bong instead of the reality of a world turned upside down.

"Dunno," Whizzer said. "We was on a maneuver and that's about all I remember."

"How'd we get up here, anyway?" said Elmer Eldreth, and Littlefield saw that though his hand was still bandaged, the wound on his shoulder was closed and the flesh undamaged, though his uniform had a small hole in it.

"Great," Cindy said. "The story of the century and my eyewitnesses are blind."

"Just be glad nobody else was killed," Littlefield said. "As far as I can tell."

A boy approached from the edge of the woods. He wore neither a uniform nor a period outfit of the civilian attachment. His gray eyes were wide, cheeks pale, hands shaking.

*Looks like he's still got his wits about him. At least he has enough sense to be scared.*

"Hey, Bobby," Cindy said, and the sheriff saw a glance of recognition and secret agreement pass between them. "You okay?"

Before Bobby could answer, Littlefield asked, "Did you see what happened?"

The boy shook his head. "Nothing but smoke."

"They overloaded their battery," Cindy said. "Went 'poof' like a magician's sleight of hand."

"Vernon Ray's gone," Bobby said.

"Gone?" Littlefield said.

"They took him."

Littlefield was about to ask who had done the taking, but then realized there was only one "they." Kirk's Raiders might have beaten a retreat from the battlefield, but the war was far from over.

"Where did they go?" Cindy asked, but Littlefield already knew the answer. He'd known it all along, just as Cindy had accused, but he'd avoided the truth because it was troublesome and painful.

*It always goes back to the Hole and the darkness under the world.*

If ignoring it didn't make it go away, maybe he could solve the problem the old-fashioned way: kill it quick and bury it clean. He'd had a bead on the colonel back at the park, had aimed true at an imaginary bull's-eye on the tunic-covered chest, but his mistake had been shooting the dead man in the heart.

Because it turned out the colonel didn't have one.

Capt. Davis hustled up, his saber pointed toward the ground. "The Tennessee boys didn't follow the script," he said.

"They ain't supposed to be in until tomorrow," Stony Hampton said, swatting at a sweat bee that hovered in the fading gun smoke.

"That's what I mean," Davis said.

"Let me check that pistol again," Littlefield said to him.

The captain frowned and gazed down the tracks as if a steam locomotive had hauled off half his brains. He passed the gun to Littlefield, who checked the chamber and saw that all the cartridges were intact.

"He fired it," Cindy said. "And I doubt he had time to reload."

"Invisible bullets," Bobby said. "Everybody's shooting blanks."

"At blank targets," the sheriff said.

Littlefield passed the gun back to Davis, who holstered it and began rallying the troops for the march back to camp. They grumbled a little, as if content in their drowsiness, but they gathered their gear. Elmer Eldreth collected his hat and musket, tipping his canteen and taking a generous gulp.

Capt. Davis led the desultory soldiers down the track. Bobby ran after his dad, said something to him, and received a lazy nod in response. Bobby jogged back to where the sheriff and Cindy stood on the tracks, reconnoitering the woods.

"Like nothing ever happened," Cindy said.

Littlefield couldn't resist. "There goes your Pulitzer and your book deal."

"I've still got my camera."

"If there's anything on it. I have a feeling when they get back to the park, they'll find Chalky Watkins strutting around fresh as a rooster, wondering where the hell everybody went. And that woman in the civilian camp will be flexing mugs of fresh coffee like some backwoods Martha Stewart."

"That horseman got killed, remember?"

"Sure, but I'll bet there's not a scratch on him now, and Perry Hoyle will write it down as a heart attack or stroke. It's almost like nothing's changed, a return to balance."

"Except Vernon Ray's gone," Bobby said, and he turned to Cindy. "Your 'replacement' theory. To balance things out."

"That means one got away," Cindy said.

"What are you two talking about?" Littlefield said. Capt. Davis and his Home Guard had gone around the curve and were no longer visible, though Davis's tired commands were audible as he herded the troops back to Aldridge Park.

"It ain't over," Bobby said. "That was the calm before the storm."

"The anticlimax," Cindy said. "To trick these macho clowns into letting loose with a bunch of testosterone and rage so Kirk's Raiders could sponge up the energy. Like a haunted battlefield where the ghosts linger long after the screams have died away and the blood has soaked deep in the dirt, feeding on the long memory of pain."

"We've covered all this before," Littlefield said. "So does this mean they got what they wanted?"

"Only if you're willing to give them the boy," Cindy said.

Littlefield gazed through the trees that were rooted and fed by the black skin of the mountain, the shadows under the kaleidoscopic canopy seeming to eddy and swirl like obscene molasses. He thought of his dead deputy, Sheila Story, and his little brother, other sacrificial lambs thrown on the altar of his ego and failure.

*You feed the monsters and they go away and leave you alone.*

*Even if the outcome carries a little collateral damage.*

*At least you walk away.*

*You walk away.*

"I guess there's nothing else for it," Littlefield said, then asked Bobby. "How do we get to the Hole from here?"

Bobby pointed to a slight part in the scrub, where jackvine and poison oak strangled a stand of leafless saplings. The path was barely wide enough to allow passage to a rabbit or raccoon, much less a grown man. But the gate was strait and the way was narrow. Or so said a book Littlefield had burned six years ago along with a certain contaminated church over in Whispering Pines.

"I don't suppose I could talk you into staying out of it?" Littlefield asked Cindy.

"No," she said, adjusting the camera on her shoulder as if preparing for a hike. "But if it makes you feel any better, I'll keep it off the record."

"You could never translate all this into English."

"Enough talking," Bobby said, heading for the animal path. "My best friend's up there in the Jangling Hole with a bunch of dead guys."

He slipped into the tangled brush and was swallowed by the woods of Mulatto Mountain.

Littlefield stared at Cindy as if fully seeing her for the first time, as a colleague, a partner in crime, and a woman, and he wondered if he'd always looked at people in his life as ghosts just waiting to happen. Her eyes were as blue as the sky, flecked with gold that might have been borrowed from the autumn poplar or the sun. She blinked first.

"History is written by the winners," she said, sneakers crunching the gravel as she hurried after Bobby.

"Or the survivors," Littlefield said, but he was the only one around to hear it.

## CHAPTER THIRTY

Pearl had took sick since the shenanigans of the night before, and Hardy figured a day in bed would do her good, not to mention get her out of harm's way in case Kirk's bunch paid a return visit.

He'd forgotten he'd set the tea kettle on the stove to make her a cup of that fancy Darjeeling hippie-sounding stuff. When it broke steam and erupted in a whistle, he about jumped out of his skin, thinking it was the shriek of one of those contrary creatures from the Hole. He'd scalded his thumb while pouring the hot water, and now balanced the cup and saucer as he made his precarious way up the stairs.

He skipped the thirteenth step, where the drummer boy had been shot the night before. There was no blood, no bullet holes in the wall, nothing to mark the confrontation between Earley and Kirk's Raiders. If not for the musket that had wound up at the far end of the hall, Hardy would have written off the incident as a dream, though that damnable rattling of the snare drum still echoed in the stairwells of his memory. At least Pearl and Donnie had been protected from the sight of the ghosts, though his wife's imagination had done worse things to her than her eyes ever could.

And Donnie had no imagination worth worrying about.

Donnie's room was quiet, which meant his son was either coloring again or else he was sleeping, or maybe just sitting cross-legged in the corner and rocking back and forth as he sometimes did. Hardy was almost past the room when he saw the opened door and the black wedge that filled the space leading behind it.

The door had been locked from the outside when Hardy had gone down to the kitchen. He'd checked it twice to make sure. Pearl might have taken Donnie into the bedroom to comfort him the way she had when he was six and the nightmares came. Except she'd been snoring loud enough to wake the dead, compliments of the blue pills the doctors had prescribed her in February, when the latest round of tests had resulted in the suggestion of a state hospital stay for Donnie.

Hardy swallowed hard and kicked the door wide with the toe of his boot. It squeaked open and Hardy slopped some of the tea on his overalls. The room held nothing but the little table with its scattered crayons and papers, the rumpled cot in the corner, and a plastic water tumbler. Hardy set the saucer on the table and picked up the lone drawing on it. He angled it so it caught the light leaking from the hall.

Stick figures. A man and a boy.

Marching toward the Hole, which held smears of red and yellow in its dark squiggles as if the devil was serving up hot peppers for dinner.

He hurried down the hall to his bedroom and checked on Pearl. The hand-stitched quilt rose and fell with her breathing. Maybe merciful God would let her sleep through it all. Hardy took the musket from the closet, knowing it was as impotent as the slack, wrinkled meat between his legs, but like that part of him that had sired Donnie, its presence gave him comfort nonetheless. The Bible offered a little less, but he tucked it in his overall pocket anyway, just to feel the weight of the words.

As he made his way back through the hall, he was troubled by two things. Something had unlocked Donnie's door and then led Donnie down the creaky stairs and past Hardy in the kitchen without being seen. Well, there was a third thing, too. The Hole had come unplugged and hell had let slip a few of its occupants.

From the porch, he surveyed the pasture and the twin ruts that led to the far gate. The dew had long since dried and the cows were grazing with their heads toward the west, working the last of the season's grass as if storing the sweetness against the dead taste of winter hay. A lone buzzard circled high beneath the clouds, lazy and patient.

The rumble of heavy equipment oozed down from Mulatto Mountain as if the ancient stacked granite was being shaken to its foundation. He thought he heard a snare cadence in the diesel-fueled throbbing, but it might have been his own erratic pulse fluttering against his eardrums.

The musket had grown heavy by the time he reached the woods, and he considered tossing the Bible to ease his load. He thought about that little inspirational picture he'd seen in the doctor's office, where there were footprints on the beach and the bit about where there was only one set of footprints and it turned out Jesus had carried a man across the sand for a while.

There was no mention of where they both were headed or why Jesus wouldn't allow the fellow to rest for a minute, but that was the way of things. You just kept walking, no matter the burden.

Entering the high church of trees, he shivered. The temperature had dropped about 20 degrees and the advance scouts of December had grown a little bolder, baring their teeth in the shadows. This was a time of year for digging potatoes and setting aside cabbages, hauling in the feed corn and piling it up in the barn crib. Autumn was a season of dying, and the weak wouldn't see it through.

Budget Bill Willard's machinery was rumbling away, carving up the mountain and changing it forever. In a few years, there would be no Mulatto Mountain. Only Elkridge, with a fancy embossed sign down by the highway, and a stone entryway with a steel gate that could be lifted by punching in a code. Hardy wondered if the Hole would still be there, Kirk's Raiders sleeping under the million-dollar houses that dotted the slopes.

*Time passes and human greed outlasts even the eternal.*

But when it came to sins, Hardy carried enough of his own. Pride went before a fall, the Good Book said, and he'd never figured out whether that meant pride led to trouble or whether you better throw over your pride before it got the best of you. Maybe pride was just another form of greed, but one thing Hardy knew, the Hole wasn't taking his boy without a fight, even if Hardy had to march right down in there and wrestle bare-handed with Kirk and his entire troop.

He could have avoided the construction area, but that would have meant cutting below the ridge and climbing a steep, rocky incline on the north slope, where the laurel grew tangled and tough. He didn't want to waste either the time or the energy, and he didn't intend to let anything stand in his way, even a bulldozer. He emerged from the logging trail onto the turnaround, where Budget Bill Willard had planned to place the clubhouse for the resort. A dump truck was parked on the gravel, idling as it awaited a small steam shovel whose jaws plucked at gray boulders.

The Caterpillar bulldozer was higher on the slope, digging its thick, rusty blade into the dirt, turning up stumps and stones. It hadn't taken long for Budget Bill to replace Carter Harrison, and the raw road was much closer to the ridge than it had been during Hardy's last visit. Bill's crew was making good time.

Hardy followed the fresh cut of the road, ignoring the clanky steam shovel. Budget Bill's pick-up was off to the side in some weeds. The cab was empty, and Hardy hoped the sawed-off developer was away checking out property lines or maybe taking some of those photographs of the mountaintops he was able to parlay into calendars and postcards. Hardy followed the loose soil until he was near the bulldozer, and then realized the new road was barely a hundred feet from the Hole.

The air was charged with the static of a coming storm, though only a few clouds dotted the horizon. The ground throbbed under Hardy's feet as he ascended the road bed, and the roar of the big diesel engine shouted down the forest noises. Ahead was a gap in the laurels where he could duck into the woods and reach the cave. Hardy thought he would make it without being seen when one of the Caterpillar's treads locked and the machine swung around sideways.

Budget Bill was in the cab, working the dozer's levers, his hands encased in White Mule work gloves. He eased down the throttle and a tuft of black smoke spilled from the smokestack. As their eyes met, understanding and horror dawned on the developer's face.

*He thinks I've gone squirrel-shit nutty and that I killed Carter, trying to stop the development. And he reckons he's next.*

Hardy nodded at Budget Bill and patted the musket barrel, letting him think the worst. He let a grin creep up one side of his face, enjoying the developer's torment. He considered the steep hike remaining to reach the Hole. Even if he made it without his heart exploding, he wouldn't have much wind left to take on a haunted platoon before Kirk and the mountain took whatever little bit was left of his son's mind and soul.

He pointed the musket toward Budget Bill, not bothering to aim.

Budget Bill eased back on the levers and raised his hands like a prisoner in a war movie. Hardy eased the barrel of the musket back and forth, motioning for Bill to dismount. Bill reached for the ignition but Hardy shook his head. Bill climbed down, eyes flicking back and forth as if considering escape.

Hardy met him when he reached the ground and yelled over the rumble of the diesel engine. "How do you run this contraption?"

Bill, perhaps sensing if he let Hardy take the bulldozer he could escape with his life, made a pulling motion. "Left bar forward, right for back, brake in the middle."

"Like an old Massey Ferguson tractor," Hardy said.

Bill nodded, though Hardy suspected the developer didn't know the first thing about Massey Fergusons. Bill would have probably agreed that the sun rose in the south and the Tooth Fairy was real if it would keep Hardy's finger away from the trigger.

Hardy settled in the cab seat, laid his gun across his lap, and pulled back on the throttle. He yanked the lever–Budget Bill, who was skidding down the muddy road as fast as his stunted legs could carry him, hadn't lied to him–and the dozer lurched into the saplings and strewn granite stones, grinding toward the Hole.

CHAPTER THIRTY-ONE

The Jangling Hole was cool, the air fetid. Vernon Ray was just past the reach of daylight, beyond the spot where the rubble had settled during the long-ago cave-in. The throat of the underworld was now open, the slumbering lungs taking a deep breath of the outside universe as if starved for light and life.

The dead soldiers were resting around an unseen campfire. They no longer appeared solid, except for Kirk, who crouched near the cave's mouth and surveyed the edge of the woods. Another soldier, whose cheek bore a deep scar, stood just beyond the opening, his musket at the ready. Vernon Ray adjusted his kepi and blinked into the darkness, expecting the icy pierce of a bayonet or the muffled detonation of a deadly powder charge.

The ground trembled with the drone of heavy equipment, and a rock kicked loose from the cave ceiling and bounced near Vernon Ray's feet. A shower of moist dirt sprinkled on his shoulder.

"You warm enough?" one of the men said, and the words echoed a couple of times before dying in the rumble of heavy equipment.

"You can talk," Vernon Ray said, and laughter erupted around the circle, mimicking the low rumble of machinery.

"Yeah, but you can't rightly hear," said another soldier. His kepi was pulled low over his forehead, but white bone glinted dully where his chin should have been.

"Leave the boy alone," Kirk ordered, before turning his gaze back to the forest outside the cave. His voice was the same as the one Vernon Ray had heard in his head during the rain-shed encounter.

Those words rose from the depths of his memory like a drowned corpse bobbing up from a watery grave: *We don't belong together.*

The soldier to the left of Vernon Ray was scraping his spoon against a tin plate, dredging up air and scooping it toward his moss-covered face. The moss parted, revealing a black maw, and the spoon entered. After a brief slurping, the spoon pulled free, dribbling bits of gooey mud. The spoon hit the plate again, combining with the rattle of hardware and the cleaning of muskets in a jangle of activity that had given the Hole its name.

There were three soldiers between Vernon Ray and the opening. Kirk was one, the sentry the second, and the last lay sprawled behind Vernon Ray, propped up on the stump of an arm. Shattered bone emerged from a ragged sleeve packed with rancid, discolored meat. The stench of corruption mingled with the mildew and mud and the acrid smoke that arose from somewhere below.

Vernon Ray thought of running for daylight, leaping the soldier behind him and plowing past Kirk. But he wasn't sure his legs would work anymore. The Raiders had marched him up the mountain under the cover of gun-smoke, somehow diverting the attention of his dad's Living History group.

The bullets had whizzed past, manifesting into solid things, the battle made real for a short stretch of the morning. The ghost soldiers could have killed him, or let him get shot by friendly fire, but instead they had taken him prisoner.

So they wanted him alive for a reason.

"Here come Eggers," the sentry shouted.

Several of the soldiers reached for their muskets and Kirk rose to his feet and moved to the edge of sunlight. Vernon Ray shifted away from the dark depths of the tunnel that promised its own special brand of gravity, one that would suck and tug until all light was defeated. He knew better than to trust his depth perception in the Hole, and the grinding of the bulldozer's steel against ancient granite added to his disorientation.

From his vantage point, he could see Donnie Eggers approaching the Hole, grinning like a rabid possum and tapping two sticks against his thighs as he juddered up the slope. Branches slapped at his face but he seemed oblivious to the welts raised in his flesh. His cotton shirt was torn, naked toes covered in mud, his hair greasy with sweat. Donnie's wild eyes were fixed on the cave as if the darkness inside it held vast pleasures and joys.

"Go back," Vernon Ray whispered.

"Ain't no going back," Kirk said, though Vernon Ray's words had barely been audible.

That's when the corporal came out of the trees, floating over ferns and galax and jackvine. It was the man from the railroad tracks, the one with the CSA canteen. Earley Eggers. Decades dead and as hellacious and rebellious as ever.

"All right, boys, we got one more battle," Kirk said, and though the command was issued loudly enough to carry over the bulldozer that was crashing through the trees on the back side of the ridge, the soldiers rose with a languid reluctance. The man with the stump lifted himself by his wounded limb, gangrenous flesh dropping from the effort.

Boneface with the kepi was grinning, but Vernon Ray couldn't tell whether it was due to nervousness or the fact that his lips had long since melted away to dust. The soldier with the red kerchief and crusty blue tunic drifted toward the mouth of the cave, moving his legs as if his spirit still harbored memory of needing them. The preternatural platoon was mustering around their leader, taking a stand, black eyes flinting tiny sparks of hellfire. They were misfits, losers, a band of outcasts that the world had no room for, a coalition of the damned whose camaraderie had survived the grave.

*We don't belong together.*

And one of them had broken ranks. The deserter, Eggers.

No wonder they were riled.

But that didn't mean the innocent should suffer. Every war had its collateral damage, every conflict its unintended targets. If Cindy Baumhower's law of balance was correct, then Earley's return should end the war, at least for this go-round.

But Donnie might reach the Hole first, and Kirk might decide a living Eggers was better than a dead Eggers, and fresh blood might be welcome.

Donnie was close enough that Vernon Ray could see a strand of clear drool dangling from one corner of his idiot grin. Donnie's head bobbed as his wrists flexed in a fluid grace that defied the spastic jerking of his legs and shoulders. He was stamping out the vintages of his mental isolation, marching to the beat of an indifferent drummer.

Earley was mostly solid, though ripples of light played in his limbs as he staggered toward the Hole. His face was like dishwater, sloshing around the soulless eyes.

Kirk rubbed his beard, standing with broad shoulders squared and one hand on the hilt of his saber, his silhouette dark against the spilled shaft of sunlight. Muskets rattled as the Raiders tamped sulfur and brimstone into their barrels.

"Want them dead or alive?" Boneface asked Kirk.

"Let him go," Vernon Ray said. "He never belonged here."

Kirk angled his head around, then around, until he was facing Vernon Ray, though his boots and medals were still pointed toward the forest. Kirk's words were nearly lost in the roar of the diesel engine and the cracking of tree limbs, but Vernon Ray wasn't sure whether they were spoken or were voiced by the dank wind oozing up from the depths of the cave.

"Nobody belongs nowhere," the voice said, reverberating in Vernon Ray's head as if his skull were a granite sheath.

Donnie was less than 30 feet from the cave now, eyes bright with fevered hope. He would reach the Hole before Earley. And the oddest part was that Donnie, who was alive, appeared to fade and become less substantial the nearer he got, while Earley grew more solid and heavy, his scuffed boots now flopping over the ground.

The grinding, splintery thunder of the bulldozer swelled louder as the earth machine ascended the ridge.

"Vernon Ray?" came a shout from the edge of the forest.

*Bobby . . . .*

CHAPTER THIRTY-TWO

Bobby had raced ahead of Cindy and the sheriff, anxious to find Vernon Ray before Kirk and the goon squad siphoned him so deep into the Hole he would never return.

At least not in any recognizable, useful, *human* way. Donnie Eggers had been only half gone, according to the rumors, and an intangible half of him was trapped lurking somewhere in those black depths. Vernon Ray's fate might be far worse.

Bobby wasn't sure what he would do when he got to the Hole, but he slowed enough to scoop up a fist-sized stone from among the fallen leaves. *Th'ow it, doof*, Dex repeated in his head.

And if what Dad said were true, Vernon Ray was more than his best friend, more than the guy who tried to kiss him, more than a fellow survivor of the Dysfunctional Family Circus. Vernon Ray was his brother by blood. That carried extra obligation, and Bobby was willing to risk death, or whatever passed for death in the depths of the Hole, to rescue V-Ray.

When he entered the clearing in front of the Hole and beheld that terrible orifice of rock, dirt, and darkness, the sun ducked behind a clump of clouds and stretched a shadow over Mulatto Mountain. Earley Eggers staggered toward the Hole like a wayward son returning to the family doorstep.

The cave was still and empty, at least from the few feet Bobby could see of its interior. The entrance seemed like a solid wall of black glass, and he imagined that if he made it close enough to hurl his stone, the wall would shatter like a midnight mirror into a thousand sharp pieces.

*And what would be behind it?*

Donnie didn't slow down. The man-child took staggering steps toward the Hole as if navigating a sheet of ice with cinder blocks on his bare feet, but he moved forward with determination and strength. Earley's movements were almost in perfect rhythm with Donnie's, as if the two had undergone the same parade drills and now were locked in a unison of muscle memory.

The bulldozer chuffed and trembled in the woods, tearing up trees as it made its inexorable assault on the ridge. Donnie was almost to the entrance now, Earley about 20 feet behind him. Donnie had dissolved and faded so that Bobby was able to see gray slabs of mossy granite through his body. Donnie was ten feet from the Hole when a command issued forth from the cave: "Halt!"

Bobby didn't recognize the deep and chilling voice, but he would have bet his entire run of Silver Surfer comics that it belonged to Col. Creep. Donnie and Earley both stopped, though Donnie continued to tap out his quiet cadence, his head bobbing up and down.

"Vernon Ray?" Bobby shouted again, and he heard the reporter and the sheriff hollering after both of them, then the bulldozer burst through the line of laurels and clanked into the clearing, a wild-eyed Hardy Eggers at the controls.

The sheriff stood near the stump where the boys had been smoking cigarettes a week ago. He held his pistol in his hand as if he were the star gunslinger in a shoot-em-up western. Bobby looked down at the rock in his hand, then at Hardy's musket.

*Crapola. Am I the only one who isn't packing heat?*

Just when Bobby thought the situation couldn't get any weirder, Capt. Jefferson Davis jumped out from behind a boulder near the cave, his saber flashing in the filtered sun. He grabbed Earley and yanked the dead, ragged scarecrow of a soldier close, pressing the saber to Earley's neck. The captain's Rebel yell temporarily drowned out the rumbling bulldozer.

Hardy stood in the cab of the idling bulldozer and his musket swiveled from the cave to Earley, then to Jeff Davis. The sheriff's pistol did likewise. Cindy Baumhower had appeared at the sheriff's side, and her camera lens also tracked between the various targets.

The commanding voice boomed from the cave again: "Looks like we have us a standoff."

CHAPTER THIRTY-THREE

There was motion at the mouth of the cave, and a hunk of shadow broke itself free and stepped forward.

It was the man in the cavalier's hat, the ratty ostrich plume flailing in the October breeze. Littlefield aimed his Glock at the man, and then remembered they'd already played out that scenario and all Littlefield had to show for it was an empty shell casing. Except the man–Col. George Kirk, if he believed Cindy–appeared more substantial than he had down at the park, as if submersing in the Hole had revitalized him in the same way that heated natural springs restored spa visitors.

The dead colonel seemed calmest of all, as if defeat or victory led to the same fate. The veins in Jeff Davis's temple were turgid and purple, his teeth bared in a rictus of madness. Littlefield didn't know what would happen if Davis drew his saber across Earley's throat, but he had a feeling that Kirk wouldn't like it. And though Kirk held only a saber himself, he had a group of soldiers backing him up who had already proven they would follow him to hell and back.

A click beside Littlefield startled him, then he heard the whir of machinery and realized Cindy was focusing her camera. "Quit it," he said.

"You do your job and I'll do mine," she said.

*Sounds simple, except I'm not sure what my job is at the moment. I can't tell whether this situation calls for an undertaker, a psychiatrist, or an exorcist in a Sherman tank.*

Treetops shook as the bulldozer plowed toward the clearing, and the growling of the big Cat engine added extra tension to the scene, setting Littlefield's teeth on edge.

"Give me my soldier," Jeff shouted at the colonel.

The colonel merely stood with one hand on his saber, studying the assembly as if he were defending a fort surrounded on all sides. Jeff's hostage, who Littlefield now recognized as the man he'd seen vanish in the lumberyard, appeared slack and resigned, like a scarecrow dangling on a cold and lonely winter pole.

The hostage looked as solid and healthy as the colonel, except for his eyes, which had no whites. Littlefield wasn't sure what would happen if Jeff drew the saber across the dead soldier's throat, but he imagined a Pandora's box of horrors spilling out from the wound, nasty stinging creatures and fanged bats and tiny, scaly dragons.

Bobby, who had stopped when the colonel emerged from the Hole, edged toward the opening and paused again near Donnie. "Vernon Ray! Are you in there?"

Metal clanked against stone, and the bulldozer's treads rattled and squeaked as they fought for traction. Donnie's hands moved up and down as if drumming in accompaniment, then the autistic man took a stiff stride toward the colonel. Bobby grabbed him and tried to tug him backward, but the man was too strong. Donnie shook free, knocking Bobby to his knees, and lumbered toward the colonel.

"Donnie," the sheriff shouted, taking a step forward bit unsure where his loyalties lay. "Get back here."

"You're only getting one, but not mine," Jeff said to the colonel. "Which one is it going to be?"

Col. Kirk folded his arms across his chest as if he had all the time in the world, which Littlefield supposed he had. Then the colonel lifted his head and gazed at the sky as if remembering what it was like to breathe autumn mountain air. Aside from the cantankerous bulldozer, the moment was almost peaceful.

Bobby scrambled to his feet and cupped his hands against his mouth. "Vernon Ray?"

The colonel ignored him. Instead, his head swiveled toward Earley. "Desertion is a hanging offense, Corporal."

"Take him and hang him, then," Jeff said, pressing the saber deeper into the solidified ether of Earley's neck. Littlefield saw a black sliver open in the supernatural skin and wondered if Jeff Davis was committing a crime.

*Assault with intent to kill? Hard to make that one stand up in court when the victim was already dead.*

Folklore said if you wanted to kill a snake, you had to chop off its head and wait for sundown. He was considering giving Col. Kirk one more opportunity to take a bullet and die like a man, but before he could force himself to pull the trigger, the bulldozer burst forward, roots and branches dangling from its raised blade. Dirt and wet leaves sprinkled from its treads as it plowed ahead.

Hardy Eggers tilted the throttle full ahead in a burst of black smoke. Littlefield started toward the bulldozer and showed his palm, even though he didn't expect the crazy-eyed old man to obey his command to stop. From the way Hardy wrestled with the levers, Littlefield wasn't sure the man could have put on the brakes if he wanted to. And Littlefield wasn't about to climb over those churning treads to reach the cab.

Hardy was pale and sweating, one white eyebrow twitching in anxiety. He eased one of the levers forward and the bulldozer slowed as he motioned Bobby away from the Hole. "I told you damned kids to stay away."

"My friend's in there,"' Bobby said.

"I can't worry about your friend," Hardy said, tugging up one of his overall straps and pointing his musket into the Hole. "I got to save my boy. What's left of him, anyways."

"They want Earley," Bobby said. Littlefield took advantage of Hardy's distraction to close in, and Cindy stuck to him like an unwanted shadow.

"They done tried to take him but Earley ain't going back. He's done his duty."

"But somebody's got to pay," Bobby said.

"Kirk needs a replacement," Cindy said. "The law of mass and energy."

"I follow a different law," Hardy shouted. "The Bible says an eye for an eye, blood for blood, a burning for a burning."

"There won't be any more blood spilled here," Littlefield said, though he doubted if the black stuff oozing from Earley's neck counted as "blood." "Not while I have anything to say about it."

"Why do you think you'd have any say?" Kirk thundered.

"Give me back my boy," Hardy yelled.

"Give me back *my* boy," Jeff yelled.

Kirk's head swiveled back and forth between Earley and Donnie as if making a decision, though his skull appeared too lolling and loose, as if his spine had shattered during the cave-in and the long decades hadn't knitted the bones back together.

Just before the beetle-black eyes could settle on a new recruit, Vernon Ray stepped from the shadows of the cave, though it looked to Littlefield as if some of the shadows still clung to him like old rotted rags. A snare drum bounced against his hip as he walked to the colonel's side and stood at attention as if awaiting orders.

His left hand held two drumsticks and his right palm was facing out as he saluted.

## CHAPTER THIRTY-FOUR

"Run, Vee," Bobby yelled, not understanding how his friend–brother–could stand there with the Hole at his back like a giant mouth. Vernon Ray acted as if he hadn't heard, as though the people gathered around him were toy soldiers on a make-believe map. Bobby expected gunfire to erupt at any moment, and since the boys in the Hole seemed to have hoarded enough munitions to last several centuries, Bobby would bet on Kirk's Raiders to carry the day.

"Come here, son," Jeff shouted, momentarily relaxing his grip on Earley and letting his saber tilt down.

Donnie spazz-marched in place, apparently excited by the presence of the snare drum, but Bobby held him by the waist. Hardy, perched in the bulldozer seat, put his musket to his shoulder and stared down the barrel at Kirk.

Knowing the legendary inaccuracy of Civil War-era weaponry, Bobby figured V-Ray was as likely to take the bullet as Kirk was. Kirk had already spent his share of time on the mortal plane, and Vernon Ray might get cheated of his own go-round.

"We'll let them choose," Kirk said, his lips scarcely moving but his voice making a duet with the bulldozer engine. He put a pale hand on Vernon Ray's shoulder. Bobby imagined the colonel's flesh was as cool and cloying as the dirt in the cave.

"Don't go AWOL, soldier," Jeff shouted.

Vernon Ray snapped off a mocking salute in his dad's direction. "Reporting for duty, *suh!*"

Donnie took another trembling step toward the Hole, and Hardy's musket exploded in a flash of smoke. The musket ball must have been aimed at Donnie's twitching legs because it kicked up a spray of mud several feet in front of them.

Hardy's shot triggered a chain reaction, and Bobby froze. Littlefield fired his pistol and Col. Kirk's tunic erupted in a blossom of murky oil. The colonel looked down with no expression, eyes as dead and cool as the Jangling Hole that had infected them with its unwholesome lack of light.

Earley Eggers escaped from Jeff Davis's grip, going to smoke, leaving Jeff–*Daddy?*–to clutch at the evaporating fibers of his spectral hostage.

Bobby sprang toward Vernon Ray, who stared out at the woods like a lone sentry of the soul, watching and waiting for an end to the forever war.

Kirk clutched the wound in his chest, taking his hand away and staring at the sludge that dripped from his fingers as if finally realizing that he had been dead a long, long time. The colonel staggered backward toward the welcoming darkness of the Hole.

"Get over here, you goddamned little homo," Jeff screamed, expecting his orders to be obeyed without question. Vernon Ray tilted the snare drum against his waist and rolled his sticks into playing position.

"*Guh-ruk,*" Donnie barked, wobbling uphill toward Kirk.

Bobby glanced back, tightening his grip on Donnie's waist, wondering if Hardy Eggers or the sheriff were about to fire again, but the sheriff and the reporter were running toward the Hole and Hardy had tossed his rifle aside, gunning the bulldozer engine and lurching forward in a titanic creak of steel, rust, and rage.

Bobby was juiced by adrenaline instead of diesel, but he let out his own blast of internal combustion, shrieking in a mimic of Jeff Davis's Rebel yell. Bobby pushed past Donnie, giving him a shove as if he were a linebacker interfering with a touchdown run, and launched himself toward Vernon Ray, who didn't seem to recognize him.

*Dang, they've already got him . . . .*

Kirk fell to his knees just beyond the mouth of the cave, and a skeletal arm reached out as if to drag him to safety. Bobby hoped the sheriff wouldn't shoot again, because he and Vernon Ray were exposed targets. And the monumental jangle of steel inside the mountain suggested that an army was massing to defend its borders.

Vernon Ray struck the drum head a solid blow, and then delivered a left-handed roll that seemed to fill the sky like midnight thunder. Bobby was closer now, ducking low in case bullets flew, planning to drag Vernon Ray away from the mountain that wanted to swallow V-Ray and Donnie and Bobby and maybe the whole living, breathing, hateful world into the cold, endless sameness of its belly.

"Come on, Vee," Bobby said, reaching for his friend.

He clutched a sleeve, but Vernon Ray shook free and continued drumming.

Vernon Ray stared ahead, unblinking, not seeing the guy who was there for his first Incredible Hulk plastic model, his journey reading "The Lord of the Rings" trilogy, his first chipped tooth from a skateboard accident. Bobby's best friend had forged a new bond, an unspoken alliance with something no comic-book writer could ever dream up. The snare cadence rumbled through the forest and across the hills, calling all creatures to muster.

But the cadence was drowned by a different rolling storm, that of the bulldozer growling its own battle cry.

CHAPTER THIRTY-FIVE

The sticks were light and strong in Vernon Ray's hands, the kepi tucked tight and proud. Vernon Ray straightened his spine as much as he could, facing the full-frontal assault as bravely as he could.

Dad was running toward him, waving his saber and calling him an idiot faggot, face so twisted in rage and fear that he looked like an escapee from the criminal psycho ward. Dad's uniform was torn and filthy, and Vernon Ray would be blamed for it. Dad would dress him down, commandeer the kepi Col. Kirk had given him, and take away the beautiful and resonant snare drum that was as comforting as a mother's heartbeat in the womb.

He was out. Dad would call him "homo" and "faggot" until the end of time, or at least until Vernon Ray ran away or took up cutting himself until he got the nerve to check out for good, maybe with razor blades in the bathtub or by making one final trip to The Room, loading one of Dad's collector Smith & Wessons, and painting the history books, maps, and artifacts with a red-and-gray shower of blood and brains.

Bobby touched him—

"Get away," Vernon Ray said, retreating two steps but keeping the drumroll strong and steady. His colonel was wounded and the boys were helping, and maybe Vernon Ray could buy some time for them. Dad and the sheriff were closing in, but it was the bulldozer that worried him most–the enemy had brought out the heavy artillery for this one.

"You're spaced out, dude," Bobby said, reaching again.

Vernon Ray backed up another step, and then the colonel was beside him, swaying back and forth, pressing his hand against his wound to stem the flow of ichor.

The lost leader's face squirmed, as if the space between skin and skull was occupied by worms instead of meat. But his right hand held his saber, raised in defiance of those who sought to destroy what they couldn't understand.

Tears welled in Vernon Ray's eyes.

At last he understood the colonel's recruiting pitch, and he repeated it now to Bobby.

"We don't belong together," Vernon Ray said, only it had a different meaning out here under the blue sky and golden treetops and the all-seeing but dispassionate eye of heaven.

"Sorry about this," Bobby yelled, and Dad was screaming, the bulldozer was chuffing and choking, the sheriff was barking unheeded orders, the reporter was taking pictures of it all, and Earley Eggers had returned to smoke, finally released from service to return home. The Raiders jangled their weaponry in the Hole, packing sulfur and brimstone for a final siege.

Bobby looked down at his hand, and Vernon Ray saw the rock. His best friend raised his arm, winging his elbow in the motion that had struck out Vernon Ray thirty-six times in a row on the baseball diamond. But Vernon Ray didn't miss a beat. Or, rather, the sticks didn't miss a beat, because now they seemed to be driving his hands, lifting them, rolling his wrists.

He was no longer playing the snare drum. It was playing him.

The colonel stepped in front of him just as Bobby flung the chunk of granite. It struck the colonel's forehead with a sickening crunch of bone, knocking the cavalier's hat from his head. By emerging from the Hole, Kirk had made himself vulnerable.

*Sacrifice.*

*Giving your life for a belief.*

*Surrendering to a cause greater than yourself.*

Vernon Ray finally understood, and he changed the cadence to sound the retreat. Glory and honor were found as much in defeat as in victory. Maybe more so, when the war was senseless and never-ending.

*We don't belong together.*

*We're not of this world, we don't belong, so we might as well do it together.*

*Not so lonely that way.*

Vernon Ray stepped back, tears leaking from his eyes, blurring the sad, frightened face of Bobby Eldreth. The colonel was dead, at least for now, though his uniform was turning to dust and his flesh was evaporating into the milk of mystery and yesteryear.

"Queer," Dad yelled, slashing his saber at the air as if he could cut a path between their great gulf.

"Don't go in there, son," the sheriff yelled.

Hardy Eggers, high in the bulldozer's cab, squinted at the Hole as if it were an old enemy, pushing the machine to its limit, black smoke boiling from its pipe. Donnie Eggers–another who didn't belong–knelt in the mud, head bobbing as if he could still hear the snare over the rumbling diesel motor.

Vernon Ray imagined Donnie would continue to hear the muster call long after the battle was over, and would wake in the night and seek its direction in the wind.

Then the cool, comforting embrace of the shadows took him, and he marched backward into the Jangling Hole, home at last, free to be, belonging.

Drumming his heart out, the sticks dancing in his hands like old friends and lovers, the troops rallying around him.

Dad was mouthing insults that were drowned by the bulldozer. His last glimpse of daylight was the sheriff yanking Bobby away, and Vernon Ray wished he could say good-bye and tell him of a love lost, or maybe a love never known, but in the end Bobby belonged to that other world.

The last thing he saw was Bobby struggling against the sheriff's grip, reaching toward Vernon Ray and the Hole.

Then the bulldozer blade smashed into the granite boulders framing the cave, a cruel cannonade into the gates of Kirk's stronghold. Stones loosened, soil spilled down, the phantom soldiers let loose a desperate moan as they prepared to die all over again.

As the earth showered down around him, Vernon Ray played on.

CHAPTER THIRTY-SIX

Halloween had passed, but its shadow clung to the mountain where two boys walked the ridge.

Dex kicked in the dirt, looking for souvenirs. Dex would love to have a bone, a junky piece of rusted metal, maybe even Vernon Ray's little Rebel cap, anything to prove he'd trespassed and defied yellow tape that blared "Police Line–Do Not Cross."

Bobby wished Dex would find something, because they all wanted proof that the Battle of Mulatto Mountain had actually happened.

Well, not everybody. The sheriff seemed perfectly happy to make it all disappear, but the reporter made sure it didn't get buried along with Vernon Ray. Her digital photographs had all been blurred and smoky, and Hardy Eggers, after making bail on a vandalism charge, had invoked his right to remain silent and was likely to keep it for the rest of his life.

Jeff Davis was the picture of the bereaved parent, so shaken that he'd cancelled the Stoneman's Raid re-enactment, though he'd been spending most of his time locked away in the room that housed his Civil War memorabilia.

Bobby had gone over to the Davis trailer once, when his mom had sent him with a bean casserole, that staple of southern comfort in a time of sorrow. Bobby heard Jeff talking to himself behind the door but hustled out before things could get weird. Dad was acting like Dad again, so Bobby saw no need to go questioning lineage and patriarchy. He had enough on his mind.

Like the pile of rubble around them and whatever path Earley Eggers had walked as he made his way home.

"So what really happened, man?" Dex said.

"I done told you," Bobby said. Dex was getting on his nerves. Life without a best friend was hard on a guy. Dex just didn't understand the real stuff, and talking to him about emotions was like talking to a chicken about the price of eggs.

"Yeah, sure, a bunch of baloney about ghosts," Dex said. "I know you're just making it up to get in Karen Greene's panties."

In truth, he couldn't meet Karen's eyes in the hall between classes. Whenever he did, he thought of Vernon Ray trying to kiss him.

"I'd rather have V-Ray back," he said, studying the mounds of heaped dirt, stumps, and rocks. The heavy equipment brought in to search for Vernon Ray—or his body—was still parked around the clearing, though it had been three weeks since the runaway bulldozer had closed the Jangling Hole for good.

"I got to admit, it's kind of creepy that they didn't find him," Dex said. "I mean, you saw the Hole. It couldn't have been more than 10 feet deep. Where could he have *gone*?"

Bobby had wondered the same thing, but he didn't know how to explain that maybe some people just weren't made for this world. They came into it fresh and whole and good, but the world wasn't ready for them.

Or maybe Vernon Ray was right: if you were different, you didn't belong.

Bobby gazed across the ridges that stretched in the distance like brown waves of a dirty sea. Autumn was giving way to winter, and soon even the brown would be a memory as all turned to gray.

"I guess he went everywhere," Bobby said. *And I hope you fit in there.*

He picked up a rock and tossed it toward the closest gash in the soil. It bounced off an upturned tree root and settled on the black skin of Mulatto Mountain.

"You read too many comic books, dude." Dex dug in his jacket pocket and pulled out a cigarette pack. "Want a smoke?"

Bobby shook his head.

Dex lit his cigarette and looked at the sky, where a dark swell of clouds were bloodied by the sundown. "Thunder?"

Bobby nodded again, a stone in his throat. He knew the suffocated rattle of a snare drum when he heard it

*The beat goes on . . . .*

"We better get out of here before it rains," Dex said.

"Yeah." Bobby turned away from the disturbed rubble of the

Hole and headed down the mountain.

Rain would be okay. It would come in silver with a liquid *tatta tatta tat*, beating its ancient pulse across the skin of the Earth. It would pound like a million drummer boys, so that Vernon Ray's lonely rhythm could be lost among them. It would bathe the uncertain grave of the Jangling Hole. Rain would smooth the heaps of loose dirt, rain would sweep away the scent of decay, rain would wash the world clean.

Most of all, rain would veil his welling tears.

# THE END

## OTHER BOOKS BY SCOTT NICHOLSON

Solom #1: The Scarecrow
Solom #2: The Narrow Gate
Solom #3: The Preacher
Liquid Fear
Chronic Fear
After #1: The Shock
After #2: The Echo
After #3: Milepost 291
After #4: Whiteout
Disintegration
Drummer Boy
McFall
Kiss Me or Die
Speed Dating with the Dead
The Skull Ring
The Home
Creative Spirit
October Girls
Scattered Ashes
Monster's Ink
Thank You for the Flowers
They Hunger
Bad Blood (Spider #1)
Cursed (with J.R. Rain)
Dirt
Grave Conditions

Scott Nicholson is the international bestselling author of more than 30 books. He lives in the Blue Ridge Mountains of North Carolina, where he tends an organic garden, strums guitar, and practices armchair Taoism.

Visit   www.AuthorScottNicholson.com   or   email   him   at hauntedcomputerbooks@gmail.com.

Made in the USA
Las Vegas, NV
28 January 2025